"DO NOT REMAIN HERE TOO LONG AND TAUNT THE EVIL POWERS WHICH RULE THIS HOUSE."

Such was the grim warning from the bent old man who had first told Enid of the legend of the Jade Princess: a ghostly figure, garbed like an Oriental, who always left a lingering trace of jasmine in the air to mark her passing.

This sweeping epic novel of exotic romance and mystery brings the legend to life, as young Enid attempts to solve the baffling riddle of her sister's death. And, under the spell of the strange and beautiful Orient, she meets EDMUND PORTER, patriarch of the Porter family, whose murdered wife, it is whispered, has returned as the Jade Princess; STEPHEN PORTER, Madge's husband, brooding, ill-tempered, seemingly unconcerned by his wife's death; CHRISTOPHER PORTER, his brother, reckless, irresponsible, with a taste for danger—and possibly murder; CHARLES MILANO, charming and attractive, but with a shrouded past; and SONYA CHEN, who seems to know more about the Jade Princess than she is willing to tell.

JADE PRINCESS

JADE PRINCESS

Clarissa Ross

PYRAMID BOOKS   NEW YORK

JADE PRINCESS

A PYRAMID BOOK

Pyramid edition published April 1977

Library of Congress Catalog Card Number: 77-72093

Printed in the United States of America

Pyramid Books are published by Pyramid Publications (Harcourt Brace Jovanovich, Inc.). Its trademarks, consisting of the
word "Pyramid" and the portrayal of a pyramid, are registered
in the United States Patent Office.

Pyramid Publications
(Harcourt Brace Jovanovich, Inc.)
757 Third Avenue, New York, N.Y. 10017

To my friends Ronny and Mort Bernstein.
And to the memory of Mort's father,
Mortimer Bernstein.

one

It was one of those bleak, late afternoons in February characteristic of London. A sinister mixture of fog, smoke, chemicals and temperature had compounded to produce a thick, yellow smog. Traffic was slowed to a near halt and the great old city on the Thames had become a place of ghostly moving objects. Pedestrians braved the streets at a decided risk and groped their precarious ways through the five o'clock traffic and thick mist.

Enid Branch was one of those braving the thick fog. She had left the modern skyscraper where the insurance firm for which she was a secretary was located and hurried down in the elevator only to find that the fog ridden streets were almost impassable. This caused her much frustration as she had an early dinner appointment with her elderly, bachelor uncle, David Branch.

It was the first time she'd had a meeting arranged with the old gentleman in months and she knew he hated to be kept waiting. To complicate matters the Clarion Restaurant was a good four blocks from her office building. She slowly made her way along the street with many other unfortunates in a similar plight and hoped that her Uncle David would also be kept late by the fog. This was her only hope!

At twenty-four Enid was something of a veteran of living and working in London. She'd lived alone in a small flat near her work since her half-sister, Madge, had married and gone off to distant and glamorous Hong Kong to live. It was somehow to be expected that the vivacious, Titian-haired Madge would be the one to meet a millionaire exporter and capture his heart. That had been three years ago although it seemed a lot longer. Enid gave a tiny shudder as she stood with others by a curb and waited for an opportunity to cross the street. The bobby directing traffic was furiously blowing at his whistle and trying to move the various vehicles along.

She stood gazing blankly into the thick, yellow mist and thinking about Madge. For Madge was dead! She still found it difficult to believe that she would never see the lovely, warm-hearted Madge again. But the word had come from Hong Kong and that was why she was having this meeting with Uncle David.

It shamed her that at first she had felt jealous of her older half-sister's good fortune. To marry a handsome, rich, young man and go live in a fabulous house in the Orient had seemed the ultimate of any girl's wishes. Madge had made the transition into that magical world as if she had always expected this to happen to her. And perhaps she had!

Enid knew she was very different from her outgoing half-sister. Yet she had plenty of dates and enjoyed the company of young men. Unlike Madge she had no wish for an immediate marriage and so she had been careful not to date any one of her many beaux regularly. She wanted to live on her own for a while longer until she was quite certain of the type of life—and the sort of husband—she wanted.

The bobby turned to her group of pedestrians and blew his whistle at them, furiously beckoning them to make the crossing. She stepped off the curb with the group and they slowly made their way to the other side. This brought her within a half block of the restaurant.

She moved on slowly keeping an eye out for the restaurant front, fearful of missing it in the thick fog. Once you missed your bearings in the awful mist you could really wind up lost. Enid had her mother's brownish hair and large hazel eyes in an oval face. Her long eyelashes enhanced her lovely eyes and she had a full-lipped mouth of perfect form. Her nose was finely shaped and she had a bright smile which often shone thanks to her keen sense of humor. But she felt no humor now on this bleak evening after receiving the sad news of Madge's death.

All at once she halted and then looked towards the orange glow of two large windows. They were the windows of the Clarion Restaurant and she went inside.

The headwaiter, a tall, dark man, bowed to her. "You are meeting someone, Miss?"

"Yes," she said. "Mr. David Branch." She had only been to the large, comfortable restaurant with its wood-paneled walls once before. And then as her uncle's guest.

The headwaiter smiled knowingly. "Of course! Mr. Branch is waiting for you! Just come along!" And he led her through a maze of circular, white-clothed tables, most of them occupied, to a table at the mirrored rear wall where Uncle David rose to greet her.

She stepped close to him to receive his usual greeting kiss on the cheek. She apologized, "The fog made me late!"

"And no wonder," Uncle David rumbled with a sympathetic look on his florid face. "It's a filthy night!" He was her late father's older brother and was retired from the army. He still kept his military bearing and his round face was decorated by a flourishing, gray mustache to match his thick head of iron gray hair. He saw her safely seated and then ordered drinks for them.

Enid told him, "I appreciate your seeing me."

His pleasant, florid face showed regret. "Only sorry I wasn't in town when you first tried to reach me. Had a fortnight in Scotland with an old army comrade."

"I understand," she said.

He frowned. "But what a shock for you! To receive the sad news about Madge and have no one to share it with. My duty as the only member of your family surviving. Sorry, I failed you."

"I don't think of you as having failed me," she said. "I'm only sorry to be bothering you with this. But with mother and father both dead you are the only one I can turn to."

He eyed her kindly. "And you were right to do it. I want to help. Dashed! I'd have been angry if you hadn't let me know!"

Their drinks were served. And she said, "I have the letter from Madge's husband."

Uncle David frowned and blinked as he recalled, "Fine looking, chap! I thought she'd made a good match!"

9

"I'm sure that she did," Enid said as she lifted her handbag from an empty chair and began a search of it for the letter she'd received from Stephen Porter in far off Hong Kong. Though Madge had only been a half-sister they had been very close. They had shared the same father and with the death of Enid's mother when Enid was only fifteen the older girl had assumed the role of foster mother to her.

They had barely left home to work when their father had succumbed to a sudden heart attack. This had left the girls alone except for David Branch. The bumbling, good-hearted old bachelor had done his best to watch over them in spite of his almost constant traveling.

Now he asked Enid, "What precisely happened to poor Madge? Did she die in childbirth or something of that sort? She was always so healthy!"

"I know," Enid said, producing the brown envelope in which the letter had come. "Her husband has given me no details at all." And she passed him the letter.

He fished reading glasses from his pocket, placed them midway on his nose and fumbled with opening the envelope. He pulled out the single sheet of expensive paper and studied the short, neatly written letter. After he'd read it, he put it down with an indignant look on his red face. "Dashed little information here!"

"I know!"

He frowned as he gazed at the letter again. "Beyond his curtly informing you that Madge is dead and asking that you come out East to settle her affairs he says nothing."

"He does mention that his London agent will be holding a cheque to cover my expenses," she pointed out.

Uncle David returned the letter to her and in an annoyed tone said, "Yes, but I still think the letter is cold and abrupt! No hint of sympathy beyond the formal, 'I regret to inform you,' and no suggestion of how your sister died."

Enid's lovely face was shadowed as she put the letter back in her handbag. "I know. I was tempted to wire for more facts and then I decided to wait until I saw you."

Her uncle sighed. "Is there some reason for his not telling you what caused her death?"

"I've been wondering about that. Perhaps she met with

some sort of accident and he found it too painful to recount the details."

Uncle David sipped his drink. "Possibly. In fact anything is possible though I confess I do not understand it."

"He seemed such a wonderful young man."

Her uncle gave her a sharp glance. "Appearances can be deceiving. At the time I worried that Madge had not known him longer."

"Nearly half a year."

"Hardly long enough," the old man said. "At least not in my day. But he seemed such a wonderful catch I hesitated to interfere. It seemed that Madge was suddenly being given all the riches which she so surely deserved."

"I felt the same way," Enid agreed.

Her uncle's face was a study in concern in the subdued lighting of the cafe. He said, "I suppose I should have seen more of him before I gave my blessing to the match. Should have talked with Madge about it."

She leaned across the table and touched his large hand with her own slim one. "You mustn't have regrets. I'm sure dear Madge's death was no fault of her husband's. We shouldn't be presuming him guilty of anything."

"But the letter? So unsatisfactory!"

"Undoubtedly because of his grief," Enid suggested. "Grief can cause one to behave oddly."

"True," Uncle David said. "That is perhaps the answer. I suppose we shall know the whole story in due time." He glanced at her with questioning eyes. "Do you propose to accept his offer and go to Hong Kong?"

"I have asked my supervisor and he is willing to let me have a three-month leave," she said. "I think that should give me plenty of time."

"More than enough," the gray-haired man said. "You can fly there from London in a matter of twenty-odd hours. So you have made up your mind to visit Stephen Porter!"

"Yes," she said. "Especially under the circumstances. I do want to find out what happened to Madge. I'd also like to see how and where she lived. And there are her personal things such as family jewelry and photos which she had. They won't mean anything to her husband, but they do have a definite value to me."

David Branch sighed again. "I'm not sure I like the idea of your going out there alone."

"Why not?"

He hesitated. "I mean, should there be anything peculiar about the manner of Madge's death you might be placing yourself in danger."

Her lovely hazel eyes widened. "Nonsense!"

He raised a cautioning hand. "Perhaps. And then perhaps not. You don't know what happened to Madge and he has been most wary of telling you in his letter. I think this might well be construed as suspicious."

Enid had briefly thought the same thing herself but had forced the doubts from her mind. She could not afford to entertain them if she were to make the journey of discovery to Hong Kong.

Now she tried to sound completely casual as she told the old man, "I'm not at all worried about that. I'm sure Stephen will have a complete and satisfactory explanation for me. I'm most worried about visas and shots and packing!"

"Routine," her uncle said with the placid calm of an experienced traveler. "I can help you with all that. But I can't be in Hong Kong to watch over you."

She smiled. "I won't need that if you'll only help me before I leave. I'll need to buy suitable clothes and there are so many things."

"Have you visited his agent yet?"

"No. I wanted to talk with you first," she said. "But I'll go see him tomorrow if the fog lifts."

"Mustn't have anything happen to you," her uncle worried.

"Nothing will," she said, with more assurance than she felt. And to change the subject she added, "You spent some of your army time in Hong Kong, didn't you?"

He nodded and perceptibly straightened in his chair as he became the army major again in memory. "I was assigned to duty on the island before the Second World War. Just good luck I was transferred from the Crown Colony before the Japs came and took it over."

Enid was interested. "It was captured during the war, wasn't it?"

"Grim business," Uncle David said, tugging at his gray mustache as he remembered. "Canadians came to augment

12

the garrison there. Poor blighters didn't have time to get any idea of the lay of the land or how to defend it before the little yellow men were upon them! They put up a courageous defense but a doomed one! In the end Hong Kong was taken over by the enemy."

"Have you been there since the war?"

"No," he said. "I have met a few people who have. They tell me it's changed greatly. The island is dotted with tall skyscrapers now. The streets are busy with traffic. Only a small section of the old city still exists and they predict that within a few years the westernization of that section will be complete."

"So I won't be going to a strange, exotic land!"

"You will," her uncle warned her. "For all the tall buildings and modern ways it is still an Oriental city. Behind its modern facade you will still find it a place of mystery. It takes time to understand the ways of the East. You must guard against deception, from being shortchanged and swindled in a street bazaar to being suavely lied to by some seemingly upstanding citizen."

She rebuked him, "You're still afraid that Stephen Porter may not be all that he seemed to be!"

"I'm not thinking only of him," her uncle said. "I know the Orient. I have lived there. It has beauty and many fine people, but there is another world not so well known to the Westerner. A world into which the Westerner can be trapped and twisted in character!"

"You're trying to frighten me!"

"No. Trying to make you understand. The small islands of Hong Kong hold three million people. It is a fantastic, exotic mixture of nearly every group in the East and many from the West. It lies only a few hours by boat from Macao, still the headquarters of the Orient for smuggling of all sorts. Be it drugs or gold or precious stones, they are readily available for a price in Macao!"

Enid said, "I doubt that I will leave Hong Kong. I plan to see Stephen Porter, settle Madge's affairs and come straight back to London."

David Branch said, "I still have one or two old friends there. I will look up their names and addresses, and I shall

13

send them letters of introduction for you. At least that is one way I may be able to assist you in your mission."

"I would appreciate that," she said sincerely.

"I shall attend to it at once," her Uncle David said as he motioned to their waiter. "And now let us order dinner."

So it was settled. She applied for her leave of absence and called at the palatial offices of Stephen Porter's London agent where she was given a sealed envelope containing a sizable check—more than enough to cover her needs for the journey, Enid decided. There was no question that Stephen Porter was generous.

Then came the last-minute flurry of visas, health shots, and packing. She had scarcely time to think until she found herself one morning at the London airport with Uncle David loyally standing by. It was a bright, sunny morning and the jet in which she was to make this long journey stood waiting on the asphalt runway a short distance off, shining and sleek.

She turned to her uncle. "I'll write you as soon as I've arrived and have found out a few things."

The gray-haired man had his hat in hand. "I shall be waiting for that letter," he promised her. "Is Stephen Porter aware of which flight you are using?"

She nodded. "Yes. I sent him a cable and told him the time. I also requested that someone be there."

"By all means," her Uncle David agreed. "And you have the names and addresses of my friends?"

"I have," she said. The call was given for her flight and she gave him an anxious look. "I must go now!"

Uncle David showed a worried look on his round, mustached face. He took her awkwardly in his arms and gave her a parting peck on the check. "Take care!" he said. "I'm not sure about that fellow!"

She nodded and with a hint of tears in her eyes turned and hurried to join the others heading for the plane. In her haste she dropped the flight bag which she was carrying. As she stopped to pick it up she became aware of a tall, handsome, dark-haired man who swooped down a hand and, rescuing the bag, offered it to her with a smile showing on his squarish, tanned face.

"Thank you," she said breathlessly and hurried on.

14

"My pleasure," the young man assured her in an accent which could not be anything but American.

The attendants were there to guide them to their places on the great jetliner. Diminutive Indian girls in colorful saris offered an initial touch of the East. Enid was shown to a window seat midway in the big airship. She had no sooner seated herself than to her pleasant surprise the tall, young American arrived to take the seat beside her. He thanked the Indian girl attendant who had a special smile for him.

He bowed to Enid and sat beside her, saying, "I had no idea we'd meet again so soon."

For no reason Enid knew she was blushing as she replied, "Nor did I." And she added hastily. "It was good of you to help me."

"Nothing," the American said, studying her with his keen, black eyes. "You're British."

"Yes."

"I'm American. Since we're going to be seat partners may I introduce myself. I'm Charles Milano and I'm going back to Hong Kong where I've been assigned as a news correspondent."

"I'm happy to know you," she said with genuine pleasure. "I'm also going to Hong Kong. But only for a brief visit."

He raised his dark eyebrows. "Excellent! We'll be going all the way there together. Is this your first trip?"

"It is," she said. "I'm rather excited about it."

"Interesting place," the young American agreed. "A strange blend of yesterday and today. It has its dark side streets and its modern thoroughfares, its sampans in the harbor and its fine European hotels rising up above the city. I think your poet Kipling used to talk about Mandalay as the place where East meets West. I'd say today it is Hong Kong."

Enid listened to him with growing interest. "You must know a lot about the city being a newspaperman."

He nodded with an amused look on his manly, tanned face. "We find out what we can."

At that moment their conversation was interrupted by the announcement that the jetliner was taking off. It rose into the air with hardly a tremor and passed through the bottom cloud base. Then it climbed what she assumed must be double the height to glide nobly above the white clouds in endless

15

sunshine. The passengers relaxed and Charles Milano asked her permission to light a cigarette.

He told her, "It will be dark in a few hours."

"Dark?" she echoed in surprise.

He gave her another amused look. "Yes. By about two o'clock British time we'll be heading into darkness. We're on our way to meet the night and traveling at some speed."

"I'd forgotten the time zones," she said. "It's my first time on a really long flight." She added. "My uncle was stationed in Hong Kong in the British Army, but that was years ago."

"I see," the American said as he enjoyed his cigarette. "Are you on your way to meet relatives now?"

"A relative by marriage," she said cautiously. Though her first impressions of the young man were favorable she did not think she should tell him too much about her mission. Especially as she was so uncertain of what she was going to encounter when she reached Hong Kong. The mystery of her half-sister's death was still to be explained.

"I see," the young man said, fortunately exhibiting no more curiosity about the subject. "We're flying over Europe now and we'll be making our first stop in Beirut in a few hours."

The excitement of departure over, Enid began to feel somewhat sleepy. Charles Milano was helpful in assisting her to adjust her seat back and then place a pillow behind her head at just the right spot to be comfortable. She closed her eyes, listened to the steady drone of the great plane and the subdued murmur of conversation drifting to her from the mixed group of passengers close to her.

She was thinking of Hong Kong and what she would say to Stephen Porter when he met her at the airport. She had no doubt that the good-looking widower would come to personally greet her and give her the details of Madge's sudden death. She hoped there would be no awkwardness between them and again she found herself troubled by the weird manner in which he had written her. No wonder poor Uncle David felt uneasy about her safety!

These were the thoughts drifting lazily through her mind when she fell asleep. She slept for a couple of hours and when she wakened she was told by Charles Milano they were about to land in the Lebanon airport of Beirut. There was a

16

ripple of anticipation among the passengers in the plane at the prospect of being on land for a while.

With a wise smile, the American newspaperman warned her, "Don't expect too much! Mostly it's sticky, hot and shabby!"

She glanced out the window and in the darkness suddenly saw a myriad of twinkling lights along with a giant new moon above. The plane prepared for landing and in a moment they touched the ground and came to a smooth halt.

Charles Milano stood up and warned her, "Don't leave anything in your seat. Things have a way of disappearing here."

She thanked him and rose, clutching her airbag with her newly purchased camera and other items in it. They waited in line to leave the plane and make their way to the large, empty airport. They were in an immigration area guarded by Lebanese police who spoke in Arabic. Announcements came over a loud speaker system high in the shabby walls first in Arabic and then in English.

Charles Milano handled himself with assurance and ordered them drinks. Enid realized she was fortunate to have the experienced newspaperman as a guide. Most of the other passengers were mulling about, complaining or bewildered while they sat at a table in comparative ease.

She said, "You know this place well."

"Fairly well," he agreed. "I spent some months here. The bazaars of Beirut are the headquarters for much of the smuggling in the world. Diamonds, illegal munitions, gold and drugs. You can name any contraband and be almost certain it moves through here."

"I had no idea," she said, impressed.

"Now that the Arab countries have plenty of money they are interested in heavy arms, such as planes and tanks," he said. "They aren't that easy to smuggle."

She asked, "Is there any smuggling in Hong Kong?"

Her companion looked wise and said, "Macao!"

"Macao?"

"That's a Portuguese colony. An island just a short way from Hong Kong. Everything is wide open there, including smuggling."

He went on to tell her about Macao and the criminals who

17

made their headquarters there. He explained that both the Crown Colony of Hong Kong and mainland Nationalist China frowned on the illegal activities of Macao but were able to do little about it. Vice, it seemed, had to have a fortress and Macao was it.

Enid found the airport hot and oppressive and was grateful when they were called back to the jetliner. As they boarded the craft she noticed that some of the passengers had changed. Within a short period they were soaring high above the Arabian Sea. She read a novel she'd brought with her and once again slept for a little.

They landed at the airport in New Delhi. She and Charles Milano wandered about the pretentious airport and studied items of Indian craft in the shops catering to air travelers. Charles spoke cynically of the country which had won its independence of England. She found his views surprising for an American. He appeared to think they had been much better off as a colony.

With a teasing smile she asked him, "What about America? You were also a colony once. Don't you think you are better off with independence?"

The newspaperman shrugged. "That's a different situation altogether."

When they boarded the plane again there was another small turnover of passengers. She realized that she and the young American newspaperman were becoming good friends. A note of casual easiness had come to their relationship. She was enjoying his company and she had an idea he also liked being with her.

They were well along in their journey as he turned to her to say, "You'll soon be seeing the peak of Mount Victoria."

"Mount Victoria?"

"Yes," Charles Milano said. "You know the official name for Hong Kong is Victoria. Some of the islands were handed over to Britain years ago. And in 1898 other island territory and a small section of the mainland was leased for ninety years. Nationalist China has been wanting the leased land back but it seems a good bet that this won't happen for the term of the agreement."

"What then?"

"If worse comes to worst," the newspaperman said, "I'm

18

sure the population could settle on the islands which Britain owns. But I'd expect that some arrangement would be made so that wouldn't be necessary."

She smiled. "I imagine some of the British firms have been in Hong Kong for years."

"They surely have," he agreed. "There is a saying in Hong Kong that all influence begins in the Jockey Club, the Hong Kong Shanghai Bank, Her Majesty's Government and the firm of Edmund Porter and Sons."

Enid reacted as he spoke the name so familiar to her. She said, "I'm going to Hong Kong to meet one of the Porter family. At least I assume it is the same family. The man I'm meeting is Stephen Porter."

Surprise flashed across his tanned face as he repeated, "Stephen Porter!"

"Yes. Do you know him?"

Charles Milano took on a strange, guarded air. He said, "Yes. I've met him. I know his cousin, Christopher, better. How do you happen to be friendly with Stephen Porter?"

There was a tension in his question which at once upset her. Awkwardly, she explained, "He was married to my half-sister, Madge. She died recently. I'm coming out to settle her affairs."

Charles Milano stared at her. "I see," he said quietly.

Still flustered, she said, "Since you were living in Hong Kong and know Stephen Porter you must have heard about my half-sister's death."

The handsome, dark man said guardedly, "I seem to recall hearing something about it." His tone was as evasive as the letter she had received from Madge's husband. What could it mean?

two

There was silence between them for a moment during which the plane droned on in the background. She gave the young American a searching look as she said, "You must know the circumstances of my half-sister's death."

Charles Milano only looked more uneasy. He said, "I did not have the pleasure of meeting her."

"But you know the Porters," she said. "Surely you must have heard about her death from them or read of it in the local papers."

The journalist hesitated and then said, "I was away from Hong Kong for a few weeks. I recall the incident took place during my absence. So I really know very little about it."

She gave him a serious look. "I know absolutely nothing! I thought it strange that her husband did not write me in some detail. That is one of the reasons I've made this trip."

The American's handsome face registered sympathy. "I'm sorry," he said. "I wish I could help you but I can't. I think it would be best if you heard about all this from Stephen Porter directly."

She could tell by his manner he knew more than he was telling her. But she also could see that he was determined to reveal no more than he had. She would have to go into this personally with the husband of her late half-sister.

"I expect he will be meeting me," she said. "I only knew him for a short time. Is he popular in Hong Kong?"

"The Porter family have a secure social position," Charles

20

Milano replied, offering an answer which was not entirely satisfactory.

"You say you know his cousin?"

"Yes," he said. "Christopher Porter is a member of the family exporting business. He is my favorite, though some people are fondest of old Edmund Porter, grandfather of Stephen and Christopher. He is in his early eighties but still active with the business."

"I see," she said, carefully. "And you don't approve of Stephen?"

"I didn't say that!"

"But you didn't mention him," she pointed out. "In this instance I'd say the omission is significant."

Charles Milano glanced down at his folded hands. "Let us say I don't know him too well."

She was not satisfied by this but she knew there was little else she could ask the newspaperman. He apparently had strong personal reasons for not wanting to show any interest in the man who had married Madge. Considering this, in view of the other instances, it wasn't too promising.

The plane's motors took on a different sound and it began to slow down and prepare for a landing. The young man gave her a worried glance. "For what it's worth I live at the Hong Kong Hilton. You can usually reach me there or leave a message for me."

"Thank you," she said. "I'll remember that. The Hilton."

"Yes," he said, his eyes still fixed on her. "I'm sure we'll meet again."

"It will depend on how long I remain on the island," she said.

"You will remain to learn about your sister's death," he said.

"That may not take long."

There was a strange expression on his handsome face as he replied, "And then again it could take longer than you think."

She was about to ask him just what he meant by this when some islands came into view set in the purple of the ocean. She said, "Is that Hong Kong?"

"Those are the Communist-owned outer islands," the young man beside her said. "See, there's Victoria mountain ahead!" And now they were hovering above the city of her destination and finally settling down on an air strip surrounded by one of the most beautiful views in the world.

There was a bustle aboard the plane as everyone prepared to land. Again she found herself waiting in line. Charles Milano had taken a position directly behind her.

He said, "The airport is a busy one. I'll remain with you until you meet Stephen Porter."

"He should be here," she replied. "I sent him a cable."

"No doubt he will be," her new friend said, though he did not sound convinced.

At last she stepped outside and thoroughly enjoyed the mellow, warm air. She crossed to the airport buildings and the customs and immigration counters with Charles Milano at her side. There was a slight delay while her visa was stamped and her bags examined and during this time she became parted from the young American who had chosen to go through another wicket. All around her there was a movement of people talking in many languages.

She was waiting for Charles Milano to join her and wondering where Stephen Porter might be when she was suddenly conscious of a stout Chinese in a white linen suit and Panama hat who was slowly walking towards her. He had a moon face with gray eyebrows. The almond-shaped eyes set deep in the big sallow face were sharp and now they were focused on her.

The old Chinese came forward to her and removed his hat to reveal a head of close-cropped iron-gray hair. In a voice which held the lilt of Chinese but whose words were perfect English, the old man said, "Do I have the pleasure of addressing Miss Enid Branch?"

"Yes," she said, startled that the elderly Chinese should have picked her out from the crowd so easily.

He bowed gravely. "I am Wong Lee, partner to Edmund Porter, the grandfather of Stephen Porter. I have seen your photograph in one in which your late half-sister and Stephen also appeared."

She said, "So that is how you knew me!"

"Yes," the old man said carefully. At close range she could see the many tiny wrinkles in the sallow face and since he was a partner of the senior Edmund Porter, who was over eighty, she felt it quite likely that the stout Chinese in the linen suit could be over eighty as well.

"Where is Stephen Porter?" she asked.

The old man, his Panama hat still clutched in a chubby hand, showed no change of expression as he said, "Stephen had to travel to Siam on an urgent business matter. His cousin, Christopher, is absent in Macao, so it fell to either Edmund Porter, his daughter-in-law, or his adopted granddaughter to meet you. Edmund Porter is feeling unwell today and he did not think it seemly to have one of the women greet you so he asked me to look after you."

Enid listened to the long, very solemn explanation and felt that it gave her something of an insight into the Chinese mind and character. The elderly Wong Lee was taking this mission most seriously and went to much more trouble than any European might have under the same circumstances to explain just exactly why he was there.

She said, "It was good of you to come."

"I am delighted," the elderly Wong Lee said, returning his Panama hat to his gray head. "I have the Porters' Bentley sedan with me and will have a boy gather up your baggage and see it safely installed in the car."

"Thank you," she said. "Everything is right here." She indicated the two large bags and a smaller one which had come safely through customs.

Just then Charles Milano rejoined her. Seeing old Mr. Wong Lee, the young American smiled and said, "I did not expect to see you here, Mr. Lee."

"Nor I you," the old Chinese said. "You know Miss Branch?"

"We met on the plane coming here," Charles said. "I had an idea Stephen Porter was meeting her."

"Stephen is in Siam," Mr. Wong Lee said. "I am taking Miss Branch to Porter House."

Charles said, "Then she is in excellent hands." He turned to her with another smile and said, "Remember. I'm at the Hilton Hotel."

"I won't forget," she promised. "And thank you for your kindness to me during the flight."

He shook hands with her. "I consider myself lucky having such interesting company. Enjoy Hong Kong!"

23

"I'm sure I shall," she told him.

With that Charles Milano nodded and left her. At the same time the elderly Wong Lee had been giving instructions to a slim Chinese youth in the sing-song native tongue. The youth promptly placed the small bag under his armpit and with a heavy bag in each hand trotted off towards the exit.

The stout old Wong Lee assured her, "He will take them directly to the car and place them in the boot safely. The chauffeur will be waiting to drive us to Porter House."

She joined him as he walked slowly along with the throngs of people of all nationalities moving towards the exit. She spoke loudly to be heard above the din of multilingual chatter taking place around them, saying, "Hong Kong appears to be a true melting pot of peoples."

"It is that," the old gentleman in the linen suit agreed. "When Stephen Porter's grandfather and I first formed the export company which still is highly successful it was a small place compared to today. Shipping was our only contact with the West in those days. Now much of the passenger traffic and a great deal of freight comes by airplane."

He led her out to the parking lot where the huge white Bentley stood proudly among a number of smaller and lesser cars. A young Chinese chauffeur in uniform and cap bowed and held the rear door of the Bentley open for them. Once he was installed in the comfortable rear seat with Enid at his side, the old gentleman uttered instructions to the chauffeur in the same sing-song Chinese which he had used before. They drove out of the airport and through the streets of a city which Enid felt contrasted the modern and ancient in a more enchanting manner than she had ever experienced before. Perhaps it was the Oriental tone of the ancient which made it so much more impressive.

The elderly Mr. Wong Lee told her, "The Porter House is located on the southeast corner of Hong Kong island. Edmund Porter built it years ago on a green slope at Shek-O, just facing Big Wave Bay."

"It sounds fascinating," she said.

"It is peaceful and away from the city," the old man agreed. "Three generations of Porters have lived there."

"And where do you live?" she asked.

"Nearby in a more modest establishment," the old man said. "I am a bachelor and my needs are few."

She turned from the exotic sights of the street through which they were driving to say, "Of course you knew Madge."

The old man nodded. "Of course."

"Her death came as a great shock to me."

"I'm sure it was a shock to all of us," the old man agreed.

"I know very little about it."

The round, moon face of the old Chinese betrayed little expression. "You are here now. Soon you will know everything."

Enid knew at once by his manner that he was not prepared to discuss her half-sister's death any further. Why did they all wish to avoid the subject? What was there about Madge's death which caused them to at once dry up and say no more? Would she have to wait until Stephen Porter returned before she learned the truth from his lips?

She asked the old Chinese, "When is Stephen Porter expected to return?"

"If he completes his business in Siam as expected he will be back in Hong Kong tonight."

"I am anxious to meet him again and question him," she said.

The stout old man in the white linen suit and Panama hat nodded solemnly. "Of course," he said. "That is quite understandable."

They drove on leaving the city for a winding road which followed the coastline. Eventually the car turned into a side road on the left flanked by white brick gateposts and they followed a half-moon road which opened on a vast area of lawns, orchid trees and on the left a large grove of casuarina with magpies chattering merrily in their branches.

Set in the midst of all this was a white house of Victorian architecture with the familiar gingerbread trellis trimmings of the era. The house was four stories high and sprawled out to left and right with three-story wings. It had an impressive entrance of double doors and was set close by the ocean atop a high cliff—the perfect location for what were probably the richest family in all Hong Kong! It was here the vivacious Madge had come to live and to mysteriously die!

The car came to a stop at the front entrance of the great house and the old Chinese told her, "We will get out here and the chauffeur will take your bags inside by another entrance."

The chauffeur held the car door open for them and they stepped out and crossed the flagstone path to the front door. Almost as if by magic it opened as they approached it and a tall, cadaverous-looking man with long white hair stood there in dressing gown and shirt open at the neck to greet them. She guessed at once this must be the grandfather of Stephen Porter.

The octogenarian confirmed this by stretching out a palsied, thin hand and telling her in a weak voice, "I am Edmund Porter."

She took the thin hand in hers. "How do you do, Mr. Porter," she said. "I hope I am not being a bother to you."

The old man stepped back with a troubled look on his wrinkled, hollow-cheeked face. Rheumy eyes studied her from beneath shaggy white brows.

Edmund Porter said, "By no means. Stephen was anxious that you come here. I have been wracked by a recurrent spell of a malaria I contracted years ago. That was why I was unable to meet you today."

"It is quite all right," Enid assured him. She turned to the elderly Wong Lee who was standing silently behind her. "Mr. Wong Lee took care of me very well."

Edmund Porter glanced nervously at the stout Wong Lee and told her, "I was certain he would. That is why I had him act for me. Did you have a pleasant journey?"

"Yes," she said. "I was fortunate in meeting an American journalist who claimed to know your grandson, Christopher Porter."

The old man frowned. "What is the fellow's name?"

"Charles Milano," she said. "He's assigned to Hong Kong."

Edmund Porter stood, his trembling hands at his sides, as he considered this. "The name means nothing to me and I think I know most of the accredited newspapermen on the island. Did you ever hear of him, Wong Lee?"

The stout old Chinese said, "Yes. He is not with any one publication. He is here as a free-lance writer. Many of his stories are sold to American publications and never read here."

"Then I would not know him," the palsied Edmund Porter said, dismissing the young man as though not worthy of his interest. And to Enid he added, "I have had a room made ready for you on the third floor. It is not far from the room occupied by your sister and my grandson after their marriage. I trust you will find it suitable."

"I'm sure I shall," she said lightly.

"Perhaps you would like to look at it now," the old man said. "If it does not appeal to you I can find you another. May I say it was occupied by your sister when she first came here. She used it fairly often when Stephen had to go away on business and she found herself alone."

Before Enid could make any reply to this, an aristocratic, straw-haired woman of late middle age came into the room. She was dressed elegantly in a pale blue dress and she had a hawk face. One could say at once this was a person of determined character. She came towards Enid with a glacial smile and extended her hand.

"You must be Miss Branch here from London," the older woman said.

"I am," Enid agreed, shaking hands with her. "And you are Stephen's mother, I'm sure."

The woman lifted her eyebrows. "Is there such a great resemblance? I have always thought that Stephen resembles his late father."

Edmund Porter spoke up impatiently. "It is true that Stephen resembles my son who was drowned in an unfortunate boating accident."

Enid saw at once that the two older people apparently did not get along too well. It was perfectly understandable, they lived under the same roof no matter how large the house. And Eleanor Porter was of a younger generation than her father-in-law.

Enid said, "I understand Stephen will return tonight."

Edmund Porter scowled. "Perhaps. They use planes for everything today. In my time it would have taken two weeks to cover the ground Stephen does in two days now."

Eleanor Porter was studying Enid with appraising eyes.

27

"You are a much more retiring type than your late sister," she ventured.

"Half-sister," Enid corrected her politely. "We were very close though, like real sisters. And actually I'm much like her in temperament though I often appear quieter on first meeting. I was stunned to learn of Madge's death."

"It made the entire house sad," Eleanor Porter said though there was not much feeling in her words.

"Were you here when it happened?" she asked.

An odd look flashed across the face of the older woman and she rather hastily said, "Yes. I was. But that is something you would best discuss with my son."

"I see," she said quietly. Then she turned to Wong Lee and told him, "I thank you for your help."

"A most enjoyable task for me, Miss Branch," the stout old Chinese said with a bow.

She then said to Edmund Porter and his daughter-in-law, "I will go upstairs and rest and freshen up some if you don't mind."

"I'll show you the way," Eleanor Porter said with cool graciousness. "Your half-sister always spoke of this house as being utterly Victorian and out-of-date. Do you think this is so?"

She glanced about her at the huge rooms with their rich Chinese tapestries on the walls, the heavy silk curtains at the windows and the furniture and ornaments all rich in Oriental design. She said, "It is Victorian but with a difference. Your decorating gives it a quaint and pleasant atmosphere."

The hollow-cheeked face of Edmund Porter showed approval. The old man said, "I built it as a copy of my father's place in Dorset. It was a fine house and so is this."

"Though hardly in keeping with Hong Kong," his thin daughter-in-law said with some acidity.

The stout Wong Lee spoke up at this point and told Enid, "There is one part of the estate charmingly in keeping with the atmosphere of the island. In the gardens between the main house and the edge of the cliff there is a summer house of Chinese design."

"That does sound interesting," she said.

Old Edmund Porter dismissed this with a gesture of his crippled hand. "It is a miniature teahouse, nothing more. A suggestion of the architect who built this place. I sometimes regret that I ever had it built!"

"Nonsense!" Eleanor Porter said in her arrogant fashion. "Wong Lee is right. The summer house is perhaps the one quality bit of architecture on the estate." And to Enid she added, "Do come along with me."

Enid followed the tall, very erect woman up the stairs which were covered in rich carpet. She recognized that Eleanor Porter was probably the dominant member of the family group. And she could not help wondering how the strong-willed Madge had made out with her domineering mother-in-law. She would be surprised if there hadn't been clashes between the two.

At the first landing Eleanor paused by a window which looked out on the ocean and the gardens. She told Enid, "You can look out here and get an excellent view of the tea-house."

Enid did and was delighted with what she saw. The summer house had been constructed like a true teahouse and was most ornate. She said, "That is the sort of thing I expected to see everywhere."

"There are some structures like it in the ancient section of the town," the older woman said. "But they are becoming more scarce every year."

They ascended the next two flights of broad stairs. Eleanor took her along a wide hall to an open door which led to a large bedroom with a canopy bed and dresser and other furniture in black ebony with Oriental decoration. The drapes of the room were white with pale blue dragons as a pattern. And the thick carpet on the floor was also of white and blue dragon design.

The older woman said, "I think you will like this room."

"How can I help it?" she asked and she noticed that her luggage had been carried up and neatly set out for her to unpack.

"I'll leave you now," Eleanor said. "You have two others of the family still to meet. My nephew Christopher and my adopted daughter, Sonya Chen."

Enid said, "Yes. Madge wrote me that there was a Chinese girl in the house. About Stephen's age."

"Yes. Both my son and my adopted daughter are extremely

29

fond of one another. They could not be any more close if they were of the same flesh and blood."

"Has Sonya Chen been here long?" she asked.

"We adopted her when she was three," Eleanor Porter replied. "She is twenty-six now."

"I look forward to meeting her," Enid said.

"She was educated in the mission school and college here," the older woman said. "Then we sent her to Columbia University in New York to get her master of arts degree. I'm sure you will like her."

"I'm sure I shall," she said.

The formidable Eleanor Porter left her and she at once began to unpack. It took a while and she paused now and then to take stock of the room and glance out the window at the gardens and the sea beyond. A tramp steamer moved lazily across the horizon issuing black smoke from its stacks. In the garden the teahouse looked smaller from the greater height of the third floor.

One of her pleasant discoveries was that she had a complete bathroom attached to her room. The house was not at all Victorian in this sense as the bathroom furnishings were modern. Evidently the house had been renovated from time to time.

When she finished unpacking she took a shower and put on a thin print dress and arranged her hair. The warm, pleasant weather here was in utter contrast to the cold, February fogs she'd left behind her in London. She saw there was a huge fan installed on the ceiling of her room and its great blades whirled around silently to keep the room cool.

Eleanor Porter had mentioned that Madge sometimes used this room. This gave her a strange feeling, a sensation that something of Madge was still within its walls. The vibrations of her dead half-sister might yet be somewhere in this room attempting to make themselves known to her. And still she did not know the circumstances of Madge's death.

There was a light knocking on her door and she opened it to find herself face to face with a Chinese girl of great beauty. The girl looked a trifle frightened as she stared at her in silence. Her dark hair was cut short but attractively set off her pleasant-featured face. Her almond eyes met those of Enid.

"I am Sonya Chen," she said in a soft, pleasant voice.

"I'm so happy to meet you," Enid said. "Do come in."

Hesitantly the girl entered. She was dressed in a gown with a high collar in Chinese design. It was of some crimson silken material with a yellow pattern at collar and sleeves and down the front.

The Chinese girl said, "You do not look at all like her!"

"You mean like Madge?"

"Yes."

She smiled thinly. "I have been told that before. We were only half-sisters. But we were much alike in disposition."

Sonya Chen said, "Stephen asked you to come here?"

"He felt that I should."

The Chinese girl looked frightened. "I think he was wrong. There is nothing you can do for her."

"I know that," she said. "But she was my sister. I wanted to come and learn what happened and how she spent her last days here."

"You should have remained in London," Sonya Chen said tensely. "This is not a house one should visit."

Startled by the girl's strange talk, she said, "I don't think I follow you."

"There is evil here!" the Chinese girl said earnestly. "Madge knew about it but she could not escape it!"

Enid stared at the girl. "What sort of evil?"

Sonya Chen shrugged. "Can evil be always explained? It is often enough to know it exists! And now you have come here to place yourself in the shadow of the same danger!"

"Why should I be in danger here?"

"Everyone is," the pretty Chinese girl said unhappily. "It is the house! This grim old house! There is a curse on it!"

Enid was finding it hard to believe the girl's outburst. "You amaze me," she said. "I was told you were educated here and in the United States. You speak English perfectly and yet you seem to be filled with superstitious fears!"

The girl's almond eyes flashed with disdain. "The evil I fear is not some native superstitious thing! It has nothing to do with my being Chinese! It is a different sort of fear! Born of your western world! Born of this house with its phantoms!"

"Phantoms?"

31

Sonya Chen hesitated and then her frightened air changed to one of weariness. She said contritely, "You must forgive me! I am overtired these days! I let myself be carried away. You must forget all that I said!"

Enid told her, "That will not be easy."

"You must!" the girl implored her. "I get these foolish notions. It is right that you should not share them. Do not tell my foster mother of my wild ramblings."

"But they had to mean something!" she told the girl accusingly.

"A product of my frayed nerves," Sonya Chen went on to explain in a taut voice. "I teach school in Hong Kong. It is not an easy task these days. The students question everything! I find myself harassed and weary by the end of the day. Then I come back here and it is so bleak!"

"I don't see it as bleak," Enid said. "I agree the house is of an old design but I think it pleasant."

The almond eyes were solemn. "You do not know it yet."

Enid frowned. "Did Madge feel the same way about this house that you do?"

"It frightened her," Sonya Chen said.

"Why?"

"You will find out," the Chinese girl warned her. "And then you should leave before you are trapped."

Enid said, "You talk in riddles. Why can't you tell me plainly why you are afraid and why you think I should not have come here?"

"You will have to ask my foster brother," the Chinese girl said. "He brought you here. You must ask Stephen!"

"I will as soon as I see him," she exclaimed. "But can't you speak more frankly in the meantime?"

"No."

"At least tell me how Madge met her death! No one has told me as yet."

Sonya Chen showed fear again. She moved towards the door to leave. "No, I can't do that!" she protested.

"Why?" she demanded.

"Stephen would not want it," the Chinese girl said in a voice filled with terror. "He is the one to tell you! Let him explain the evil which all of us here know and fear!" And she hurried out leaving Enid standing alone in dismay!

three

Enid had not been prepared for the emotional display offered by the Chinese girl. She had always had the idea that
Orientals went to great lengths to conceal their feelings yet
Sonya Chen had been shatteringly dramatic in her telling of
the fear the old Victorian house inspired in her.

And the Chinese girl like all the others seemed terrified to
make any reference to the manner in which Madge had met
her death. Enid felt she had travelled half-way around the
world to meet with nothing but frustration. It was maddening.

The house was silent again and she did not feel at ease in
her room. She decided to go downstairs and investigate the
garden and the teahouse before it was time to join the others
at dinner. She made her way down the stairs, passing a small
Chinese woman in a dark pajama suit with short cropped jet
black hair. The woman paused on the stairs with politely
bowed head as she went by her on the way down. Enid decided the woman was a servant in the house, which by its
size, must require many.

Reaching the lower floor she found open French doors and
made her way out to the lawn. It was to be expected that the
teahouse would draw her attention first. She crossed to it and
admired its teak construction and the steps leading up to its
interior. It was eight sided with open windows all the way
around it and had a pagodalike top covered with some sort
of shining gold paint.

33

She stood admiring its intricate design for a few moments before attempting to enter it. And as she stood there she unexpectedly was overtaken by a chilly sensation of fear. She actually trembled there in the warm sun. There was no reasonable explanation for the sudden eerie feeling—and it passed almost as soon as it came. She stood there at a loss. As a child she recalled an aunt speaking of experiencing terror and commenting that it was like someone walking over her grave. She thought of this long-forgotten remark now and wondered why it should come to her mind.

She put it down to the strange mystery surrounding Madge's death and the reluctance of everyone to talk about it with her. With an effort she shed the grim mood and mounted the steps to make an examination of the shadowed interior of the teahouse.

The moment she stepped inside the building with its pungently scented wood construction, she was aware of its coolness compared to the warm air on the lawn. She stood a moment staring back at the rear of the old Victorian house. And she saw that it did have something of an ugly look. It belonged neither to the quaint Oriental style of Hong Kong nor to the architecture of the present. It was a monument to an old man's memory of the house in which he had lived years ago in England.

"Why have you come here?" The question was put to her sharply in a rasping, harsh voice which came from the shadows.

Enid wheeled around quickly. She had not been aware there was anyone else in the teahouse. Now staring into the shadows at the other side of it she saw the outline of a figure.

The figure moved and came out of the shadows and it was the white-maned and palsied Edmund Porter. He had a grim look on his hollow-cheeked face as he told her, "Did you know this was one of Madge's favorite places?"

"No," she said.

"It was," the old man said, coming over to her. "I told her she came here to brood. It was a joke of course. But now I wonder if there mightn't have been something in it."

Enid said, "It has a cool and quiet atmosphere. A good place to think."

Edmund Porter's ravaged face showed approval and he

34

raised a twisted hand in a benediction. "Now that is a much better choice of word. This is a good place to think. I come here to remember. These days the past becomes more and more vivid to me. A failing in the old."

She said, "I think everyone has a right to their memories."

He nodded slowly. "We are bound to our memories whether we like it or not."

"I didn't mean to intrude on you," she said, feeling sorry for the withered old man who must have once been strong and handsome and a powerful force in the colony.

Edmund Porter shook his head. "No harm done. I was on the point of leaving. Wong Lee is staying to have dinner with us. An unusual gesture on his part, he lives very much to himself. He is in talking with my daughter-in-law. Eleanor talks enough for two and is bound to keep him busy. I have heard all she has to say and so came out here for a moment of quiet."

"I enjoyed meeting Mr. Wong Lee," she said.

"And I'm certain he liked you," the old man said. "If he hadn't he wouldn't be staying for dinner. He and I were the original partners in the firm which still bears my name today and is carried on by the family and Wong Lee."

"He has no wife or family."

"No. He has preferred to remain a bachelor and devote himself entirely to the firm."

Enid said, "He is so vigorous. It is hard to tell what his age might be."

Edmund Porter's cadaverous face showed a wan smile. "He is of my generation which means he has to be over eighty. I do not know his exact age. He never told me. But he has kept his health while I have become a wreck."

She was embarrassed. "It's not all that bad. You are active for a man of your age except for the palsy."

An expression of pride flashed across his ancient face. "They still call on me when there is a particularly knotty problem to solve. And I'm grateful to find I'm sometimes needed."

"But Stephen and Christopher are the active managers."

"Yes," he said, not sounding as happy as he had a moment before. "I often wish I had trained Sonya Chen, my adopted

35

granddaughter, for a role in the business. It would have been better for her than teaching, and better for the firm."

"Couldn't she still make the change?"

"I have discussed it with Stephen and he is willing to take her on as a partner. But Christopher has rebelled against the idea. He thinks she would cripple the business with her decisions. So I have done nothing about it."

"She is a refreshingly beautiful girl."

"You have met her?"

"Yes. She came to my room for a few minutes."

The old man looked to be lost in memories as he said, "I was attracted to her loveliness when she was only a child. That is why I adopted her. All my life I have been a lonely man with a thirst for beauty." He gave her another sharp glance. "You know that I lost my wife when she was still young and very beautiful?"

"No, I didn't," she said.

"I have been a widower these many years," Edmund Porter said. "Losing Regina—that was my wife's name—was a bitter experience for me. I then gave all my love to my son, Stephen. But Stephen was never close to me. And he met an untimely death. Today I place my hopes in his son, Stephen, who was married to your sister."

"And Christopher?" she said.

"Was sent here from England by his father. He was not doing well in the old country and his father felt he would do better here. And he has."

"His father was your nephew?"

"Yes," Edmund Porter said. "Which makes Stephen and Christopher cousins as well as partners in the firm. Happily they seem to get on well enough."

Enid suggested, "Perhaps it would have been better if Stephen had married Sonya Chen rather than my sister. Sonya would have understood the islands and their ways."

"I thought of that often," the old man said frankly. "But no one can dictate who will love whom. Sonya and my grandson did not love each other. Nor do she and Christopher have a strong relationship. In fact, neither of them likes the other."

She was on the point of asking him about Madge and how she'd met her death. But something warned her that this

36

would be useless. The old man had evaded answering this question before and he would surely do so again. Instead she moved away from him to glance out at the ocean and say, "I'm sure Madge must have loved this view."

Edmund Porter nodded. "As a matter of fact she did mention that this was the chief attraction of the teahouse for her. The view is magnificent. Much closer than the one from the main house."

"Yes, it is."

"Like most everyone else she disliked the main house," the palsied old man said bitterly. "It does not matter that it represents my only tie with my homeland. That it is the one thing which takes me back to my good boyhood days. If they had their way the place would be torn down and some new, modern structure put up. I'm sure that will happen as soon as I'm gone!"

She turned to him again. "It is a rather different sort of house," she said. "Even ugly. But then many Victorian houses were ugly."

"This is an almost exact replica of the one I knew as a boy," the old man said tensely. "Madge might have been happy here but she chose to let the others turn her against it."

"Does Stephen feel the same way about the house?"

Edmund Porter spread his hands. "Who knows what is in Stephen's mind? I'm sure I don't. In that way he is much like his late father. I think he dislikes the house but puts up with it in silence." He paused and then added, "I think perhaps we ought to both go inside now. Dinner will soon be ready and Eleanor does not like to be kept waiting."

So she allowed him to escort her into the house again where they joined Eleanor and the stout, old Wong Lee in the richly furnished living room. They were soon joined by Sonya Chen and Christopher Porter. It was Enid's first meeting with the bluff, friendly young man.

Christopher came to her at once. He was exceptionally tall and wore horn-rimmed glasses. He had a loose-featured but pleasant face and a thatch of disorderly brown hair which he wore long enough to cover his shirt collar. He had twinkling eyes and an easy flow of conversation.

37

Shaking hands with her, he said, "Stephen told me you were coming."

"He kindly made it possible," she said.

Christopher paid no attention to this, saying, "He needs you here because of the tragedy concerning Madge. I'm glad you were able to make the journey. Will you be able to stay long?"

"I have a few months leave of absence from my job in England," she said.

"Excellent," Christopher said. "That gives you plenty of time. I'm sure Stephen will invite you to remain for a while. He ought to be here tonight soon after dinner. His plane is scheduled to arrive shortly."

"I'm anxious to talk with him again," she said.

"I'm sure you are," the brown-haired young man agreed.

She had no further chance to talk with him. At that moment Eleanor came over to join them and as usual dominated the conversation. They shortly moved on to a dining room which adjoined a verandah. There were numerous French doors along the length of the dining room which, if the occasion required, could give access to the verandah. On this particular evening many screened windows were open and the result was the dining room was cool and airy.

Sonya Chen had changed to a lovely brocaded white gown with a high collar in Chinese style. It appeared her entire wardrobe had been tailored to conform with certain modes of Chinese dress. The girl with the flashing almond eyes was quiet and nervous at the table. Eleanor was loud and opinionated while old Edmund Porter and his nephew, Christopher, talked a good deal to each other about business affairs which were of no interest to the others.

Enid found the ancient Mr. Wong Lee on her right and he proved to be an excellent conversationalist for which she was grateful. She needed some strong stimulation on this first night with the Porter family. And all the while she waited nervously for the missing Stephen to put in an appearance. For it appeared that only from him would she learn the truth about Madge.

She turned to the old man near the end of the meal and said, "I understand your chief interest is the firm which you helped found, that you have little time for anything else."

The moonfaced old Wong Lee said, "Your description of me hardly does me justice. I am a bachelor and I live alone but I have other interests. I attend a certain temple, I enjoy the reading of philosophy and I serve on a local council whose object is to help the lot of the peasants living in the harbor on their sampan boats."

She smiled. "I was sure you weren't one of those hard-driving businessmen we have in the West."

The old man chuckled. "I know the type and I must admit I have a grudging admiration for some of their traits. But I think of a parable by the philosopher, Liehtse, whenever I am tempted to emulate them. Have you heard the parable of 'The Man Who Only Saw Gold'?"

"No."

"It is a simple one," Wong Lee assured her. "There was a man of Ch'i who desired only to have gold. He dressed up properly and went out in the early morning to the market. He went straight to the gold dealer's shop and snatched the gold away and walked off. The officers arrested him and questioned him. "Why, the people were all there," the policeman said. "Why did you rob them of gold in broad daylight?" And the man replied, "I only saw the gold, I didn't see the people." In my case I prefer to think of people rather than only gold."

"I like that," she told him. "The Chinese have a simple way of explaining things."

"We are an old culture," Wong Lee said. "My father once gave me a credo. He told me, 'Be firm in your acts, but easy in your heart. Be strict with yourself but gentle with your fellow men.' I have tried to remember it and apply it in my life."

She asked him, "Did you often talk with my late sister, Madge?"

The old man's round face betrayed no expression. He said, "She and I had many conversations. She was a lovely young woman."

"I'm glad she had you as a friend."

"I was happy to know her," the old Chinese said. "And her loss has grieved me."

Enid said, "I don't know much of her life here but I have

39

been told that she didn't like this house. That she came to fear it."

"Many have," Wong Lee said.

"Why?"

"There are as many reasons as there are people who fear it," the old man in the linen suit said. "Perhaps the house has become a symbol for those who need something on which to concentrate their hatreds."

"I'm not sure I follow you," she said. "Edmund Porter says that she liked to go and sit by herself in the teahouse. That doesn't seem like Madge. She was an outgoing person who always liked to be with others."

The old Chinese shrugged. "Perhaps life in Hong Kong made a change in her."

"I can't think it did."

"The teahouse has a special significance," Wong Lee said. "It is of the Old China just as this main house is of the Old England. You should show interest in it while you are here. It is an unusual structure."

"I must visit it again," she said.

The dinner party broke up and the tall, slyly charming Christopher came to her and, leading her a few steps from where she was standing talking to Wong Lee, told her, "I've been on the phone. Stephen's flight from Siam is going to arrive late."

"Oh!" She was let down.

The twinkling brown eyes met hers and the white-suited Christopher suggested, "Since Stephen won't be here I think it would be fun for me to show you a bit of Hong Kong at night."

She shook her head. "I think not. I only arrived today. I'm weary and I should be here when Stephen does arrive."

"You won't see him until midnight, if by then," the persuasive Christopher said. "That gives us more than a couple of hours."

She was as wary of this suave young man in the horn-rimmed glasses as she was of the idea. She was afraid of Christopher without really knowing why.

She said, "I'd rather stay here."

"You'll be here most of the time," he argued. "Let me

show you some of the city tonight while I have a chance. I'm normally too busy to be an excursion guide."

She gave an embarrassed smile. "It's not that I don't appreciate your offer." Then she had an idea. "If I should go can Sonya Chen come along?"

The tall man showed a bored look. "She won't. She goes up to her room every night with her books. And she doesn't approve of me."

"Why not?"

"I barred her from becoming one of the firm," he said. "I'm not strong for women in business. I like them as social creatures."

"I work for an insurance firm in London," she told him. "So you can't approve of me."

He gave her one of his disarming smiles. "Come on. You needn't be afraid of me. Don't play games! Let's ride into the city for an hour. I promise to bring you back early."

She tried to get him off the subject but in the end he won. She agreed to go in to Hong Kong for an hour if he would bring her back in time to talk with Stephen. She told Eleanor of her acceptance of the invitation and the older woman's hawk face showed cold disapproval of the idea.

Eleanor stood very erect and said, "You will find Christopher to be a spoiled young man who expects to get his own way most of the time."

"He was very persistent about my going in to the city," she admitted.

"I'm sure he was," Eleanor said grimly. "Just keep in mind what I've said and don't allow him any easy victories."

She blushed. "I won't forget."

"If Stephen comes while you're gone I'll tell him you won't be away long," Stephen's mother said.

"Please do that," Enid said. She went to say goodnight to Wong Lee and the others.

Wong Lee bowed to her and said, "Our friendship will grow. People who make friends easily are shallow friends."

There was fear in Sonya Chen's manner when Enid bade her good night and said she was going in to see Hong Kong with Christopher. The Chinese girl whispered, "Do not tell him anything of what I said to you today. Promise!"

41

"Of course," she said, surprised. "You may depend on me."

Old Edmund Porter was worried about Stephen's late arrival. "Confounded planes! They may save time but when they crash everyone dies. We've had several plane wrecks here in the last few years. I've tried to get Stephen to use the ships for travel but he refuses."

Enid said, "I'm certain Stephen is safe. I understand the plane left its destination late."

Christopher suggested she get a wrap as the nights could be cool and they would be driving in an open car. He led her out into the moonlight where his cream-colored Jaguar stood waiting. Enid knew it would be an extremely sophisticated girl who would not be charmed by the combination of attentive young man, dashing sports car, exotic setting and moonlight. And she was not all that sophisticated.

The tall young man saw her seated comfortably on the cushioned leather front seat and then got in behind the wheel beside her. He started the engine—it was so quiet she couldn't hear it—and with a smile her way, he said, "We couldn't afford to miss celebrating this first night of our meeting."

As he drove away from the house in the moonlight, she said, "Do you think it all that important?"

"I've been waiting for the moment," he said. "You don't seem a stranger to me. Madge told me about you often."

She glanced at him and saw that the breeze which was making her own hair unruly was ruffling his long curly locks as well. She said, "Then you and Madge became close friends?"

He was driving fast with his eyes on the beam of the headlights on the road. "I was her best friend."

"Better than Stephen? Her husband?"

He kept staring ahead. "Husbands aren't always that understanding."

"I wouldn't know," she said. "But if you knew Madge so well why didn't you tell me more about her?"

"That's Stephen's job."

Upset, she replied, "Everyone tells me that. I don't know why you won't talk about her to me. Tell me about how she died!"

42

"I told you, that's Stephen's job," he said and he gave her a brief glance as he made the car speed along. "Let's forget Madge for a little and talk about you!"

She put the shawl over her head and asked him, "Don't you have any speed laws here?"

"Not in this end of the island. This is for the people of privilege. And the Porters are high-ranking officers of that class."

"So it seems," she said. "But I don't want to be in a wreck my first night here!"

"I learned to drive with Stirling Moss!" the young man said cheerfully.

"That doesn't surprise me. But you're not on a race track!"

"You're not married," he said. "At least you haven't any wedding ring."

"Madge must have told you I wasn't married."

"She might not have known."

"I had no secrets from her," Enid said, bracing back against the seat as they veered wildly around a short curve on the road which followed the shore.

"Engaged?"

"No."

"Man-hater?"

"No."

"What then?"

"I like to be my own person," she said "I'm not ready for marriage yet."

He gave her a knowing smile. "Neither am I."

"And I'm not the type for affairs," she was quick to tell him.

"A pity," Christopher said. And then he eased the speeding Jaguar as he told her, "Also a pity I have to slow down. We are coming into the city. From now on I cease being a gay young blade and become a stodgy tour guide. And you have only yourself to blame!"

Enid found herself laughing at him. It was impossible not to like the young man though she felt wary of him at the same time. But she soon realized what he had meant by the magic of the city at night.

The streets of Hong Kong were the most enchanting night streets she'd ever seen. The advertising signs of Hong Kong

43

were in neon shades new to her. There were none of the harsh colors in use. Instead they presented a galaxy of crowded Chinese ideograms in neon signs of pale violet, pink and green. The mystery of their meanings also added to the pleasure they gave her.

Christopher drove the open car slowly along the busy street and she could smell sandalwood, frying onions and a kind of odd sweet scent she had never known before. He parked the car and took her to a busy bar. There were many types present in the softly lighted, smoke-filled place. Certainly it was a mixture of East and West. She was enchanted by the pretty Chinese girls in their cheongshams with high stiff collars and skirts slit from the hem up as far as the beauty of the wearer's leg would allow.

Christopher was mildly amused by her enthusiastic reactions and took her on to a tiny side street restaurant where he insisted that she eat only with chopsticks.

She faced the bowl of food with dismay and cried, "I can't do it!"

"Try," he said. And he deftly went at his food with his own set of chopsticks.

Enid followed and only managed to get a little food to her mouth. But what she managed to eat was delicious. It was a tasty mixture of chicken and walnuts. At last it was time to leave. She reminded him that the tour was to be of only an hour's duration.

"I can't show you Hong Kong in an hour," he complained as he led her back to the cream Jaguar.

She laughed. "I didn't ask to see the entire city. I've enjoyed what I've seen."

As they settled in the car to drive off she glanced towards the street and from an alley nearby she saw a Chinese in a dirty linen suit of Western style, staring at them. There was something in the way he was watching them that bothered her. She noted the long scar on his cheek and the fact that he was lurking a few feet from the sidewalk in the shadowed alley.

She tugged at Christopher's arm as he started the motor and in a taut voice said, "That man in the alley! He's been glaring at us."

Christopher gave a careless glance in the direction of the alley as he headed the car out into traffic. He told her, "I

44

didn't see anything special about him. Hong Kong is filled with hard-looking characters like that. We have an underworld, you know."

"He was giving us special attention," she maintained.

The young man at the wheel gave her a mocking glance and said, "He probably intended to slit our throats and rob us."

"I don't think that's funny," she said.

"Sorry," Christopher replied contritely. "Come to think of it, it wasn't. Bad joke. Forgive me."

"What about the underworld?" she asked.

"We have a little of everything," he said, as he drove on more swiftly with the city now behind them. He told her, "Take a look back over your shoulder and see the skyscrapers lit up against the sky. It'll remind you of London."

She looked back and saw the tall buildings with their lights. "A lot different from the tiny restaurant we were in."

"The old and the new," he said lightly.

She settled back against the seat. "I hope Stephen's plane arrived and he is at the house when we get there."

"Is it all that important?"

"It is to me," she said.

He drove on in silence, swiftly now that they were on the road with hardly any traffic again. She understood this road served the mansions of the European rich who lived on this end of the island. They all owned shorefront property and lived in the same fashion as the merchant princes who had first made their fortunes in fabulous Hong Kong.

Without warning Christopher brought the car to a screeching halt and pulled it over to the side of the road. He gave her a stern look. "Something important!" he said.

"What?" she asked, wondering what was wrong.

"I find myself in love with you," he replied and in the same unexpected fashion took her in his arms and held her close while he gave her a passionate kiss.

It took her seconds to realize what was happening and when she did she pounded at him to let her go and succeeded in breaking away from him.

"That was a miserable trick," she said accusingly.

"I'm in love with you," Christopher replied as if that gave him license for whatever he had in mind.

45

"Don't be a fool!" Enid said with anger. "I'm in no mood for your silly games. I expected you to be an adult."

The young man went pale with anger and in a surly tone, said, "Silly games? Come now, don't be so coldly British."

"And don't you be so forward," she cried.

His reply was to angrily turn on the engine and wheel the car back onto the road and begin driving towards Porter House at a mad speed. She sat tensely in the front seat of the open car expecting every moment that it would skid off the curving road and plunge over the cliffs into the moonlit ocean.

But his boast about being a good driver had not been an idle one. The car sped on through the night. Then suddenly ahead she saw men in white appear from the bushes on either side of the road. Christopher saw them at the same instant. In a tone which was close to a wild shriek, he warned her, "Duck! Duck down!"

She did, throwing herself down onto the floor of the front seat as he bent almost under the wheel. Then she heard a weird sound and there was a splintering of glass with some of the sharp fragments coming down on her!

four

Enid screamed her fear and remained crouching on the floor of the roadster as it careened drunkenly from left to right and then back again. Christopher Porter had raised himself up to a bent position over the wheel as he miraculously managed to keep the wavering car under control. Shots rang out from behind them and she had a feeling that at least one or two of the bullets must have come close to his head. Undaunted he drove on until he had the skidding car under control once more and they were speeding along the curved shore road.

She dragged herself up onto the seat and saw that the windshield was shattered and its metal supports twisted. It was from this that the splinters of glass had showered down on her. Christopher's face was pale and grim as he kept his eyes on the road ahead.

"What happened?" she asked in a quavering voice.

"Old trick," he muttered grimly. "And it almost worked."

"What do you mean, trick?" she demanded, becoming less frightened and increasingly annoyed at the danger to which he'd exposed her.

"That fellow you pointed out on the sidewalk. I should have paid more attention to him," Christopher said without looking at her. "He and his henchmen strung a taut wire cable across the road!"

"A wire cable! I didn't see anything!"

"Neither did I until the last minute. That's why I cried out for you to duck! The cable was meant to sever our heads or wreck the car. Preferably both. As it is they've made a fine mess of my Jag!"

"We're lucky to be alive," she reprimanded him.

"I know," he agreed. "The cable was stretched from a tree on one side of the road to one on the other. If the cable hadn't snapped the car would have turned over. We'd have died in a flaming wreck or they would have finished us!"

"They?"

"Chinese thugs," Christopher said, slowing the car a bit. It was difficult to drive without the windshield. She pressed her hands to her hair.

"Why would they do such a thing?" she demanded.

He shrugged. "Robbery? Who knows?"

"I think you do!" she accused him. "They must really hate you to set a trap like that."

"Everyone makes some enemies," he said as he slowed the car down to turn into the side road leading to Porter House.

The tropical night with its soft air and scented aroma had suddenly taken on a sinister atmosphere. The lush flowers and trees under the stars seemed to hold a menace which had not been present before.

She said, "The man looked at you with true hatred. What did you do to him?"

"Who knows? Bested him in some business deal perhaps. These Chinese are strange people. You'll find that out." He brought the car to a halt before the front door of the house and for the first time eyed her anxiously. "You aren't cut? There was a lot of flying glass for a moment."

"I don't think so," she said. "There are small fragments on my dress. I'll shake it when I get out of the car. What about you?"

"I have a way of escaping serious injury," he said with that reckless smile returning to his face again. "I didn't even lose my glasses."

She gave him an accusing glance. "Your luck may run out one of these days."

"If we'd stayed parked a while longer those fellows might have gotten weary and given up. You should have been more understanding."

Enid got out of the car and said, "Only you would have the nerve to say that!"

He leaned towards her. "I want us to be friends!"

"You haven't made it easy!"

"Sorry," he said. "It's my way. No finesse. But give me another try. And one more thing, don't say anything about what happened inside. Especially not to Stephen if he's there."

She noted the urgency in his voice and was more than ever convinced that he was mixed up in some sort of dangerous game which he wanted to keep from the others in the family.

"I nearly lost my life," she said. "Why shouldn't I mention it?"

"It will do no good and cause me trouble," he said. "I'll get the car out of the way early in the morning and have it fixed. No one need know unless you tell them."

"You're asking me to be a confederate in concealing what happened."

"All right. I am," he said impulsively. "I'm sorry if I offended you. But do be a good sport about this."

She hesitated. "I'll think about it," she said at last.

The brown-haired man's infectious smile returned and he said, "You won't regret it. I can be a good friend or a bitter enemy." And with that rather unusual comment he drove off towards the rear of the house.

She stood there for a moment stunned at his impudence and more than a little angry. She brushed her dress to make sure no small splinters of glass remained on it and she also ran her hands through her hair for the same reason. Later she would examine her clothing more closely and take a shampoo. Just now she had to enter the house and carry off the situation in some way.

She opened the heavy door and let herself inside. For a moment she felt the area there was deserted but suddenly Eleanor Porter emerged from the shadowed doorway of the living room. The regal older woman advanced across the foyer to her and studied her with her piercing eyes.

"Stephen has not yet returned," she said.

"Oh?"

"I worry about my son on these night flights," the older woman said. "But I dare not show it since my father-in-law is always in a panic. You know that Stephen's father was

49

drowned when the seaplane he was in crashed into the ocean."

Enid said, "This is the first time I've heard the details. I took it to be a boating accident since I heard he'd drowned."

"No," the grim older woman said, compressing her thin lips. "He was on his way from one of the outer islands in a seaplane. It suddenly burst into flames. Both he and the pilot escaped. But they were killed by sharks before they could be rescued."

"How awful!" Enid said with sympathy. "No wonder Stephen's grandfather worries about him."

"All Edmund Porter cares about is that the line goes on," Eleanor said bitterly. "He thinks only of Stephen. He offers me no pity for the loss of my husband. Nor does he give me credit for having acted as the mistress of this household all these years."

Enid said, "I'm sure he must appreciate it. He only fails to mention it."

"There are many things he doesn't mention," the older woman said, her shadow reflected against the wall of the dimly lighted foyer. "He was sorely disappointed when your sister died without giving him a great-grandson."

They were back to the subject of Madge's death and yet she knew that the older woman would balk at giving her the information she was anxiously awaiting concerning the death. She said, "Madge was good with children. She would have made an excellent mother."

Eleanor Porter's hawk face wore a sarcastic look. "We'll never really know that, will we?"

"No," she said quietly. And then she asked, "What about Stephen's grandmother? I take it she has been dead a long while."

"A very long while," the stiff Eleanor said. "Come with me." And in a surprisingly abrupt manner she waved Enid to follow her across the foyer into the living room where only one table lamp broke the shadows. The older woman halted before a large oil painting which was mostly in shadow and, pointing to it, said, "That's a portrait of Regina, Stephen's grandmother."

Enid studied the portrait as well as she could in the almost dark room. It was a three-quarter study of a young woman of commanding beauty and yet possessed of a strangely Oriental cast of features. The woman in the portrait had thick black hair in a coiffure often seen in Asian women, and her delicate features and faintly olive skin enhanced the impression that she was Oriental. To complete the illusion she wore a gown with a high collar in the same style as the adopted Sonya Chen seemed to favor now.

Enid turned to the older woman and said, "She was a beauty."

"Yes, she was," Eleanor replied coldly.

"And she almost looks Chinese."

The hawk-faced mother of Stephen sniffed in her arrogant fashion as she gazed at the portrait with a faint air of disgust. "That's not so strange. She was part Chinese."

"Really?" Enid was surprised, she'd not heard this before.

"Edmund Porter met her here in Hong Kong and married her," Eleanor said. "She was what is called an Eurasian. She had a Chinese mother and a British father. They weren't too well accepted socially in those days. Of course it is all different now."

"I should hope so," Enid said. "She looks lovely and intelligent. I'm sure she must have been a good wife to Edmund Porter."

"Some say that losing her broke his heart," Eleanor replied with a grim look. "I rather doubt it. He cares more for himself than anyone else. But she did bear him a son, who became my husband and Stephen's father."

Enid said, "Edmund Porter must think a great deal of Stephen."

"He does," the older woman agreed. "And when he is in a sentimental mood he refers to his Regina as the Jade Princess. That is what we all call her now as a result of his ramblings. The Jade Princess of Porter House."

"So Stephen does have some Chinese blood."

Eleanor looked upset. "There is no hint of it in him. Nor was there any in my late husband."

"I think it a good thing," Enid said. "It should help the Porters here with their business."

"They do well enough," Eleanor said. "Christopher is the black sheep. How did you make out with him tonight?"

She took a step away to gain further concealment from the

shadows as she told the older woman, "I was strict with him. I remembered your warning."

"You will do well to keep it in mind," Eleanor said. "He fancies himself as something of a ladykiller and I doubt that he works hard enough for the firm to justify his being kept on. But old Edmund has great family loyalty and Christopher is a Porter."

Enid wanted to avoid discussing her evening with the young man. She had promised him not to mention anything about the frightening incident in which the car had almost been wrecked. So to quickly change the subject she glanced up at the portrait of Regina again and said, "You didn't tell me about her death."

Eleanor advanced towards her with a grim majesty. "She vanished."

"Vanished?"

"Yes. She had a cousin ill on the mainland. She left her son at home and took a boat and wagon to the hills on the mainland where her cousin lived. She never reached there and she never returned."

"What happened?"

"No one really knows," Eleanor said in her stiff way. "Edmund Porter's theory is that she was robbed and then murdered by Chinese bandits hiding in the hills."

"Was that likely?"

"Things of a similar nature happened all the time. It seemed that this may well have been her fate. It was a grim blow for Edmund Porter. And it marked the beginning of the legend."

"The legend?"

"Of the Jade Princess," the older woman said with asperity. "Her ghost is supposed to haunt this house. I thought Wong Lee might have told you. He is said to have remained a bachelor because he lost Regina to Edmund Porter. They were both in love with her and partners in the same company."

"A strange story," Enid said with awe.

The tall Eleanor nodded grimly. "I have been told that Regina broke many hearts in her time. And they claim she is jealous of any attractive female who comes to this house. Her phantom appears and tries to drive them away."

"Does anyone believe that to be anything but a romantic fable?"

The hawk face of the older woman studied her in the shadows as she said soberly, "There are many who have seen the Jade Princess, myself among them. But you must never speak of her ghostly appearances to Edmund Porter. Such talk infuriates him."

"And no wonder," Enid said, defending the old man. "He loved Regina and he would not want people talking about her ghost and how she met her death."

"I suppose not," the older woman said. "But you remain here long enough and I promise you that you'll receive a visit from her."

"It is something I can well do without."

"So can we all. But these things do happen."

Cold chills played about her spine as she heard all this. What a strange place it was! And she had yet to learn how Madge died. She was suddenly very weary.

She said, "I must go to bed."

Eleanor was staring at her in a strange way and then she reached out and touched the hair on the side of her head which was nearest. The older woman withdrew her hand and held her palm out for Enid to see a tiny fragment of glass sparkling in her palm. She said with satisfaction, "I saw it glistening in your hair."

Enid at once knew a moment of panic. She did not want to break faith with Christopher and tell about the murder attempt on them. Uneasily, she exclaimed, "I have no idea where it came from!"

"Broken glass," the older woman said, glancing at the tiny, sparkling object. "It probably fell from some balcony in the ancient section of the city. They have all sorts of cheap ornaments hanging from their windows and balconies. I have no doubt Christopher took you strolling there."

"Yes," she said, relieved that the older woman had provided an explanation for the awkward discovery. "I found it glamorous."

"Tinsel glamor!" Eleanor Porter said sourly. "I would gladly give it all up to return to England and spend my final days there."

"Why don't you?"

The older woman raised her eyebrows and said coldly, "I will not desert my son. With the loss of his wife he needs me more than ever before."

"Of course," she agreed hastily and felt it was time to manage a discreet retreat. The arrogant old woman standing there in the shadowed room with her made her uneasy. Also it was very late. "Now, if you will excuse me, I'll go up to bed."

Eleanor nodded. "Stephen will see you in the morning."

Enid bade her goodnight and then hurried up to her room. The many happenings since her arrival at Porter House had left her in a state of confusion. She was shocked that no one had offered to tell her about the manner of Madge's death after she'd made such a long and strenuous journey to learn the facts. And with all the tensions in the ancient, white Victorian mansion she worried that her half-sister might not have been at all happy there. Surely there was a sense of the sinister about the place which was upsetting.

Her room was warm despite the soft whirring fan in the ceiling. Some sort of giant night bugs were hurling themselves against the windows, attracted by the room's lights. She quickly drew the shades and noticed that her bed had been turned down and her nightgown set out.

She bolted the door to the hallway and then proceeded to undress and prepared to take a shower and shampoo her hair at the same time. She was thankful that only a small bit of the broken windshield had remained in her hair and she could not help wondering what Christopher was doing about his damaged car. She also wondered how he had come to make enemies so bitter they would attempt to murder him in this way.

With a tiny shudder she stepped under the shower. By the time she'd finished with her hair and dried it as well as she could with a towel it was getting late. She was struck suddenly by the accumulated weariness of her long day and night. She literally collapsed into the waiting bed and fell asleep quickly.

Her sleep was dreamless and deep. But she was wakened to the shadows of the big bedroom by what she thought was someone calling her name softly. She sat up, still partly in a

54

sleepy daze, but certain she had heard someone call out to her.

Wide-eyed she stared into the shadows and asked, "Who's there?"

There was no immediate reply. But after a few moments she was aware of another sound like the soft rustling of silk. For some weird reason this sent a cold fear through her.

Now she was fully awake and frightened. She gazed into the darkness with the silence pressing in on her. Again she called out and again there was no reply. But she thought she saw a figure dart quickly across the room at the foot of her bed. She reached for the bedside lamp and turned it on. As she did so she caught a glimpse of a closet door closing and a thin hand vanishing.

She threw back the clothes and got to her feet. She was convinced that someone must have made an entry to her room and crossed to the closet for a hiding place. She moved to the closet door and stood before it hesitantly. It was of step-in proportions and many of her clothes had been hung in there. Now she feared that some intruder had also taken refuge in the closet.

Her voice had a tremor in it as she demanded, "Who is in there?"

Again there was no reply and she stood there worrying that perhaps it had all been a bad dream. But the movement of a figure in the darkness, the slowly closing door and the thin hand were too vivid in her mind's eye for her to be mistaken. What to do?

Her dilemma was resolved by a light tapping on the door which led from the corridor. Her attention was now diverted to this other door and with fearful eyes still on the closet she moved slowly toward it.

"Yes?" she asked, leaning close to the door.

"I was passing by and I heard you," a familiar voice told her. "You sounded frightened. Can I help?" It was none other than Christopher in the hallway.

She at once unbolted the door and opened it to find the tall young man standing there in pajamas and dressing gown. He stepped into her room at once.

Enid pointed to the closet door and said, "I'm sure I saw someone in the shadows and they vanished in there. I turned on the lamp just in time to see a hand vanishing as the closet door was shut."

The cynical Christopher's eyes gleamed with amusement behind his thick glasses. He ran a hand through his tousled brown hair. "I'd say that calls for an investigation on my part."

"Please be careful."

He gave her a lazy grin. "I'm an expert at handling intruders. You should have more confidence in me." And he moved over to the closet and hurled the door open.

She took a step nearer and could see no one inside the dark closet. "There's a light. The switch is by the door."

Christopher found the switch and turned it on. Next he stepped into the closet in which almost her entire wardrobe was hanging. He probed behind the clothes and then emerged from the closet to offer her an amused look.

"Are you sure you didn't have a nightmare?" he asked.

Her cheeks flamed. "Quite sure!"

He shrugged. "No one in there. You must have had a visit from a ghost. Come to think of it you're exactly the sort of person the Jade Princess might resent. She's made a brief call to let you know she doesn't want you here."

"I don't believe that!" she said defiantly, beginning to worry that her imagination might have betrayed her.

Christopher Porter's eyes met hers and there was an odd gleam in them as he said quietly, "Don't be too quick to question our phantom. Madge didn't."

"What do you mean?"

"She saw the Jade Princess many times. She told me so," the tall young man said, turning off the closet light switch and closing the door.

Fear and confusion took hold of her completely as she went to him and pleaded, "Tell me about Madge! What happened to her? You claim to have been her best friend."

He shook his head gently. "Not my place. I have to keep peace in the family. Stephen will talk to you in the morning. It is her husband's right to break the news to you."

She stood there trembling. "I have heard she often used this room."

"Perhaps. I wouldn't know," Christopher said. "Did that old battle-axe question you about our night in the city?"

56

"You mean Eleanor?"

"Who else?"

"She asked me some questions."

"I hope you gave her the right answers. You didn't tell her about what happened to the car?"

"No," she said, staring at him and wondering if he hadn't deliberately come by to find this out. It was merely a coincidence that he had come at an opportune moment.

"Good girl," the tall man said, patting her on the arm. "My advice to you now is to get back to sleep."

"I'm not sure that I can."

"Leave your bed lamp on," he advised. And he started for the door. "And don't forget to put the bolt back in place."

"I won't," she said uneasily as she followed him to the door which led to the corridor.

He gave her another of those mocking smiles. "Believe me, your greatest danger probably lies in bounders like myself prowling about in the night. The bolted door is terribly important." He gave her a wink in parting.

Some of her fear vanished in the rage which she felt at his cruel taunting. She quickly closed the door on him and shoved the bolt in place. Then she leaned weakly against the door with tears of frustration in her eyes.

He had treated her like some sort of idiot after she had been considerate enough to keep her promise in saying nothing about the bizarre accident which had climaxed their night in Hong Kong. And there were his insinuating comments about Madge though he refused to tell her anything about her dead half-sister's experiences in the old mansion.

She started back to bed and then hesitated part way to the closet door. She went to it on impulse and opened it to inspect it for her own satisfaction. Switching on its light she stepped inside, and she was astonished to find the tiny room filled with an aroma which surely had not been there earlier. Her nostrils were filled with the odor of an exotic perfume with what seemed a jasmine base. The phantom might have vanished but the odor of her perfume remained!

Enid's lovely face reflected her shock at this eerie discovery. Why had Christopher not mentioned it? Perhaps he had assumed the perfume was hers, emanating from her clothing hung in the closet. Or perhaps he had chosen to ignore it.

With a feeling of having met utter defeat she turned off the closet light and shut the door. She returned to bed but followed Christopher's advice in leaving the bed lamp on. After propping up the pillows she lay against them for a long while thinking of the strangeness of it all. She had journeyed so far in such a short space of time and now she found herself in an old mansion filled with mystery and hostilities.

It was inevitable that she would think about the young American journalist who had been so helpful to her during the plane journey from England. Christopher appeared to be the only one of the Porters friendly with the pleasant American. She remembered that Charles Milano had mentioned being a guest of the Hong Kong Hilton and decided she would attempt to contact him there as soon as she'd talked with Stephen Porter. As soon as she learned something about Madge's death!

These were the thoughts filling her mind when she at last dropped off into a restless sleep. The sleep lasted until morning when she was wakened by a light tapping on the door of her room. She rose and put on a dressing gown and went over to open the door.

A diminutive, old Chinese woman in black stood there with a tray. "Breakfast for Missee," the elderly servant in the black kimona said gravely.

"Thank you," Enid said. "Just place the tray on the table by the window."

The old woman nodded, carried out her instructions, and left the room with quiet dignity. Enid washed and sat down to the ample breakfast. It was evidently a custom of the house to serve breakfast in the guest's rooms.

From her chair she could see the gardens and the ocean beyond. She noted that the spare, white-clad old Edmund Porter was already standing out by the golden-domed teahouse giving one of the gardeners instructions about caring for the flower beds surrounding the eight-sided summer pavilion.

She thought about this thin, palsied Englishman and the stout Wong Lee. They had been partners for more than half a century and according to Eleanor had loved the same woman. But it was Edmund Porter who had won Regina. She

58

wondered what the two men had been like in those days and what a different sort of place Hong Kong had been.

When she finished breakfast she put on a plain yellow linen dress. She studied herself in the dresser mirror and thought she looked a trifle weary. But this was not surprising in view of all she had gone through. Not the least being her experience with the ghostly intruder in the middle of the night.

Satisfied that she looked well enough she finally made her way downstairs. The first person she met was Sonya Chen. The pretty Chinese girl bowed to her shyly.

"I hope you have enjoyed your room," Sonya Chen said. The almond green eyes were fixed on her nervously.

It at once came to Enid's mind that the Chinese girl might have been her mysterious intruder the previous night. If so, how had she so completely vanished? And the Chinese girl was not wearing the jasmine scent which Enid recalled so well from the closet.

"I was awake some," she said carefully. "I take a while to get used to strange rooms."

Sonya Chen nodded, those eyes still fixed on her. "It is a strange old house. I was terrified when I came here as a youngster. Sometimes I think I have never gotten over that first feeling of fear."

"You remember first arriving here?" Enid asked.

The pretty Chinese girl nodded. "Yes. My impressions were fantastic and out of proportion, but I do remember. The great golden dragons which stand on either side of the front door seemed real to me. I shrank from them and cried with terror. Grandfather Edmund had to carry me inside."

"I noticed the dragons," Enid said. "They are ornamental but could be frightening to an imaginative youngster."

"They were for me," Sonya Chen assured her and, clutching a thick stack of books under her arms, said, "I must rush now. Otherwise I'll be late for my class."

"I'll see you later," Enid called after Sonya as she hurried out.

She turned to find herself facing Christopher. He made a good-looking figure in his spotless white linen suit. He smiled at her. "You look much more rested this morning. Did you get back to sleep after the unhappy interruption?"

"Yes. I followed your advice and left the lamp on."

59

The tall young man with the horn-rimmed glasses chuckled. "Ah! Nothing like the glow of an electric lamp to dispel demons! I always recommend it."

"Do you?" she said, deciding it was not a subject she wished to enlarge on with him.

His Panama hat in hand, he moved towards the door and then turned to say, "You'll be interested to know that Stephen has returned. He will be wanting to see you."

At once anxious, she asked, "Where can I find him?"

Christopher gave her another of his mocking smiles. "Easy! Go straight down the hall to the rear of the house. You'll find him in the chapel with his mother and Grandfather Edmund. They are very strict about morning prayers. I'm the only atheist of the family."

With this startling bit of information he went on out leaving her standing there stunned.

five

Enid was never certain whether Christopher was telling her
the truth or not. The black sheep cousin of Stephen appeared
to enjoy teasing her. Now she stood in the foyer not knowing
whether to follow his instructions or seek out someone else.
In the end she decided that he might be speaking the truth.
Many of the older English mansions had their own chapels
and the venerable Edmund Porter had wanted the great white
house to be the replica of a fine British country house.

With some trepidation she made her way down the bright
wide corridor with its shining hardwood floor and teak walls.
The walls of the long passage were lined with colorful
paintings of ancient China. She judged that the works were
rare and of great value. Probably the mansion contained a
fortune in art and furnishings.

As she reached the end of the corridor she heard voices in
what seemed to be ordinary conversation. She felt she would
not be interfering with the worship of her hosts and so went
on. A moment later she made her way through an arched
doorway to a small chapel. It had a half-dozen pews on either side of it, a raised altar and lectern. There was even a
pipe organ with the ornamental pipes reaching up above it.
The total effect was enhanced by a stained glass window of a
New Testament scene high in the rear wall, the rays from the
multicolored representation of shepherd and sheep shining
down from the shadows of the arched, gothic ceiling of the
chapel. The three were standing at the back of the chapel

ready to leave. On seeing Enid, Eleanor touched her son's arm to advise him of her arrival. Stephen had been engrossed in some serious discussion with his grandfather. Now he turned from the old man and, seeing her, his handsome face lit up.

"My dear Enid!" he exclaimed and came forward and took her in his arms and kissed her chastely on the cheek. "It is strange you should first find me here," he went on as he released her. "It was here in this chapel we held the burial services for Madge."

She said quietly, "It is a lovely chapel. One would never suspect it existed here, even though it is a large house."

Edmund Porter's cadaverous face showed pleasure. He said, "It was constructed after the main house was built. A small wing added on. I built and dedicated it to the memory of my wife, Regina."

Before she realized, she came out with, "The Jade Princess."

The old man's face darkened. "Some have called her that. But I assure you she was a devout Christian lady. She would have been proud of this chapel."

Stephen spoke up at once, advising the old man, "Enid meant no offense. She has heard Grandmother Regina called the Jade Princess because of her exquisite beauty."

Eleanor told her son, "You and Miss Branch go along. Your grandfather and I will follow. I know she is anxious to talk with you."

"True," Stephen said, and linking an arm in Enid's he said, "Come with me." He led her along the corridor and then to a side passage where his study was located.

Not until she was seated in the rather somber study with its book-lined walls, broad desk and leaded glass window did she have much chance to study Stephen Porter closely. She had known him as the carefree beau of her half-sister and then as Madge's happy bridegroom. Several years had gone by since that halcyon period and both the years and the tragedy which had occurred had obviously taken a toll of the young man.

Stephen was still handsome. But he was thinner and older looking. Somewhere in the still young face there lurked the shadow of Edmund Porter's emaciated countenance. The first hollows and lines were beginning to appear ever so slightly. His hair also seemed to have receded somewhat and he was pale, in contrast to his robust cousin Christopher.

With his hands behind his back, Stephen began to pace the width of the room in front of her. Frowning, he said, "This is a sad errand for you."

"One I never hoped to make," she agreed.

"I know how you must feel," he said, continuing his pacing. "But I want to make it clear that Madge and I had the happiest of marriages. There was no trouble between us."

She looked up at him with forlorn pleading on her lovely face. She said, "I can wait no longer to hear the details of her death. No one will speak to me about what happened to her. They have continued telling me that the news must come from you alone. Why?"

He halted and stared at her frowning. "I'm sure I can't say."

"Tell me!" she implored him.

Stephen Porter's face was grim. In a taut voice he informed her, "I can only say she vanished."

Enid gasped. "Vanished?" And she stood up.

"Yes." His eyes met hers and it seemed to her there was a hardness in them she had not seen there when she'd known him in England.

She said, "Your grandmother vanished! Murdered by bandits in the hills, so your mother told me. I can't believe that the same thing happened to Madge."

He shook his head. "No. Madge's case was quite different. As you know she was very fond of swimming."

"She was an excellent swimmer."

"Too much so for her own good," the handsome widower said. "We have a small wharf here with some pleasure craft. Madge often went down there to swim by herself. The rest of us would be off in Hong Kong at work and my mother hates sea bathing. I warned Madge not to be too adventurous and I asked her not to go out in the ocean alone but to wait until I or some of the others were here."

"Go on."

He sighed. "Though Madge and I got along well she was all too often headstrong. And she was particularly strong-willed in this. She disobeyed me and went alone to the wharf many times."

"And?"

"One afternoon she took the smaller of our motor launches out. A sudden, angry squall came up. She was too far out to make it safely back to shore. No one really knew where she was. When I returned home and she could not be located I went down and found the boat missing."

"Where was it?" Enid asked, feeling as if she might faint at any moment.

"You look pale," Stephen said. "Better sit down." And he helped her into the chair and then poured her a glass of water from a pitcher on his desk and handed it to her. "Sip that."

"Thank you," she said weakly. "Please go on." And she wet her dry mouth with a sip of the water.

"We went out in the larger launch and found the smaller one a mile or more out on the water. It had overturned and there was no sign of Madge."

Enid's eyes were wide with the horror of it. "But surely she could have kept herself afloat and clung to the boat! She was a champion swimmer."

The handsome man's face wore a weary expression. "She believed that. But she didn't know the kind of sudden, wild squalls we get in this part of the world. The waves must have been mountainous. She didn't have a chance."

"What about her body?"

"It was never found. That also is not astonishing. The waters are infested with sharks."

She sat there trembling. "Poor Madge!"

"I was beside myself," Stephen told her. "I made at least a half-dozen futile journeys looking for her, thinking she might have been rescued by some other passing craft. But it wasn't to be. The sea engulfed her and that was the end."

"I can't believe it!" she said.

"I know," he agreed, seating himself behind his desk and gazing at her sadly. "I felt exactly the same way. I waited for weeks before having the memorial service here. Before I gave up!"

Her eyes met his. "So her death was in keeping with the legend."

He frowned. "What do you mean?"

"The legend of the Jade Princess. Isn't it said that your grandmother returns to frighten off any other young woman who comes here to take her place as mistress of the house?"

"Who told you that wild story?" he asked angrily.

"Your mother."

This made him hesitate. He sat back in his chair. "I'm sorry to say that mother has a superstitious streak. You mustn't pay too much attention to her."

"She seems a very realistic type to me," Enid said. "Yet neither she nor any of the others would tell me what you have revealed just now."

"I suppose they felt it was properly my place to give you the facts."

Enid gave him a searching look. "Were the authorities satisfied with your theory of Madge's death?"

His face crimsoned. "Of course. I called in the police and the proper authorities at once. They all agreed it was a regretable accident."

"So a second young bride vanished from this house."

"Years apart and in an entirely different manner," the handsome Stephen protested.

"Still, there is the coincidence," she said. The first shock of what she'd heard now over, she was finding herself skeptical of the story.

"If you want to look at it that way," he said somewhat impatiently.

"You had a memorial service for her?"

"In the chapel. And there is a stone to her memory in our private burial ground on the estate."

"A memorial stone and no body under it?"

"That is not so unusual," he told her. "It is often done in the case of drowning victims whose bodies aren't located. In fact, there is a stone to my grandmother near that of Madge's."

"I'm sorry," she said. "I find it macabre."

His expression was sympathetic. "I worried about that. It's one of the reasons I wished you to come here and learn the story for yourself."

"I see," she said.

"I understand you have met all the family," he said. And

65

then in a different tone, he added, "and that Christopher took you out on the town last night."

She said, "It was a little less than that."

"At least you made a start of seeing our island. Later I shall look forward to the pleasure of showing you more of Hong Kong."

"I have not planned to remain here long," she said.

He protested. "You must stay a while. Wong Lee will also wish you to be his guest. He is like one of the family."

Enid nodded. "Mr. Lee was good enough to greet me when my plane arrived. I think he is a wonderful old man."

"He is highly respected on the island," Stephen Porter assured her. "He and my grandfather were responsible for organizing one of the largest export firms here."

"I know," she said. "My plan is to remain here long enough to take care of Madge's personal effects and then return to London."

The handsome, dark man said earnestly, "I was hoping you might stay here much longer than that. There are things I'd like to hear about Madge when you two were growing up together. I know little about your family. Our courtship was a whirlwind one, you'll remember."

"I do remember," she said. "We have few relatives left. Only Uncle David in London. He served in the army out here for a little and so I believe he still has a few friends in Hong Kong."

"Madge didn't tell me," he said. "You should try and look those people up."

"I plan to," she said. "I also met an American journalist on the plane, a Charles Milano. He seemed to know your cousin Christopher."

At the mention of Christopher the young man seated at the desk looked unhappy. "I think I know Milano," he said vaguely. "Christopher has a lot of acquaintances. Some of whom don't meet with my approval."

She was surprised by his words. She said, "Charles Milano was very nice to me."

Stephen Porter at once became apologetic. "I didn't mean to imply anything against him. I was speaking of Christopher's friends in a general way."

"I see," she said quietly.

Stephen got to his feet and glanced at his watch. "I'm due at my office for a meeting in a half-hour. I'd like to give you more time but I simply can't at this moment. We can talk when I return this evening."

"Very well," she said, rising.

He came close to her. "My mother has the key to the room in which I placed all Madge's things. I could not bear to see them. I would appreciate your going over whatever is there and keeping what you wish."

"I will," she said.

He was studying her earnestly. "You remind me of Madge in many ways though you are not physically like her. Something in your manner. I have been very lonely. It will be good for me to have you here."

"Thank you," she said. "It was kind of you to arrange for my coming here. I doubt if I would otherwise ever have had a chance to see this part of the world."

"Madge wanted you to visit us."

"I couldn't seem to get away when she asked me," Enid said. "And suddenly it was too late."

The handsome man sighed. "If I had ever dreamed it would end as it did I would never have brought her out here. Unhappily we cannot see what is ahead for us in this life."

"Perhaps that is best," she said. "One would rather leave it to fate."

He saw her to the door and in a low voice, said, "One more thing. My mother is a difficult woman. Try not to let her bother you. Unhappily she and Madge did not get along well."

"I suspected that."

He frowned. "I think that was one of the things which often drove Madge from the house. She sought the grounds and the ocean as a sanctuary where she could be alone."

Enid made no comment on this as he escorted her to the front area of the old mansion once again. But she felt it significant that he had mentioned the trouble between the late Madge and his mother. This had not come as a surprise to her knowing Madge's high spirits and the cold disposition of Eleanor Porter. The two had been opposites.

Stephen Porter left for the city of Hong Kong in a big black limousine driven by a Chinese chauffeur. She went out to stroll in the gardens for a little and try to get her thoughts straightened out. The account of how Madge had met her death had come as a shock.

More than that it struck her as lacking in conviction. No one had witnessed the boating accident nor had anyone found her half-sister's body. Stephen seemed to accept the matter without question. And yet there was a certain strangeness about this disappearance of a wife of a Porter in the same manner in which Regina Porter had vanished years ago. True, in one case it was supposed to be a boating accident and in the other murder by hill bandits. Yet there was a definite parallel in the two deaths, it seemed to her.

She strolled towards the cliffs so that she had a view of the wharf with the pleasure craft tied there. It must have been in one of these boats that Madge had met her death. By Stephen's account the boat had turned over amid giant waves but Madge had been an excellent swimmer. She ought to have been able to save herself. This fact alone made Enid suspicious of the events which had led to Madge's death.

Yet why would Stephen Porter bring her to Hong Kong if he had anything to conceal about the tragedy? Wouldn't normal caution warn him that she might become dubious and ask awkward questions? Or perhaps he'd done it as a grand gesture to prove to himself that he couldn't possibly be suspected of any wrongdoing?

She tortured herself with these questions as she strolled along in the warm sunshine. Was she being fair to Stephen in her sudden impulsive feeling that he was in some way to blame for Madge's death or at the very least hiding from her something of the true facts concerning the tragedy.

He showed the ordeal of having lost his wife. And he seemed genuinely desirous of her staying on at Porter House for a while. Was this part of the crafty plan of someone responsible for his wife's demise or was it a case of genuine kindness on his part?

Where did Sonya Chen fit in the puzzle? It was plain the lovely Chinese girl was very fond of Stephen. Had there been a triangle of which most of the others in the old mansion were unaware? She was positive Christopher knew more than he was saying. And she couldn't think of any way she'd get that wily young man to talk freely. Perhaps if she caught him sometime when he was drinking. But that was only a slim chance.

Even though it was possible, she could not make herself believe that Madge had drowned. That was the big hurdle. All her other doubts stemmed from that. And so she found herself concerned that Madge might have been murdered. It was a terrifying thought but one she could not reject. And what to do about it?

Memory of the intruder in her room the previous night and the aroma of jasmine perfume in the closet still haunted her. Had she seen the ghost of the long dead Regina? The jealous Eurasian beauty who did not want any other attractive woman to rule Porter House. But that was only a legend. She could not let herself be influenced by legends!

Bad enough to have her imagination run riot as it was doing now. She had strolled all the way down to the wharf and now she found herself confronted by a wizened little man in work clothes and a battered straw hat who had come up over the side of the wharf where he'd apparently been working on one of the craft tied up there.

The monkey face with a stubble of gray beard showed a smile, revealing several yellow fangs. In a jaunty voice the little man informed her, "I'm Ben Larsen. I look after the boats for Mr. Porter."

"I'm glad to know you," she said. "I'm a visitor here."

The little man squinted at her in the bright sunshine and ventured, "I guess you must be the one from London. Sister to the late missus."

She nodded. "Yes. Madge Porter was my half-sister."

"She was down here often," the little man said. "A fine woman. But I saw her failing in those last months before we lost her."

Enid stared at the little man, startled by his words. There had been no word of Madge failing from anyone else. She asked him, "You mean she was looking ill?"

"Thin and ill," Ben Larsen assured her. "Though I must say she was a beauty to the last!"

"No one has mentioned any illness to me," she said. "I was told she was drowned when she went out in a boat and a squall came up."

"I wasn't here that day," the little man with the monkey

69

face said with regret. "Wish I had been. But there was a Yankee ship came in with some old shipmates of mine on it and I sort of stayed in Hong Kong for a couple of days and nights. I'm from the States."

"I can tell that by your speech," she said.

"I always regret I wasn't here," he went on. "I might have warned her about going out. You can always tell when one of them squalls is coming up. I think she must have had an idea it wasn't safe. And I often wonder if she knew she was in a bad way from some sickness and went out there into the storm on purpose."

Enid gasped. "You think she might have deliberately sought death?"

"That's about it," the little man said. "I was devoted to her. But I could tell she wasn't happy. Two or three times I came down here and found her alone and crying."

"Crying?"

"Like her heart would break," the little man said. "I always went away for a little so she wouldn't know I heard her. And when I came back again she'd act as if nothing was wrong."

Enid was stunned by this information. She said, "Madge was always a happy, carefree girl!"

Ben Larsen nodded. "She was when she came here."

"But she changed?"

"I saw it happen. Especially in the last year."

"Why?"

"Like I said, I think she was a sick woman," the little man in the work clothes said.

"If she'd been ill she'd certainly have seen a doctor," Enid said. "And why wouldn't Stephen Porter have noticed and been concerned?"

The little man rubbed his chin sagely. "It could be he's so taken up with other things he didn't take the time to notice. That Stephen is his grandfather's son. The main thing in his life is the business. I'm not saying he wasn't fond of the missus in his own fashion. But he was away a lot of the time and she was lonely."

"I can understand that."

"And the Lady Eleanor, if you'll pardon me calling her

70

that," Ben Larsen said with disgust, "she didn't like your sister and made it hard for her. Not to mention that the China girl expected to marry the boss and took it grim when he brought back a British bride."

"Sonya Chen actually thought he would marry her?"

"Sure she did," the little man confided. "And so did old Edmund. That China girl is the apple of his eye. He was married to a half-China girl himself once. You must have heard about that."

"Yes," she said. "I have. She vanished mysteriously. They say she was killed by bandits in the hills."

The little man nodded. "I guess it almost sent old Edmund Porter mad. If he hadn't had his son he would have lost his mind. But it changed him. He was a strong man and his health failed. You've seen his hands shake?"

"Yes. He has a bad case of palsy."

"And he built that chapel in memory of his wife. Funny thing, the only one around here lately who could play the organ for services was your sister. The missus played every Sunday morning when old Edmund had us attend service. Now we don't have any organ music but he makes us go to service just the same. Drunk or sober on a Sunday morning you have to be there!"

"Madge played organ and piano well," she agreed. "And she was an excellent swimmer. That is what makes me wonder about her drowning."

The little man with the monkey face showed a crafty look. "May I say, Miss, I've often thought the same thing."

"Perhaps if you are right about her being ill that might explain it. But why wouldn't the others know she wasn't well?"

Ben Larsen said, "She was a great one for smiling and putting on a good front. I guess I was one of the few who knew she cried a lot when she was alone. And of course she and Mr. Christopher were good friends. And he's the kind to keep you cheered up. A lively sort."

"A little too lively for my liking," she said.

The little man winked. "A bit wild, Miss. He's a strange one. None of the others can control him."

"I've gathered that," she said. "And also that there is a lot of tension in the house."

71

"The wisest one of all is that old fella, Wong Lee," the handyman said earnestly. "He lives on the next estate. By all accounts he was the brains which started the Porter firm and he has more money than any of them."

"I liked him," she said and then she quickly returned to the subject which troubled her most. She said, "You think that my sister may have deliberately gone out and committed suicide?"

Ben Larsen looked uneasy. "I wouldn't want to be quoted."

"You won't be," she said. "I promise you that. I'll never let on we had this conversation. If anyone sees us from the house and asks me, I'll tell them you were giving me information about the islands."

"And that I can do," he said enthusiastically.

"You are serious when you suggest Madge was a suicide?"

He hesitated. "I began to wonder when they brought back the boat. She didn't show any damage to speak of. Nothing to make it look as if she'd turned over by accident."

"You're saying Madge might have dropped over the side and for reasons of his own Stephen Porter claims to have found the boat upside down in the water?"

Ben Larsen looked wise. "He was in the search craft alone when he found that boat. It wouldn't have been impossible for him to turn it over and make it seem like an accident before he tried to tow her in."

Enid found herself trembling. "Why would he do such a thing?"

Ben Larsen considered. "To save a scandal, maybe. He's a prominent man in Hong Kong. It wouldn't be good for his reputation to have people whispering his wife killed herself."

"No, it wouldn't," she agreed in a small voice as she debated whether the determined Stephen would have gone to such lengths to protect the family honor.

The little man eyed her craftily again. "Then there's another thing."

"What?" she asked breathlessly, not knowing what new revelation he'd offer next.

"They never did find her body."

"Is that unusual?"

"No," Ben Larsen said. "But if a body had been found

we'd have known for sure she was drowned. This way—" he halted and shrugged.

Her eyes widened. "You're saying she might never have gone out in that boat? Someone might have set it adrift empty?"

The monkey face was solemn. "I've heard of such things."

"If she wasn't drowned she could have been murdered," Enid said in a taut voice.

"You're saying what I've been thinking," the little man said.

"Who would want to murder her?"

He shrugged. "I can't tell you that. Everyone has enemies."

"That is true," she agreed, thinking of the close call she and Christopher had the previous night at the hands of his foes.

The little man glanced up towards the cliff and the great Victorian house towering on it. He said grimly, "I think old Eleanor capable of murder. And she hated the missus."

"Surely not Eleanor," she protested.

"Who else?" he wanted to know.

"Sonya Chen? You say she was hurt and jealous at losing Stephen."

The little man shook his hands. "I don't see her as being violent. I could be wrong."

"Christopher?"

Ben Larsen nodded. "He's the one I suspect most. Him or some of his crowd. Because Mr. Stephen neglected her to look after his business, she spent more and more time with that Christopher and his no-good bunch."

"How could she be so indiscreet?"

"He has a way with women. Better watch him, Miss."

"I will," she said. "It seems we've exhausted all the possibilities. What about Stephen Porter?"

"The boss?"

"Yes."

The little man moved about nervously. Then he said, "I can tell you this. He can have a vicious temper at certain times. I've seen him in one of his tempers. It would frighten you."

"Why should he be angry enough at Madge to want to kill her?" she asked.

Ben Larsen looked wise. "I can only think of one reason."

"What?" she asked.

"He might have found out she'd been overly friendly with that Christopher, if you know what I mean."

six

Enid was unable to restrain a startled gasp at this comment of the garrulous Ben Larsen. She saw the sly look on his simian face as he studied her reaction. Then she finally managed, "You don't really think Stephen had any such motive?"

The boatman spread his bronzed hands. "If the master had any such notions I'd say he was wrong. Your sister was a fine woman. But seeing how friendly she was with that Christopher he might have had some dark suspicions. And they could have led to a dark deed, if you follow me."

"I do," she said in a taut voice. "I'm sure it couldn't have been that way."

"Probably not," he agreed.

She gave him an appealing look. "You have a good chance to find out the real facts. If you learn anything more while I'm here please tell me."

"I will."

"There surely is something strange about Madge's death," she went on. "And you're mentioning her crying spells and that she looked ill suggest something was seriously bothering her."

"Right," the little man agreed.

"I'll be staying here for at least a week or two, maybe longer," she went on. "And I'll talk to you again."

"Do that."

"I'm sure there is more to find out."

"Very likely, Miss," Ben Larsen said. "And one thing

more. I'd watch myself while I was here if I were you. There may be those who resent your being here. Who are afraid of what you may find out."

She was impressed by the warning in his tone and the look of concern on his wrinkled face. She said, "I'll remember that."

"Come back again," the boatman said. "You'll find me down here or at the boathouse."

"Thanks," she said and she turned and started back up the embankment to the lawn of the great white mansion. Once again she found her thoughts whirling in confusion. What she had heard from the ancient boatman had only served to further underline her suspicions and her fear that Madge had been murdered by someone and all the others were trying to cover up the crime.

When she reached the house the grim Eleanor was waiting for her. Stephen's mother said accusingly, "You were down at the wharf!"

Her eyebrows raised slightly. "Yes. Why? Is there some reason why I shouldn't go down there?"

Eleanor's hawk face showed a hint of embarrassment. "No," she replied quickly. "Though I don't fancy it down there myself. Especially after what happened to Madge. And she was forever down there. I only meant to warn you against that Ben Larsen."

"Warn me?"

"Yes. That apelike little man prefers to talk rather than work. He'll wear your ears away with his stories if you let him. Worse than that, he's a gossip. I don't know why my son keeps him on."

"Perhaps because Larsen is good at his work with the boats," she suggested.

"I hope he is useful for something besides talk," the older woman said vindictively. "What did he have to say to you?"

Enid was certain she sensed an uneasiness in Eleanor Porter's manner. It seemed very likely the older woman was afraid Ben Larsen might have told her too much about the way Madge had been acting before her mysterious drowning.

She said, "He just talked about the boats and asked me some questions about what London is like now."

"Is that what he talked so long about?" Eleanor comment-

76

ed with a hint of sarcasm in her tone. "He took long enough to do it."

"He is talkative."

"I detest him!" the older woman snapped. Then she held out a key to her. "My son asked me to give this to you. It is the key to the room where he had Madge's things placed."

Enid nodded. "He mentioned he'd be giving me the key." And she took it.

"The room is on the upper level, the fourth floor. Just at the head of the landing. You probably ought to go up there and begin going through everything."

"I suppose so," she said reluctantly, not happy at the prospect of the task.

"Stephen could not face going over everything and I want no part of it. You are obviously the one to do it. You are the other most interested party."

"True," she said in a small, unhappy voice.

"I think you should start at once," Stephen's mother went on in her arrogant fashion. "The longer it is put off the worse it is for everyone."

"I suppose so."

"The things you don't wish to keep can be sent to some charity," Eleanor said briskly. "We have many needy people in Hong Kong."

"I'm sure of that," she agreed.

The older woman gave her a meaningful look. "Also I think the sooner things are gone over and sent out of the house the better it will be for my son. You may not realize it but Stephen still grieves a lot over Madge."

Enid could not help but wonder about this. Perhaps it was because Stephen's mother feared he might break down under the burden of a murderer's guilt that she was so anxious that all things associated with Madge be removed from the old mansion.

She said, "They were very much in love until the end, weren't they?"

"They were," Eleanor said grudgingly. "Though I don't hesitate to say that Christopher attempted to cause trouble between them."

"He did?"

"Yes," the other woman said tartly. "He paid far too much

attention to Stephen's wife. Tried to turn her head with his flattery. Nothing would have suited him better than to have had her turn from Stephen to him."

"Madge was always a loyal girl," she defended her half-sister. "I'm sure she must have made your son a devoted wife."

"I'm not saying she didn't," Eleanor said lamely. "I just point out that Christopher made a most disgusting play for her affections."

Enid said, "Then her drowning must have been a bitter shock to him."

"To Christopher?" Eleanor gave a dry, mirthless chuckle. "It is evident you don't know him well. He cares for nothing or nobody but himself. It would be a strange day when he'd grieve for anyone."

"He is very self-centered," she agreed. And then anxious to escape the dragonlike Eleanor she said hastily, "I must go upstairs and make a beginning."

With these words she left the older woman and hurried up the several flights of stairs. She wanted to escape and be alone for a little as much as anything. The prospect of facing the room filled with her half-sister's things was not inviting but she needed some quiet in which to think. Going over Madge's possessions would at least offer her that.

When she reached the door on the fourth floor landing and inserted the key in the lock her hand trembled slightly. But she knew there was no turning away from this important task, so she forced herself to open the door and enter the room with its musty smell of having been closed for some time.

The first thing she did was wend her way between trunks, suitcases and boxes and find a window which she opened. She had felt faint on first entering and now she stood breathing in the fresh air and gradually losing some of her nervousness. The room looked as if everything had been placed in it hastily. In some cases dresses had simply been draped over the backs of chairs.

Far down below she saw the yellow dome of the teahouse in the garden and beyond it the embankment leading down to the wharf, the boathouse and the ocean. Eleanor had shown herself to be afraid that Ben Larsen had revealed too much about Madge's death. There could be no mistaking the older woman's behavior.

Eleanor's grim comment on the relationship between Madge and Christopher had also not been lost on Enid. And once again she had the uneasy fear that Stephen, either through imagined or real unfaithfulness on Madge's part, might have been driven to murdering her. But this suspicion was balanced by her belief that a loyal Madge would never have given her husband such a sordid motive. And she found herself left only with the harrowing belief that Madge had been the victim of a murderer without being able to guess who the murderer might be or why.

Enid crossed over to a suitcase which she recognized as one which Madge had brought to Hong Kong from England. It had once belonged to Enid and she'd given it to her half-sister during some last-minute packing. Now with a deep sense of sorrow she knelt before the suitcase and opened it. She found it filled with an assorted lot of items.

There were some sweaters, white gloves, several silk scarves and under the carefully packed scarves a photo album Enid recognized. She took it out and skimmed through its contents. There were snapshots of herself and Madge and their various boy friends, all carefree and smiling. Reminders of happier days.

Her eyes filled with tears as she hesitated over one snapshot and then another—this golden past of their lives in London together now so sadly far away and lost. She put the album down and it was then that she saw the leather bound diary. This was new to her and she picked it up with a feeling of tenseness. It was dated for the previous year, and though she had never known Madge to keep a diary perhaps she had taken up the practice to break her loneliness in this grim old mansion.

She opened the square leather book and saw that not every page was written on, but the writing that was there was surely in her sister's hand. Her neat, clear handwriting had always been one of the things in which Madge took a personal pride.

Enid read an entry which said, "August 7th. Rain all today and yesterday. Must get away from house. Cannot stand it."

The entry ended with that and there were several blank

pages, then on August 12, Madge had written, "Saw the phantom again last night! It followed me across the garden. Stephen refuses to listen to my fears concerning it. Old Edmund in a rage when I told him. Only Christopher understands."

Enid turned the page of the diary with a growing excitement. There was an entry for August 18, "Feeling unwell again. I dare not mention it. Stephen's mother hates me and shows it. Sonya hates me and conceals it. I have no one to turn to. Stephen refuses to hear me say anything against either of them. Christopher away in Macao. If only he would get back!"

So there had been a strong association between the two! Enid realized this with some dismay. She found another entry, this one dated September 3. It read, "I spent an afternoon with Wong Lee at his house. What a fine old man he is and how unlike Edmund Porter. I think he understands my problem but he was kind enough not to mention it. However, he did speak briefly about Christopher."

Enid gazed down at the diary with stricken eyes. It was almost as if the dead girl were indicting herself. The items in her diary could only suggest that she had fallen in love with Christopher, that the wily cousin of her husband had tricked her into having an affair with him. The diary was underlining Enid's worst fears.

She skimmed the other pages and saw there were no more entries. Not that it really mattered. She had read enough to cause her grave concern. She carefully wrapped the small book in one of the silk scarves and made up her mind to take it down to her own room and conceal it there. She did not want anyone else to read it just yet, especially not Stephen.

But even as she considered this she worried whether he might already have read it and been driven by it to the edge of madness. It seemed to her if he had and felt the diary in any way condemning he would not have left it there for her to read. Perhaps he didn't even know about it. His mother had suggested that he'd placed all the things in this room soon after Madge vanished. In his grief he had not been able to give any attention to her belongings. At least that was his mother's story.

With the wrapped diary in her hand, she got up from the

suitcase and moved across to where some summery dresses were draped on the back of a plain chair. The moment she drew near the dresses she recognized a familiar scent—the same jasmine perfume which had lingered in the closet of her room the previous night following the visit of the phantom!

With a trembling hand she lifted a beige dress and the fragrance of the perfume became stronger. There was no question it was the same perfume she had noticed following the macabre appearance of the phantom.

Had the Jade Princess also visited this storage room? Or had Madge by some chance adopted a perfume which had also been used by Stephen's grandmother long ago? Enid did not know what to think. She put the dress down quickly and, feeling she'd experienced enough for one afternoon, turned to leave the room.

She carefully locked the door of the storage room, placed the key in her pocket and went on down to her own bedroom. There she hid the diary away carefully in a pocket of one of her own suitcases. She had barely finished this when she heard her name called from the hallway.

Still upset by her discoveries, she went out and found Eleanor standing on the stairs, a short distance from the landing. Enid asked the older woman, "What is it?"

"You are wanted on the phone," Eleanor said.

"Oh?"

"You can take it on the phone down at the end of this hall," Eleanor said, indicating the phone table.

"Thank you," she said, and she hurried to the phone and lifted the receiver, saying, "Enid Branch speaking."

A jovial voice at the other end of the line said, "I would have recognized you anyway." And she knew it was the American journalist, Charles Milano.

Glad to hear from him, she said, "How kind of you to call me."

"I said I would," he told her. "Are you nicely settled in?"

She hesitated. "To a degree."

"That's a trifle evasive," he told her. "I've phoned because I happen to be out at this end of the island. I wondered if I dropped by and picked you up we might have a short drive and drink together."

Enid could not conceive of turning down the invitation. She

needed to talk with someone she could trust and needed to do it badly. She said, "I like the idea. How soon will you be along?"

"I can be in your driveway in ten minutes," Charles Milano said.

"I'll be there waiting for you," she told him.

"On my way," he said happily and hung up.

Feeling heartened simply by hearing his voice, she went back to her room and freshened up a little. Then she went down the stairs to the foyer. Old Edmund Porter was standing there in conversation with his daughter-in-law, Eleanor. They both gave her a surprised glance.

"Are you going somewhere?" Eleanor wanted to know.

"Yes," she said, trying not to show her nervousness. "That call was from the American journalist I met on the plane coming over here. He wants me to go out with him for a short drive."

"Do you know anything about this fellow?" the older woman wanted to know.

Edmund Porter's cadaverous face was grim. "Have to be careful about strangers here."

"It's all right," she assured them. "Charles Milano is well known. And he told me he's a friend of Christopher's."

Eleanor gave a small groan. "That is no real recommendation. I promise you!"

"Christopher knows all kinds of dubious people," Stephen's grandfather complained.

Enid was determined. She said, "I don't know about the other friends Christopher may have but I do know that Charles Milano is a respected journalist."

"You will be back for dinner?" Eleanor said.

"Of course," she answered. "Just don't worry about me." And she went on out into the sunshine aware that she had been followed by their looks of disapproval.

She took a stand by one of the golden dragons which guarded the door on either side and which had produced such grim nightmares in Sonya Chen when she had come to the old mansion as a child. The dragons were done in some sort of metal in great detail and had apparently been kept carefully gilded over the years.

A small white car came into the driveway and halted before the door. Genial Charles Milano stepped out of it and greeted her with a smile. "Those dragons are fantastic. Beauty guarded by the beasts!"

She smiled in return. "Impersonal guardians!"

"We may as well get under way," he said. "I'd like to take you to a place in Hong Kong and that's quite a little drive."

"I've promised to be back in time for dinner," she told him as she got in the car.

"No problem about that," the young American said and he shut the car door and then went around and seated himself behind the wheel and they drove away.

She said, "I didn't expect to hear from you so soon. I'm glad you called."

They had reached the main roadway which followed the shore and he gave her a brief glance and smile as he said, "I had an idea you might be. Especially after your adventure with Christopher last night."

Her eyes widened. "You mean the car?"

"What else?"

"How do you happen to know about it?" she asked the young man at the wheel. "He made me promise to tell no one."

"Christopher and I are close friends."

"You must be."

"He has the car in the city getting it repaired now," the journalist said.

"Did he tell you why those people did such a thing? Why they tried to kill us?"

"No," Charles said, keeping his eyes on the road.

"There must have been a good reason."

"Christopher can be arrogant when he likes. I imagine he has made enemies here."

"He was very mysterious about it," she said. "I warned him earlier that an evil-looking man was watching us from an alley as we got in the car."

"It is also characteristic of Christopher that he doesn't like to take advice," Charles Milano said.

"His family seem to think him reckless and careless about the friends he makes."

"They're probably right," he agreed as they drove along

83

the picturesque road with its palm trees, green fields and blue bay in the distance.

"Old Edmund Porter was even concerned about my meeting you when he heard that you were a friend of Christopher's."

Charles smiled again without looking at her. He said, "I trust you vouched for my character."

"As best I could."

"What do you think about the Porters now that you've met them?"

"I don't know what to think."

"Interesting," he said. "And about your half-sister's death?"

"I'm very bewildered and frightened," she said. "Stephen gave me a report of her drowning which I find less than convincing."

"So?"

"I've questioned him and the others and I can't help thinking that something is being concealed, that I haven't been told the truth."

Charles said, "That is why I refused to discuss the matter. I felt it best you should hear it from Stephen first."

"No one would discuss it with me. Only Stephen talked about it and what he said didn't satisfy me."

They crossed a bridge and now the skyscrapers of the city came into view a distance ahead. The young man at the wheel asked her, "Have you come to any conclusions?"

"One. Which I don't like to think about."

"Care to tell me?"

She hesitated. "I don't know. You are a friend of Christopher's."

"What has that to do with it?"

"Maybe a lot. I gather that Madge and Christopher became very close friends."

"That is probably true," he said, slowing the car to ease by some cyclists on the road.

"I'm afraid their friendship may have triggered a jealousy in her husband which resulted in his murdering her."

Charles Milano gave her an interested look. "That's a strong statement."

"You asked me to honestly tell you what I've been thinking. There you have it."

84

He said, "You think Madge was murdered?"

"Yes."

"Stephen needn't have been the killer," the young man from the United States said. "There may have been others in the house who hated her enough to want to see her dead."

"I realize that," she said. "But when you get to other suspects it is too confusing. At the moment I can only think of Stephen Porter as the possible killer."

"He's almost too obviously a suspect," Charles suggested lightly.

"I don't know," she admitted worriedly. "I'm in a bad mental state about it all. That's why I'm glad you called me."

"I was afraid you were in for some shocks."

"You knew I was," she chided him.

"And then when Christopher told me about your close call last night I decided I'd better see you," he said.

"I'm grateful."

"Christopher admires you. He gives you credit for not telling the others. He's in trouble most of the time and this would not have helped him."

"I gather that he's a constant worry to the family," she said. "I wonder old Edmund doesn't send him back to England."

"They don't want him back in England," Charles told her. "There was some nasty business about passing bad checks. If Christopher hadn't come out here he might have landed in prison."

She was shocked. "That bad?"

"I'm afraid so," the young journalist said. "He hasn't made any sort of confession to me, I hasten to say. But I heard the story from an especially reliable source."

"And you think it true?"

"Yes."

"Aren't you uneasy about being his friend?"

Charles shook his head. "No. For all his faults Christopher is an interesting fellow. No doubt that is why Madge liked him so much. He's not straightlaced like Stephen. And the Porter family are so loyal where family are concerned they'll see him through any trouble he might get in here."

"I gather he counts on that."

"I'm sure he does. He gives only a little time to the

business. He has a taste for gambling both here and in Macao and he's probably run up some bad gambling debts. That is what last night may have been all about."

She said, "You think they may have tried to kill us because he owes them money from gambling?"

"The operators of the gambling casinos are rough types," Charles told her. "They have to make their customers pay one way or the other or everyone would end up owing them money."

"If Christopher knows that, he should be more cautious."

"Caution isn't part of his nature," the young man at the wheel said as he slowed the car again.

They were now in one of the exotic, narrow streets of a truly Oriental nature, the sort of thing which Enid had expected from Hong Kong. As the car moved slowly along in the heavy traffic of pedestrians, rickshaws and small cars she noted the small shops with their colorful signs and the rickety apartment houses above them. From many of the windows Chinese faces gazed down at them.

Charles said, "We'll park the car down here and use the alleyway to the waterfront."

She gave him a questioning look as he stopped the car. "Where are you taking me?"

He gave her another of his boyish smiles. "To a place you must have read about and surely must see."

"Oh?"

He helped her out of the car and locked it. Then he led her along the busy street filled with the sound of voices chanting in sing-song fashion. They were clearly in one of the native districts.

He held her by the arm as he led her down a narrow, steep alley whose cobblestones made it difficult for her high-heeled shoes. She gasped and asked him again, "Where are we going?"

Charles was like a delighted youngster. He said, "I'm sure you must have read Richard Mason's novel *The World of Suzie Wong*. I'm taking you to the modest waterfront hotel which served as the setting for his story."

"Really?"

"Yes. The book is not very popular here in Hong Kong.

Especially with the great union of British families. They don't approve of miscegenation."

"Edmund Porter was married to a woman who was half Chinese."

Charles nodded. "The Jade Princess. You've heard about her?"

"Yes."

"Have you seen her ghost?"

"I'm not sure," she said. "I saw something. But whoever or whatever it was vanished leaving only a scent of jasmine perfume behind."

"At least that was something," the young man said. "The Porter family are very touchy on the subject of the Jade Princess. They prefer not to talk about her. You must have found that out."

"I did," she said as they reached the end of the alley. They came out near the entrance of the Luk Kwok Hotel which was located between the landing stage and the British Sailors' Home. They went inside the modest bar which was empty except for the bartender and a young American sailor accompanied by a pretty Chinese girl. These two were seated at a corner table in the shadows and so entranced with each other they didn't even look up when Charles and Enid entered the bar.

Charles pulled out a chair for Enid at a table not too far from the entrance of the bar. Then he sat down and ordered drinks from the stout barman who had come strolling over. She glanced around and saw a large and many-splendored jukebox, one of the posters advertising the book pinned up on a gray wall, along with a rather hideous modernistic painting on an opposite wall. Decorating the bar was a large bowl of Siamese fighting fish.

In a low voice, she asked Charles, "Isn't this a brothel?"

"Not officially," he replied. "Single girls may not sit here but you can bring a girl in from the outside. Many do, and the rooms upstairs are almost constantly rented."

Enid made a face. "What about Suzie Wong?"

"They talk about her as if she were a real person. The story is that her marriage failed and she is back living in Hong Kong and heavily into dope. But she will have nothing

87

to do with any other man. Lomax is supposed to send her regular living allowances from London."

"And of course it's all pure make-believe!" Enid exclaimed.

Charles shrugged. "So much of Hong Kong is make-believe that one small legend more or less really doesn't matter."

The bartender came over with their drinks and Charles paid him. She took a sip of the fruit juice concoction heavily laced with rum. She could not help but agree with the young journalist that they had arrived in a city of pure fantasy.

She was about to make a comment to this effect when her eyes strayed to the entrance and standing there in the shadows she saw a familiar face and figure. She was so upset she gasped aloud. For the man she saw glaring at her from the shadowed entrance hall was the same evil-looking fellow with the scar she'd seen in the alley the previous night. Christopher's enemy!

seven

Charles heard her small cry of alarm and saw her frightened face. He asked, "What is it?"

She nodded towards the entranceway but by that time the ugly Chinese with the scar had quickly vanished. She said, "Out there! I saw the man in the dirty white suit who spied on Christopher and me last night!"

"Out there?" Charles said. And he at once jumped up and went out to the hallway. He also vanished as he went on to the street in search of the mysterious scarface. He returned a moment later with a puzzled look on his good-natured face. "I didn't see a sign of anyone to fit your description outside."

Enid said bitterly, "You wouldn't! He knew I saw him and he'd lose no time getting away."

Charles frowned. "You're sure it was the same man?"

"Yes. It isn't the sort of face one forgets easily," she told him with a tiny shudder.

"I didn't mean to question you," he apologized. "But the light isn't that good in here. I wondered if you might have made a mistake."

"I think not."

"Perhaps I shouldn't have brought you here."

"It's not your fault. This is one of the places I wanted to see. I can tell people who've read the book I've actually sat in the bar."

Charles continued to look uneasy. "A lot of strange people

89

live in the area around here. I consider it safe enough especially in the daytime. But you never can be sure."

She said, "I can't see why he should have anything against me."

"You were with Christopher."

"Would that be enough?"

"I'm afraid so," Charles said worriedly. "These people are crafty about collecting debts. They're not above kidnapping the wives, children or girl friends of their debtors."

Enid heard his troubled explanation with new fear. By merely being in the company of Christopher she might have exposed herself to this sort of danger. No wonder the family had been concerned about her going out with him.

She said, "Are you really serious?"

"I'm afraid so," he said. "But it is daylight. Police do patrol the streets. We should be all right."

She thought of the dark, narrow alley they had to venture before getting back to his car. And she said, "Perhaps we ought to leave at once."

Charles looked embarrassed. "We can't very well."

"Why not?"

He raised his hand in a gesture of resignation. "I didn't tell you before. We're supposed to meet Christopher here."

She was shocked. "We are what?"

"I told Christopher I'd bring you here about this time," the journalist said. "He said he'd come and meet us."

"It's news to me!"

"I should have told you earlier," the young man said in an apologetic tone. "I didn't expect anything like this to happen."

Enid said, "I still think we should leave at once."

"I can't," Charles said. "Not if you were right about that man. If he's in the area I'll have to wait here and warn Christopher."

She said, "Can't you phone him somewhere and stop him coming here?"

"I wouldn't know where to reach him," the American journalist said. He consulted his watch. "He ought to be here at any minute."

She stared at the clearly troubled young man and said, "You have great loyalty to Christopher."

90

"We're friends."

"What about he and Madge? Did you often see them together?"

The man across the table from her at once looked wary. He hesitated, "I met them occasionally. They used to go out to dinner together. Stephen travels a lot. Madge was left alone a good deal of the time."

"Too much of the time for her own good perhaps."

"Maybe," he said cautiously.

She gave him a sharp look. "In her diary, which I was reading before I came out, I found more references to her missing Christopher than to missing her husband. She was continually complaining when Christopher was away from Hong Kong."

"Interesting."

Her eyes met his for a long moment of silence, then she asked, "Do you think she and Christopher were lovers?"

Again he showed a hesitancy to answer. He said, "Stephen told you what happened to your half-sister. She's dead. Why not be satisfied with that?"

She was amazed by his reply. She said, "I'm afraid that is not possible. Not while I have any doubts as to how she met her death."

"You may regret your curiosity," he said quietly. The bartender had ambled over to them again and was standing by expectantly. "Want another drink?" Charles asked.

"No."

"I'll have one," he told the bartender and waited until the stout man had left their table before he warned her, "I'm only trying to keep you out of trouble."

"You haven't begun too well, bringing me here," she rebuked him.

"Sorry."

She suddenly had a new thought and it wasn't a pleasant one. She stared at the young journalist across the table and said, "I see what happened to Madge as the result of a triangle. I've been suspecting that her husband might have killed her out of jealousy. But Christopher could have murdered her for the same reason. I should have thought of that before."

"No!"

"How can you be sure?"

91

Charles hesitated. "I know they cared deeply for each other."

"What about Stephen?"

"I think Madge fell out of love with her husband soon after she came to live here."

"It doesn't sound like her."

The bartender brought the young journalist's drink over. Charles paid him. Enid noticed with some uneasiness that they were alone in the big, drab gray bar now. The young American and his Chinese girl friend had silently vanished somewhere. Probably to one of the rooms above.

Charles took a big drink from his glass and then put it down. He seemed to be growing more nervous as the minutes passed. He drummed the fingers of his right hand on the table. Then he suddenly said, "Maybe we'd better leave."

"Why have you changed your mind?" she asked.

"I have an instinct about some things," he said. "I don't like the feeling this place gives me at the moment." He finished the rest of his drink.

She was about to stand up when Christopher appeared in the entranceway and came into the bar. He was wearing a neat, white suit and a Panama hat. He smiled at her and took a seat at their table.

"Sorry to be late," he said.

"I was beginning to worry about you," Charles told him. "Enid thought she saw a friend of yours in here. The man with the scar."

Christopher gave her a look of dry amusement. "I'd hardly call him a friend."

"It was the same one who watched us from the alley last night and you said later tried to wreck the car."

"Didn't do a bad job of it either," Christopher replied. "The car will be laid up for a while. They've ordered new parts and rented me another car in the meanwhile."

Charles asked him, "Did you see the fellow?"

"I met him in the street," Christopher said. "That's what kept me late."

"What about him?" Charles wanted to know.

"We had a talk," the brown-haired man with the glasses said. "And I'd say we came to an understanding. I've promised to drop by the casino tomorrow."

Charles frowned. "It was foolish of you to make any promises to pay if you don't intend to keep them. That will only make them more vicious than ever."

"Order me a drink, dear boy," Christopher said. "A gin and tonic! And let me do the worrying, please!"

Charles crimsoned but he rose from the table and went over to the bar to order the drink. Enid found herself alone at the table with the errant Christopher.

She said, "Are you continually in trouble?"

He laughed. "It gives life some flavor."

"A sour flavor as far as I'm concerned," she said. "That man came in here and gave me a look of hatred I won't forget easily."

"You mustn't worry about it. I have that matter settled," he said.

"I can't help thinking that if I hadn't gone out with you last night he wouldn't even know who I was, or have the least interest in me."

"Don't you enjoy being the focus of attention?" Christopher asked.

"Did you put Madge in the same danger by exposing her to those thugs to whom you owe gambling debts?"

He gave a soft whistle. "I suspect my friend Charles has been talking a little too much."

"It was time someone warned me," she told him. "I didn't believe what they said about you at the house. Now I realize they were telling the truth."

"You are wrong to be so prejudiced," was his mocking reply.

Charles came back with his drink and sat it on the table before him. The journalist said, "I think I'd better start back with Enid. You were so late arriving we've stayed here longer than I planned."

Christopher told him, "No need for you to worry, old boy. I have my rented Jag. I'll take her home."

Charles didn't look pleased at the suggestion. He said, "I promised she'd be there in time for dinner."

The lanky, brown-haired man downed his drink in a long gulp. Coughing slightly he rose and said, "I'm ready to leave at once."

Charles turned to her. "Does this suit you?"

She was on her feet. "I suppose there's no need for your driving way out there when Christopher is going in any case. Thank you for the tour."

The young journalist smiled wryly. "I'm afraid it didn't turn out all that well." And giving his attention to Christopher, he asked, "Where is your car?"

"Up behind yours," he said.

"All right," Charles said. "We can all go back up there together. Safety in numbers."

"No need to worry," Chrisopher told him. "I have that problem settled."

"I want to be sure," the journalist replied firmly. "We do have Enid to consider."

"By all means let us consider Enid," Christopher said in his mocking fashion. He waved to the stout bartender as they left the place and told her, "Well, you've seen the home of Suzie Wong. Something to tell your friends about."

"It has been an experience," she agreed.

They went back out onto the street and up the dark, narrow alley with its mixture of grim odors. The men walked on either side of her and she knew that Charles, at least, was grim and tense. Christopher seemed to take everything in the same jaunty fashion. She felt a deep relief when they reached the busy street where the cars were parked.

Christopher had a blue Jaguar much like the one which had been damaged except for its color. Charles saw her safely in the car before he drove off on his own. Christopher headed the Jaguar along the narrow street to another one not quite so narrow or crowded which led to one of the broad, modern avenues. From there it was only a short drive to the open roadway leading to the other end of the island.

At the wheel Christopher teased her, "I think Charles was put out by my taking you over."

"I doubt it," she said. "You saved him a long drive out and back."

"He likely considered being in your company worth it."

She told the young man at the wheel, "You have a bad habit of taking too much for granted."

"You think so?"

"I do," she said. "And don't count on working your charm on me as you did on Madge."

94

"Your half-sister was glad to be my friend."

"And where is she now?"

Christopher gave her a glance of reproval. "That wasn't a nice thing to say."

"It's what I'm thinking. I'm wondering just how much your friendship cost her."

The tall man with the horn-rimmed glasses kept his eyes on the road as he drove on at his usual reckless pace. He said, "I think you've been taking the family's talk against me too seriously."

"I wonder."

"If Madge were here at this moment she'd give you a much different picture of me than the one you seem to have."

"No doubt. I'm sure you tricked her into believing in you. That doesn't mean you are what you pretend to be."

"Few of the family are," he said dryly. "Why don't you ask Stephen a few more questions? Ask him if he really neglected Madge and whether that made her turn to me. I'll be interested in hearing what he has to say."

She made no reply to this and for a little while there was no conversation between them. Within a surprisingly short time they arrived at the front door of the white Victorian house flanked by the two golden lions.

"Thank you for the drive back," she said and let herself out of the car.

"I'll see you at dinner," he said and drove on towards the asphalt parking area.

Enid went inside and upstairs without encountering anyone. She took a quick shower and changed into a flimsy gown suitable for dinner and the evening. Then she went down to join the others in the family who were standing out on the patio having cocktails. A quick glance told her that Christopher had not yet joined the group.

Eleanor was standing there looking formidable in a pale green dress and holding a drink. She eyed Enid blandly and said, "So you did manage to get back."

"I said I would," she told the older woman.

Old Edmund Porter was seated in a white chair of wrought-iron construction. He smiled weakly for her benefit. "It is nice to have you here," he said. "You brighten the place."

Stephen, who had been hovering in the background until this moment came forward to greet her. He looked grim and he said rather abruptly, "I saw you drive in with Christopher."

"Yes. Just a short while ago," she said, taking it all casually. "I see he hasn't gotten down here yet."

Stephen's handsome face wore a look of annoyance. He said, "Often he doesn't join us. Can I get you something?"

She asked for a gin and bitters and he had it brought to her by one of the servants. She took the drink and said, "Charles Milano drove me in to Hong Kong. We met Christopher and he kindly offered to drive me back here."

Stephen said, "I'd like to discuss a few things with you in my study after dinner."

"Of course," she said, wondering what he would have to say to her.

It didn't take her too long to find out. Dinner proved a tedious affair with Christopher coming to the table at the last moment and leaving almost as soon as coffee was served. Several times he caught her eye across the table and gave her one of his mocking smiles.

When the meal was at the end she dutifully followed Stephen to his book-lined study. Like most of the other rooms in the old mansion it was air conditioned. He gestured for her to take a chair while he stood before her importantly with his hands behind his back.

He said, "You haven't been in this house very long. But I expect you've been here long enough to know there is not too much peace among us."

She looked up at his stern, handsome face. She said, "I gather you mean there is strife between you and your cousin."

"Christopher and I are completely at odds," he said. "I ought to have made that clear from the first."

"I think I rather guessed it."

Stephen frowned. "My cousin had an unfortunate hold over Madge. He did everything in his power to turn her against me."

"Why?"

The man standing before her shrugged. "Basically because

96

he hates me and could not bear the happiness Madge and I had."

She said, "I went through some of her things today. I found a diary with some entries in it."

Stephen at once showed upset. "What sort of entries?"

"Some of them were strange."

"Strange?"

"I mean they bore out what you've just said about your cousin having a strong power over her. She seemed to think of nothing but him."

"I didn't know she wrote of him in a diary," Stephen said in a tortured voice. "May I see it?"

"I'd rather not show it to you, just yet," she said.

He was clearly taken aback by this reply from her. He said, "What do you mean?"

"Simply that I think it best to complete reading it myself before turning it over to you or anyone else. I have an idea she did not ever want you to see it."

"Probably not."

"And I'm worried about the mystery surrounding her death," she went on. "It may be that the diary will give me some clues to what really happened."

He frowned at her. "I told you what happened."

She corrected him. "What you *believe* happened. You may have been deceived."

"I think not!"

"I want to be sure," she said.

"Suppose I order you to hand over that diary," he said.

"I'd have to refuse."

He stared at her. "I did not bring you out here to cause more trouble."

"I have no wish to do that. But I loved my sister. I do not understand what changed her so and how she came to her death. I'd like to find out the truth."

Stephen Porter turned away from her to pace up and down nervously. Then he halted and said, "I have tried to spare you any pain I could."

"Why do you say that?"

"Because I have not told you that Madge proved to be an unfaithful wife, obsessed with a hopeless devotion for Christopher. I think that was what led to her death. It was as much a suicide as anything else."

Enid was not too surprised by his outburst. She had guessed most of this for herself. But it was important to have him verify what she had only assumed to be true.

She said, "You think she took that boat out in the storm purposely."

"Yes."

"It doesn't seem like her."

Stephen's face was haggard. "What you don't seem to understand was how much she changed. You would have believed it if you had been here."

"Was any of it your fault?"

"I loved her even after I found out about her and Christopher."

"You could have sent him away," she suggested. "Would that not have ended things between them?"

He made a frustrated gesture. "I begged my grandfather to send him away. But grandfather refused. He promised Christopher's father he would give him a haven here. If Christopher returned to England he'd be put in prison."

"Didn't you try to reason with her?" she asked.

"I never gave up hope," he said. "I kept trying to win her back to the day of her drowning."

She heard his words filled with pain and felt that he must be speaking the truth. Yet she still was not satisfied. Still felt she had not been given all the facts.

She said, "You needn't be afraid of Christopher exerting the same spell over me."

"I think that is what he is after," he warned her.

"I'm aware of what he is. I can't think why Madge didn't see it also."

"She saw it and didn't care."

"Then she wasn't the Madge I knew."

"I keep telling you that," he said. "While you are here I would be grateful to you if you'd avoid his company as much as you can."

"He is a member of the household."

"I understand that. I know you must be civil to him while he is here at the house for my grandfather's sake. But there is no need to be taking these excursions into Hong Kong with him."

She said, "I didn't expect to see him today. I actually went into Hong Kong with another friend."

Stephen's handsome face was bitter. "I know. My mother told me. It was Charles Milano who came here and picked you up."

"Yes. We met on the plane coming here."

Stephen said, "And Milano and Christopher are staunch friends."

"They seem to be," she agreed.

The tall, dark-haired man had taken a stand before her again and in a tense voice, he said, "As I understand it Charles Milano told you he was a journalist."

"Yes."

"He lied."

She was stunned. "Lied?"

He works for no newspaper here."

"He is a free-lance writer. He sends his stories back to the United States."

Stephen waved this aside. "I have friends among all the foreign newspapermen here. Charles Milano has no credentials with them. They consider him a fake."

"A fake?"

"Yes. Whatever his business is in this part of the world it has nothing to do with journalism. I made it a point to find this out."

She was on her feet. "I'm sure you must be mistaken." She had felt from the start she had a friend in Charles Milano. If he were a liar and a fake she must really stand alone. Yet she had been worried by the conversation between him and Christopher when they'd met at the Suzy Wong bar. There had been a strong suggestion that they were mixed up in some criminal business as partners. The journalist had given Christopher some sharp warnings about breaking his word with the thugs who'd been threatening him.

Stephen said, "I understand that you accepted this Milano at face value. But I have to let you know the truth about him."

Wearily, she said, "Very well. Until I know more about him I will not see him again."

"All this is for your own good," Stephen said. "I do not wish to give you orders."

"I understand."

"I want us to remain friends," he went on earnestly. "And when you leave I would like to have you satisfied that I did all I could to make Madge happy and save her."

Enid said, "It's not easy to adjust to a situation so complicated. At least I know some things that will help guide me. I'll try to get through Madge's belongings and be ready to leave soon."

"I don't want you to hurry," Stephen implored her, his manner changing. "We are all lonely here. Your presence is most welcome."

"I doubt that," she told him. "I seem to be adding to the bitter conflicts which already exist within your family. I have no wish to do that."

"Just avoid Christopher when you can."

"I will," she said. "Is that all?"

"Unless you wish to remain a while longer and tell me about your life in England when you and Madge were growing up," he suggested. "There are many things about her past which she never told me."

She said, "Sorry. I don't feel up to talking about such things tonight. I have a headache."

He looked disappointed. "That's too bad. Another evening, perhaps."

"Perhaps," she said, not wishing to make any strong promises.

He showed her out of the study and she went upstairs to her room at once. In her room she gave way to her despair. Tears filled her eyes and she slumped down into an easy chair as she considered all that Stephen Porter had revealed to her. The triangle which included Madge and Christopher had existed just as she'd suspected. And for some weird reason Madge had given her love to Stephen's ne'er-do-well cousin.

What shocked her even more than this was Stephen's contention that Charles Milano was a liar, that he was not in Hong Kong as a journalist but for some nefarious business which he preferred to keep secret. And Christopher was a partner with him in whatever it was.

Probably the two had tried their hand at beating the gambling combine which flourished in Hong Kong. Although the operations of the casino were kept underground, unlike those on the island of Macao, there were literally dozens of gambling places in the city. If Christopher and Milano were in debt to the casinos it could mean serious trouble and perhaps death for them. That would explain the presence of the ugly man with the scar and the attempt on their lives which had ended with the white Jaguar being damaged.

She had not told Stephen about this incident though she had mentioned the diary to him. She had no special purpose to protect Christopher but she'd been so stunned by the revelations about Charles Milano the car accident had been temporily erased from her mind.

She didn't think it was all that important. Later she would mention it to Stephen. She saw that she would have to keep very much to herself for the balance of her stay in the old mansion. She wryly remembered her uncle's warning about not trusting those she met in the Oriental city and she was ready to admit that he had been all too correct.

She sat in the chair as dusk overtook the room. She thought about it all and found herself still completely confused. For a while she had pictured Stephen as the villain. She'd seen him as the scorned husband who might have murdered his wife in a fit of jealousy. Now this didn't seem to fit any longer.

The emerging villain was Christopher with perhaps Charles Milano as a cohort. Stephen was now cast in the role of the wronged husband who fought to retain the love of an errant wife to the very end. At least this was the story which he had told her. And he had been convincing enough to sway her from her previous assumptions.

The room was in darkness and somehow she found the shadows held comfort for her. They protected her from the harsh reality of all she'd learned in the old mansion. She got up from her chair and crossed slowly to the window. She pulled the curtains aside and stared out at the grounds below.

There were few stars and no moon on this dark night. But after a moment her eyes became accustomed to the darkness and she was able to make out various objects in the garden. She saw the teahouse and the rows of small oramental bushes

101

which were set out around it. Edmund Porter had given a great deal of time and money to making the teahouse and the garden a place of beauty.

She had the odd feeling that in some way he had erected the teahouse as a moument to his beautiful Eurasian wife who had vanished so mysteriously. Vanished just as in a different way Madge had years later! The old Victorian mansion was surely a place of tragedy and mystery.

It was while these thoughts were going through her mind that she suddenly saw a figure come out of the teahouse. She strained to see in the blackness of the night and was sure that the figure was slim and feminine. Whoever it might be came directly to below her window and stood gazing up at her. Enid suddenly felt her throat contract in sheer terror for it seemed that the ghostly face looming up towards her from the shadows was the wan face of the dead Madge!

eight

The haunting face was visible for only a moment and then it disappeared, leaving Enid stunned. Her reaction to this eerie experience was completely unplanned. She turned from the window and raced across the dark room and out the door into the corridor. Then she made her way down the several flights of stairs with frantic haste.

Finding a set of French doors leading out to the garden area she flung them open and stepped out into the warm, flower-scented, tropical night. She glanced in the direction of the teahouse and taking her bearing from it knew she must be almost directly in the same spot where she had seen the phantom Madge.

She stared around her in the darkness, cold with fear and trembling, despite the soft warmth of the night air. Somewhere out here she had seen this ghostly figure which now appeared to have dissolved into the darkness without a trace. She nervously took a few steps in the direction of the teahouse. Perhaps the weird fugitive had taken refuge there.

Enid was nearing the teahouse when she heard the sound of heavy breathing from behind her. Before she could wheel around to see who it might be, her throat was seized by savage hands and she found herself gasping for breath. She clawed at the hands of her unseen attacker without avail. Suddenly her head began to spin and a sickening giddiness overtook her. The ground swayed under her as she dropped to her knees still feebly attempting to free herself from the unrelenting grip of those wiry fingers. Then she knew no more. With a tiny moan she lapsed into unconsciousness.

She stirred and then turned over on her back so that she was stretched out on the grass staring up at the stars. She was vaguely aware of a voice, of someone urgently pouring words out, words she was not able to comprehend. And she wearily decided it was very stupid and she would not even listen. She shut her eyes.

Then a hand on her shoulder shook her violently and she was forced to make the effort to open her eyes. She gazed up into a face which seemed familiar, though slightly out of focus. And then as her senses became sharper she saw the face more clearly. It was Sonya Chen, old Edmund Porter's adopted grandchild.

The Chinese girl urgently shook her again and said, "You must listen to me!"

"What!" she croaked in a voice unlike her own and was surprised that it hurt her to utter this single word.

"You are not dead!" There was relief in the other girl's voice.

She awkwardly lifted herself on an elbow and in an indignant tone managed, "Of course I'm not dead. What made you think I might be?"

"You were stretched out here on the grass. So still! I was sure you were dead."

Enid was becoming more herself with every passing moment although with increasing clarity of mind she was more aware of the pain in her throat.

She lifted a hand to caress the aching area and asked, "Did you see anyone running away from me?"

Sonya Chen shook her head. "No."

"You must have," she replied almost accusingly as she struggled to her feet with the other girl's help.

"I came out to stroll in the darkness as I often do," Sonya Chen said. "I stumbled over your body."

Enid was dazed and weak. She gazed at the frightened expression on the face of the pretty Chinese girl and tried to decide whether she was telling the truth or not.

She said, "I was attacked! Someone tried to throttle me."

Sonya Chen looked more scared. "I cannot help it. I did not see who it was."

Enid touched her hand to her aching neck again and gazed around her in the shadowed night. "I saw a figure down here. I came to try and locate it and this happened to me."

"You'd best come inside."

She gave the Chinese girl a sharp glance. "You say you come out for a late night stroll often?"

"Fairly often."

"Have you ever seen a phantom figure out here? A ghost?"

Sonya Chen continued to look frightened. Taking Enid by the arm she said, "It is not a time to talk of such things. You must come inside."

Enid realized she was not about to get any more information from the terrified girl and so she obediently allowed herself to be led back towards the great Victorian mansion looming like a phantom in the night. There were lights at several of the windows and also at areas of the ground floor.

The first person they encountered when they went inside was Christopher Porter. The lanky man with the horn-rimmed glasses came towards them with a look of surprise on his bronzed face. He said, "What's going on?"

Sonya Chen gave him an angry look. "She was attacked in the garden. Someone tried to choke her."

Christopher eyed Enid with concern. "Is that true?"

"Yes." Somehow she felt that he was acting his role in this little drama, that perhaps he wasn't all that surprised.

He said, "Thank goodness something has happened for which I can't be blamed. I just came down from my room to have a midnight snack and drink. Did you see who it was?"

"No," she said miserably.

"You look a wreck," the young man said. "Sit down." He helped her into a nearby chair. "I'll get you a stiff drink of brandy. That will help." He turned from her to go over to the sideboard against the opposite wall and pour her the brandy.

She leaned back in the chair, fearful that she might faint again. And she saw that Sonya Chen was slipping away from them out of the room. It made her worry and debate whether the Chinese girl might have been guilty of the attack on her. But surely those powerful hands could not have belonged to the slender, dark-haired girl.

Christopher came back with the brandy and urged it on her. "Drink it all down." he said.

Almost automatically she did as he told her. The burning liquid slid down her aching throat and she nearly choked. But within a few seconds she surprisingly felt a good deal better. She handed him back the empty glass. "Thanks," she said in a weak voice.

Christopher was studying her with a stern expression. "Why did you go out there in the dark alone?"

He was showing great concern, impressing her with his interest in her. Was this how he had managed to win Madge's confidence and eventually her love? Enid reminded herself she must be wary of the suave Christopher.

She said, "I had a good reason."

"There can't be any good reason for something as silly as that," he told her. "You don't know the place or the hazards that well."

Before Enid could answer him they were interrupted by the appearance of Stephen with Sonya Chen following after him. Now it became clear to her why the Chinese girl had so quietly slipped away. She had gone to summon Stephen and let him know what had happened.

Stephen was wearing a dark dressing gown over his pajamas and his hair was ruffled as if he'd been awakened from a deep sleep. He came straight to Enid, ignoring the presence of Christopher in the room, and asked her, "Are you all right? Should I call a doctor?"

"No," she said. "I don't need a doctor."

Christopher addressed his cousin, saying, "She went out into the garden and someone tried to choke her."

Stephen's handsome face was dark with anger. He told the lanky man, "I'm only too aware of what happened. I don't need your assistance. Nor does Enid." And he turned to her and said, "Are you well enough to come along with me?"

A trifle startled by the turn of events she nodded, "Yes. I think so." And Stephen helped her to her feet and placed an arm around her to steady her as they left the room.

She did not have a chance to see Christopher's face as they went out, so she had no idea what his reaction might be. Meanwhile Stephen guided her up the several flights of stairs to her own room. He opened the door, turned on the lights and saw her over to an easy chair. When she was seated he sat on the the edge of a nearby table and, gazing at her, grimly began to question her.

"Why did you venture into the garden alone so late at night?" he wanted to know.

"Didn't Sonya tell you?"

"No."

She hesitated. "I saw a figure. A ghost."

He frowned. "A ghost?"

"Yes. A ghostly face stared up at my window. Then the phantom vanished. I went down to try and find it."

Stephen's tone was stern. "You say a ghost? What sort of ghost?"

"The face I saw belonged to my half-sister," she said.

His reaction was one of shock. He stood up staring at her. "You saw Madge!"

"I think so."

"It had to be your imagination playing tricks on you," the handsome Stephen countered.

"It's a face I know well," she said quietly.

"It's impossible!" he sputtered. "I expected you to tell me something about the Jade Princess. That you'd seen her ghost. There's been too much of that loose talk. But what you have to offer is even more ridiculous."

She said, "I'm sure it was Madge. She looked wan and fragile. Exactly as you might expect a ghost to look."

Stephen said, "And so you went downstairs and outside because of this flight of fancy on your part?"

"I wanted to see if she might still be down there."

"I doubt she was ever there."

"How can you be sure?" she asked him. "Perhaps her ghost is trying to reach me. Or attempting to tell me something."

The handsome Stephen gazed at her in grim silence for a moment. "I don't suppose I can change your foolish notions about ghosts wanting to contact you," he said. "But at least I can give you sound advice about going out alone after dark. You mustn't ever do it again. It can be dangerous here."

"I found that out."

"You are lucky to be alive," Stephen went on. "Hong Kong has its share of thieves. These islands are not only the homes of the affluent. We have a harbor filled with sampans, crowded with people living so near the starvation level there is not enough food left floating around to attract the gulls. Notice when you drive by next time. Hong Kong harbor has no sea gulls. And that is why."

"You're saying I was attacked by a thief?" she asked.

"It is the most likely explanation. The watch you are wearing, the pin on your dress. Both are valuable enough to warrant the attention of one of the criminal element."

"No one warned me."

"I did not think it necessary," he said. "You know that Christopher consorts with the underworld. There is no telling what kind of character he might have lurking about the grounds for a meeting with him."

"I thought of that," she said. "But he seemed very worried about me when he was questioning me."

"That could be a pose on his part," Stephen warned her. "You can't believe anything he says or does."

Her eyes met those of the dark man as she said in a level voice, "Could it be he who attacked me?"

"I don't know," Stephen said with a sigh. "I'd hardly expect that of him. But I can't say it isn't possible."

"I would suspect him before anyone else in this house," she went on. "Whoever it was had cruelly strong hands."

"I prefer to think it some intruder," the handsome man said.

"Or perhaps the ghost itself," she suggested. "Who knows the power of a phantom's grip?"

Stephen lifted a protesting hand. "I wish you wouldn't talk of phantoms."

"Why not?" she said. "I'm sure I saw Madge's ghost tonight. And nothing you can say to the contrary will change my mind."

"I see," he said, with a grim resignation. "You are going to stay with your version of things. I only ask that you not repeat it to the others. It would be bound to upset my mother and my grandfather."

"Very well," she said. "I'll say nothing to them."

Stephen asked, "Did you mention this to Sonya or to Christopher?"

"No."

108

"That is good," he said with obvious relief. "Do you feel better now?"

"Yes."

"Do you mind my leaving you alone?"

"No," she said. "I'll be all right."

He started for the door then turned rather awkwardly to say, "I'm sorry about this. I wish it hadn't happened. You will be cautious in future?"

"You may be sure of that," she said, rising.

She followed him to the door and as soon as he went out she bolted it after him. She leaned against the door, her mind filled with troubled thoughts. It had been a night she would not soon forget. Not only had Charles Milano been exposed to her as an impostor, she'd also been made aware of Christopher's evil deeds. Then to cap all this, she had seen what she could only believe had been Madge's ghost.

The pale, tortured face of her half-sister remained vivid in her memory. Had a phantom Madge come back to warn her of some danger? Or had it been an attempt of the lovely, wan ghost to let her know her death had been the result of foul play?

She moved across the room slowly, her mind still racked by these suspicions. She had heard so much about the jealous phantom of the Jade Princess that she might not have been surprised to encounter that legendary beauty. Indeed, she had an idea the ghost of the long dead grandmother of Stephen had visited her the other night. There had been the moving shadow and then the scent of jasmine left in the closet.

Could it be that one phantom had sent her out to make a search in the night and she had been attacked by a second one? By the jealous Regina, old Edmund Porter's beloved Jade Princess?

Enid finally went to bed still tormented by these speculations. Because she was thoroughly exhausted she slept soundly despite the strange ordeal she'd gone through. And she did not awaken until the maid knocked on her door the next morning to announce that breakfast was being served.

It was another of the perfect, sunny days which Enid had come to expect of Hong Kong. She pondered over the changes which were supposed to have taken place in Madge and wondered why these had come about. Surely Stephen must have been a good husband even though a good deal of his time was necessarily dedicated to his business. Why had Madge turned against him?

When she finished breakfast she dressed and went downstairs. She met Stephen's mother in the front hall. Eleanor looked unusually concerned for her. The normally arrogant woman was almost a trifle apologetic.

She said, "Stephen told me of your going out for a stroll last night and being attacked."

"Yes," she said, warily, not sure just how much Stephen had told his mother. Not likely he'd mentioned the ghost since he'd warned her about any references to it.

The older woman sighed. "We have come to a fine day when our own grounds can no longer be called safe."

"I feel all right this morning," Enid said. "I was more frightened than anything else."

Eleanor's hawk face was shadowed by her concern. "From the accounts given me by Sonya Chen and Stephen you were on the grass unconscious for a while. The result of having been throttled."

"It sounds worse in recalling it," Enid said. "It all happened so quickly I hardly realized my danger until I blacked out."

The older woman leaned towards her confidentially. "You can put it down to Christopher. He's the one responsible for having all sorts of dangerous people turning up here. I think he associates with the scum of the islands."

"I should blame myself mostly," she said. "I should have known better than risk the gardens alone in the dark."

"A few years ago you would have been perfectly safe."

"Things change."

"They do around here," Eleanor said ominously. "I'm sure that Stephen gave Christopher another lecture last night."

"I hope I haven't made things worse between them," she worried.

"You couldn't do that," the older woman said. "We all wish that Edmund would send that young man away from here but he refuses."

Enid said, "He's a very old man. Probably he thinks that Christopher's evil is exaggerated."

"I think you are right. Christopher has a way of getting

110

around people. But you mustn't allow it to happen with you as it did with poor Madge."

It struck Enid that Stephen's mother was showing more fondness for Madge in death than she had in life. It was a grim irony of the situation which existed in the old mansion. Christopher seemed to be quite alone with all the others joined against him. Was this fair?

Enid said, "Do you honestly think Christopher had that much power over Madge? She was the sort of person not easily swayed."

"You should have been here," Stephen's mother said with indignation. "She turned her back on my son and became that rascally cousin's devoted slave. It was sickening. She always took Christopher's part when there were any arguments. And you can be sure there were plenty of them."

"I think that very odd," Enid said.

"We all felt the same way. Especially Stephen. And though he is my own son I might as well say that any girl would have been lucky to have him as a husband. Madge didn't appreciate him at all."

She said, "I'll continue going through her things today."

"Not a pleasant task I'm sure," Eleanor Porter said.

"One that has to be faced," she replied.

The older woman looked at Enid's throat and said, "I can see the red marks still there."

"Fortunately they don't hurt as they did at first," she said.

"Stephen asked me to speak to you about seeing a doctor. He wants you to feel quite free to do so if your throat is bothering you."

"No," she said. "Let's not make too much of it. I will be fine. I was stupid enough to go out alone in the darkness. I deliberately placed myself in danger. I won't let that happen again."

"You are our guest," the older woman said. "We should have taken better care of you. I think you are being most generous with us."

"Not at all," Enid said.

She then went back upstairs to her own room to get the key to the attic room where all Madge's belongings had been placed. She had left it in the same suitcase with the diary which she had found. She opened the door of the closet

111

where the suitcase was kept and to her amazement saw that the bag had been opened and its contents strewn roughly over the closet floor.

Kneeling down she tried to restore some order to the chaos. Almost at once she found the key and the scarf in which the diary had been wrapped but the diary itself was missing. Someone had brazenly entered her room, gone through her luggage and stolen the diary.

She sat before the open suitcase considering it all. And she was almost certain that Stephen was the only one she had told about the diary. If so, then she must turn to him to explain the robbery. But as she thought about it more it seemed that she had made some reference to the diary to either Charles Milano or Christopher. If that were the case her range of suspects increased widely.

It was another frustration at a moment when she was not feeling too much like enduring such setbacks. She had only skimmed through the diary and not studied it enough to come to any firm conclusions about it. Now it was gone with all the secret thoughts Madge had written in it gone as well.

With a sigh of dismay she closed the suitcase and put it back in the corner of the closet where she had first left it. She should have found a better hiding place for the diary. But it had never struck her that anyone would come into her room and steal it. Nor had it occurred to her that she would be the object of an attack, yet she had been.

It seemed that someone was especially anxious to keep the facts of Madge's death a secret. Her presence in the old mansion was threatening that someone and meant that she was being placed in danger. She had suspected this from the first but she had not looked for violence to follow so quickly.

She returned to the attic room with a feeling of despair. Whatever she might discover of value in solving the mystery of what had happened to her dead half-sister could only result in more danger for her. It wasn't a pleasant thought. And yet the memory of that ghostly face gazing up at her from the darkness made her vow to go on with the search.

This morning she tackled some boxes which contained books that Madge had brought out from England and had no real value or interest for her at the moment. When she had gone through these she spent nearly an hour going over a trunk full of clothes. Madge had always enjoyed dressing well and the wardrobe she'd left behind was extensive.

There was a packet of letters, some of them written by herself, and kept by Madge. Then some snapshots, most of them fairly old. A few even dated back to the London days and Enid smiled ruefully at the likeness of her younger self in one of these.

There were snapshots in color and of later vintage showing Sonya Chen and old Edmund Porter standing together smiling, a grim likeness of Eleanor picking roses in the garden and several snapshots of Stephen standing by the big black Bentley. But it was the one on the very bottom of the group which interested Enid most.

She stared at it as she recognized the familiar faces of Madge, Charles and Christopher in it. All three of them were on a motor launch, standing smiling at someone who was taking the snapshot. And from the background of the snapshot, in which the boathouse was clearly evident, Enid was sure that it must have been taken down by the wharf.

It jarred her because it showed her there had been a definite link between Madge, Charles and Christopher. Only last night she had learned that Charles was not the journalist he had pretended to be for her benefit. She was left wondering what his real business was and how he had become such close friends of Christopher and Madge.

But who had taken the snapshot? Surely not one of the family. Not with them feeling the way they had about the errant Christopher. They had likely enlisted one of the many servants to take the picture. And of course the most likely one would be Ben Larsen, the ugly old boatman whom she'd met when she first arrived at the estate.

Perhaps Ben would have some story to tell her concerning the snapshot. If he knew anything he would surely talk; he enjoyed gossiping. With all this in mind she decided to abandon her task for long enough to go down and talk to the old boatman.

She locked the room and, with the snapshot in her pocket, made her way downstairs. She went out and crossed the very area of the lawn where she'd been attacked the previous night. It seemed so safe and pleasant now, that it was impos-

113

sible to believe she might have met her death on the very spot.

As she drew near the teahouse she saw a figure inside its shade. It was old Edmund Porter standing there in the attitude of someone lost in thought. He did not seem to notice her as she passed by. He continued to stand there with his ancient eyes gazing off into space and a sort of vacant look on his wrinkled face.

She continued walking by the house without any sign of recognition from the old man. She had an idea the others might have kept from him the account of the attack on her. Probably this was wise since it would only distress him. On the other hand he was far from senile and had a right to know what was happening on the grounds of the mansion. She could only leave it at that. If he mentioned it to her she would discuss it with him.

All but the part about her seeing the ghostly face of Madge. She had promised Stephen she would not mention phantoms to the old man. It evidently upset him because of the repeated references to the ghostly appearances of the Jade Princess, his wife, Regina, of long ago.

By all accounts he had never been a truly happy man since his lovely Eurasian wife had vanished in the hills between Hong Kong and the mainland.

Enid reached the path leading down to the wharf. She found herself becoming more tense as the moment for questioning Ben Larsen arrived. She had a strange feeling that the old boatman would know the details about the snapshot and perhaps be able to tell her more about the roles Charles and Christopher had played in Madge's life, not to mention her death.

When she reached the wharf there was no one in sight and her heart sank. She had rushed down feeling sure the old man would be there and now it seemed she was to be disappointed once again.

She stood there on the gray timbers of the ancient wharf and listened to the water slosh against it. The smaller boat was tied there and it bumped against the wharf with the motion of the waves. Far out in the bay a tramp steamer was making its way across the horizon.

She was about to give up and return to the house when she

glanced in the direction of the boathouse and saw its door open and the old man emerge from it. She at once waved to him and he returned her greeting with a wave of his own. He hurried across the rocky beach and then climbed up onto the wharf to join her.

She said, "I almost went back without seeing you."

The old man with the apelike face tipped his marine cap and showed a smile on his battered features. "I was working in the boathouse, Miss. I don't have many idle minutes."

"So it seems," she said.

"Are you enjoying your stay here, Miss?" he said, peering at her with near-closed eyes in the bright sun.

She at once sensed a certain tone in his voice. And she said, "Did you hear about last night?"

He nodded. "Aye."

"I thought so," she said. "Who told you?"

"One of the servants," the old boatman said. "Chinese fellow. Word spreads around them fast."

"I gather that," she said.

"Claimed you were almost choked to death."

"I was."

The old man spat in anger. "What sort of creature would harm a nice young lady like you?"

"That's something I'd like to know," she said.

"I wish I'd been around last night," Ben Larsen said. "I sometimes am. But last night I was up the shore working on a boat belonging to another of the English families. I worked late and stayed there all night."

She said, "But the news was waiting for you when you came back here this morning?"

"It was," he admitted. "Heard it when I had my second cup of tea in the kitchen."

"I've come to you because I think you may be able to help me," she said.

"Any way I can," he assured her.

She took the snapshot from her pocket. "Do you recognize this?"

The old man reached for it with his gnarled hands and studied it nearsightedly. Then he said, "I should recognize it, Miss. I was the one who took it!"

"I thought you might be," she said.

115

"I remember the day," the boatman went on as he stared at the snapshot. "It was the first time that other chap showed up here."

"You mean Charles Milano?"

Ben nodded. "That was his name. And I remember he only stayed a while. And after he left the missus and Mr. Christopher got into some kind of argument about him. They had a regular battle of words you might say."

nine

"They quarrelled?" Enid said in surprise.

"Yes, Miss."

"You say the argument was about Charles Milano?"

The old boatman nodded. "If that is the chap's name."

"Did you hear what they were quarreling about?"

The old man gave her a sly look and rubbed his grizzled chin. He said, "I'm not one to listen when I shouldn't. But they were making such a fuss I couldn't help but hear some of it."

"So?"

"Missus Madge was saying that Mister Christopher should not trust this other chap. That he was counting on him too much. And Mr. Christopher kept shouting that it was all right, he knew the fellow could be counted on."

She frowned. "Counted on for what?"

"I don't know that," Ben Larsen said. "I expect it was some sort of business venture."

"Why should Madge worry herself about Christopher's business ventures?"

The boatman shrugged. "I can't say. Unless she wanted him to go on his own and leave the family firm. He and Mister Stephen have never got along."

"I'm well aware of that," she said. "How did the battle between Madge and Christopher end?"

"After a while they calmed down," Ben Larsen remem-

117

bered. "And Mister Christopher must have gotten his way because that Milano fellow came back here again a few times."

"Did Madge and he seem to get along then?"

"Yes," Ben Larsen said. "There were no more arguments. And the missus and he seemed real friendly." He handed her back the snapshot. "But they never asked me to take any more snapshots of them."

She took the snapshot and put it in her pocket. "Did you ever talk with this Charles Milano?"

"No," Ben said. "He never came down except with the others. And he only came once or twice with the missus when Mister Christopher was away."

"So there's not much else you can tell me about them."

"I'm afraid not."

She gave a deep sigh and gazed out at the calm blue waters of the bay. "I've been thinking of what you said the other day. And I can't convince myself that Madge would deliberately go out there in a storm."

"Struck me as strange," the old man agreed.

She gave him a sudden glance. "What would you say if I told you I'd seen Madge's ghost last night? That it was the sight of her phantom face which took me out onto the grounds alone."

Ben's face showed awe. "You saw her ghost!"

"Yes. And so let myself be led into danger."

"I'm not all that surprised," Ben said.

"You're not?"

"No, Miss," he said earnestly. "You see, I've seen her ghost myself."

Enid was once again shocked. "You have?" she exclaimed.

"Yes," the elderly boatman said. "I didn't mean to speak about it for fear of upsetting you. But now that you claim you've seen the ghost yourself I can tell you my experience."

"Go on," she urged him.

"It was late one night," he said. "I'd been working on an engine in the boathouse. I came out here and started up the path to the lawn. I'd only gone about halfway when I saw her coming down. Walking straight towards me, she was. I can tell you it gave me a start!"

"Then what?"

"I turned and came back down here," the old man recalled. "I couldn't bear to come face to face with her."

She stared at him. "And you haven't told anyone?"

"Not a chance!" he said emphatically. "If I did they'd say I was drinking. That old woman, Eleanor, has her heart set on getting rid of me and I'm not going to give her any excuse."

"But you should have told Stephen. Let him know what you had seen."

"I wouldn't risk it," old Ben said. "But I did see her. No doubt about that. It was a clear night without a touch of fog or anything and she was coming, gliding down the path. At first I thought of the Jade Princess—her ghost is part of the story of the house—but it didn't take me long to see it was the late missus."

"How long was this after she was drowned?"

Ben considered. "Maybe a month or six weeks after."

"So we've both seen her," she said grimly. "I wonder if others have and like us have been afraid to say so."

"Sounds more and more as if she were murdered," Ben Larsen said. "That's why she's not at rest in her grave."

Enid gave him a knowing look. "You mustn't forget there was no grave."

"Right," he agreed. "Her body was never recovered."

"Did you see her ghost only once?"

"Yes," the old boatman said in an awed voice. "And I promise you I don't want to see it again."

"Nor do I," she said quietly. "I guess I'll have to discuss it with Stephen. Do you mind if I repeat what you've told me?"

The simian face registered unhappiness. "It could mean the end of my job here."

"I'm sure it won't," she said. "In fact I'll make him promise that the information won't be used against you."

"If he tells the old woman she'll want me discharged," Ben worried.

"I'll see that he doesn't," she promised, not entirely sure she could keep the promise but needing his consent to discuss the ghost.

"All right," Ben said reluctantly. "But I'm putting my job in your hands and no mistake about that."

"I won't let you down," she said. "Like myself you do want to find out what really happened to my half-sister."

"The missus was always pleasant to me. I liked her," Ben said. "And if anyone did wrong against her it should be known."

"I feel exactly as you do," she said. "I'm not sure how Stephen Porter will react to the ghost business but I have to test him with it."

She remained a few minutes more with the old man and then started back up the path to the lawn above. She had found out a few things of importance, perhaps the most astounding being the confession of Ben's that he had also seen Madge's ghost. The thought of the pale ghost made her shudder involuntarily.

There could be a risk in discussing the ghost with Stephen, especially if he'd been responsible for Madge's death in a fit of jealous rage. But she had to test him and get his reaction. With the additional information she was gathering, her suspicions were beginning to turn more towards Christopher or even the mysterious Charles.

It still troubled her deeply that she had been so completely taken in by Charles Milano. She had not questioned his statement of being a journalist and she had actually begun to like him. Now it turned out he was a friend of Christopher's and probably up to some crooked scheme with him.

When she reached the lawn once again, she saw that the elderly Edmund Porter was still in the teahouse but that he was no longer alone. The old man was now seated and with him was the equally elderly Wong Lee. The sight of the stout, placid Chinese partner of the Porter family made her feel somewhat better. She had enjoyed meeting Wong Lee and felt he might be someone she could turn to if she needed help.

When she reached the teahouse she halted and went up the several steps to its interior. The two elderly men, one cadaverously thin and the other extremely stout, rose to greet her.

She said, "I hope I'm not interrupting you."

"By no means," Edmund Porter said, and with a sweeping gesture of a thin hand he indicated an empty chair. "Please sit down for a little. We will be grateful for your company."

Wong Lee smiled and bowed to her. "It is a pleasure to see you again, Miss Branch. One of the benefits of being a neighbor to my old friend here is the opportunity of meeting his guests. A good neighbor is a found treasure."

She accepted their invitation to sit down and said, "How near is your home, Mr. Lee?"

The stout Chinese said, "I own the adjoining property. But the entrance to my house is a distance along the road. When the Japanese took the island over they reached this house first. One of the servants came through the heavily treed area of our properties to warn me. As a result of Edmund's friendly gesture I was able to find a hiding place and later make an escape to one of the fishing boats which eventually landed those of us who'd escaped on a British warship."

Enid turned to the emaciated Edmund Porter and said, "You were taken prisoner, Mr. Porter?"

"Yes," he said. "Though I must say I was given better treatment than most. My importance to the islands was not lost on the Japs. I traded them some small favors for comforts."

She asked, "Where was Stephen at that time?"

"He was in England with his mother," the old man said. "And his father was in the army. I heard little from them. Overseas mail did not arrive for a year and then it trickled in. I received my first letter from my daughter-in-law two years and three months after I entered internment. Many were worse off than that. In all the period I received four letters. One time it was known that a lot of mail had arrived but it was held up four or five months because the Japanese claimed they were short of censors."

Wong Lee said, "I made my way to Bombay, India, and spent the war years there. We have an office in Bombay and I assumed control of it and was able to make some excellent profits for the firm in spite of the war."

Old Edmund chuckled. "It's a fact. Wong Lee came back with the news that business had been better than ever for the firm outside of Hong Kong and Singapore."

"It must have been a frightening time," Enid said. "Now the war seems so far off. Did you have any Red Cross in your internment camp to see you were treated properly?"

Stephen's grandfather nodded. "A Mr. Zindel from the Swiss Organization was in charge here. We had one great tragedy in which he played a major part."

"What was that?" she asked.

He said, "It was in October, 1942, that the Japanese decided to transfer a number of British prisoners-of-war to Japan to work in the mines. They boarded the *Lisbon Maru* but when some distance off the Chinese port of Ningpo, the ship was torpedoed by a United States submarine. This was bad enough, but as the ship began to fill with water the Japanese battened the prisoners into the holds. Many were able to fight their way out, but the Japanese opened up on the swimming men with machine guns. It was a terrible story, and I was present at the trial of those concerned. The captain of the ship showed great distress. The traditions of the Japanese navy, and of the sea, were very different to those of the hated military. The captain agreed there was no excuse for the action taken against our troops, and I'm glad to say those who were caught and held responsible were duly punished."

Wong Lee said, "Punishment did not bring back the lives lost."

"Unhappily, no," Edmund Porter said with a sad look on his thin face. "The Red Cross man, Mr. Zindel, tried to get a list of survivors, but through no fault of his own it wasn't accurate."

"You were both lucky to have survived," she said.

"We were," Wong Lee agreed. "I was the more fortunate thanks to Edmund."

"Many younger men lost their lives," Edmund Porter said. "It was ironic that my son survived the conflict without any injury at all only to die with a business associate in a plane crash years later."

"Your daughter-in-law told me about that," she said. "It was very sad."

"Fortunately I have Stephen, my grandson, to carry on," Edmund Porter said proudly. "And he has done well."

"I'm sure he has," Enid said politely.

Wong Lee was staring at her and now he said, "It is tragic that he had to lose his beloved wife."

"Most unfortunate," she said, feeling that the old Chinese had not brought the subject up merely to make polite conversation. Again she had a feeling that he knew more about the manner in which Madge had met her death than he was willing to let on.

"Madge was reckless," Edmund Porter said. "She spent too

122

much time in the ocean. She should have known better than to take the boat out in the face of that oncoming storm."

"I still find it strange," she said carefully. "Back in England she was not that fond of the seashore."

"It was Christopher who got her interested in boating," Stephen's grandfather said bitterly. "She would have done well to avoid him. But they became close friends."

Wong Lee asked Enid, "Have you completed the task of going through the late young lady's effects?"

"Not yet," she said. "It's a difficult task."

"Of course," the old Chinese said with sympathy.

"You mustn't rush yourself," Edmund Porter told her. "It is good to have you here. My grandson needs company at this time to take his mind off the tragedy."

She said, "One thing I'd like to ask. Where is my sister's grave?"

Edmund Porter stood up and indicated a path through the woods on the left. "If you will follow that path you'll find a clearing. The graveyard is in the clearing."

The stout Wong Lee gave her another knowing glance. "You realize her body is not buried there."

"I know," she said.

Still standing, old Edmund Porter said, "Neither is the body of my beloved Regina. Yet I erected a stone there in her honor. Stephen had a similar gravestone put up for Madge."

"I must go take a look at it," she said, rising.

"It is only a short distance," Stephen's grandfather said. "When you have seen it perhaps you'll honor two old gentlemen by returning to the house and taking lunch with us."

"I'll be happy to," she said.

The stout Wong Lee was on his feet again. "You have not yet honored me with a visit to my home," he said. "Would you find it convenient to join me for tea tomorrow afternoon if I send my chauffeur over to get you?"

"I can think of no reason why that shouldn't be all right," she said. "And I'd like to see your home. You're very kind."

"On the contrary," Wong Lee said. "It is you who will be doing me an honor."

She left the two old men standing in the teahouse and made her way across the lawn to the path which Edmund

Porter had pointed out. She was puzzled by the manner in which Wong Lee had referred to Madge's death and she had an idea he might reveal some unknown facts to her when she had tea with him the following afternoon.

Old Edmund Porter appeared blissfully unaware that there was a good deal of mystery associated with the way in which Madge had died. She had also noticed his visible emotion when he'd made the brief mention of the loss of his beloved Regina. Even after the long years since she'd been killed by mountain bandits he deeply mourned her. It was odd that Wong Lee, who was also supposed to have been a suitor of the Jade Princess, had shown no emotion at all when she had been mentioned.

Enid made her way through the tropical growth so very different from an English woods. The path was winding and the trees on either side of it shaded it from the strong sun. There was a sweet scent in the air which she suspected must come from some unseen tropical flowers growing in the shadows of the palms.

As she walked slowly along a multicolored bird rose from its perch in one of the trees and flew ahead of her with a belligerent squawking at being disturbed. Then all at once she found herself in a clearing about thirty feet in diameter. The clearing was circular and she thought it a strange place for a cemetery. Yet Edmund Porter had chosen it for this purpose.

There were perhaps a dozen gravestones of various sizes and ages standing guard over neat green mounds. It took her only a moment to pick out the large one with facing angels at its top which was inscribed to the memory of Regina Porter, beloved wife of Edmund Porter and mother of Stephen.

Her heart was pounding as she finished reading the words worn with time. She knew that Madge's gravestone could not be far distant and even though Madge was not under it, the moment of discovering her grave sent cold chills through her. She was trembling and could not help herself as she approached the newest of the gravestones almost directly behind the one erected to Regina.

Her real moment of shock came when she drew close enough to the stone to read its lettering. It was plain white with black lettering but some vandal had battered the lettering with heavy stones so that the inscription was almost too blurred to be readable. The stone itself had been cracked by the fury of the unknown vandal and stood there with an injured dignity.

She saw the stones where the vandal or vandals had dropped them. And she stood staring at the damaged stone wondering who would commit such a macabre act and why? Surely it had to be someone who hated Madge.

She was so stunned by her discovery that she did not realize she was no longer alone until a hand reached out and touched her arm. She wheeled around with a frightened scream to find herself gazing up at the mocking face of Christopher.

"Really gave you a bad shock, old girl," he said in his taunting way.

"What are you doing here?" she demanded angrily.

The eyes behind the glasses were cold. "I might ask you the same thing," he said.

She was still upset as she sought to deal with him. She said, "I came to see Madge's grave."

"Very thoughtful of you," he said with a hint of sarcasm. "I saw you taking the path and followed you."

"I'd expect you to be in the city," she said.

"Things aren't always as we expect," was his cool reply.

She could sense a new hostility in him and began to fear for herself being alone in this remote place and at his mercy. She said, "Look at the gravestone."

He did and gave a low whistle. "What do you know. Someone must have it in for poor Madge."

"It's a disgusting act of vandalism even though she isn't buried there."

"Without a doubt," Christopher said in his casual way. "I have an idea Stephen will be upset that you've seen this."

"He'll be upset in any case," she said.

The tall, brown-haired man eyed her from behind the heavy glasses. "Hasn't it ever struck you that Stephen may hate Madge more than anyone else? That he might have done this himself?"

She gazed at him with shocked distaste. "Not very likely after his having the stone erected here."

"His grandfather made him do that," the tall man said with a crooked smile. "Stephen does what his grandfather

125

suggests. So he had the gravestone put up here. Whacking it with the stone could be his own idea."

"I don't believe you."

"I didn't expect you to," Christopher said. "I know you have been properly warned against me. Beware of Christopher, the leper. I know my reputation with the family."

"Then you must know you've earned it."

"By the way," Christopher said. "My friend, Charles, is much taken with you. He thinks you're delightful."

She said, "You both must have had a good laugh at me behind my back. When you see him again, tell him I know now the papers he works for and I'm not impressed."

Christopher arched his eyebrows. "Ah! So Stephen has filled you in about Charles as well. Obviously he wants to turn you against both of us for his own purposes."

"He was kind enough to warn me," she said. And she took the snapshot she'd found with Madge, Charles and Christopher standing in the boat smiling and handed it to him. "Do you remember when that was taken?"

He studied the snapshot. "A long while ago," he said.

"It's too bad Madge chose to make friends of you two and turn against her husband," she told him angrily.

The brown-haired man gave her an annoyed glance. "Has it occurred to you that she might have done that in an attempt to protect herself from an obsessively jealous husband?"

"I don't see Stephen in that role."

"Try thinking about it," Christopher advised. And he handed the snapshot back to her. "You may want to show that to Stephen."

"I may," she said, taking it.

"See how he reacts," the young man said. "You may be surprised."

"It would take a lot to surprise me now," she told him. "And by the way did you ransack my room and steal the diary belonging to Madge I'd left there?"

"What kind of a thing is that to say?" he replied in pious protest.

"I'm sure I told you about it being there."

"Madge's diary would not be of the slightest interest to me," he said.

126

"I'm not at all sure of that."

"You may take my word," he said. "And by the way, if you are smart you won't mention this vandalized tombstone to old Edmund. He's liable to go into a rage and it might not be too good for Stephen."

"I'll do as I see fit," she said, though she had already made up her mind to keep the news of the vandalism for Stephen's hearing alone.

"I'm going on trying to be your friend," Christopher said in his mocking fashion. "Even your British prudery won't discourage me, devastating as it is."

She crimsoned. "I'm not asking for your friendship nor do I want it," she said. And with that she made up her mind to try escaping from the unhappy position in which she found herself. She quickly stepped past him and headed for the path.

"What's your hurry?" he called after her in that cruel tone of mockery.

There were tears of frustration in her eyes but she made no reply to him. Nor did she turn to look behind her. She kept walking straight back towards the house. Apparently he had no intention of trying to prevent her from leaving or even of following her. As she made progress along the shaded path she began to feel less uneasy. At last she stepped out into the sunlight of the lawn again.

Eleanor Porter was waiting in the foyer of the white mansion, to greet her. "I saw you go out to the graveyard and shortly after Christopher followed you."

"Did you?" she said. "It wasn't a rendezvous if that is what you're thinking."

The older woman was grim. "I hoped that it wasn't. Did he try to bother you out there?"

"Only with his usual mockery," she said.

"He knows better than to lay a hand on you when he can be caught," Stephen's mother said. "But you mustn't trust him. If you hadn't appeared I was ready to go out there and protect you."

"Thank you," she said. "I managed very well on my own."

"After what happened to you the other night I'd expect you to be more cautious," Eleanor said.

"I'm trying to be," she said. "Where are your father-in-law and Mr. Lee?"

"In the screened patio at the other end of the house," the older woman said coldly. "They are waiting for you to join them. They're having their lunch out there."

"Yes," she said. "I promised I would have lunch with them."

"You needn't cater to them any more than you wish," Eleanor said. "Those two old men are spoiled with everyone at their beck and call."

Enid said, "It was their genius which founded the firm. Aren't they entitled to some rewards?"

Her reply took the grim Eleanor by surprise. The older woman swallowed hard, then said, "I suppose so."

She quickly went upstairs and freshened up and then went back down again to join the two old men. As she reached the bottom of the stairs she saw Christopher coming striding across the lawn. She did not wait for him to enter the house but hurried down the long side corridor to escape him.

When she reached the patio she discovered the two old men seated at a white-clothed table waiting for her. Edmund Porter rose and saw her seated at the place which had been set there for her.

He said, "Did you find Madge's gravestone?"

"Yes," she said, trying to sound casual, not wanting him to find out what she'd discovered.

The stout Wong Lee gazed at her across the table with interest showing on his broad face. "It must have been a difficult moment for you."

She met his glance. "I did feel upset."

"Quite natural," Edmund Porter said. "I thought later we ought to have gone with you. Then Christopher came by the teahouse and I suggested he go and see you were all right."

Enid was shocked. "You sent Christopher in there?"

The old man was unperturbed. "Yes. He's a bit of a bounder but one must make use of him as the occasion occurs. This was a time when he could be useful."

"Thank you for your consideration," she said, no longer certain now how she ought to feel about Christopher following her. He had not told her he'd done it at the old man's request. She had blamed him wrongly as he insisted she often

128

did. Was this true? Had she allowed herself to swing too far in an opposite direction and be unfair to him?

The stout Wong Lee was studying her again and with the air of a man who had read her thoughts, he said, "Young Christopher is a difficult person to judge."

ten

As soon as Enid finished having lunch with the two old men, she excused herself and went back upstairs to the task of going over the belongings of the dead Madge. It was a grim business but she persisted at it in spite of the afternoon heat. Her nerves were on edge because of the several things she had discovered and she was anxious to see Stephen and talk with him.

It had surprised her to learn that Christopher had followed her because of a suggestion from Edmund Porter. She still did not understand the relationship between the two, though perhaps family loyalty was sufficient in the old man's case for his tolerating Christopher. As for herself, she did not know whether to brand him all villain or not, as in most cases he had some redeeming qualities.

She felt that Wong Lee had attempted to give her a hint as to his feelings about the reckless young man. And she looked forward to her visit at the neighboring mansion of the old Chinese. It seemed almost certain that he would have more to tell her about the Porter family.

Little had she guessed when Madge had left England to marry Stephen that it would end as it had. The vandalism of her half-sister's gravestone was another shocking discovery to be added to the already long list.

She kept at her task in the stuffy room until she had barely time to change and shower and see Stephen before dinner.

She felt it important that she talk with him as soon as she possibly could.

When she came down the main stairway, immaculate in a rainow-hued gown with a low back, her hair neatly arranged, and wearing a single strand of pearls, she was fortunate in meeting Stephen in the main foyer. He was wearing a white linen suit, his usual garb when he returned home from the firm's headquarters in Hong Kong.

The tall, dark man smiled in greeting her and said, "I trust you've had a pleasant day."

"A pleasant lunch at least," she said, standing with him. "I joined your grandfather and Wong Lee on the patio."

"They can be fine company when you get them talking about the old days here," he said.

"We had some war reminiscences," she said.

"They can tell a few stories."

"The balance of the day I spent upstairs," she went on. "I've almost finished up there. And then I paid a short visit to the family cemetery."

"Did you?" he said, almost uneasily. "Then you've seen Madge's grave."

"Yes. Have you been out there recently?"

"No."

"I think you ought to go."

"Why?"

"I have my good reasons," she said. "In fact, if you'll take a few minutes before dinner I'll be glad to return there with you. There is something I'd like to point out."

His eyebrows raised. "Really?"

"Will you take the tour with me?" she asked.

"All right, if you insist," he said, seeming puzzled.

As they crossed the lawn together in the direction of the path, she said, "I won't keep you too long."

"No problem," he said. "My grandfather can pour the drinks for the cocktail hour. Or perhaps Christopher will be on hand. I think he spent the afternoon out in his boat."

"He was here," she said. "I saw him at noon. He followed me out to the graveyard, but on your grandfather's instructions."

Stephen frowned. "Grandfather has a lot more confidence in him than I have. Did he behave all right?"

"Better than usual," she said. "Though he does like to taunt me."

"That seems part of his nature," Stephen said.

They had reached the beginning of the shaded path through the tropical growth and she gave him a knowing glance. "I want to ask you about something else."

"What?"

"The diary of Madge's which I found and didn't have a chance to read through completely."

"What about it?"

"Someone came into my room and ransacked it and stole the diary from a suitcase where I'd hidden it."

He looked shocked. "Who would do such a thing?"

"I've been wondering. I recall telling only three people about it. Charles Milano, Christopher and yourself."

The handsome face showed a frown. "If you told those other two you can be sure they're somehow mixed up in the theft."

"Naturally that was my first impression," she said. "But I thought I ought to discuss it with you."

They were walking more slowly now as the path had become narrow and twisting. He said, "I'm glad you mentioned it, I'll do what I can to try and get it back for you."

"I doubt I'll ever see it again," she said. "In the diary Madge had written some of her most intimate thoughts. Whoever stole it didn't want me to have time to analyze what those writings might mean."

"Unquestionably," Stephen said but without too much enthusiasm. She at once began to wonder whether he might have had some strong personal reason for stealing the diary.

He asked her, "May I ask why you are bringing me out here?"

"Yes," she said. "There is something I know you ought to see."

"Such as?"

"Better for you to see for yourself," was her quiet reply.

They reached the clearing as the sun was about to set. She led him directly to Madge's gravestone and let him gaze at its vandalized face in dismay.

"Who would do that?" he gasped.

"I've been asking myself that."

He gave her an angry look. "Was it done before Christopher turned up today?"

"Yes. If he's to blame for it he must have done the damage at some earlier time. But I don't think he's guilty. He seemed to be genuinely startled by what had happened to the gravestone."

Stephen knelt before the battered headstone and felt its surface with his fingers. "Someone must have used a heavy weapon to do such battering."

She bent and lifted the large, pebbled rock which she had found by the gravestone and which showed signs of having been used as a rough hammer. She held it out to him. "I'd say it was done with this."

He took the stone and weighed it in his hand. "Most likely," he agreed in a grim voice. "But why?"

"Someone had to hate Madge a good deal."

"Who?" he said, staring at her in what appeared to be genuine astonishment.

"You ought to know a lot more about that than anyone else," was her suggestion.

He stared thoughtfully at the stone in his hands, then tossed it to one side. He looked grim. "You say Christopher was taken aback."

"Yes."

"He's the only one I can immediately think of, unless one includes Charles Milano. And they seem to be in all their dark schemes together."

She said, "The stone wasn't like this when you last saw it?"

"Certainly not."

"Which must have been shortly after you had it installed?" she said.

He stood up, still staring at the broken stone as he said, "Grandfather insisted that I have a stone put up."

"And you didn't approve?" She recalled what Christopher had said. That Stephen had not erected the stone in the role of a heartbroken husband but on his grandfather's explicit instructions.

Stephen eyed her warily. "Let us say I did not approve of it to the same extent that my grandfather did. He had put one here for Regina even though her body isn't here. He felt Madge should have no less."

133

"And you?"

He shrugged. "I likely wouldn't have done it if Edmund hadn't kept harping on it. After all, we didn't find her body. The gravestone is resting over an empty grave."

This agreed exactly with what Christopher had told her and made her wonder whether it might be wise to believe at least some of the things the errant young man said.

She said, "A woman could have done this damage, by using the stone."

"I suppose so."

"Without question. What about Sonya Chen?"

The question caught him off guard and he crinkled his brow. "Sonya Chen did not hate Madge."

"Madge took you from her," Enid suggested.

The handsome man dismissed this with an angry wave of his arm. "We were never romantically interested in each other."

"Are you speaking only for yourself or for her as well?"

"For both of us," he insisted. "She has been like my sister. And anyway she is not a violent person. She wouldn't do a thing like this."

"Sometimes people surprise us," she said. "They repress a violence which is very real."

"Not in Sonya's case," he said blithely. Too blithely for Enid's liking. "I take it this is what you wanted me to see." He indicated the vandalized headstone.

"Yes. I hope you'll forgive my drawing it to your attention."

"I would want to know," he said. "As a result of this I'll delve into a few dark corners. I may come up with the answer."

She said, "I wish you'd think about the stolen diary also. I'm certain that has importance."

"I will," he promised. And taking her by the arm, he added, "Probably we ought to go back now so we won't be missed."

Enid saw the sense of that. If any of those who were regularly on hand for cocktails were guilty it would be better for them to remain ignorant of this excursion they'd made to the private cemetery.

On the way back, Stephen said, "I'd like you to come into the city and see our warehouse and headquarters."

"I'd enjoy it," she said.

"What about tomorrow afternoon?"

"Sorry," she said. "I have already promised to have tea with Wong Lee."

"Well, that is something you should do also," the tall man agreed. "His house is a treasure chest of Chinese antiques and art."

"I understand he fled the islands during the time of the Japanese invasion," she said.

"Yes," Stephen said. "But he was fortunate the general who was billeted in his house was also a lover of antiques and so nothing was harmed."

"He was lucky," she agreed.

"The general didn't have such a happy fate," Stephen went on. "When he knew that Japan had surrendered he killed himself in the traditional way, by committing hara kiri on a bamboo rug in one of the adjoining sheds. He was too considerate a guest to have his blood soil any of the fine rugs in the main house."

They reached the lawn and as they began to cross the short area to the house, she looked up at him and said, "That last day you saw Madge. Did she say anything which suggested that she might have been going to take her life?" Perhaps it was the recounting of the suicide of the Japanese general which had led her to ask this question. If Madge had gone out into the storm deliberately she must have had a reason. And the reason might offer a solution to the entire mystery surrounding her death.

Stephen's handsome face crimsoned. "She didn't say a thing to me."

"She must have said something."

He looked more annoyed. "No. As a matter of fact we weren't on speaking terms. Hadn't been for a while."

She stared up at him as he strode towards the house. "You didn't make that clear before."

"I'm sure I must have mentioned it," was his protest.

"I would have remembered if you had."

"Anyway I don't think it important," he said, as he held the door open for her to enter the entrance foyer.

135

She said, "I think it is. Why weren't you speaking?"

"For many reasons."

"Christopher?"

"Among other things," he agreed. "Now let us end these stupid questions and go in and join the others."

It seemed strangely appropriate that Christopher should be presiding over the cocktail hour. He stood there, smiling, wearing a late-style fawn suit. Old Edmund Porter and Eleanor were seated in wicker chairs while Sonya Chen, in a crimson Chinese gown, stood alone on the patio nursing a glass of wine and staring out at the bay.

Christopher deliberately made a big thing of the arrival of Enid and Stephen. He exclaimed, "Ah, latecomers! We've missed you two. What will you have?"

Stephen gave him an ugly look. "I'll make my own drink," he said.

Christopher didn't seem to mind the look at all. He accepted it as if it had been a compliment and turning to Enid said, "And I shall make a drink for the lovely young lady. What is your pleasure, my dear?"

Enid knew he was mocking them but could not help admire his nerve. To help save a difficult situation, she said, "I'll have a whiskey and soda, please."

"On its way," Christopher said, turning to prepare it.

From her chair Eleanor gave her a bleak look. She said, "Was my son showing you the grounds?"

"Yes," she said, not wanting to enter into a general discussion on the matter.

Stephen had prepared his drink and now he turned to his mother and said, "Enid was especially impressed by the gardens around the teahouse."

"Done under my direction," old Edmund Porter spoke up proudly.

Christopher came towards Enid and handed her the drink. His eyes holding that familiar mocking gleam, he said, "And done to perfection, I may say. There are no gardens quite like them anywhere else in Hong Kong."

Edmund Porter's thin face lost some of the pleasure he had shown earlier. The old man sipped silently at his drink. To avoid Christopher she decided to move out on the patio and stand with Sonya Chen. The lovely Chinese girl showed nervousness as she stood beside her.

Enid said, "You are studying the bay. It has many moods, I'm sure."

Sonya Chen gazed at her with those almond eyes and told her, "The bay makes me feel lonely. I do not like the water."

She said, "I wish Madge had felt the same way."

"Your half-sister was fond of boating and swimming," the Chinese girl said. "She spent much of her time down at the wharf."

"So I've been told," she said. "Could it be that she wished to get away from the house?"

Fear flecked the almond eyes. "I cannot answer such a question," Sonya Chen said.

"Or is it that you prefer not to answer?" Enid suggested.

Eleanor announced that dinner was ready and so they all went off to the dining room. During dinner Enid noticed hat the errant Christopher teased Edmund Porter mercilessly whenever he could. He mocked the old man's opinions about the island politics and business. The strange part of it was that the proud old man did little or nothing to defend himself.

When dinner ended she and Stephen walked out of the dining room in each other's company. He said, "About that visit to the office. Why not come the day after tomorrow?"

"Very well," she said.

"I'll have one of the cars bring you in," Stephen said. "You can come in time for lunch at the Hong Kong Club and then after you've seen the plant, do a little shopping on your own before returning here."

"That sounds pleasant," she said.

"I'll send my limousine for you around eleven," was his promise. And then he added, "I'm sorry I was a little angry with you earlier. But my patience has been tried badly. You saw how Christopher behaved at cocktails and dinner."

She said, "He seems to enjoy tormenting your grandfather."

Stephen looked grim. "I blame grandfather for much of it. He doesn't need to keep Christopher here. Had he been turned out long ago as he deserved, Madge and I would never have quarreled."

Eleanor joined them at this moment and ended the rather confidential nature of their conversation. At old Edmund Porter's request Sonya Chen went to the stereo and put on some records. She chose some recordings of the D'Oyly Carte Company doing Gilbert and Sullivan. This pleased him. Christopher had vanished somewhere and Enid decided that all the others must be happy that he had. She remained with the others listening to the music until ten. Then the party broke up and Enid went up to her bedroom.

She lingered by the window staring out at the splendor of the Oriental night before going to bed. Now that she was alone she began to feel strangely tense. It had been a trying day which had left her more bewildered by what was going on around her than she had been before. At last she changed into her nightgown, put out the lights, and got into bed.

But it took a while before she slept. And when sleep did come it was filled with bizarre dreams. She dreamt she was in the private graveyard studying the battered headstone over Madge's grave. She heard a slight sound of movement from behind her and when she turned she was terrified to find the slim figure of the long dead Regina, the Jade Princess, standing over her and holding the rock which had been used to vandalize Madge's headstone.

The Jade Princess looked exactly like her portrait except that there was an expression of supreme hatred on her lovely face. Now she bore down on Enid with the rock and Enid dodged away from the makeshift weapon screaming. She was still screaming when she wakened to the darkness of her bedroom.

She sat up in bed and the first thing she was aware of was the scent—the scent of the jasmine perfume which seemed to fill the bedroom. Since she associated this scent with the ghost she stared into the darkness with frightened eyes seeking some sign of the phantom figure.

"Enid!" Her name was called softly from somewhere in the distant darkness.

She reacted to the whispered sound of the voice as if an electric shock had gone through her. She asked, "Who is it? Where are you?"

Only mocking silence answered her. As she reached for her bedside lamp she heard a door close softly but did not know

138

whether it was a closet door, or the one leading to the hall. She was certain she had bolted the door which gave access to the hall.

Turning on the lamp she hastily slid into her slippers and crossed to the hallway door. The bolt had not been put in place. She found this hard to believe. She was so certain she'd taken care of this. So her intruder could easily have used this door. Belatedly, she slid the bolt into place.

The room reeked of jasmine and now she moved across to the dresser where the scent seemed strongest. And to her utter amazement she saw that someone had used her lipstick to write in large letters, "Sussex, July, '71." This gave her another jolt. In 1971 she and Madge had spent their final summer holiday together in Sussex.

Now there was this reminder of that final vacation there on the dresser mirror. Her heart pounded as she stared at the message and recalled the way her voice had been whispered. What did it mean? Was a dead Madge trying desperately to get through to her?

She was standing there speculating on this when she heard a sound from the other side of the door leading to the hallway. She rushed to the door, pulled the bolt and threw it open to see something familiar on the floor.

It was Madge's missing diary! She bent to pick it up and at the same instant heard the sound of soft, yet rapid footsteps as someone ascended to the floor above. Without a moment's hesitation she plunged forward and up the flight of stairs in time to see a vanishing figure in a flimsy negligee.

"Stop!" she called out and raced down the hall.

The figure did not hesitate but reached a doorway and entered it. There was the sound of a door closing and Enid found herself angrily trying to open the door.

"Open up!" she cried. "I know there's someone in there."

There was an eerie silence from the other side of the door and she thought she could hear someone there breathing tautly and waiting for her to go. She told whoever it was, "I won't leave!"

She'd barely called this out when another door opened and old Edmund Porter appeared in pajamas and nightgown. In a querulous voice, he demanded, "What is going on here?"

"Someone ran into this room and locked the door," she told him.

The thin grandfather of Stephen eyed her with amazement. "That is my foster-granddaughter's room. Sonya, will you please open the door!"

There was no response. Still clutching the diary to her, she said, "You see!"

Edmund Porter scowled and rapped on the door. "Sonya, I demand that you open this door."

After a moment's waiting the door opened hesitantly and a frightened Sonya in a thin, blue nightgown gazed out at them contritely.

The cadaverous face of the old man was flushed with annoyance. He asked the girl, "Sonya, what have you been up to?"

She was trembling as she told them. "I meant no harm! I left Madge's diary at her door."

Edmund Porter turned to Enid. "Is this so?"

"Yes," she held up the diary as evidence. "But she ran away as soon as she did it."

The old man asked Sonya, "Why did you run away?"

"I did not want her to know I had it," Sonya said in a frightened voice.

"It was stolen from my room," Enid explained. "Taken before I had a chance to properly go through it."

Edmund Porter turned to the girl again. "Did you steal the diary from Miss Branch?"

"No!" Sonya wailed unhappily. "When I came up to my room a little while ago I found it on my bed. I knew that it belonged to Miss Branch."

"And so you took it back to her?" he said.

"Yes," the Chinese girl said. "I was afraid she might blame me for taking it in the first place and that is why I ran after I set it down by her bedroom door."

The old man turned to Enid saying, "I think that sounds reasonable enough."

"It does as far as it goes," Enid said.

"Aren't you willing to believe that Sonya is telling the truth?" he asked.

"I am," she said. "But before the diary was returned there was someone in my room. I smelled the scent of jasmine."

140

"The Jade Princess!" burst from the Chinese girl excitedly without her being able to help herself. And then when she saw the reaction to her words on the face of the ancient Edmund Porter she bit her lip.

The old man turned to Enid again, "What is all this about a scent of jasmine?"

"If you will come to my room I'll show you," she said.

Edmund Porter eyes her reluctantly and then said, "Very well." And to Sonya Chen he added, "You come along as well. I want this fully straightened out!"

The Chinese girl obeyed him with her head bent downward. She followed the old man and Enid along the hall and down the stairs. It struck Enid that they made a quaint trio and she hoped that they would not rouse any others in the house.

When they reached her bedroom the perfume had almost evaporated. Yet there was still a slight hint of it in the air.

Edmund Porter sniffed and said, "I can't smell anything."

Enid thought this was deliberate on his part although she had been told that some older people lost much of their sense of taste and smell with advanced age. Perhaps it was true in his case.

She pointed to the dresser mirror. "You can't deny that message. It was written there in the dark by the phantom with the jasmine scent."

He read the several words and asked, "What is the meaning of the message?"

"Madge and I spent our last vacation together in Sussex," she said. "I'm probably the only one here who knows that."

He asked irritably, "How can you be sure of this?"

"What do you mean?" she said.

"I mean Madge could have told Stephen, Christopher or anyone here about that vacation," he said with annoyance.

"I doubt that she'd bother mentioning it," Enid said.

"Don't be too sure of that," the old man replied. And he turned to Sonya and asked, "Did Madge ever tell you about taking a vacation in Sussex?"

The frightened almond eyes avoided Enid as the girl said to the old man, "No. She never said anything about Sussex to me."

Edmund Porter turned to Enid once more. "I think we can assume my foster-daughter is telling the truth."

Enid said firmly, "Someone was in this room. Someone wrote that message!"

"It was not I!" Sonya Chen said with desperation.

"Maybe not," she replied. "But I heard you outside a moment after."

"I can't help that," the Chinese girl said. "I had nothing to do with the message. I was never in this room until you brought me here just now."

Enid felt weary. At this moment she could not decide whether she should believe the Chinese girl or not. At last she said with resignation, "Very well. It must have been someone else."

"Thank you," old Edmund Porter said with grim coldness. And he told his foster-daughter, "You may go back to your room. And if you have anything else to deliver, speak to me about it first."

"Yes, sir," the Chinese girl said respectfully and bowed and hurried out of the room.

The thin old man now turned to Enid and said, "I have every reason to believe the girl is telling you the truth."

"I'm also inclined to believe her," she said.

"Sonya does not lie. It was stupid of her to leave the diary without an explanation. She should have knocked on the door and told you how she came by it."

"I agree."

The old man said, "No doubt the culprit who stole the diary in the first place left it with Sonya in the hope of shifting the guilt to her."

"That is quite possible," she said. She indicated the lip-sticked message on the dresser mirror. "But what about that?"

Edmund Porter's expression was bleak. "I don't know. I'd guess someone was trying to frighten you."

"Frighten me away before I can learn the truth about Madge's death," she suggested.

He scowled again. "There was no mystery about that. The girl was obstinate in going out in the face of the storm. She died as a result."

Enid decided to risk the old man's anger with another

question. She said, "When I mentioned jasmine perfume, Sonya Chen at once cried out the name of the Jade Princess. Was the intent to make me believe that she left this message here?"

Fury showed in his pale blue eyes and he snapped, "The legend of the Jade Princess is pure fantasy. I will ask that you not mention it again in my presence."

"Very well," she said with a sigh. "So we are left with no explanation of who was in here?"

"I cannot be responsible if there is a practical jokester under my roof," the old man said.

"I do not find a message from the dead any sort of joke," she replied.

His answer was to shrug and walk out with ancient dignity. She followed him and closed the door and bolted it. Then for the first time she gave her attention to the missing diary which she still clutched. She opened its cover and read the inscription in her half-sister's handwriting, "Diary of Madge Porter." And then she began to turn the other pages and as she did so her shock increased. Every page with a written message had been torn from the diary, only blank pages now remained.

eleven

And so she was left tortured with fresh doubts.

Her sleep that night was wretched and tormented by eerie dreams in which dark, phantom figures played a sinister part. And when she awoke to the sunshine of the next day she was more than ever convinced that this seemingly placid paradise was anything but that. Concealed in its shadows there was an ugly drama still being played out.

The dark-garbed and respectful female servant came with her breakfast tray. She sat by the window and consumed the ample meal wondering what it all meant. The message written in lipstick was still on her dresser mirror as a reminder of the previous evening and the diary with all its vital pages removed sat on her bedside table.

There was a knock on her door and she looked up from her coffee to say, "Come in."

The door opened and Eleanor came in with a tense air. She was wearing one of the dark, shapeless dresses which she seemed to favor. And as she came to stand before Enid it was apparent that she was a large, powerful woman with hardly any excess fat on her big frame.

Eleanor hesitated and then said, "My father-in-law tells me you were bothered during the night."

"Yes."

The big woman said, "I simply cannot understand it."

"Nor can I."

144

Eleanor said, "However, I agree with him that you should not blame Sonya Chen. She is not capable of devious tricks."

"I'm quite able to believe that," she said. "And yet I wonder who is responsible. For that message on the dresser mirror for example."

Eleanor turned and studied the lipsticked message. Then she glanced at Enid again and said, "This was done while you were sleeping?"

"I was wakened by an intruder in the room. I smelled the jasmine perfume. When I turned on the light the intruder left by the door over there. And I read this message. It was only a few seconds afterward that Sonya Chen came by the door with the diary. That is why I followed her and accused her."

"It had to be a coincidence," Eleanor said with her brow furrowed.

"So it appears."

"You did not have the door bolted?"

"I was sure that I had bolted it," Enid replied. "But when I tried it the bolt had been slipped."

"That doesn't seem likely," Eleanor said. "Poor old Mr. Porter is very upset. More so than he let on to you. I think one of the reasons is that he fears these happenings will revive the legend of the ghostly Jade Princess."

"Sonya mentioned the Jade Princess and I saw that it upset him," Enid agreed.

"It always has," Eleanor assured her. "The loss of his beloved Regina was as shattering to him as losing Madge was shocking to my son. He has never really recovered from it, they tell me. Never been the same sort of person since. I do not want Stephen to be so scarred and yet the danger is there."

Enid got up from her breakfast tray and touched a napkin to her lips. "It would seem that someone wants me to leave here. And this same someone wants to cover up the truth about what happened to Madge."

The older woman showed concern. "We all know what happened to your half-sister. What can you mean?"

"I mean what you have chosen to accept doesn't satisfy me," she said. "I had hoped in coming here to make things a little easier for Stephen."

"We had all hoped that."

She gave Eleanor a resigned look. "Yet it seems to have worked out rather differently. My presence here is upsetting to everyone. So it would seem that the best thing I can do is quickly finish sorting out Madge's belongings and take the plane back to England."

There was a short silence on the part of Stephen's mother. Then she spread her hands in a gesture of acceptance and said, "It could be that you are right. It is too bad. I'd expected that your presence here would cheer Stephen up. But I agree that he only appears more tense."

"I know that," Enid said. "And Christopher does not help. I'm to see Mr. Wong Lee this afternoon and Stephen has invited me to lunch and a tour of the company headquarters tomorrow. Following that I will plan to leave Hong Kong."

Eleanor said, "You have been here such a short while."

"It seems long enough to me," she said. "And if I'm not to learn any more about what happened to Madge I know it is best for me to leave." It was a defeatist attitude but it was how she felt at that moment.

"I'm sorry," Eleanor sighed. And yet as Stephen's mother left the room it struck Enid that the older woman was not all that upset to see her go.

Later Enid cleaned the dresser mirror, not wanting the phantom message to be found by the maid. Then she went back upstairs to the macabre task of going through the balance of her dead sister's belongings. And while she worked at the task she could not help being haunted by the wan face which had drawn her to the dangers of the garden the other night. She could not accept that the face had been a product of her troubled nerves. She had seen Madge somehow returned from her watery grave.

She finished sorting the things which she would take and those which would be left behind for Eleanor to dispose of. Probably the things would be given to some local charity—the older woman had suggested this. Enid was quite agreeable to the plan, anxious to put all the unpleasantness behind her.

When she reached her bedroom she saw that it had been put to rights. The bed was neatly made and the dresser dusted and everything carefully set out. She packed some of Madge's things in one of the suitcases and included the dam-

146

aged diary which would have very little meaning now. But she decided to take it in any case.

She had lunch with old Edmund Porter and Eleanor on the patio. She noticed the thin man's palsied hands appeared to tremble more than usual. He tried to keep up a conversation but every so often he lapsed into silence and his thin face took on an almost haunted expression.

Towards the end of the meal the old man turned to her to say, "This is the afternoon on which you are having tea with Wong Lee."

"Yes," she agreed.

He nodded approvingly. "I'm sure you will find the experience enjoyable."

"I look forward to it," Enid said.

"His antiques alone are worth a fortune," Eleanor said. "This house is barren by comparison with his."

Old Edmund Porter glanced at her with annoyance. "I do not think that a good comparison. The thing is that he has added extra pieces over the years while I have scarcely bought anything. My late wife, Regina, furnished this house as you see it today. I have never wished to add to or change the way in which she decorated it. Wong Lee has had no such restriction in mind and so has added freely to his household furnishings and collection."

Enid said, "I consider this house to be decorated with exquisite taste."

"Thank you," the old man said.

"Was Wong Lee always so stout?" Enid wanted to know.

The old man showed a sad smile on his thin face. "Yes. Wong has always been stout just as I have always been thin. But when we were younger the contrast was not so noticeable. With the years he has added weight and my illness has made me rather grotesquely thin."

Enid smiled. "I cannot think of either of you as being different from what you are."

Eleanor spoke up, "There has been change. When I first married Stephen's father Wong Lee was not nearly so stout and Grandfather Edmund was fairly well padded and rugged looking."

Edmund Porter sat back in his chair. "My illness has finished me. I'm lucky to be alive."

Nothing more was said. She left the table a few minutes afterwards and went back to her room. She wrote some letters to friends in England, including her uncle, and then rested a little before changing into a yellow linen dress for tea. She went down at the appointed time and waited on the doorstep only a few minutes before an ancient Rolls Royce appeared with an elderly Chinese chauffeur in dark uniform. It was Wong Lee's car sent for her.

She took her seat in the comfortable car which she judged must be at least twenty years old. She guessed that Wong Lee must have bought it shortly after the Second World War. It was almost a collector's item now and seemed in excellent shape.

The drive to the fawn stucco mansion on the adjoining property took only a short time. When they reached the rambling house with its red-tiled roof the amiable Wong Lee was standing there waiting to receive her. The old man took her hand and kissed it most courteously before he escorted her up the steps and into his treasure-packed home.

Enid had never seen anything to compare with it. If she had any criticism it was that the house was too filled with Oriental art. And for her, the very soul of this sort of art depended on its having enough space.

The fine lacquered furniture was set off by equally priceless decorative pieces in bronze, chinaware and jade. Fine carvings were matched by beautiful silk screens and delicate paintings. One wandered from room to room as though in a museum. She barely gasped out her admiration for a life-sized Buddha only to walk a few feet further and be just as much thrilled by a dainty carving of the same figure in ivory.

She turned to a smiling Wong Lee and said, "How have you managed to collect all these things?"

The stout man was gratified by her appreciation. He told her, "It has been the work of years. One of my main interests."

"That is easy to understand. And the money you must have poured into these things!" Her hand rested for a moment on a lovely, earthenware jar with a cover.

He said, "That is of the T'ang Dynasty, I have tried to specialize in that era."

She gazed at him in admiration. "And all the while you have been a businessman as well as an art collector."

Wong Lee smiled. "Not to mention the interruption of the war years."

Enid said, "Mr. Porter told me about the general who was billeted here—the story of his also being a collector and so taking care nothing happened to your precious art works. That was most fortunate even though his suicide was a sad affair."

The stout man said, "I have a theory that the atmosphere of beauty with which he found himself surrounded hypnotized him to the point where be became a servant to it. In the end he destroyed himself rather than attempt to destroy the beauty around him."

"That may be how he felt," she agreed.

"We will have tea on the balcony," he said, leading her out to a screened balcony with a white marble table supported by gilded dragons. It was shady and quiet and they were at once served by an elderly man who vanished the moment his task was completed. Wong Lee poured her tea and offered her some dainty cakes with an exotic flavor.

She said, "These are wonderful!"

"I'm fortunate in having an excellent kitchen staff," he said.

"I'm sure you are," she replied and then she looked out at the lawn with its tropical trees serving as a background. She said, "This is so different from the Porter house. It is so peaceful here."

"You miss that feeling over there?"

Her eyes met his. "Yes. Don't you?"

"If I'm to be completely honest, I do."

She said, "You and Edmund Porter are so different. Yet you have been partners over the years."

"Through all sorts of times," Wong Lee agreed. "Many of them difficult. But our stars seemed destined to follow the same path. Perhaps you have not been told this, but we both fell in love with the same young woman."

"Regina."

"Yes."

"She was part Chinese, wasn't she?" Enid said. "And very

beautiful. Edmund Porter has a painting of her on the living room wall."

"He has made the house a kind of temple dedicated in her honor," Wong Lee said. "But at one time Regina was on the point of marrying me rather than Edmund."

"And she changed her mind?"

"Yes," the stout man nodded. "She was a creature of whims. Never able to be quite sure what she wanted. Generous and gentle yet filled with a restlessness. She was courted by dozens of young men before she agreed to marry Edmund. And she loved every moment of it."

"Do you think things might have turned out differently if she had married you?"

Wong Lee's broad face became grave. "Yes. I think so. I'm not saying they weren't much in love. But he did not understand the Chinese side of her nature as I would have. Had she been my wife I would never have let her go off to the hills to see her cousin. But she demanded that Edmund allow her to go and he would not refuse her anything."

"You would have."

"For her own good," he said. "She took only one decrepit old servant along for company and to drive the cart they were traveling in. It was a mistake. Too late Edmund realized this."

"I don't know any of the details," she said. "Only that she vanished, just as my half-sister vanished. And no one seems to know much about or want to discuss that ill-fated event."

"The death of Madge was like history repeating itself," he agreed.

She leaned forward to him earnestly. "You have known the Porters for years and you knew Madge. What do you think really happened? Do you believe this story they have concocted about Madge going out in that small boat in the face of a storm?"

Wong Lee showed no expression for a moment. Then he lifted a plump hand and said, "The Porters are a strange family."

"I know," she said unhappily. "So at war with themselves. I think Christopher tried to win Madge's love and her husband became aware of it and was madly jealous."

The old man said, "Jealousy is a Porter trait. Even after

Regina married Edmund, he remained possessive and jealous of her. I do not think he ever trusted me where she was concerned, and I was his business partner and closest friend."

She listened incredulously. "Edmund Porter continued to be jealous of you?"

"To the day of his wife's death," Wong Lee said. "I was absent on a business journey. In those days we traveled by wagon and ship. It took a long while. When I returned to find she had vanished he first angrily accused me of having arranged some rendezvous with her."

"He thought that?"

"Unhappily, yes," the old Chinese said. "It took some effort on my part to convince him otherwise. And when she still did not return he gradually accepted the belief of the local authorities that she had been kidnaped and slain by hill bandits. Only then did his attitude change towards me. Since that time he has never doubted me."

"And you think that Stephen has the same jealous streak?"

"It would not surprise me," Wong Lee said.

She gave him a searching look. "Has it ever occurred to you that Stephen might have killed my half-sister through jealousy?"

"It has crossed my mind."

"And have you come to any conclusion?"

"It is difficult to tell," Wong Lee said. "Madge was a friend of mine. I think she trusted me. And while she enjoyed Christopher's company during the lonely times when Stephen was away I don't think she was fooled about his being a thorough rogue."

Enid said, "Do you think Madge and Christopher became lovers?"

The old man was slow in replying. Then he said, "I have an idea there was some strong link between them, especially towards the end. Whether they actually became lovers or not I cannot say."

"I'm sure that Stephen thinks so and so do some of the others."

"Christopher could also be capable of murder," Wong Lee pointed out. "The last day I talked with your half-sister she looked pale and ill. She made some references to a quarrel

151

she and Christopher had. It was over some companion of his, a Charles something."

"Charles Milano."

"Yes. That is the name. From what I gathered Christopher had been associated with this fellow in some business deals of an illegal nature. She'd warned Christopher against him and he'd refused to listen. She put up with the man being around and then they quarreled again. She was very upset about this second angry scene between them."

"You say she looked ill? Do you think it was a matter of nerves or that she might be physically unwell?"

Wong Lee said, "I knew her for the several years she was here. In the final months there was a marked physical deterioration in her."

"That surprises me," she said. "Madge always had good health."

"The climate here is not kind to many people."

"That could be the answer," she said. "But it doesn't explain what happened to her in the end. No one wants me to find out. In the time I've been here several strange things have happened." And she went on to detail these things ending with the account of the message on her dresser mirror and the return of the stolen diary by Sonya Chen.

Wong Lee listened and then said, "You are being made the target of some weird attack. But I do not think Sonya Chen is mixed up in the plot in any way."

"Stephen's grandfather says that and I'm ready to accept it," she said tensely. "But who wants to be rid of me and why? And did I see Madge's ghost the other night or was it also some sort of trick?"

"That is difficult to say," Wong Lee commented carefully. "The house has had the reputation of being a place of ghosts. Since the death of Regina, the Jade Princess has been said to return."

"I'm familiar with the legend."

The old Chinese went on, "Whoever wishes to be rid of you, may have been inspired by the legend of the Jade Princess to make you the victim of other ghostly manifestations."

"Go on," she urged him.

He frowned. "You speak of the troubled atmosphere at the

Porter mansion. And you are right. Things are not all as they may seem there. They were not properly sorted out when Madge arrived to take over as mistress of the house. It is a place dedicated to the past. You have spoken of being much impressed by the teahouse in the garden."

"Yes. It is the one definitely Chinese thing about the house and grounds."

"I agree. It was not built there too long before Regina Porter vanished. Edmund has made it a kind of shrine to her. I do not think the word shrine too strong. A great deal of all that goes on in the family comes from the influence of that teahouse."

"I think that is true," she said. "Anyone can see Edmund Porter lives in the past."

"In a way his life ended with that of Regina's," Wong Lee agreed.

Enid said, "I hardly think Stephen was that devoted to Madge."

"Who can tell?"

"I'll admit I can't," she said. "I'll also admit I'm baffled by all I've encountered. I plan to pack my bags after tomorrow and leave as soon as possible. I've given up hope of ever knowing the true facts about Madge's death."

The old Chinese gave her a troubled glance. "Would Madge be satisfied to have you do that?"

She said, "I can only believe that she brought on much of the trouble she experienced."

"And so you will give up trying to help her?"

"How can I help her? She's dead. The dead are beyond help."

"But not beyond being avenged," Wong Lee said. "If she was done wrong by would she not want you to even the score?"

Enid smiled bitterly. "It is my feeling that the odds in this game are against me."

"That may be true," Wong Lee said. "But we Chinese are inveterate gamblers. It is our curse."

"So I've heard."

"If I were in your place I would make a last gamble that the truth might yet be discovered."

"You're saying that I remain in Hong Kong?"

"There is a great deal to see," the old man said. "You have barely left the house next door since you arrived. You have much to see."

"I don't think I can easily slip into the role of a tourist," she said with a sigh. "This other thing weighs too heavily on my mind."

He smiled. "You would appear to be merely a tourist but I would do all possible to assist you in solving the puzzle which is bothering you. I, too, have my own theories about what may have happened to Madge."

She eyed him for a moment in silence, then said, "I'll think about it. But I'll make no promises."

She remained about a half-hour more with the old Chinese and then he had his chauffeur take her back to the Porter mansion.

When she entered the foyer she found Eleanor there. Apparently waiting to greet her, the older woman said, "You have been to Wong Lee's."

"Yes. I had a most interesting time."

"My father-in-law has asked that I send you to him," the older woman said. "He is in the teahouse and asks that you join him there."

Enid was surprised. "Are you sure?"

Eleanor looked at her oddly. "Of course I'm sure. I am not one to indulge in practical jokes. I consider such things in bad taste."

"Very well," Enid said. "I'll go see what he wants."

"Thank you," Eleanor said coldly and left her.

In a puzzled frame of mind she went out to the teahouse. As she crossed the lawn she spotted the old man seated in his favorite chair in the pavilion with the gilded dome. He was gazing out at the bay and did not seem aware of her approach.

She climbed the steps and went over to him and said, "You wanted to speak with me?"

Edmund Porter glanced up with surprise. "I swear I did not hear you until you spoke. You gave me a start."

"I'm sorry," she said.

He waved her to a chair by him. "Sit down. I asked to have you come to me because I received a phone call soon after you left."

"A phone call?"

"Yes." The old man's faded blue eyes were fixed on her and there was a new sharpness in them. "Sonya Chen phoned me from the school where she teaches."

"About what?"

"About last night."

"What did she have to say?"

The thin face revealed a bleak smile. "I can tell you are most interested."

"Naturally."

"She remembered something."

"What?"

"When she entered her room and found the diary there she also noticed something else by it. A kind of medallion which she had never seen before. But she was no much upset by the discovery of the diary she paid no attention to the medallion."

"And?"

"This morning she thought of it again and went to look for it," the old man said. "But the medallion had vanished. She searched for it and could find it nowhere."

Enid frowned. "You say a medallion?"

"Those were her words," the old man said. "I presume she means some sort of medal. She claimed it was bronze in color and about the size of a silver dollar."

"Did she give any other description of it?"

"Yes," he said. "She told me there was a likeness of a young woman in a sports outfit running on its face along with some words in Latin around its edge."

Enid gasped. "It can't be!"

Edmund Porter was watching her closely. "What?"

"When Madge was in private school she excelled in sports. She received a bronze medal for winning a race for the school. It looked exactly like the one you say Sonya Chen described."

"Amazing!"

"Frightening!" she said. "How could that medal have gotten to her room with the diary?"

"An interesting question," the old man mused.

"I didn't find the medal among her things. I'd forgotten all about it until you mentioned it just now. Slowly it all came back to me."

The old man said, "Sonya Chen was worried that it might have importance."

"Is there any chance it is still in her room?"

"None at all," he said. "I had Eleanor go up and search for it herself. She came down to tell me that Sonya was right, the medallion has vanished."

Enid said, "It was left there to give substance to the diary being returned. As if Madge had returned it herself and vouched for it by leaving the medallion."

"And later removing it?"

She said bitterly, "Aren't ghosts supposed to be able to do anything? Someone is having a very good time torturing me with these macabre tricks."

"I'm sure Sonya Chen has done no more than report the truth," the old man said.

"I agree," she told him. "I'm sure someone else is behind this."

"We must talk to Stephen about it," the old man suggested.

"I plan to," she said, rising to leave.

Edmund Porter asked her, "Did you have a pleasant time at Wong Lee's?"

"Yes. He has a magnificent collection of art and antiques."

"He devotes himself to it," Stephen's grandfather said. "And what did he have to say about me?"

"About you?"

"Come now," he told her, "you don't need to spare me. I know that old partner of mine. He did not spent an hour with you and not express some opinion about me."

She was surprised that Edmund Porter should put the question to her so abruptly. She said, "He spoke of your long years of being in business together and your friendship."

"And what else?"

She shrugged. "He mentioned your dead wife and said that you and he had once been rivals for her hand. That your Jade Princess had been very popular."

The old man nodded grimly. "I was certain he'd tell you that. He never gave up loving her, you know. Of course he did nothing about it after she married me. But the deep feeling was there. I always knew it."

156

"You could not hate him for that."

"I found myself near to hating him when I lost her," old Edmund said in a taut voice. "I guess right then I blamed the whole world. I was mad for a little time."

"But that is all in the past," she protested.

"Yes," he said with a grim nod. "Lost in the past." And he looked away from her and gazed out at the bay again. She stood by him in silence for a moment and sensed that he was also lost in the past with his thoughts and did not want to talk to her any longer. As quietly as she could she left him.

twelve

Darkness cloaked the old, white mansion and its grounds. Stephen had been late returning for dinner and it was not until after the meal was over that she had sought him out and told him she had some urgent matters to discuss with him. He had pleaded some important long distance phone calls and had not come to her until the night was well along.

Now she and Stephen walked on the cliffs above the wharf and the boathouse. Behind them one could see the many lighted windows of the mansion and down below in the boathouse a single window showed light. Stephen informed her that old Ben, the boatman, sometimes lived in a room in the boathouse. Far out on the bay the red and white signal lights showed from a tramp ship. Above in the dark sky there was a great pattern of stars but no moon.

Stephen had invited her out for the stroll. It was the first time she had ventured onto the grounds after dark since the macabre attack on her. But with the tall, handsome man as her companion she felt safe enough. Although the thought had once flashed accross her mind that he might be her secret adversary, she had quickly pushed it aside.

He halted on the cliff path just above the wharf and turning to her said, "I hope you approve of my idea of strolling out here. It is a lovely night."

"I shall remember these warm nights when I return to the cold of London in March," she said.

"Have you decided to leave? So soon?"

158

"I have gone through Madge's things. What else is there for me to do here?"

He gazed down at her earnestly. "You might remain to fill the void left by Madge."

She was startled by his words. She stared at him and said, "You must know I can't do that."

"You can in your own way. If you wish."

"How do you mean?"

Again his eyes met hers in deep seriousness. "I find a lot of Madge in you, even though you are much different in looks and personality. There is a something about you that speaks of her."

"And?"

"I think I've fallen in love with you," was his next astonishing statement. "I've hinted this to you before. I can say it openly now."

"Stephen!" she reproved him. "You're trying to be nice to me. You're not serious."

"I am. I can think of no better way of bringing back some brightness to this old place than by having you remain and become my wife."

"That's a flattering offer," she said bitterly. "But you above all others should know why I can't accept it."

He frowned. "What do you mean?"

"Surely you're aware that while I'm planning to return to England I'm going with my mind upset. That I'll be leaving here convinced that Madge did not meet her death as you and the others insist. I think she was the victim of a murderer who has chosen to harass me and make me decide to leave."

"And just who do you suspect might be Madge's killer?" His voice had gone suddenly cold.

Aware of his anger but ready to stand up to him, she said, "I haven't decided. I think you could help me if you would."

"How?"

"In many ways," she said. "But for your own reasons you want the mystery to remain a mystery. Christopher and Charles Milano and others are mixed up in it. I'm properly confused and willing to admit that there's little hope of my ever finding out the truth. That's why I've decided to leave."

"And my offer doesn't interest you?"

"Under the circumstances how could it?"

He looked at her without betraying any expression. "You do plan to come have lunch with me and look around Hong Kong tomorrow?"

"Yes. It will give me a chance to do some last-minute shopping."

"I'll have a car pick you up about eleven," he promised. "I'm anxious for you to see the building we occupy. And then we'll have lunch at my club."

"Very well," she said.

He went on evenly, "About the events of last night. I can only tell you that I suspect Christopher. You may have noticed he did not come to dinner this evening."

"I thought he might be away on business."

"If he is it is on his own," Stephen said grimly. "He comes and goes as he pleases thanks to my grandfather's tolerant attitude towards him."

"Christopher may well be to blame," she said. "Maybe he also killed Madge. I have no way of being any more certain of that than of anything else."

"Madge fell for his false charm. I hope he hasn't also included you in his victims?"

"Never," she said with a grim smile. "I'll admit he has a rogue's way of making himself liked. But from the first night he took me for a drive I've known the sort of person he really is."

Stephen sighed. "I wish Madge had found out." And he began to walk slowly back to the great house with Enid at his side.

"You don't think she knew him for what he is?"

"If she did, she shut her eyes to it."

"That doesn't sound like her."

"Madge changed. You're not taking that into account," he argued.

"I wasn't here to see the change," she told him. "So I can't be any judge of her state of mind."

"It was not good, I promise you that," the handsome man at her side said.

They strolled along in silence for a little. She thought how many times she had been envious of Madge's good fortune in winning such a husband. Now by a strange twist of fate she was being offered the same opportunity to be the wife of Ste-

160

phen Porter. And it was something she couldn't even allow herself to consider. That was the irony of it. Not with all her doubts concerning Madge.

They reached the French doors and were about to enter when one of the male servants appeared out of the shadows and spoke urgently to Stephen in Chinese. She stood by watching his worried reaction and heard him reply in the same sing-song manner without any apparent effort. It was obvious that Stephen must have grown up from childhood able to converse in this other language.

He turned to her and said, "There is a problem in the garage. One of the cars is apparently going to need extensive repairs. This fellow has asked me to have a look at it."

"Don't let me stop you," she said.

"I should only be a few minutes," he told her. "I can join you in the living room."

"Please don't hurry on my account," she hastened to say. "I think I'll go upstairs to my room. I'll be getting up early tomorrow and I feel weary."

"All right, then," Stephen said. "But be ready when the car comes for you at eleven."

"I will be," she said. "Goodnight and thanks."

"Goodnight," he said, studying her intently for a moment. "I'll look in the living room when I come in, just in case you change your mind." And with this as a final word he walked off in the darkness in the direction of the garage with the other man.

She watched him go with the realization that she really still knew very little about him. She might try to convince herself that her short stay at the old mansion had given her the keys to all its occupants, but it simply wasn't so.

She stepped inside and found the large living room was deserted. A single lamp on a table near the exit to the hall supplied the only light in the big room. As she went its length on her way out she paused before the portrait of the first mistress of the house. She looked up into the happy face of the lovely Regina.

The black-haired girl in the painting had broken many hearts including those of her husband and Wong Lee. She had used the charm of her mixed heritage to betwitch the young men of her time. Sadly, in the end she had fallen a victim to her own mad need to follow her every whim.

Wong Lee blamed old Edmund Porter for being a weak husband. The old Chinese insisted that he would not have let her go on such a dangerous journey. But perhaps that had been the way fate had ordained it. Regina was given her every wish, even though the last one meant her death.

Her mind wandered to the present and Madge. Had Stephen also been a weak husband? Had he too readily allowed Christopher the opportunity to be with Madge during his absences on his many business trips? It would have been much wiser for him to have had Madge accompany him instead of allowing her to remain at home open to temptation.

With a sigh she moved on. The foyer was also deserted. It seemed that everyone in the mansion had gone to bed early leaving the ground floor empty. She was about to start up the stairs when she heard a low sound, almost like a moaning from far down the hall. She halted on the steps, gazing over the railing anxiously, as she attempted to locate the sound and what it could be.

It came again and this time she realized it came from a long distance down the hall. As the sound continued she recognized it as the low rumble of deep organ notes being slowly sustained. With the recognition an eerie chill shot through her. She had been told that Madge was the only one in the house who could play the organ. That since her drowning the organ had not been used at the weekly services led by old Edmund Porter.

Yet the organ was being played now! There was no doubt of it. She could hear it clearly. Like someone caught up in a spell she turned and slowly descended the stairs and set out down the long dark hall towards the ancient chapel from which the organ music was coming.

She moved along at a set pace neither looking to left nor right. She was deep in a trancelike condition induced by her fears. Gradually she reached the very end of the hall and then stepped through the archway into the tiny chapel.

A single candle burned on the altar and from its wavering glow she could barely see that there was someone clothed in black seated at the organ. The person presiding at the organ

162

swayed from left to right and back again as the majestic instrument responded to the touch of trained fingers.

Enid stood there enthralled by the music and trembling with fear at the same time. Then abruptly the organ music ended in a series of disjointed chords and the player swung around. Enid found herself standing there staring up into the face of her dead sister. It was a pale, sorrowful Madge who looked down at her from the shadows.

It was too much! Enid gave a small, pitiful cry and collapsed. Her terror melted away in the black velvet of her unconsciousness. She had no idea how long she lay there before she came partially to and realized she was being lifted from the floor and carried somewhere. She was vaguely conscious of a female voice offering a cascade of terrified Chinese and a male voice replying curtly, almost roughly.

Moments transpired and she was being deposited gently on a lounge in a side room off the hall when she opened her eyes to see an upset Stephen gazing down at her.

"What happened?" she murmured.

"You might very well tell me," was his reply. "You gave me a bad scare when I found you."

She was still in a daze. "Found me?"

"Ah Kem found you when she went to put out the candle on the altar. It is one of her nightly tasks," Stephen said. "She found you stretched out by the entrance to the chapel and came screaming to me."

Now remembrance came back to her and she sat up with horror on her lovely face. "The chapel! Madge!"

"What are you talking about?"

She stared up at him frantically. "I saw Madge at the organ. Playing it!"

Stephen really looked grim. "Come now. You've gone overboard this time. Given your imagination too much play. No one has touched that organ since Madge was drowned."

"She was playing it tonight. I heard the music and it took me down there. And I saw her!"

"Please!" he said with grim patience. "I know you are badly upset about Madge. You were foolish enough to go down to the chapel alone and your bad nervous state took care of the rest."

"You think that?"

163

"It is all I dare think," he said wearily. "The main thing is that you weren't hurt in this neurotic adventure. You have to curb yourself of these ideas for your own good."

Still feeling shaky she got to her feet. "You're being very male and insulting."

"I'm sorry."

"I did hear organ music and I did see Madge."

"Anything you like," he said with a deep sigh. "Just so long as you'll go to bed now and not roam anywhere about the house for the balance of the night."

She said, "You think I'm some sort of neurotic freak, don't you?"

"Let's not argue," he said.

"I won't argue," she told him. "And I thank you for coming to my aid. But I won't go back on what I know to be true. I'm sorry it offends you. But that is the way it has to be." And with that she made a brave show of walking past him and up the hallway to the stairs.

Once again her sleep was haunted by nightmares in which the pale, tortured face of her sister appeared. And she woke the following morning determined to leave Hong Kong after spending this final day in the city as guest of Stephen. She could not picture herself finding out the truth about Madge and the most sensible thing seemed to be to leave the sinister atmosphere of the Porter mansion and return to London.

She had a leisurely breakfast and did some packing. Then she dressed for her luncheon engagement with Stephen. There was no one else around when the limousine came for her. She sat back in the rear and relaxed as she was driven in to the heart of the great Oriental city.

The winding road along the bay was lovely in the daytime. But she could not forget that night when she and Christopher had nearly been caught in a trap set by his enemies. Had the plan worked they would surely both have been killed on her first night in Hong Kong.

Soon they were in the bustling city driving slowly along a narrow street lined with boutiques. There were stalls selling beaded bags, others dealing in leather belts and slippers, or junk jewelry and Mao fashions. They drove on past the Thieves Market of Cat Street and then proceeded to a more

Western area of the seething city whose population seemed to be growing continually.

The limousine came to a stop before a huge skyscraper of white cement and glass similar to those in any great city in the West. The chauffeur let her out and guided her to the large glass doors of the entrance. Inside a petite Chinese girl sat at the receptionist desk and politely inquired whom she wished to see. When Enid let her know it was Stephen Porter she was meeting the girl showed a flutter of excitement and at once called his office. She waited a few minutes longer and an elevator door opened and a pleasant-looking young man of European extraction in a neat, brown suit stepped out to welcome her.

"Good morning," the young man said with a pronounced Scottish accent. "I am Martin Douglas, personal assistant to Mr. Porter. I'll take you to his office at once."

She walked with him to the elevator and as they made the ascent to Stephen's private world, she said, "This is a very modern building."

Martin Douglas nodded. "It is only about five years old. Some of the original buildings are still on the waterfront and we keep them for secondary purposes. But this is the headquarters for all our business in Asia."

The elevator stopped at the eleventh floor and they left it to find themselves in a large reception room. The young woman at the desk here was also British. She smiled at Enid as they went on to the inner office where Stephen presided.

Martin knocked on the door and when Stephen answered he opened the door for her and showed her in. Stephen rose from behind the large desk which was the chief piece of furniture in the room and came to greet her.

"You had no trouble finding me," he said.

"No. I'm very much impressed with your building," she said.

The handsome, dark man showed a pleased smile. "We have made some progress since the original days of a few wooden warehouses by the docks. Both Wong Lee and Grandfather Edmund are uneasy in this new atmosphere. They come here as little as they can and when we have some meeting which they must attend we hold it in one of the old offices in a dock building."

She advanced to the broad windows which gave a magnificent view of the city and harbor below. She studied the older buildings by the docks, the harbor filled with sampans and the ferry boats moving lazily in different directions.

"A fantastic view," she said.

"I'm glad you like it," Stephen said. "I'll take you on a brief tour of the building and then we'll go to my club for luncheon."

He kept his word in that the tour of the building was brief. She found the packaging plant to be impressive. And she was equally fascinated by the great boxes of tea being labeled and shipped to all parts of the world. The firm of Porter and Lee had taken on any number of products, although in the beginning their staple line had been tea.

When the tour was over she was whisked in a limousine to a staid red brick building a few blocks away. Inside the doors of the building the atmosphere was that of England. Perhaps closer to the feeling of Victorian England. The quiet club rooms with their potted plants, leather chairs, great chandeliers and fine carpets could have been transplanted from a Victorian London. And except that many of the members wore white linen suits, their appearance was that of a well-to-do class of British businessmen.

They went directly to the dining room in whose sterile, air-conditioned gentility no voices were raised and even the sound of dishes was subdued. The headwaiter guided them to a window table which had a decent view of the bay. The sunshine streaming in was pleasant since it was balanced by the frigid air conditioning.

When they had ordered and were having preluncheon drinks Stephen stared across the table at her with a worried look on his handsome face. "I hope you are enjoying yourself."

"Very much," she said. "Though I find it hard to believe I'm in Hong Kong. This could be back in London."

"The members try to keep that atmosphere," he said with a tired smile. "We have to cling to something of our tradition."

"I like it for contrast," she said.

His eyes met hers. "Feeling any better about last night?"

She said, "What do you mean?"

"Are you still as certain that you saw Madge's ghost?"

166

She hesitated and then said, "Yes, I think so."

He looked pained. "And you plan to leave as soon as you can book passage?"

"I called the airline office today," she said. "They think there is a cancellation for Friday."

"Two days off! You'll be leaving that soon?"

"I think it best."

He sighed and stared down at his half-finished drink. "When you first came here I had high hopes that you might remain for a long while."

"I'm sorry."

"I'm as much to blame as anyone," he said with a disarming frankness. "I've not done all I could. I know you aren't satisfied with the facts of Madge's drowning. Yet there's little I can do. I don't want to open the subject with the authorities again."

Enid gave him a speculative look. "What I can't understand is why you were so willing to accept a weak sort of explanation in the first instance."

He kept staring at his glass to avoid meeting her gaze. In a taut voice, he said, "That was probably a bad mistake in judgment on my part. Now I'm surely paying for it."

"And you are willing to pay?"

He looked up at her unhappily and said, "I feel there is nothing else I can do."

The waiter brought their luncheons and the discussion was interrupted. They never did get back to talking such basics again. Instead their talk drifted to Hong Kong and to things Chinese.

Enid smiled at him. "One thing I've never seen here in any section of the city is a Chinese with a pigtail. As a little girl I grew up thinking they all wore them. I mean all the males in their native China. Another illusion shattered."

He said, "About sixty years ago they were declared illegal. The Chinese are thorough about such things. The police either cut the offending pigtail off at the point at which it joined the head, or cut the head off, at the point at which it joined the body."

"That would be quite permanent," she said with mockery.

Stephen went on, "Actually the pigtail is not a really ancient appendage in terms of Chinese history. They don't appear in the ancient scrolls. Research has shown the pigtail was introduced in China in about 1644. In that same year the Japanese introduced China to tobacco. Probably a coincidence. But in those days a pigtail in short form was worn by sailors in the British navy and in the navies of some other countries."

Enid listened to him over their tea, finding his talk interesting. It saddened her to think that her excursion to Hong Kong was ending in failure, that she would always have doubts about Madge's death and also about whether this man seated across from her was a murderer or not.

He said, "You seem lost in your thoughts."

"Sorry," she apologized. "I have a tendency to daydream."

Stephen smiled sadly. "There's nothing I can say or do that will persuade you to remain here longer?"

"No."

"I see," he said. He glanced at his wristwatch and said, "I dislike mentioning it but I have an important meeting in about a half-hour. I must get back to the office."

She touched her napkin to her lips. "Don't keep yourself late on my account."

"I won't," he said. "As I understand it you want to do a little shopping before you return to the house."

"I would like to shop a little," she agreed.

"You probably ought to take the ferry over to the Kowloon side of the harbor, but you might find the Nathan Road shopping area too crowded and confusing."

"I think I can find enough to interest me in this part of the city," she said.

Stephen considered. "There is the Ocean Terminal shopping center which I think excellent. My suggestion is you browse about the city for a while. When you have completed your shopping take a taxi back to the plant. Tell the receptionist who you are and she will arrange for a company car to drive you home."

"I don't want to be a nuisance," she protested.

"I won't be troubled at all," he assured her. "I'll set it all up as soon as I get back. And then when I see you at home tonight you can tell me all about your exciting day."

She smiled ruefully. "I'm sure it won't be all that exciting."

They left the club together and got into the waiting limousine. She remained in the car until they reached the narrow streets where the shopping bazaars were. He dropped her off on Cat Street.

"Watch yourself!" was his final advice. "You can find rare bargains here and you can also be cheated expertly."

"I'll remember," she said.

He got into the car again and was driven off. She found herself alone in the crowded street with the air full of sing-song chattering and scents strange to her nostrils. She spent some time sampling the wares of a tiny jewelry shop whose ancient owner looked exactly like a jolly little Buddha. She studied sets of earrings for pierced ears while he hovered at her elbow.

"Fine earrings," the jolly-faced little yellow man said. "First class price."

She found a pair in the shape of Chinese letters which she liked. She gave them to him to package. "These will do," she said.

The little man made much of her purchase. "Good luck letters!" he said with a broad smile as he handed her the small box with the earrings and took her money. "Would you like jade ring?"

She shook her head. "Nothing so ambitious. I have a limited budget."

The pot-bellied Buddha in a dirty linen suit followed her out into the street. "Can give you real bargain, Missee!"

"No!" she said, becoming embarrassed, sure that everyone must be watching them. She moved swiftly on and after a moment he dropped back with a forlorn expression crossing his wrinkled face.

Actually she realized that she had no need to worry. There were similar dramas of bargaining going on all around in the crowded streets. This was Oriental Hong Kong where women still wore coolie styles and cradled children in shawls strung on their backs. She passed herbal shops which dispensed potions to put in your tea which were supposed to relieve various ailments. She passed Man Mo Meal on Hollywood Road and knew from reading the guide book this was the oldest Chinese temple in the colony. There was a sign on it welcoming visitors to view its Buddhist gods and see their gold-plated thrones.

169

She debated going in and decided against it. Instead she turned down an alley where street merchants were displaying their wares in pushcarts. Again she was surrounded by natives talking shrilly in their own tongue. She realized that mostly foodstuffs and special Chinese delicacies were being touted by these merchants.

Since this sort of shopping did not interest her she was about to turn and go back to the other street. Then suddenly she saw something which froze her with fear and changed all her plans. Down at the bottom of the alley a girl, obviously of Western extraction, was bargaining with one of the vendors. The girl turned to look up the alley and it was then that Enid received a terrifying shock. The face of the girl staring up the alley was the face of Madge!

It took her a few seconds to get over the first frantic surprise which she felt. Then she waved and cried out, "Madge! Madge! It's Enid!"

The girl continued to stare at her and then turned and with a few quick words to the pushcart vendor took her purchase and hurried off in the other direction.

By this time Enid was trying to make her way to the vanishing girl. She pushed and elbowed her way through the crowds in the street, ignoring their stoical glances and occasional complaints. She could think of nothing but getting to that phantom figure. The frustration of being held back by the flow of humans all around her was maddening.

"Please! Let me by!" she cried as she came between two elderly women, pushing them out of the way. She raced down the cobblestones of the alley until she reached the pushcart where she was sure she'd seen Madge.

"Who was that girl?" she demanded loudly of the vendor.

The old woman behind the pushcart merely looked baffled and uttered a lot of words in some sing-song dialect. It was apparent that she spoke no English. Enid turned to stare in the direction in which the phantom figure had vanished. There was no sign of her now. It was hopeless!

thirteen

She stood there feeling thoroughly miserable and defeated. Was her mind playing tricks on her so that she saw the dead Madge's face everywhere she looked? For a few seconds she'd forgotten that Madge was dead, her body lost in the waters of the bay. All she'd been able to think of was reaching her sister and talking to her. Now the momentary excitement had passed and she was left with only frustration and doubt.

The old woman had another customer for her oranges and was no longer paying her even the slight attention of staring at her. Enid took a step into the narrow street along which the phantom figure had disappeared.

She felt a touch at her elbow and, startled, turned to look into the incredibly wrinkled face of an oldster smoking a clay pipe and dressed in black from wide-brimmed hat to his shabby shoes. This short, thin ancient was smiling up at her.

"Look for missee?" he asked.

"You speak English," she said gratefully. "Yes. I'm looking for the girl who was here at the stand. She bought some oranges and went somewhere down this street. Can you tell me where?"

He held out a yellow hand. "Five Hong Kong dollar!"

"I don't care about money. I'll pay you!" she told him eagerly.

The thin hand was still there before her. "Five Hong Kong dollar!" he repeated.

She saw that nothing was going to happen until she paid

him the money. She quickly opened her pocketbook and counted out the five Hong Kong dollars and passed them to him. With annoying slowness he accepted the money, folded it in his trembling hands and then carefully stowed it away in some inner pocket.

"Quickly!" she said.

"Come," the old man told her. And he started down the narrow street. She followed, not sure that he was even taking her to the right place. But she had no choice but to gamble on this.

He padded along and then as they came to another dark side alley he turned and beckoned for her to follow. The alley was filthy and there were no shops, only a few doors leading to squalid tenements. He halted before one of the open doors.

"Missee up there," he said. "Top floor!"

"Thank you," she said, wondering if he were playing a trick on her. She could very well reach the upper floor and find no one there or some natives who would only be bewildered by her appearance. But again she had no choice but to take his word and hope he'd turn out to be right.

She stepped into the fetid hallway and started up the first flight of rickety steps. It was almost totally dark on the stairway and the only voices she heard from behind the doors at the landing were speaking Chinese. She started up the second flight.

As she slowly made her way up the second stairway she speculated on her reason for being there. She had come in pursuit of a phantom young woman who looked a double for Madge. What sort of English girl would live in a place like this? Surely no one whom Madge or the Porters would know. It would have to be someone who had descended into the underworld of the exotic city and no longer was accepted in the Western colony.

Another landing and more doors, and again the sounds of Chinese voices from the other side of those doors. Wearily she started up the third flight. She made her way slowly, grasping the railing, becoming more convinced each moment that the old Chinese had deceived her and tricked her out of five dollars.

She was close to the third landing when she heard the

familiar voice. It was someone whom she knew speaking in English. And at once it came to her. It was the errant Christopher whom she was hearing.

Shocked, she halted and listened intently. Her search had led her to Christopher and this made her wonder if by any chance Madge might still be alive and in hiding with Stephen's evil cousin.

Christopher's voice could be heard in a scornful tone from the other side of the door at the top of the landing. He was lashing out at someone, telling them, "I can't depend on you! You let us down the last time!"

"It will be all right this time," an older harsh voice insisted.

"The damn mainland police nearly overtook you last time," Christopher went on angrily. "And if those Reds had captured you that would have been it! We'd have been finished!"

"I know," the other man with the harsh voice lamented. "That is why I got rid of the stuff. I didn't dare keep it on board."

"The stuff was worth fifty thousand pounds," Christopher told him. "We can't have any more such losses."

"The ship is in good shape," the harsh voice told him. "We can really move fast now. The new engines solved all our problems. I promise you."

"You promise! But I have to stick my neck out with the people in Macao."

"Give me this single chance," the harsh-voiced one begged him.

"Suppose I do use you again," Christopher railed at him. "What about the loss?"

"You can take half my share until the debt is paid. It oughtn't to take more than four or five good trips between the island and here to square everything."

"I'm not sure I can trust you to manage one," Christopher said, moving a distance away so that she took the few steps to the landing to be sure and hear him. She stood trembling, with her ear pressed against the door. Then Christopher's voice came less clearly, "We have new competition for the American market. The Mexicans are letting brown stuff seep across the border. The market for opium and heroin is more competitive every week now."

"There will be no more slip-ups, no more losses," the harsh-voiced one promised. "And I'll pay back what I owe. What could be fairer than that?"

Christopher began to complain in a low voice. She could not make out what he was saying. But now she was realizing with horror what she had stumbled into. Christopher was a leader or at least a full-fledged member of some drug-running gang. That was the illegal traffic he'd entered into with Charles Milano!

That explained the underworld enemies who had tried so hard to kill both her and Christopher when they were driving back to the house on that first night. She had followed a phantom Madge and been led to the errant Christopher. But why not? For if Madge was alive, as Enid was beginning to suspect, where else would one expect to find her but with Stephen's wicked cousin?

What to do? She was helpless alone. Her best plan would be to get out of this place, mark it carefully, go to the office and somehow get in touch with Stephen. When he heard what she had to tell him he would be bound to look into the distressing business. Either he'd send the authorities or come himself with suitable protection and investigate what Christopher was up to.

She was shaking with fear and nauseated by the fetid atmosphere of the place and her reaction to what she'd just discovered. She was about to turn and grope her way down the stairs when suddenly hands seized her from behind and she found herself struggling to save herself from being choked.

Her involuntary scream of, "No!" rang out in the small hallway, as the battle between her and her unseen assailant went on.

An instant later the door was thrown open and an angry Christopher appeared with a short, squat man behind him. By this time her attacker had her arms pinned behind her back and held her a helpless victim. There was little she could do but gaze defiantly at Christopher.

"Well, I'll be damned!" the tall man with the glasses said in a tone of genuine surprise.

"Make him release me!" she begged him.

Christopher's smile wasn't pleasant. "I certainly didn't expect to have you as a visitor. Bring her in, Ben."

174

"Righto!" A familiar voice from her attacker identified him at once as the old boatman, Ben Larsen. Enid remembered grimly that Eleanor had disliked and mistrusted the simian-like old boatman. How right she had been!

Ben shoved her roughly into the big attic room which was almost bare of furnishings except for a couple of plain chairs, a medium-sized table, and a battered old brass bed which had not been made up in a long while.

The short squat man had a gray whisker and wore a captain's cap, a dark blue jacket and some sort of dark trousers. He was studying her with interest. He asked Christopher, "Who is she?"

Christopher in his mocking fashion said, "A member of my family. Half-sister to Madge!"

"To Madge!" The bewhiskered captain echoed.

Enid still stood helplessly before them, her arms in the iron grip of the old boatman who was presenting her like some sort of prize which he'd fished from the sea. She said, "Does he have to twist my arms all this while?"

"You have been a bad girl," Christopher told her. "Why are you here spying on me?"

"I saw Madge in the street," she told him.

His eyebrows raised a little. "Really? But that isn't so surprising. You've been seeing her many places. You appear to have forgotten that Madge drowned in the bay months ago."

"I don't believe it. She's here somewhere!"

The captain gave Christopher a wary glance. "This one is full of strange notions."

Christopher nodded. "She's too smart for her own good. Had to keep prying and spying until she's finally managed to get herself in too deep."

She pleaded, "Christopher! I mean you no harm. If Madge is alive and with you, turn her over to me. That is all I ask."

"That is all you ask?" he mocked her in his familiar way. "You want me to bring back the dead!"

"That's a good one, Guv'nor," Ben Larsen chuckled. "Bring back the dead." And he gave her arms a further tug which made her moan. "Trick I learned out here, Miss," he informed her.

The captain asked Christopher, "What are you going to do about her?"

"I'm giving it some thought," the tall man with the glasses said. "Don't rush me."

Enid said, "A man led me here. He said this was where the girl who looked like Madge had come."

"Who led you here?" Christopher asked sharply.

"An old Chinese. I don't know," she said. "Please make him let me go!"

Christopher told Ben, "Take her over to the bed. Tie her to the head of it." And he turned to the captain. "You help him."

The bewhiskered man showed indignation. "I'm not in the game of kidnapping women."

"You're in all the games we play," Christopher told him nastily. "Lend a hand."

Enid again felt rage replace her despair as the tall, brown-haired man stood idly by and let the other two truss her tightly to the brass frame at the head of the bed.

She cried out to Christopher, "What have you done with Madge?"

He came and stood at the foot of the bed frowning at her. "My immediate problem is what am I going to do with you."

"I mean you no harm," she said. "If you keep me here Stephen is bound to organize a hunt for me and you'll really be in trouble."

Christopher smiled nastily again. "Do you honestly think he'd have any chance of finding you?"

She did not reply. She couldn't. She knew that he was right. Locating her in the maze of the Hong Kong underworld would be next to impossible. She was in serious trouble.

The captain and Ben Larsen now stood to one side waiting to see what Christopher might have in mind. The captain spoke up. "You can't keep her here."

Christopher kept his eyes on her and answering the captain without looking at him, he said, "I don't mean to. She'll go with us tonight."

"To Macao?" the captain asked incredulously.

The tall man gave him a sour smile. "Why not? You've pointed out she can't stay here. And I can't let her go. Let us safely stash her over on the island."

"Good idea," Ben Larsen said.

176

"Good or bad it's what we're going to do," Christopher said. And he directed himself to the captain, "You can consider yourself lucky. This young lady showing up has made it necessary for me to give you another chance. You ought to thank her."

The whiskered man's face showed mixed emotions. "I want to make the trip but I'm not sure I want her as a passenger. The Porters wield a big clout in Hong Kong. If they find out it could be bad. Kidnapping is a major crime."

"You can't afford to be choosy," was the young man's grim answer. "If you want to work for us you'll do as I say."

"Then you take full responsibility for her," the captain argued.

"She goes along," Christopher said in a tone which meant it was settled. And he told the apelike Ben, "You keep close to the captain until tonight. Come back about ten with a car to pick up Miss Branch!"

"Ten o'clock does it," Ben said, tipping his cap.

"What time do we sail?" the captain wanted to know.

"No later than eleven," Christopher said. "And let us see if you can't make the run in less than three hours this time."

The captain said, "No worry about that. She's the one I'm concerned about."

"She is my affair," Christopher shot back. "Just you keep us out of the hands of the Reds and the Hong Kong police boats and we'll make out."

"The new engines make the *Tonga* the fastest craft in her class in these waters," the captain promised.

"We'll find out about that tonight," Christopher told him.

The captain and Ben Larsen went out, closing the door after them and she was left alone with Christopher. She could not believe this new nightmare into which she suddenly found herself plunged. In spite of all that had been told her about Christopher at the house she had held on to a belief that he was reasonably decent and merely misunderstood. Now it looked very different from that. She had been unlucky enough to stumble onto the young man's illegal drug operation and he had coldly made her his prisoner. And what of Madge?

She stared at him from the head of the bed where she sat tied against the ancient brass frame. She said, "You don't intend to keep me bound up like this?"

177

He stood studying her from the middle of the bare room. "What choice have I?"

"I have always been your friend," she protested.

"When it suited you."

"I won't say a word to anyone," she promised. "Just let me go and tell me what happened to Madge."

He slowly went about the business of lighting himself a cigarette. When he finished and took his first deep puff on it, he eyed her rather sourly. "You say you won't talk about what you heard?"

"I won't! I'm ready to go back to England. I want to forget Hong Kong and everything that has happened to me here."

"You know I'm in drugs."

"I don't care what you do!"

"And Madge is dead."

"I don't believe you," she protested. "I think you are lying. I'm sure now she pretended to be dead and instead ran off with you."

He gave her another of his mocking smiles. "And left her charming Stephen? Can you picture her doing that?"

"Frankly, no," she said bitterly. "But she must have. You must have hypnotized her into doing it. They were in love. I know that. Why did you come between them?"

He flicked the ash from his cigarette. "Can I help it if your half-sister happened to be overcome by my charm?"

"She is alive, isn't she?" Enid asked anxiously. "And she was here earlier if she's not still hiding somewhere here now."

"I told you. Madge is dead," he said very casually.

"And you're lying!"

"You're not in a very reasonable mood."

"What do you expect when you have your thugs attack me and tie me up like some wild creature."

Christopher crossed the room to one of the small windows and stared out. He said, "You really ought to keep calm. You are only doing yourself harm carrying on like this. You have a long wait until ten o'clock."

She exclaimed, "You're not going to keep me tied here like this until then?"

"I have to protect myself."

"How can I harm you?"

"By escaping and talking."

178

She stared at him as he stood there finishing the cigarette and gazing bleakly out the window. All at once it came to her. She said accusingly, "I know how you gained control of Madge."

"Do you?" He didn't show enough interest to turn.

"Yes. You started her on drugs! You have heroin available. You've made her an addict. That is why she has to hide with you in the shadows."

Christopher gave her a thin smile and came over to her bedside. "I suppose you think that is clever deduction on your part?"

"No. On the contrary I'd say we've all been stupid. It should have been apparent from the start. Madge's poor health and fading looks. No wonder! Her illness and devotion to you is easily explained. You've made her your drug slave."

"If you want to believe that."

"I do," she cried. "And when I saw her at the house she was really back there. Hiding from everyone! There are probably secret passages built in that old house and that is how she managed to get in and out of my room in ghostly fashion."

Christopher looked grimly amused. "All that you are saying could be true. By the same token, the whole thing could be pure fantasy on your part. It doesn't make any difference. I'm taking you to the island of Macao with me tonight."

"You wouldn't dare."

"You heard me arrange it with the captain."

"Why take me there?"

"You will be less dangerous there," the tall young man with the glasses said. "And when I have made up my mind exactly what to do with you I'll find it easier to dispose of you in Macao than here."

She listened to his threats with growing apprehension. She knew that Macao was a lawless gambling and crime center. From the moment she'd arrived in Hong Kong she'd heard dozens of stories about the outlaw way of life on this other island. Charles Milano had been one of the first to mention Macao to her.

The thought of Charles made her ask her captor, "Do you think Charles will approve of this? He's your partner, isn't he? He won't approve of any of this."

179

Christopher studied her shrewdly. He said, "With a little luck Charles need not know anything about it."

Thinking she might have found a chink in his armor, she said, "I can't imagine him not knowing about it if you kidnap me as you plan."

The tall man shrugged and threw the butt of his cigarette on the floor and stamped it out. "Charles is not here now so we can postpone worrying about what he will think. His ideas on the subject might surprise you."

She said, "The family business wasn't good enough for you. You had to branch out into crime."

Christopher spread his hands. "What other choice had I? Old Edmund refused to honor any more of my gambling debts. I had to have more money."

"He should have dismissed you and sent you back to England long ago."

"I have no interest in England or the prison sentence awaiting me there," Christopher told her. "And I have committed myself here. So there is no turning back for me. I'm what you might describe as a desperate character."

"But why destroy Madge?"

"Madge fell in love with me."

"After you put her on drugs!"

"I prefer to think she was influenced by me alone," he said suavely. "I find your thoughts ugly. I'm going to leave you alone for awhile. I've not gagged you but I warn you that it will do you no good to cry out for help. No one in the building understands English and they are used to female hysterics from up here."

"I find that interesting," she said scathingly. "The cries of your victims?"

"More of your lovely thoughts, which I can well do without," he said and he turned and strode out of the big room closing the door after him.

Tears brimmed in her eyes. Her show of defiance had been no more than a brave front. She was frightened as she had never been before in her life.

The room was weirdly silent. She listened to try to hear where he had gone and if he were talking with anyone. She now had an idea that Madge was somewhere in the attic flat.

If so she might be so far gone in a drug haze that she would not want to show herself or attempt any conversation.

Enid was convinced that Madge was alive and a drug addict. Everything that had happened added up to that. Of course Christopher would not admit it. He did not need to. The fact that Madge had deserted Stephen and his mansion to live in this slum with his cousin was proof enough.

She listened intently and caught a murmur of conversation from one of the adjoining rooms. She could not hear clearly enough to distinguish the voices but she knew that one of them must belong to Christopher. The other was probably Madge but she could not be certain of this.

Next she tried to free herself from the rope which bound her to the brass bed. She twisted to the right and left and strained but without result. No matter how hard she tried the ropes held. At last she gave up her struggles in despair. The villainous sailor Ben Larsen knew well how to tie knots.

The boatman had apparently given up his job at the mansion or had been given a leave for a period of time. Either way he was a traitor to the Porter family and an associate of Christopher's in his criminal drug running. The crafty little man had fooled her completely with his pose of offered friendship. She saw now she had been too trusting.

Christopher did not come back into the room. Several times she heard him talking to someone in the other section of the attic. Gradually the sun sank and the room filled with shadows. Her back and arms were aching and her whole body was giving her acute discomfort. Yet it was still a long while until ten o'clock when they planned to move her to the boat.

By this time she would be missed at the mansion. Stephen would surely be sending out a search party to trace her progress in the streets and attempt to discover what had happened to her. With good luck they might find this house. But she knew this was almost hoping too much. The house was in a dark alley far from the streets where the vendors usually had their pushcarts.

Would Stephen even suspect that Christopher was behind her disappearance? Did the dark, handsome man have any idea that Madge was alive and a fugitive from all those who loved her? She thought he might have guessed it but was not

181

completely sure about it. How much did he know about the drug traffic and Christopher's part in it? All these questions were difficult to answer and had a direct bearing on the plight in which she found herself.

The room was in darkness when Christopher entered carrying an old-fashioned lamp. He set it on the table and said, "Are you in a more friendly mood than when I left?"

Derisively, she said, "Do you really expect me to be friendly?"

He stood by the lamp, illuminated by its glow. His face showed a grim smile. "No. I don't. But no harm trying for miracles."

She said, "I'm very uncomfortable. Can't you untie me?"

"That's why I'm here," he told her. "I'm going to untie you and take you to the kitchen. There is food and drink out there and a place for you to wash up just off the main room. I don't want any funny tricks."

"Such as?"

"Your trying to escape," he said. "There is only one door leading to the stairs and that's in here. And it's locked. If you want to dive out a window you won't make a good live witness. So better forget that. Just do what I tell you and things won't be too bad. Understand?"

"You can name the terms," she said wearily.

"I'm not really a cruel person," he said as he came to her and began to untie the ropes.

She gave a small sigh of relief as he quickly freed her and assisted her to her feet. She asked him, "What now?"

"The food is on the kitchen table," he said. "Go to it."

She gave him a questioning look. "You'll risk my being out there?"

"No risk," he said. "I'll be watching the only door which offers you a hope of freedom."

Knowing this was all too true she went on out to the deserted kitchen. There was some bread on the table, cut in hunks, and a jug of water. She was hungry enough to wolf the bread and she needed the water badly. She saw herself in the broken mirror of the battered washroom and thought that she looked far less weary than she might have expected. She had thoughts about making a run for the hall door but was sure Christopher would never let her reach it.

182

He was standing by the window when she returned to the big room. He at once swung around to face her. "That was plain fare but better than nothing. I wasn't expecting visitors."

She stood by the table with the lamp. "I can't give you marks for hospitality."

"Not much like Porter House?"

"No," she said. "But then I don't truly see you as a Porter. You're a renegade out to smear the family name."

He smiled. "Lovely! You sound like old Edmund."

"They'll be looking for me," she told him with a bravado she didn't feel.

"You think so?"

"I know it," she said. "This isn't going to be nearly so easy for you as covering up for Madge."

"In three or four hours you'll be in Macao."

"That won't make any difference."

"So you think," he taunted her. "I have news for you. Macao is another world."

She knew he was right but she did not dare to let him see how she felt. She said, "I have faith in Stephen."

"Stephen will never find you in Macao," he told her. "At least not in time."

There was an ominous threat in his final words which she wished she could ignore. But she knew that the odds were truly against her. Suddenly she felt she might faint. The room began to sway.

She reached for the table to balance herself and fixing her blurred eyes on him, she gasped, "You!"

There was a malicious smile on the face of the tall young man with the horn-rimmed glasses as he came over to steady her. He said, "Yes, I'm afraid I put a little something in the drinking water. I was worried you might notice it, but you didn't. A necessary precaution for your transfer from here."

She tried to strike out at him but could not lift her hands. And she slumped against him knowing she'd been drugged!

fourteen

She awoke to find herself stretched out on a bunk in a ship which was lurching precariously in heavy seas. There was a gas lamp hanging from the ceiling of the small cabin and it swayed with the motion of the ship. Her head was heavy and she found it difficult to clear her thoughts. Then she remembered that Christopher had tricked her. She'd been drugged. Her last recollection was of collapsing in his arms.

Now she was aboard the ship which was taking them to the lawless island of Macao. She glanced across the cabin and saw the simian Ben Larsen seated there with his small eyes studying her. There was a grin on his grizzled face.

"So you've come around, Miss," he said jovially.

She stared at him and then raised herself on an arm and asked, "Where are we?"

"Not too far from Macao. You slept real nice all the time in the car and for most of the voyage. No trouble at all."

Enid made an effort and sat up on the bunk. She said, "He left you here to guard me?"

"Mr. Christopher didn't want you to come to no harm," the little boatman said.

"I can imagine," she said grimly.

"Don't you worry, Miss, we'll soon be on land again. There's a little wind blowing tonight but this is nothing to an old sailor like me. Just a breeze as you'd say."

She eyed the boatman with disgust. "Eleanor Porter was right about you. She said you weren't to be trusted."

184

"Nor am I," the little man chuckled. "The old crow wasn't so stupid after all. I knew she never liked me and I used to torment her the more."

The ship gave an extra heavy roll again and the lamp above them cut a wider arc in the air. She worried that she might be ill if it kept on this way. She told the old sailor, "You'd have done better to serve the Porters faithfully. You can only wind up in trouble following Christopher."

"Don't you believe it, Miss," Ben Larsen said. "I've been in these islands a lot longer than Mister Christopher and I know more about them than he does."

"More villainy."

"If you want to put it that way," he said. "Mister Christopher has some important connections over here. You ever hear of the Triads?"

"No."

"They are Chinese gangs. Very murderous and outlawed in Hong Kong. But there are a lot of them on Macao. And we have a partnership with one of the Triads."

"You'll get your throat slit in the end," she warned him.

"Don't you worry your pretty head about that, Miss."

"If you'll get a message to Stephen from me I'm sure he'd overlook all you've done and pay you well," she said.

Ben looked all shocked innocence. "And do a double cross on Mister Christopher? Now that wouldn't be a nice thing to do, would it?"

"You'd be paid well," she insisted. "Think about it."

"You shouldn't ought to tempt me, Miss," the little man said, chuckling. "And what good would the money do me if I ended up sweating in a Hong Kong prison?"

"You wouldn't!"

"I would if I know Mister Stephen," Ben Larsen said. "He can be as hard as anyone. I can promise you that."

"You're mixed up in a drug running gang," she accused him. "You know you won't be dealt with easily if they catch you."

"If the mainland Red patrol boats get us they'd take us to China and lop off our heads. That's the penalty for dope they have."

"And you're willing to risk that?" she asked, noting that

185

the roll of the ship had become less noticeable and its engines seemed to have slowed down.

"The *Tonga* is swift now when we need her to be. The patrol boats can't catch up with us!"

"I doubt that," she said. "What about Madge?"

"You mean your half-sister what was drowned?"

She shook her head. "Don't try to make me believe that. I'm sure she's alive and living with Christopher. He's made an addict of her."

"I wouldn't know about that, Miss," Ben said.

"You really are Christopher's man," she said with contempt.

"We did some gold smuggling a while ago," Ben confided. "The Indians pay a good price for contraband gold. And there are a few rich ones willing to pay well for other goods as well." He gave her a wise wink.

"What do you mean by that?" she asked, not liking his tone or manner.

"A young lady like yourself," Ben said. "You'd be real surprised how much you could fetch on that market."

She eyed him angrily. "Do you think I'd be a party to anything like that?"

He shrugged. "You might not have much to say about it. And maybe after Mister Christopher gets you to come to terms with yourself you might be a lot more agreeable."

The little man's words sent a searing fear through her unlike any which she'd experienced before. With some difficulty she said tautly, "You mean I might not be so fussy if he succeeds in making a heroin addict of me as I suspect he has of Madge."

"You think fast," Ben said with admiration. "I'll say that for you. You pick up an idea quick."

She grasped the side of the bunk and brought herself to her feet. The ship was not rolling now and had slowed down. She said, "I feel ill. I want to go outside."

Ben blocked her way and shook his head. "No, Miss. That's against Mister Christopher's orders."

"I feel ill!"

He looked uneasy. "Sorry, Miss. I can't help it. He told me to keep you down here."

Before she could argue with him on this the door above

186

opened and Christopher came down to join them. He gave her a bleak look. "You've come around."

She said, "I feel ill. I need air."

Christopher told Ben Larsen, "Open that porthole over there." And as the little man jumped to obey him, he told her, "We've reached Macao. It's well after midnight."

"My head is reeling!" she complained.

"You'll get plenty of air in a few minutes," he said. "There's a launch coming to take us off and get us to shore."

She crossed to the porthole and took a deep breath of the fresh air. It helped her. And she could see the island and harbor of Macao close by. The harbor seemed full of ships and most of the buildings showed lights even at so late an hour.

She turned to Christopher and said, "You're quite mad, you know. Kidnapping me will ruin your other little game."

"Who will know I kidnapped you?" Christopher asked.

"Stephen will guess."

"I'll be home for dinner tomorrow night," he promised. "And I shall be one of those most upset by your vanishing. I will make all sorts of suggestions about trying to find out what has become of you."

She listened with a sinking feeling. "They won't believe you. They'll guess you were behind it."

Christopher smirked. "You think Stephen is all that bright? And as for old Edmund, I can twist him around my little finger. He'll never turn against me."

"Then he must be suffering from senility," she said with angry dismay.

"Family name is important to old Edmund."

"And you are a disgrace to that name!" she shot back.

From outside there was the sound of a motor launch approaching. Christopher went quickly to the porthole and looked out. Then he turned to inform her, "That's the launch come for us."

"I won't go!" she said, moving back.

Christopher looked pained. "Come on, now. You don't want us to have to strongarm you again. Will you come quietly like a lady or would you rather travel as cargo?"

"Don't come near me!" she cried.

His answer was to spring at her and seize her in his powerful arms. He shouted to Ben, "Get some rope and bind this vixen's wrists and ankles. And we'll need a gag as well."

Enid struggled with him all the while even though she knew it was useless. Between them they had her trussed up and gagged within a matter of minutes, and she had only managed to get herself roughly manhandled in her unhappy attempt to free herself.

Now she lay stretched on the bunk again feeling humiliated and terrified. Christopher towered above her with an angry expression on his young face.

He said, "You would have it the hard way. I hope you'll soon learn a lesson."

He took a blanket and wrapped it around her so that she might look like someone ill. The blanket covered the bonds at her wrists and ankles, and he'd pulled it up over her face to also hide the gag. It would do in the darkness. Save awkward questions.

The whiskered captain came down and glared at her in the bunk. He told Christopher, "Just as I predicted. She's still giving trouble."

"I can handle her," he said.

"And maybe blow up the whole game because of her," the captain continued his tirade. "We can't afford extra risks."

"Let me judge that," Christopher said grimly. "And let me remind you it was you who failed us last time."

"We've settled all that," the captain said, a trifle less aggressive.

"You think you have," the younger man told him. "I don't know until I've discussed it with the others on shore. They told me not to use you again. That was their last word."

"You can fix it!"

"If I do," Christopher said, "try and remember it. And be grateful."

"I'm with you," the captain told him worriedly. "You know that. But as for her, I think you'd have been wiser to drop her over the side."

"I give the orders," Christopher said.

"When will I come ashore?" the captain wanted to know.

"I should have things settled by tomorrow afternoon early," Christopher said. "I plan to fly back to Hong Kong.

188

You pick up the stuff and I'll meet you there when you arrive in the evening."

The whiskered one didn't seem to like this idea. He smoothed his short whiskers nervously. "Why aren't you going to make the return trip with me? Afraid of trouble?"

"No," Christopher said. "I want to get home early. The family will be upset about her. I don't want them to connect me with her vanishing."

"Her again!" The captain said with annoyance.

"Just do as I tell you and there'll be no trouble," was Christopher's firm reply.

Then he bent down and lifted her up and cradled her in his arms as he would a sleeping child. He walked up the several steps onto the deck without seeming to mind the burden of her at all. Ben was waiting on deck and trotted along beside them as Christopher went to get in the launch.

Christopher placed her on the deck in Ben's care as he stepped down onto the launch. Then Ben shifted her over so the younger man could take her in his arms again. Once he had her in his grasp he went to the bow of the launch and stayed there as it swiftly made its way to the docks.

There was a car waiting for them and Christopher lifted her into the rear seat and propped her up beside him. Ben rode in the front seat with the driver. She had only a vague impression of her surroundings. There was the darkness of the docks first, then the car travelled on narrow streets almost equally dark, to finally come out on a wider thoroughfare lined with the neon lights of night spots and gambling dens. The street was as busy as the average street in Hong Kong during the daylight hours.

The car abruptly turned into a dark alley and came to a halt at the end of it. Christopher lifted her out of the car as Ben opened the door of a building for them. It was a rear door which gave access to a dark corridor and a freight elevator. They boarded the freight elevator in grim silence and climbed to what she estimated must be a height of six or seven stories. When the elevator halted he carried her off and Ben hurried on ahead again.

They were in a wide corridor with a crimson carpet. Ben halted before a door with the number 712 on it. The little boatman rapped sharply on the door and while he waited for it to be answered he gave Christopher an anxious glance.

A moment later the door was opened by a grave-faced young servant in Oriental garb. Seeing Ben and Christopher he stood back for them to enter. She received the impression they were now in a lavishly furnished apartment. Christopher took her along a short hallway to a bedroom and roughly threw her on the bed, blanket and all. She lay there staring up at him frantically.

He did not remain to speak with her or make any attempt to remove the gag or the ropes which bound her wrists and ankles. He left a single bedlamp on in the luxurious bedroom and went out and closed the door.

She tried to move but couldn't do more than change the position of her feet a little. Her arms were aching from being tied behind her. And now her head was aching as well. She tried to keep calm and take note of her surroundings. She had an idea it could be helpful to her later. She apparently was in an upper suite of some sort of hotel. She imagined the plush gambling center was bound to have many hotels of this type. Macao was known to cater to a luxury trade.

She turned a little and winced with pain. Then the door opened and it was Christopher again. He did not seem nearly so tense as when they had first arrived. She had received the impression then that he was more than a little uneasy though she could not guess why.

He came directly to her and with a derisive look he removed the gag from her mouth. As he did so, he reminded her, "Just remember you brought this on yourself."

"Yes," she gasped. "I wanted to make this journey badly."

He shoved her on her side and first untied her wrists and then her ankles. He advised her, "I'd stand up and move around a little, if I were you."

"So thoughtful!" she said sarcastically and made an awkward attempt to stand on her numbed feet.

"Easy," he said, giving her support.

"Don't touch me," she snapped at him.

"I didn't want you to fall," he said, remaining close to her until he saw she was able to manage on her own.

At the first she actually staggered a little. But very gradually feeling came back to her feet and her wrists. She walked

190

across to the windows and saw they were shuttered on the outside.

She turned to him. "Where am I?"

He smiled in his mocking way. "I'd say you'd fallen in the lap of luxury. If you play smart your troubles will be over."

"It sounds too good," was her bitter reply.

"Well," he said with mock apology, "you must admit your quarters are improving."

"What is the point of all this?"

He said, "I hoped you might become more friendly towards me."

"You can forget about that," she told him.

Christopher studied her philosophically. "You are a good deal more stubborn than I counted on."

Enid told him, "I know why you took me prisoner. You were afraid I was coming too close to the truth about Madge. And that I would expose you to the family."

The young man sighed. "It would all be so easy if you were only a bit more reasonable. I'm the only one you can count on for help here."

"Then I am in a bad way," she said bitterly.

"Not really. If you'd be civil to me there would be no problem."

Enid said, "You and I can find no point of compromise. You should know that."

"Perhaps you'll feel different after you have a little time to consider things," Christopher went on easily. "Let me tell you something of your whereabouts. This is the Universal Hotel owned by a Mr. Kamasato with whom I'm associated in business."

She moved to the other side of the room, still anxious for exercise to get more feeling into her hands and feet. She said, "Then he is clearly a thorough rogue."

"He is a Japanese gentleman of much distinction and great wealth," the young man with the glasses assured her.

Enid sat on the edge of the bed and in a disgusted tone said, "I can imagine how he has gained his wealth. In the heroin trade with you!"

Christopher showed no reaction. "His wealth has come mostly from gambling and several other businesses. There is a large gambling casino on the lower floors of this hotel. But you will get to know more about Mr. Kamasato when you meet him in the morning."

"I don't care to meet him."

"Sorry," he said. "You'll have no choice about that. He is looking forward to the occasion." He paused. "Now let me tell you more about your quarters here. All the windows are guarded by heavy metal shutters. And at the end of the hall there is a door of iron bars which is kept locked at all times. So even if you managed to get out of this room you have no place to escape. This floor is set up like a fortress."

"Thank you for the information," she said with sarcasm. "It eases my mind."

"It could save you a lot of useless trouble," Christopher warned her. "A servant will bring you food in the morning. You will not be able to communicate with her since she only speaks Chinese."

Enid got to her feet and, ignoring all that he'd said, asked him bluntly, "What about Madge?"

Christopher showed a hint of anger but quickly restrained it as he told her, "Madge is dead! Drowned in the bay!"

"Liar!" she shot back.

"Think what you like then," he said. "Goodnight!" And he left the room.

She sat there thinking of her position and knowing it was truly desperate. She was a prisoner of the unscrupulous Christopher on an island far from Hong Kong—an island known for its lawlessness. From what he'd said there was no chance of her escaping from her luxurious quarters. And tomorrow he was planning to parade her before a sinister-sounding Mr. Kamasato who no doubt had some fiendish plans in mind for her.

All this because she had tried to learn the truth about Madge. Suddenly she realized how weary she was. The drugged sleep aboard the ship had not rested her but left her in a confused state. Now she desperately needed some rest before facing the ordeal of tomorrow.

She stretched out on the large bed and pulled some of the coverings over her. Despite the night lamp's being on she sank almost at once into a deep sleep. At first her sleep was untroubled and then she had nightmares in which she was fleeing from a relentless Christopher.

She dreamt of racing along streets of blackness, streets without a single light, not knowing where she was heading but hurling herself forward to escape from the unknown evil which Christopher represented. She suddenly found herself in a dead-end alley. Slumping against a brick wall which blocked her escape, she began to sob loudly.

As she sobbed there was a movement in the shadows and the face of Madge regarded her with compassion. Madge reached out to touch her arm and say, "Poor Enid! I'm to blame for all this."

She paused in her sobbing to turn in wonderment and cry, "Madge!"

And with this cry she came out of the dream and sat up awake. It was morning and an ancient old woman was shuffling about the room setting up breakfast for her on the table by the window. The night lamp was off and the drapes pulled from the windows of the room. The lower half of the windows were covered by the steel shutters but the upper sashes were open to the sky and the sun poured in through them.

She raised a hand to her temple and tried to collect her thoughts. The old woman gave her a glance and then shuffled out of the room closing the door after her. Enid groaned and then threw back the bed coverings and stood up. Her head was still light from the drugs given her the previous night.

Making her way to the modern bathroom off the bedroom she took a shower and straightened out her wrinkled clothes as best she could. She fixed her hair in a sort of fashion and used the cosmetics which she was surprised to find set out on a glass shelf of the bathroom. They were not the type she would normally use but the lipstick was right and the powder would do.

Then she went out to the breakfast table and saw that there was an ample supply of bacon and eggs, toast and coffee. She was not hungry but she knew she must get some food in her stomach to offset the effects of the drugs which were still in her system. After she ate a few mouthfuls of the food her appetite came back and she finished everything.

The room was ominously quiet and she suspected that it was soundproofed. She moved about inspecting the room and wondering when she would hear from Christopher. She was back standing by the bed when, her eyes wandering to the table with the bedlamp on it, she saw something draped inside the shade, over a thin brass support. It looked like a piece of jewelry.

She quickly reached in and retrieved the small object with its gold chain and gasped. It was a locket. A locket she had given Madge years ago when they were both teenagers. On its gold face there was a turquoise stone. With tears in her eyes again she snapped the locket open and saw the ancient cut-out snapshots on either side of the locket, likenesses of herself and Madge at that happy age.

"Madge!" she sobbed, holding the locket before her. It was like the weird dream she'd had coming true. For it could only mean one thing to her. Madge had been in the room to see her while she was sleeping.

Enid was convinced of this, certain that her supposedly dead sister must have come, no doubt in Christopher's custody, to look at her. And somehow without attracting Christopher's attention she had managed to drape the locket inside the lamp shade as a signal that she'd been there.

This filled her with a confusion of new ideas and a certain hope. If Madge were on the island, and probably in this very building, she would surely attempt to help her. Even though Christopher might have Madge deep in drugs she would still care enough to try and do something for her. Enid believed this without question. She carefully put the locket in her dress pocket and speculated on what would happen next.

She did not have to wait long to find out. The door from the hallway opened and Christopher came in followed by the old woman. Christopher glanced at the breakfast table and the old woman went over to clear things up and gather them on a tray to be removed.

Christopher gave her a jeering smile. "I'm glad you found your appetite."

"I hope the food wasn't drugged," she said.

"Still on the defensive?"

"Don't you think that wise?"

He waited until the old woman shuffled out with the tray of used dishes before he replied, "I think you would be wise to be a little more friendly with me."

"There is one way you can win my friendship," she said.

"Take me back to Hong Kong and return Madge to the family."

"Your terms are easy," he mocked her. "You only ask that I bring someone back from the dead."

"Madge is not dead!"

"You think not?"

"I'm sure of it," she said, almost ready to show him the locket and ask him if it had been left for her by a ghost. But she decided that it would be against her best interests to reveal the existence of the locket, and it might hinder Madge in any efforts to help her.

Christopher said, "You seem to forget that I was Madge's friend. She'd turned against her husband and had no one else."

"Because of you," Enid said.

"Because it was her own wish. Be willing to accept her death. Stop battling me about something which can't be changed."

She insisted, "I know she is alive and probably here with you."

He betrayed some surprise and then quickly recovered his mocking pose and said, "It is partly this unreasonableness which has caused you to be in your present plight."

"I'm sure that is the main reason for my being here."

"And you wish to pursue your search for her?"

"Yes."

"I can only say you are more stupid than I guessed," was his annoyed reply. "I am about to take you to Mr. Kamasato and I beg that you be more civil when you meet him. I have an idea he will like you and that could be important to your future."

"My future!" she said incredulously. "As your prisoner?"

"Let us call you a guest," was his suave reply. "Now if you will come along."

"I don't want to meet your friend."

His face became stern. "You are coming voluntarily or by force. Again I give you a choice."

She hesitated, trying to decide what to do. In the end she felt that she might be wise to pretend to go along with his wishes. Perhaps she might encounter Madge somewhere out there or some other sign that she was around. There was also the unpleasant possibility that Christopher might manhandle her into obeying him if she refused to join him in this. And she did not want to expose herself to any additional physical punishment.

"Ready?" he asked, abruptly.

"All right," she said in a low voice.

"Good for you," he said in an almost surprised tone. And with another warning look, he added, "And mind your manners."

He led her by the arm. They left the room and went down the red-carpeted hallway. At its end was the door of iron bars which really made the area a prison. A grave-faced Chinese man of indeterminate age unlocked the door and let them through. After they passed by he locked it again and stood guard by it.

Christopher gave her a grin. "I told you that you were in a security section of the hotel."

"Do you have many prisoners?" she asked with bitterness.

"From time to time," he said.

They turned a corner and he knocked on a wide, oak door richly decorated with panels of Oriental woodcarving. The door was opened by another thin Chinese male servant in black and wearing a black cap.

Christopher guided her inside and she found herself in what could have been any luxurious, modern office except that it was decorated with Oriental art and great tapestries and art panels hung from its walls. Before her, seated at a large desk and slightly bent forward over it, was a man of small stature, with a cruel, broad face. His hair was graying and cut short and brushed back. His forehead was prominent and his almond-shaped eyes were black in contrast to the almost jaundiced yellow shade of his skin.

Christopher presented her before the desk, "This is Enid Branch, Mr. Kamasato."

The squat man did not rise but nodded. "A great pleasure, Miss Branch."

Enid did not attempt an answer. She saw that they were not alone in the room. Gazing out the broad windows overlooking the city and harbor stood a slim, Eurasian beauty in a gown of Chinese style with a high neck. The gown was blue with a complicated design of yellow dragons. Enid thought the girl one of the loveliest she had ever seen. Her profile was of striking beauty.

Then the girl turned to give her a grim appraisal and as she did the other side of her lovely face was revealed. Enid could not suppress a shudder as she saw it. For this other half of the lovely young woman's face was scarred and destroyed as if some wild animal had drawn its claws down it and torn the flesh away.

fifteen

Mr. Kamasato took in Enid's reaction to the girl's face and a ghost of a smile crossed his broad, cruel features. He turned to the girl and harshly uttered a command in Chinese to her. The girl stood glaring at him defiantly for a moment, then with a sullen air she turned and slowly made her way out of the office.

Mr. Kamasato turned to Enid apologetically and said, "Yun sometimes can be annoying. You must forgive her bad manners."

"She did not offend me," Enid said. "I feel sorry for her. She is so lovely. What happened to her face?"

The squat, ugly man crouched over the table smiled at her and said, "You must not distress yourself about it. It was an unfortunate accident. And now she has grown quite used to her condition."

Enid argued, "But she is so beautiful. At home we would have had a plastic surgeon attend her. Surely you have such surgeons available here to repair facial scars."

Christopher spoke up, "I do not think Yun plans to have her face repaired."

"Why not?" she asked.

"She believes that the accident which marred her beauty made her more desirable in other ways," Mr. Kamasato said from behind his desk. "You also are beautiful, Miss Branch."

Enid looked at him very directly, choosing her words with

care as she said, "Not as beautiful as my half-sister, Madge, whom I'm sure you must have met."

The reaction which she'd hoped for came at once. The squat, ugly man gave Christopher an annoyed look as he spat out some angry words in Chinese.

Christopher rather gropingly chose some words in the foreign language to reply to him. Then with his face crimson he turned to her and said, "I advise you to say nothing more about Madge."

She arched an eyebrow. "Rather a touchy subject, it seems."

Mr. Kamasato had recovered from his annoyance and now he was staring at her as he said, "This is your first visit to our part of the world, Miss Branch?"

"Yes," she said.

"You have come at an opportune moment," he told her. "It happens that I am in need of an English secretary who can look after my ample correspondence with your country and America."

"I'm not in the market for work," Enid said, "I plan to return to England almost at once."

"Mr. Porter told me differently," Mr. Kamasato said.

"Then he did not tell you the truth," she said. "I am his prisoner here as you well know."

The yellow-skinned man looked bland. "We do not care to dwell on the unpleasant aspects of our day-to-day existence," he said in his flat voice with its slight accent.

Christopher turned to her and advised, "You might do well to consider my friend's offer and remain here. Salary is no object and you will live well."

"Behind barred doors," she said grimly.

Mr. Kamasato said, "A necessary precaution. For our safety. I can see that our discussion may be longer than I expected. I suggest that you both be seated and make yourselves comfortable."

Christopher pulled a chair up for her and reluctantly she sat. Christopher then sat in a chair just across from the one she was occupying, both of them facing the middle-aged Japanese.

Mr. Kamasato said earnestly, "My dear Miss Branch, a few months here might do you the world of good."

199

"Thank you, no," she said.

Christopher told her, "There are ways to make you change your mind."

"Never."

Mr. Kamasato hunched unhappily in his swivel chair and then he brought his hands up on the desk so she could see them. There were no hands but shining metal claws which protruded from the dark, gray sleeves of his suit coat. She stared at the lobsterlike appendages made of steel and felt sickened. Now she knew where the lovely Yun had suffered her clawed face. Just a swipe down that cheek with one of those claws must have done the evil deed.

Christopher smirked at her. "Mr. Kamasato was a suicide pilot in the Second Great War. He flew against the Americans in the island warfare out here."

"I was a kamikaze," Mr. Kamasato said proudly. "I'm sure you must have heard of our group. We were ready to die for the Emperor, without any thought of returning from a mission."

Her mind was full of vivid pictures of his savagely turning on the lovely Yun and destroying her beauty. No wonder the girl's face had not been repaired. She had been disfigured as a punishment of some sort by the cruel Kamasato.

Christopher intervened, "I fear Miss Branch is too young to know much about the Second World War."

"That is too bad," the man with the metal hands said. "It was a most interesting period in which to live. I was one of the fortunate ones who survived the service. However, my plane crashed and I lost both my arms to the elbow before they could drag me from the burning plane."

Enid guessed he was saying it as much for his own pleasure as for her information. He seemed to get a satisfaction in going over the account. She wondered if he might be a madman, if that accounted for his evolving from war hero to a master criminal in Macao. Had his injuries twisted his mind?

Mr. Kamasato held the metal claws close to her and asked, "Do you find them revolting?"

"No," she said faintly. "I think only of the harm of which they might be capable."

His grim, almond-shaped eyes were fixed on her. "You

would do well to dwell on that. But you need have no fear as long as you show cooperation."

"I want to return to Hong Kong!" she said in a pleading tone.

"That is quite impossible," Mr. Kamasato said urbanely. "You have only just arrived here."

Christopher leaned forward to the Japanese crime boss and said, "I think you should explain our methods to her."

Mr. Kamasato airily waved a claw at him and told the young man, "You are too impulsive, young Mr. Porter. Let me go about this in my own way."

"Whatever you like," Christopher said at once. It was plain that he did not wish to arouse the crime leader's anger.

The squat man in the gray suit got up and began to pace before Enid. He said, "Have you ever been in Tokyo, Miss Branch?"

"No," she said.

"A pity," he told her. "In spite of what you may have heard I think we are the most civilized people in the world. Take for instance our geishas. Are you familiar with the custom of the geisha?"

"No," she said again, wondering how long this preamble would last and what it might lead up to.

"Well," he said, halting, "let me explain. 'Gei' means art and 'sha' means person. Geishas are not prostitutes. They are young women taught artistically in dancing, playing a kind of flute and arranging flowers. She must also be good looking, vivacious and an expert conversationalist. She usually has a wealthy protector, whose mistress she is, but she lives in a geisha house, which is a kind of seminary in which a half-dozen girls live, supervised by a kind of mother geisha. You do not go to the geisha house to be entertained by these young women. You arrange a rendezvous and they come to meet you, perhaps in a restaurant or a hotel."

"Something like our London call girls," Christopher volunteered.

"The same and yet quite different," Mr. Kamasato said.

Hoping to bring the droning talk to an end, she asked, "Is Yun one of your geishas?"

Mr. Kamasato nodded. "She is. She tried to run away once

and had to be reprimanded. Now she knows she can do best for herself here."

"What has all this to do with me?" she demanded.

The squat man with the cruel, broad face showed a smile. "I like your spirit. Women without spirit are like wine without a bouquet. I am a long way from my native city of Tokyo but not too distant to miss its customs. I find myself wishing to have my own small group of geishas. And it would seem that a young English woman of your beauty and charm could be the star of them."

She stared at him. "At least you have made yourself clear."

He nodded. "What do you say to my offer?"

"Thank you, no," she told him.

Mr. Kamasato gave her a crafty look. "You can say that now, but in the end you will accept my offer in any case."

"You are very wrong about that," Enid said, getting to her feet.

Christopher also rose and told her, "You better listen to him."

"The point is, Miss Branch, you will do as I say no matter what your real wishes are," Kamasato told her. "It will merely require a period of preparation. We begin by restraining you and forcibly giving you a daily injection of heroin. Each day the dosage increases until after a while you have become what is known as hooked. You will be much more reasonable then."

"You wouldn't dare!" she gasped, though the very mention of heroin terrified her. She knew this was how Madge had been destroyed, to become a phantom creature lurking in the night shadows.

Mr. Kamasato showed a satisfied smile. "I dare anything, Miss Branch. Don't my metal hands prove that? I promise you that after you have been on drugs long enough your only concern and desire will be for the drugs to continue. You will do everything to receive your daily injection, even sell your body."

Christopher spoke up, "That is the hard way. It doesn't have to be anything like that if you listen to reason."

She turned to him appalled. "I soon guessed you were evil but I never thought you capable of anything like this."

Kamasato spoke again, "I have no intention of rushing you

in your decision. I would prefer that we become close friends in a rational way. But I will conquer you by the other means if I must. You understand me, I'm sure."

"I understand," she said tautly.

"I will call on you tonight," he said. "If all goes well there will be no more unpleasantness nor threats. You will leave the barred area of this floor and come live in my apartment with Yun and the others. You will have the best of everything as your position in my household deserves."

Plaintively, she turned to Christopher, "At least have the decency to take me out of this room!"

"I'll take her back now," Christopher said awkwardly, waiting for Kamasato's permission.

The squat man waved them off. "By all means, take her out. She knows what I expect. And I have no more time for you now. There is business to be looked after if you remember."

"I'll be back in a few minutes," Christopher said and then took her by the arm again and led her out.

She went with him in a kind of daze. She'd known that the interview would not be pleasant but she hadn't expected to be told of her fate so frankly at a first meeting. Worst of all she now realized that the usual reckless and daredevil Christopher was afraid of the squat and sinister Mr. Kamasato.

They walked along the corridors in silence. The guard allowed them through the barred door and then they went on to her bedroom. When they were inside she stood with her back to Christopher, trying to ignore his presence.

Christopher said, "I warned you to be pleasant with him. You wouldn't listen."

She wheeled around angrily. "You brought me here to trade me like you'd trade any other stolen object. You planned to use me to curry his favor. You're terrified of him!"

Christopher's face went red. "Don't worry about me. I'd do some serious thinking about your own future if I were in your shoes. You won't gain anything by choosing the hard way and having him make a junkie of you."

"I don't need your advice," she told him.

"It's your funeral," Christopher said with a grim look at her. "I'll warn you that Kamasato always wins."

203

"You should know," she taunted him.

"I don't torment cobras," Christopher said. "And you'd be wise to think about that."

He left after offering her this advice. She now did her stint of pacing up and down. She had met the legendary Mr. Kamasato and he'd turned out to be even more cruel and evil than she'd imagined. And he had told her what his interest was in her and what he expected of her.

Once again she thought about Madge. Was her sister in the hotel somewhere? Surely if she was and still had anything left of her former personality she would try to aid her in some way. Was it possible she'd become so broken in body and spirit that she'd merely begged to be allowed to come and spy on her while she slept? Had Madge's token offering of the locket meant not that she planned to help her, but that she was resigned to the fate awaiting her?

Had it been a final gift? A farewell offering? Enid was tortured by the possibility. She thought of Stephen and blamed herself for suspecting that it might have been the handsome young Englishman who had murdered Madge in a fit of jealousy. As she saw it now, Stephen suspected that Madge was still alive and in hiding. And he'd been trying to protect her as best he could, all the time hoping that she might return.

But it wasn't in the plan for Madge to ever return. Now Enid knew that. Christopher could not allow the degenerate he'd made of Madge to ever show herself at Porter House again. Not even old Edmund Porter could ignore that. Christopher had to see that Madge remained dead.

And he would also cleverly rid himself of being suspected of her disappearance by returning to the house in Hong Kong in time for dinner tonight. He had told her he would be among those most shocked by her disappearance. He would put on a good show.

The hours went by. She did not see Christopher again. Then the old Chinese woman came shuffling in with another tray of food for her. There was also a note on the tray which she knew had to come from the errant young man. When the old woman had gone she picked up the note and read it. It was brief.

"*Dear Enid,*" it read, "*by the time you read this I will be on a plane back to Hong Kong. I shall join the family in being shattered by your disappearance. In the meanwhile you would do well to face the new life offered you and work to become a favorite of Mr. Kamasato. If you take the opposite course he will make a heroin addict of you and you'll wind up a nameless corpse in the gutters of Macao. As always, C."*

The letter made her angry all over again. It also brought a dull panic to her. She knew what he'd written was not by any means an exaggeration. If the evil Kamasato turned her into a drug addict he would soon tire of her. Then she would be passed on to some other evil brothel keeper who would supply her habit for her services. Soon she would be too wasted and ill for even that and they would turn her out to die.

Once she was on that path there could be no going back. It was like coming up against that barred door. Once you were there the barrier could not be broken. Like Madge she would become a pitiful thing in the shadows. Only she would be worse off than Madge, for she believed that Madge still clung to Christopher. Enid knew she would have no one. So her utter destruction would be that much swifter.

She managed to eat only a small portion of the luncheon left for her. In her mind was the thought that with the coming of night she would be visited by the evil Japanese criminal. He had only to attack her with one of his claws and she would be as pathetic an object as poor Yun.

Her nerves grew more taut as the day went on. Being alone in the silent room did not help her. Several times she went into the bathroom and turned on the water faucets just to hear a sound, just to have something break the awesome silence which surrounded her.

She lay on the bed and closed her eyes in an attempt to sleep. But she couldn't. And then she heard the door open. She sat up thinking it must be the old woman with her dinner. But to her amazement it was someone else. Someone whom she'd almost ceased to think about. It was the young American, Charles Milano.

He came striding into the room with a shocked, angry look on his pleasant face. He said, "So you are here! I didn't believe it."

She sat up. "You!"

He came over to her, his face grim. "Kamasato told me

205

you were here and I didn't believe him. I thought he was talking about someone else."

Enid stood up facing him, a solemn expression on her pretty face. "Did you think he was talking about Madge?"

Charles looked uneasy. "No matter what I thought I hoped you wouldn't be here."

"Where have you been?" she asked.

"In Beirut," he said. "On business."

"On drug business," she jeered at him. "I know the kind of journalist you are now. How you lied to me!"

He frowned. "That's not important."

"You and Christopher are in this together," was her accusation. "Christopher destroyed Madge and now you both are going to make me a sacrifice to your Mr. Kamasato."

"Easy!" he raised a hand. "This room may be bugged. Most of the rooms in this house are."

"So you make a heroic last-minute entrance after it is too late to help me," she told him.

Charles seized her by the arm and in a low voice, whispered, "You'll gain nothing abusing me. Whatever I am I have more power with Kamasato than Christopher."

"I wouldn't doubt it," she whispered back. "You are as evil as he is."

"Never mind," Charles whispered. "I know all that's gone on and that Kamasato is coming here tonight."

"It must make you feel splendid," she gibed, though she too had lowered her voice to a near whisper.

"I want to save you."

"That's funny!"

"Funny or not, it is true," he said. "I haven't worked out anything yet. But I'll try."

"At least you try to make me believe you care," she said. "Christopher didn't even do that." And she took Christopher's crumpled letter from her pocket for him to read.

He took it from her and scanned it quickly, then cursed. "Christopher will double cross himself one day. He'll have finished with everyone else."

"You should know. You're his partner."

"There are differences in partners."

"I don't see any in you two."

"I'm going," he said. "But somehow I'll get back."

"Try to arrange your visit so it won't interfere with Mr. Kamasato's," she jeered.

Charles looked somewhat ill. He stood there as if debating with himself. Then he said, "You've met the girl, Yun?"

"Yes."

"She's Kamasato's number one girl."

"Is that why he maimed her?"

"A kind of branding," Charles admitted. "But Kamasato is still much interested in her."

"She looked at me as if she wanted to kill me," Enid said.

"She'll be interested to know that Kamasato is going to come calling on you," Charles said grimly. "And I'll make certain she gets the word."

"What good will that do?" she asked.

"You never can tell," Charles said. "And let me say she is a friend of mine. If she comes to you don't be afraid of her. She will not harm you."

"Do you have a gun?" she asked.

He shook his head. "Not that I can leave with you."

"You won't leave it with me," she berated him. "I could defend myself. You're no better than Christopher."

"Then I have sunk low," he said in the same whisper. And then he added, "I think I told you once I was in love with you."

"That was a joke!"

"Joke or not, I meant it then," he said. "And I mean it now. I'm not going to let anything happen to you." And with a final reassuring look for her he turned and strode out as quickly as he'd entered.

She found herself staring after him, not yet fully realizing that she had been talking with him. It was like some kind of bizarre dream in which a desired presence appeared at exactly the right moment. Or at almost the right moment. She wanted to believe that Charles was on her side but she didn't dare to.

His record wasn't that good. He'd lied to her about being a journalist and there was no longer any doubt that he was mixed up with Christopher in the drug-running ring directed by Kamasato. Now he was telling her that he was shocked at finding her a prisoner in the Macao hotel and he was going to do something about it.

207

She felt that he might be more upset by her plight than Christopher who had deliberately brought her to the island as his prisoner. But she doubted his ability to do anything to really help her. At least he'd made some kind of protest; she supposed she should be grateful for that.

Charles Milano might not be as afraid of Mr. Kamasato as Christopher, but neither would he have the power to defeat the Japanese gangster in his own domain.

The hours went by. She noticed that the old woman in black was late bringing in her dinner. And as the ancient woman shuffled about with her humped body and face hidden by her loose-fitting kimono of shabby black and a black hood Enid saw that places were being set at the table for two. Mr. Kamasato was planning to dine with her.

The old woman brought in the plates of food covered with round silver tops to keep the dishes warm. She lingered to make sure that every detail of the place settings was correct and then with a kind of moan shuffled out.

She had not gone long when the squat Mr. Kamasato appeared. He was no longer wearing his gray business suit but had on a colorful wine kimono. He bowed to her and smiled as he entered.

He betrayed his excitement when he spoke. The faint hissing sound which he'd hidden when speaking with her in his precise English earlier in the day was now much more plain when he used certain words.

He said, "Dear lady, I have taken the liberty of selecting some of my favorite dishes, cooked by the hotel's best chef especially for this occasion. Also I have a wine. A fine Japanese wine. Very scarce in Macao."

She stood aloof from him ready to refuse his invitation to join him. But she suddenly realized that by taking dinner with him she could use up a good deal of time. And if there were anything at all in Charles Milano's words, he might somehow come to her rescue before the ordeal of the night ended.

She said, "I will sit with you. I am not hungry."

"You will be," he promised, with a cunning smile on his broad face. "A beauty like you must have good food to keep her health."

"I didn't think you were all that interested in my health," she told him bitterly.

He moved to a mirror to preen himself, adjusting the kimono, and the white scarf folded at his throat. He turned to her and said, "But you are wrong, dear Miss Branch. I think a great deal more of you than that Christopher fellow who is now back in Hong Kong."

"He did fly back?"

"Yes. He deserted you," Kamasato said with satisfaction. "He knows I like you. He won't interfere."

"I'm sure he won't," she said. "What about his other partner?"

"The American?"

"Yes. Charles Milano."

Mr. Kamasato chuckled. "He is here in Macao. I told him about you and he was amused. Very much amused. He thought it a joke that Christopher should want you so much and have in the end to turn you over to me."

"That surely is amusing."

Mr. Kamasato lifted a steel claw. "You are fortunate. Christopher would not have been as kind to you as I will be. Also he is headed for a bad end. You can be sure of that."

"Charles Milano has a keen sense of humor it seems," she said bitterly.

"Amusing fellow," Kamasato said with a wink. "He has some girls here in the hotel. They keep him busy. I don't think too much of his taste in women but if they suit him . . ."

She was astounded by the arrogance of the squat, tough little man. She said, "But then you are a connoisseur!"

"Exactly," the man with the steel hands said. "Let us sit down. I'm famished."

They sat across the table from each other and she served. She saw that the main dish was a kind of charcoal broiled duck. Careful to give him a good serving, she said, "You are fond of this dish?"

"Yokitori," he said, smiling broadly. "There is nothing better." And he proceeded to eat, using the claws with great dexterity in manipulating the food.

She tried some of the duck which was excellent, along with the Japanese onions and green pimentos which went with it.

He eyed her across the table with the same hunger he had

shown for the food. He said, "You will like it here. The food is good and we have enjoyable times."

"You make it sound like a family," she said with grim humor.

"That is what we have," Kamasato said. "A fine little family and you shall be the most important one in it."

"Do you think I warrant the honor?"

"You are lovely," he said.

She looked at him directly. "Surely not as lovely as Yun was before you maimed her."

His reaction was immediate and annoyed. He scowled at her. "That is none of your affair."

"I could not help noticing."

"She was unfaithful to me. I do not stand that," the squat man said and returned to another helping of duck.

Enid said, "How can you be sure that I will not also be unfaithful?"

He gave her a grim smile. Raising one of his claw hands, he asked, "Are you willing to risk being treated in the same way?"

"No," she said tautly. "That doesn't appeal to me at all."

He shrugged. "So!"

They were silent for a moment and then she said, "What can you tell me about my sister, Madge?"

Kamasato looked up from his plate. "Nothing. I do not know her."

"I know you are lying," she said. "Why?"

"You would do well not to ask too many bothersome questions," he advised her. "The female is for the enjoyment of the male. You must be careful to remember that."

"I'm sure you'll remind me if I don't," she said. "Just the same I think Madge was here with Christopher Porter. She left me a sign that she had been here."

Kamasato frowned. "Left you a sign?"

"Yes."

His lower face covered with the duck grease, he sat back and glowered at her. "What sort of sign?"

Before she could make a reply the old woman in the black kimono and hood came shuffling back into the room and began removing the empty plates and silver covers from beside

210

the table. Enid was surprised that the ancient had returned so soon and so apparently was Kamasato. He turned and glared at the old woman.

"Old fool!" he cried. "Keep out of here until you are sent for!"

sixteen

The old woman paid no attention to Mr. Kamasato at all. She went on slowly gathering the dishes and putting them aside. All at once the scene took on an eerie quality for Enid. She sensed that something was not right. And this also seemed to hit the squat Mr. Kamasato at about the same time.

He jumped to his feet and with a cry of rage demanded of the old woman, "What sort of fool are you?"

It was the cue for a magical transformation to take place. In a second the old woman straightened and the hood fell back and it was an angry Yun who was revealed. At the same time she drew a long knife from her shabby black kimono and drove it full force into the chest of the astonished Kamasato!

He groaned and clutched both claws to his chest as blood spurted up and over the white scarf at his neck. Then he swayed and fell on his side to the floor. Enid was on her feet gazing down at his stretched-out figure in stunned consternation.

The lovely Yun knelt by the fallen man and the gathering pool of blood around him and then quickly got up. She told Enid in perfect English, "He is finished! Now we must get out of here."

"How?" Enid wanted to know.

"There is another passage besides the barred corridor," the

other girl said, keeping the scarred side of her face averted. "It is a secret passage but I know it. Come!"

Enid obeyed the slender Yun without question. They dodged out the door to the corridor and then went in the opposite direction from the barred door. They came to what seemed a dead end. But Yun pressed a secret panel in the ornate wooden walk and a door opened large enough for them to enter by bending their heads. They were then in a dark, narrow corridor.

Yun whispered, "Take my hand."

Enid asked, "Have we far to go?"

"No. But there are several steps. Watch that you do not fall and sprain an ankle."

They moved along slowly in the almost complete blackness of the corridor. The steps came and they managed them without any accident. Then Yun paused and another small opening appeared. They stepped from the opening and were in the regular corridor near the freight elevator.

Yun told her, "Charles is waiting below."

"Good," she said.

The other girl knew how to operate the freight elevator and in a moment they were on their way down. They reached the bottom floor and just as Yun had promised, Charles Milano was nervously waiting them there.

He asked Yun, "How did it go?"

"I settled my debt," Yun said. "But we must lose no time. They may have found him by now."

"Right," Charles said. And he placed a protective arm around Enid. "Feel well enough to make a break for the car?"

"Yes," she said in a taut voice.

He told her, "Once we make the car we'll be all right. It's only a short drive to the airport and I have a private plane waiting to take us to Hong Kong."

Yun looked back at the hotel as they stepped out into the alley. There was for the first time a look of fear on her ruined face as if she did not dare venture back into the world again. She lagged behind a little.

Charles looked back, "Hurry, Yun! You know we're still in danger!"

Yun said nothing but hurried enough to close the gap between them. The three of them were now well out in the parking area going towards the car Charles had waiting. Then suddenly there was blinding light and general pandemonium. A brace of moving spotlights covered the asphalt parking lot and found them.

"Quick!" Charles cried, shoving Enid out of the light and following her.

Yun still lagged a few feet behind and as a result was caught full in the spotlights. Shots rang out and she screamed and staggered.

Charles left Enid to go back to the girl. Yun had already collapsed. He leaned over her for a moment and then sprang up and raced to where Enid was cowering in the shadow of a car.

"We can't leave her!" Enid cried.

"Have to! She's either badly wounded or dead. We can't risk trying to take her with us." And he roughly shoved Enid on. They reached the car and in a moment were on their way out of the parking lot with the shots of Mr. Kamasato's guards following them.

"Will they follow us?" she asked, trembling. She took a glance out the back window and couldn't see any pursuing cars.

Charles was bent over the wheel grimly as he drove the light sports car at a furious pace, its tires squealing at every turn. "We've got a good start on them."

"They must have found Kamasato's body."

"Yes."

"Poor Yun. She saved me!"

"She was either dead or dying when I bent over her," Charles assured her. "I saw the wounds. They had to be fatal."

"She deserved her freedom."

"I'm not sure she wanted it. She faltered at the last moment. I think she was afraid of going back to ordinary living with her terribly scarred face."

"I think it could have been repaired some," Enid said.

"We'll never know now," Charles said, swinging the car around a corner with tires screeching and the car swaying at a precarious angle. "We'll be lucky if we reach the plane before the thugs arrive."

"It was your plan, wasn't it?" she asked.

"I needed Yun to carry it out."

"You knew she'd help you," Enid said. "I didn't believe you, and I ought to have!"

"Don't worry about it," he said, his eyes on the road ahead. Luckily they had met no cars as she doubted if he could have controlled the sports car if there was any danger of a collision.

They reached the airport and he drove almost to the edge of the runway. Then he told her, "Get out! And run fast with me!"

"I will," she promised.

In the next moment they were racing across the runway, hand in hand A beat-up small plane was waiting for them. The pilot, a young man, gave Charles an anxious glance. "Is everyone here? I thought there were to be three."

"There were," Charles said. "We lost one. And you may lose us if we don't get on the way."

"Get in," the pilot ordered them. "I have her all tuned up and ready. We'll be in Hong Kong in an hour."

"Let's hope so," Charles said, shoving her up into the plane and scrambling in after her.

The seats were of the most primitive sort and the interior of the plane was as bare as the outside was shabby. The pilot got in, revved up the engines and the small plane glided down along the runway with the lights showing on either side to guide it.

Charles was hunched down so he could look out one of the side windows. Suddenly he gripped Enid by the arm and said, "Look! By our car!"

She glanced out and in the lights of the airport could clearly see the car of guards from the Universal Hotel pouring out of their station wagon and coming out onto the runway with guns in hand. A couple of them made a show of racing down the runway in a hopeless attempt to catch up with the plane.

The small plane was in the air now with its engines making a loud noise. Charles slumped back in his seat, his face white, and made a gesture to indicate that they had managed it.

She shouted at him, "What will happen now? Will someone

be waiting for us at the Hong Kong airport? Will Kamasato's thugs phone ahead?"

"I think not," he said. "Kamasato was a power on Macao only. No clout in Hong Kong."

She shouted back. "There's Christopher!"

"We'll worry about him later," the young American said and closed his eyes.

Enid took the cue and followed suit. She surprised herself by falling asleep for a while despite the engine noise. She was weary and her nerves had been extended to the breaking point. Now she finally relaxed. It seemed to be only a few minutes from the time she wakened until the plane settled down at the Hong Kong airport.

They left the plane and Charles spent a few minutes in discussion with the pilot. She heard him say, "I'll let you know in the morning when I'll want you again." The pilot gave a nod of agreement to this. Then Charles came over to her.

He said, "I don't know about you but I want a stiff drink."

"A coffee would do nicely for me," she said.

"You can have what you like," the young American told her.

They found a couple of quiet stools at the end of the bar in the Hong Kong airport. The place was fairly deserted. A bored bartender served them and walked away to give them the privacy they so badly wanted.

Enid took a sip of her coffee and, in true feminine fashion, said, "I look a sight! I know it!"

Charles shook his head. "I can't believe it! In the past couple of hours you've escaped from a private prison, seen a man stabbed to death, a girl shot down and killed and almost lost your own life. And you're worried about your appearance."

"I know it sounded silly," she agreed. "It was a kind of automatic statement."

He gave her a grim smile. "As a matter of fact you look very good to me. You always do."

"Thanks," she said. "But this is not the moment for compliments."

"I got you away from Macao," he said. "Watch your step in the future. I might not be so lucky another time."

"You arrived just when everything seemed hopeless," she said.

"If it hadn't been for poor Yun it would have been hopeless," Charles said. "We needed her."

"And now she's dead as a result of helping us."

"Very likely." He downed some more of his double whiskey.

She gave him a troubled look. "What about you?"

"What about me?"

"You'll be a marked man," she said. "You were one of them and you turned traitor."

He shrugged. "I hadn't any choice."

"You didn't have to rescue me," she said.

"I wanted to."

"I know," she said, staring at his pleasant, if weary, face. "I don't understand you. Not at all. You're evil! One of the drug smugglers and I find myself admiring you."

He lifted a warning hand to silence her. "Easy on that drug talk. We're in Hong Kong now. The police here have some nasty ideas about how to treat drug runners."

"I'll be careful," she promised in a lower voice. Then she asked him urgently, "How did you get in it?"

"Money," he said. "I needed money fast."

"And now?"

"Once you're in it's not all that easy to get out. You might ask Christopher about that."

"I despise him," she said angrily.

"If it gives you any comfort, so do I," the young American said with a wry smile.

"What will happen to Mr. Kamasato's gang now?" she asked.

"There is a second in command," Charles said. "A Chinese gentleman if you stretch the term enough to call him that. His name is Wu Chang. Up until now he's been looking after the casino. But with the death of our Japanese friend he will be Mister Number One."

"I suppose he's as evil as Kamasato?" she ventured.

"There's no difference," Charles said. "All that crowd are alike. Renegades from all over the world banded together."

"Is Christopher a good friend of Wu Chang's?" she asked.

"I don't think the relationship is as close as the one between him and Kamasato. After all Chris hasn't brought Wu Chang any nice English girl friends."

She blushed. "Don't even say it."

"Charming fellow, our Chris."

"Will they connect you with the killing of Kamasato?" She asked. "I mean, can they prove you were in on it?"

"I don't think they have to."

"So you're in bad trouble."

"Not an entirely new situation for me," he said, staring at his empty glass.

"I feel responsible," she worried.

"You weren't. It was my own decision."

"You won't be able to work with them again," she said. "You won't dare go back to Macao."

Charles said, "Wrong. I'll be back there in a few days. I'll keep out of the way of the Hotel Universal gang. But I have other contacts. I'll set myself up a new deal. This time on my own. I prefer it."

"And Christopher?"

"No question he'll be one of Wu Chang's boys. Chris is not a leader for all his bravado. He lacks the nerve and he has a wide yellow streak."

"I'm sure you're right," she said, watching him with a new interest. "Have you ever thought of giving up this underworld thing and going straight?"

"Whenever I consider the possibility it disturbs me," Charles Milano said lightly. "What else do I know?"

"Stephen Porter might be able to help you."

"Not likely," Charles said. "He's Mr. Righteousness personified. I can't picture him dealing out any favors to reformed crooks."

"But when he hears how you helped me he's bound to be grateful," she said.

"That could be," Charles told her. "But I don't want his help. I'll make my own way."

She sighed. "You'll get in trouble again. And in the end they'll kill you. You know that?"

"Lives come cheap in my game," he said. "Live well and die suddenly isn't such a bad credo. Especially when you have no choice."

"But you do!" she protested.

He lifted a finger to silence her. "You are the one with the choices. And what are you going to do?"

"Do?"

"Yes," he said. "I've given you another chance. If you have an ounce of brains you'll book the first flight back to London before anything else happens to you."

"I'll have to go back to see the Porters first," she objected.

"Back to that old mansion with all its troubles and its ghostly Jade Princess," Charles ranted. "And Christopher waiting there in the shadows to kidnap you again."

"I won't let that happen again."

"You fell into the trap easily enough the first time," he reminded her.

"I know better now," she said.

"I wonder."

She suddenly frowned. "Chris will be at Porter House tonight. He plans to remain there until the morning."

Charles said, "We'll let him wait in black innocence a little longer. I'm going to take you to the Hong Kong Hilton and book you a room for the night. In the morning we'll have breakfast and I'll drive you out there. I want to deliver you personally after Christopher has gone."

"It would save an awkward confrontation," she agreed. "But I'd like to accuse him before Stephen."

"That can wait," Charles said. "The main thing is to let old Edmund and Stephen know what a desperate plight the precious Christopher placed you in."

"I'll do that," she said. "The police are probably looking for me at this very minute."

"No doubt," he said. "But they're not liable to find you without some help."

She suddenly remembered the locket in her pocket and dug for it and brought it out. She asked Charles, "What do you know about Madge?"

"Your supposedly drowned half-sister?"

"Yes."

"Nothing. That's strictly Christopher's department. If he knows anything about her he's kept it from me. As far as I'm concerned Madge drowned in the bay."

She gave the young American an accusing look. "You

knew her well enough. You were friendly with both her and Chris before she vanished."

"We weren't all that friendly," Charles said. "She barely tolerated me. She thought I was a vile scoundrel and Chris was her hero."

"Why didn't she like you?"

He arched an eyebrow. "She had an idea I was too smart for old Chris. That I bested him in a deal."

Her eyes met his. "You know that Christopher started her on heroin?"

For a few seconds he stared at her. Then he said, "Yes."

"What a filthy trick!"

"Old Chris specializes in filthy tricks. He didn't exactly subject you to a Sunday school outing."

"How badly was Madge hooked?"

Charles sighed. "I wish we didn't have to talk about it."

"I must know."

"She was hooked bad at the end," he said. "That's how Chris took her from Stephen."

"I guessed that. I'm sure she didn't really drown."

Charles said, "Don't be too sure. These hopheads do funny things. Going out in a small boat in the face of a storm would be something she might do if she were high enough."

She said, "Charles, I've seen her! I know I have."

"Ghostly faces," he said. "You told me about them. But you have never touched her or talked to her?"

"No," she said lamely.

"I'll believe she's alive when you do," he told her.

"But there have been signs," she protested. "Things left for me which only she would have."

"Such as?"

"This locket. I gave it to her years ago. Her snapshot is in it along with mine. It was left dangling inside the lamp shade. I know she somehow managed to leave it so I'd know she was in to see me when I was sleeping."

Charles studied the snapshots in the lockets. "You two were pretty way back then."

"That's not important. Are you listening to what I'm saying? If Madge isn't alive and left it, who did?"

He handed the locket to her. "Easy! Christopher."

"How would he get it?"

"Knowing him I'd say he took it from her long ago. He's probably doing this ghost business to confuse and scare you. It was through following the track of someone you thought to be Madge that you were kidnapped."

"I think Madge was up in that attic with him. But she was either doped and asleep or hiding."

"Maybe and maybe not. My guess is she drowned in the bay," Charles said.

"But you could be wrong."

"I've been around Chris a good deal lately. If she was with him why didn't I see her?"

"She may have been more careful to stay in hiding."

Charles eyed her sadly. "She wasn't nearly so nice a girl as you."

"She was my sister. I loved her," Enid said impulsively. "I want her to be alive."

"Even if she's a broken drug addict?"

"I'll find a way to save her."

"Few come back after they're as deep in heroin as she was when I last saw her," Charles warned. "This has become an unhealthy obsession with you.

She put the locket away and almost tearfully said, "I'm sure that somewhere I'll find her."

"You can't remain in Hong Kong to do that," the young American warned her. "Especially if Chris doesn't want her found."

"He knows if she is found the whole truth about his putting her on drugs will come out. It will finally ruin him with old Edmund Porter."

Charles said, "One night when Chris was drunk he told me that old Edmund knew he was a drug runner and wouldn't tell on him because of wanting to protect the family name."

"I can't believe that," she protested. "I know there is a lot of family pride but there has to be a limit. Edmund Porter would not deliberately condone Christopher in any criminal activity."

"I'm simply telling you what he told me," Charles said.

"I think it was more of his boasting with nothing to back it up," she replied bitterly.

221

"I hope you're right in everything you say," Charles told her.

"There's nothing you can tell me about Madge?"

"Nothing."

"So I'm to remain in doubt. Not know whether she's alive or dead!"

He said, "If you question her drowning I'm afraid that is the position you're placing yourself in." He glanced at his wristwatch. "Time to take a taxi to the Hilton."

She hesitated. "You think your plan is best?"

"Yes," he said, with that hidden authority which he showed so often. "I don't want you to return to Porter House tonight."

She smiled wryly. "It's thanks to you I'm here at all. I can't argue with you about it."

"I want the pleasure of having breakfast with you in the morning," he told her.

They left the stools and walked out of the now empty bar to the area where the taxis lined up for fares. Several were waiting and Charles signaled to the first one. They got in and he gave the driver the address of the Hilton Hotel. Then they settled back for the short ride.

He said, "Have you ever stayed at the Hilton before?"

"No," she said. "Will they take me? I'm in this tired outfit and I have no luggage."

"I'll put in a good word for you," he told her. "Don't forget I'm a regular guest."

The ordeal she'd just been through had left its mark on her. As they pulled up before the front entrance of the popular Hong Kong Hilton she felt apprehensive. Her fears were based on no particular grounds but more a reflection of her general state of mind.

Charles paid the driver and then escorted her into the hotel. The big lobby was almost empty when they made their way to the desk. The middle-aged Chinese who was acting as the chief night clerk regarded them blandly.

Charles said, "My friend, Miss Branch, missed a plane connection and in the mix-up she's also temporarily lost her luggage. She wishes to take a room overnight until the airline can straighten out her problems."

The clerk nodded and offered her a pen, "If you will kindly register, Miss Branch."

She put her name and the address of her flat in London with a sigh of relief. It hadn't been difficult after all. The clerk called a porter to escort her to the room and Charles came along as well.

They parted at the door of the room. He told her, "I'll call you in the morning and we can have breakfast downstairs before you return to Porter House."

"Goodnight," she said. "And thanks!"

He went on his way and she entered the modest room and prepared for bed. By this time she was tired enough to fall asleep as soon as her head touched the pillow. And she slept straight through until the phone rang in the morning. Still sleepy she groped for it and answered.

It was Charles on the line. "See you in the breakfast room in a half-hour," he suggested.

"I guess I can make it," she said with a yawn.

She waited a couple of minutes after she put down the phone and then got out of bed for a quick shower and dressed. Her outfit was showing wrinkles but it would do until she reached Porter House.

Charles, looking fit and assured, was waiting for her at the entrance to the breakfast room. He said, "I have a table reserved."

The room was almost filled but the table he had held for them was by one of the windows and was very pleasant. They also had a degree of privacy. After they were seated and had given their orders he studied her with an appraising look.

"You seem much more rested," he said.

"I am," she told him. "I think you were right. I'll be better able to face the Porters now."

"And you'll have the advantage of Christopher's being out of the way when you arrive."

She asked, "Is he going back to Macao today?"

"That is what I gathered from Kamasato," Charles said dryly.

Enid arched her eyebrows. "Christopher has a surprise awaiting him in Macao."

"I'd like to be there and see how he reacts," the young American agreed. "And of course you must paint him in his

223

true colors to the Porters. Make it so that old Edmund will have to turn him out of the house and the firm."

"I think the old man will be angry enough for that when he hears what happened to me," she said.

"I would hope so," Charles Milano agreed. "But we shall see."

The waiter came with their breakfast and their talk was interrupted for a few minutes. As Enid began the meal she found herself saddened by the knowledge that in a short while she and Charles would be parting. Perhaps forever. She knew it was wrong of her to be so fond of this young man who had lied to her and who admitted to being a criminal. But he had done her a great service and he had a vast amount of charm.

She looked up from her plate to say, "Where are you going?"

He smiled thinly. "I'll be in Hong Kong for a day or two. Then it will be back to Macao."

"You must be careful," she begged him.

"I will keep a good distance between myself and the Universal Hotel gang," he assured her. "But the sort of business I'm in demands my presence in Macao."

She gave him a direct look. "You would make me happy by deciding to change your way of life."

"You don't want me to lie to you again, do you?"

"No."

"Then don't ask me to make promises I'll probably not be able to keep," he told her. "As soon as we finish breakfast I'll drive you out to the Porter House and you'll be on your own."

"When will I see you again?"

He shrugged. "That depends on many things."

"I'll want to see you," she said. "There will be things to discuss. I'll need your advice."

"What about Stephen?" he asked. "Can't he advise you?"

"Stephen is all right," she said. "But you are the one I most depend upon."

Charles looked pleased as he touched his napkin to his lips. "I'll remember that." It wasn't a clear-cut promise he'd come back but she hoped that was what it meant.

seventeen

Enid paused at the front door of Porter House for a moment before going inside. The golden dragons on either side of the door were glistening in the bright sunshine. The old white house seemed at peace. And she couldn't help wondering what her return would mean to all those living here. Her revelation about Christopher was going to be a difficult thing for them to accept, especially for old Edmund Porter.

Charles had dropped her off at the house and now he was driving back to Hong Kong. He'd waved and smiled as he left her and the parting had brought her a certain amount of heartbreak. She knew that after what had happened the previous night she would never forget him.

She opened the door and let herself in. She was just in time to come face to face with Stephen's mother who was crossing into the foyer from the living room. The older woman halted and gasped.

"I don't believe it!" the hawk-faced Eleanor exclaimed.

"You may," Enid assured her. "I'm back."

"We've been at our wit's end about you," the older woman said. "The police are looking for you. Did you know that?"

"I was sure you'd be upset."

"What happened?"

"I was kidnapped," she said. "But it's all right. I wasn't harmed and I'm back."

"Good Heavens!" Eleanor said, aghast. "Everyone has left for the city except Edmund and me. Christopher was here last night and to give him his due, he was terribly upset about your vanishing."

"I can imagine," she said grimly.

Eleanor was all excitement. "I must call Stephen's grandfather down. And then I'll phone Stephen at his office. I believe Christopher is off on another trip today. And of course Sonya will be thrilled to hear you are safe. And Wong Lee!" The older woman went up the stairs still talking.

Enid moved across the foyer and into the living room. The house was just as elegant in the daylight as it was at night. She halted before the portrait of Regina, the glowing Jade Princess. It was not hard to understand that the strange way in which she vanished had made her a legend. As she was admiring the portrait she heard the voices of old Edmund and Eleanor on the stairs.

The old man came bursting into the room with his arms outstretched. "My dear girl," he said emotionally and took her in his embrace.

She smiled as he released her and said, "I'm sorry to be the cause of so much trouble to you all."

"Eleanor says you weren't harmed," the old man said, studying her with concern. "Is that true?"

"I managed to escape without anything more than a bad case of nerves," Enid said.

"I told you," Eleanor said, standing beside the thin, old Edmund.

Edmund guided Enid to a chair and had her sit down. "Now you must tell us all about it. Exactly what took place?"

Eleanor sat on the end of a divan, opposite her. She said, "Do tell us the facts. I want to be able to tell Stephen when I phone him."

Enid glanced up at the lined, pale face of the old man and then at the anxious features of the waiting Eleanor. She felt sorry for them and regretful that she had to bring a new burden.

She said, "My story isn't all that pleasant. As you know I was kidnapped. It happened just after I left Stephen the other afternoon."

"He blames himself for allowing you to go to the native quarter on your own," Eleanor said.

"He mustn't. It wasn't his fault," she told his mother.

"Sensible attitude," old Edmund said approvingly. "Do go on."

She said, "It began in a very strange way. I was shopping when I suddenly saw a familiar face at the bottom of the street. Madge's face."

Old Edmund looked shocked. "Madge's face?" he echoed.

"Yes. I know you all believe she drowned in the bay but I never have. When I saw what seemed to be her face I went down to speak with her. But by the time I reached the fruit stand where she'd been shopping she had vanished."

"More ghost business," Eleanor said grimly. "Nothing good can come of it."

Old Edmund raised a hand for silence. "Let us hear the girl out, Eleanor."

"Of course," Stephen's mother said.

Enid said, "An old Chinese man offered to show me where the girl I'd seen had gone. I paid him and he led me to a house in a dark alley. It was a lonely, disreputable place and I was almost afraid to venture up the stairway of the old tenement."

"But you did?" Edmund suggested.

"Yes. I made my way all the way up to the top floor of the place. At the lower floors I heard only Chinese voices but on the attic level I heard two men speaking plainly in English. I recognized one of them."

Eleanor said, "It gets more exciting!"

"They happened to discover I was there. I asked about Madge and received no satisfactory answer. And then they made me their prisoner."

"Scoundrels!" the old man exclaimed.

"Yes, they were," she said gravely. "And the main one was Christopher."

There was a weird silence for a moment and then Eleanor rose slowly and with a shocked look on her plain face asked, "Did I hear right? You did say Christopher, didn't you?"

"I did," Enid replied.

The ancient Edmund Porter had gone pale and looked like he might collapse. His reaction was the opposite of Eleanor's. He sought out a nearby chair and sank into it.

The old man gazed at Enid in despair, "Christopher has

long been a problem to me. But I can't think that he would do such a villainous thing."

"I'm not surprised! Not at all," Eleanor said shrilly. "I warned you to get rid of him long ago. I knew he was heading for something like this. And to think the wicked show he put on here last night. Pretending to be so worried about you."

Enid said, "He thought I was still a prisoner in Macao. That is where he left me. He turned me over to a Mr. Kamasato, his partner in a drug-running operation."

"Drug-running!" Eleanor repeated in consternation.

Old Edmund put a thin hand over his eyes and groaned, "He has gone too far this time."

"I should hope so," Eleanor said indignantly. "I'm going to phone Stephen at once." She shot out of the room before anyone could make a comment.

Edmund Porter lifted his head and stared at her in despair. "That young villain took you to Macao?"

"Yes," she said. "It was thanks only to the young American, Charles Milano, that I made my escape."

"Isn't that Milano a friend of Christopher's?" the old man asked.

"He was," Enid said. "When he found the plight I was in he broke his partnership with Christopher and Mr. Kamasato to rescue me."

"Milano was also one of the drug runners then?"

"Yes. He was here quite often before my half-sister vanished."

"Drowned in the bay," the old man corrected her.

"I don't think she did drown. I believe she's alive and in hiding because Christopher made a drug addict of her."

The old man eyed her dully. "Isn't that wild speculation on your part?"

"I know she became a drug addict. I haven't been able to prove she is still alive."

"I'm shocked," he said, wringing his thin hands. "I don't know what to say. For the better part of a century the name of Porter has been respected in Hong Kong and now Christopher has chosen to disgrace it."

"I'm sorry," she said. "But I have no choice but to tell you

228

the truth. If he takes a plane back to Macao this morning he'll find out that I escaped."

"He won't dare return here," the old man predicted. "He knows that even I have my limits. I would have no alternative but to turn him over to the police."

"I think he should be located and questioned about Madge," she said. "I have had signs that she may still be alive."

"It doesn't seem possible," the old man said.

Eleanor came striding back into the room. She stood before Enid and the old man with an air of importance. "I have talked with Stephen. He is leaving the office at noon and coming back here to question Miss Branch. He is very upset about what Christopher has done."

Enid rose. "I knew you all would be."

Eleanor told the old man, "And Stephen wants to discuss with you the best way to handle all this."

"The crime is so grave there is no easy way of taking care of him," Edmund Porter said. "If he shows himself here I will be forced to call the police."

"I'm glad something has made you come to your senses," the older woman said. "Until now you have been willing to let him get away with anything."

Edmund Porter waved an impatient hand to quiet her. He asked Enid, "Why do you think he captured you and took you away as he did?"

She said, "I think there were two reasons. He wanted to offer me to his partner in crime, Kamasato, as a kind of gift. I was to be kept there against my will and given drugs to break down any resistance I might show."

"The devil!" the old man exclaimed angrily.

"And I also think he wanted to be rid of me. He was afraid I might find the truth out about Madge. Find her alive."

Eleanor stared at her. "You're hardly likely to do that."

"I haven't given up hope," she said.

"We must alert the police as soon as I've talked with Stephen," the old man said. "We cannot afford to have anything else happen to you while you are a guest here."

"Please understand that I don't blame you," Enid said.

Edmund painfully rose from his chair. "I don't think we could complain if you did."

"Certainly not," Eleanor said importantly. "And a good deal of the harm came from the family's pretending not to notice the mischief that Christopher was up to."

"He is bound to run afoul of the law soon in any event," Enid said. "Drug-running is a terribly risky business."

"I gave him every chance," old Edmund lamented. "And he preferred to turn to crime."

Eleanor told her, "You'll want to go to your room and rest until Stephen comes home. I'll prepare some luncheon for you."

"Thank you," Enid said. "If you'll excuse me I do want to change. I've been in these clothes ever since I was kidnapped."

She left the old man and Stephen's mother discussing the crisis in low, grave voices. She was sorry she had had to worry the old man with the grim business but it was something in which she had little choice. Charles had recommended she handle it frankly and make no secret of Christopher's guilt. This was exactly what she'd done.

After a shower she changed into fresh clothes and then stretched out on the bed to rest for a little while she waited for Stephen to arrive. This quiet bedroom in the old Victorian house was a far different sort of atmosphere from the Hotel Universal. She couldn't help but wonder what was happening in Macao this morning.

Christopher would arrive and when he learned that she had escaped and Kamasato was dead, along with the lovely girl, Yun, he would realize that he dare not show his face at the family estate again. He would know that he was ruined in Hong Kong. And quite likely he would want to exact revenge from Charles Milano who had dared to double cross him. Enid felt sure that all the thugs associated with the Hotel Universal would be on the prowl to find Charles Milano and to even the score by killing him. Somehow she didn't think Charles would be all that easy to find or kill. He was clever enough.

She was still resting on the bed with her eyes closed when a light knock came on her bedroom door. She sat up and said, "Come in."

The door opened and framed in the doorway was the tall, handsome Stephen. His somber face told her he was deeply troubled.

"May I come in and speak to you for a few minutes?" he wanted to know.

"Of course," she said, rising. "I wasn't expecting you quite so soon."

"I left the office almost as soon as I received my mother's call," he said, coming up to her and taking her by the hands. He studied her with earnest eyes. "If you only knew how I've worried about you. Blamed myself for not keeping a proper eye on you."

She gave him a wan smile. "It wasn't that at all."

"Anyway I'm glad you're safe and back," he said and he bent to kiss her on the cheek.

"I didn't want to cause a lot of trouble."

"I couldn't think what had happened to you," he told her. "We finally came to the conclusion you must have been kidnapped."

"And I was."

"I've had the police working on the case," he said. "They traced you to the street of pushcarts but the trail grew hazy after that."

"I can well imagine," she said. And she repeated her account of seeing Madge and trying to locate her. It was then she'd been taken in custody by the errant Christopher.

"What a mad thing for him to do!" Stephen exclaimed.

She said, "He did not guess that I'd be freed."

"Apparently not. Well, he's burned his last bridge," Stephen said.

"Ben Larsen was in on it. He's one of the gang."

Stephen looked bitter. "I should have listened to my mother. She suspected Larsen from the start. But he was good with boats and so we kept him on."

"I trusted him," she admitted. "But he declared himself as soon as I was kidnapped. He laughed at the thought that he had tricked you all."

Stephen paced back and forth angrily. "Well, this is it. The police will be told. Both Christopher and Larsen will be fugitives."

"I'm sorry for your grandfather," she said.

"He is very upset," Stephen agreed. "He has been the one who insisted that we not reprimand Christopher when he did wrong. Now, he realizes what his compliant attitude has led to."

She gave the handsome man a sober look. "Of course my main concern is Madge. I still think she's alive and hiding because Christopher has ordered it. He put her on heroin and made her his slave."

Stephen frowned. "I can believe everything else. But I refuse to think that Madge is alive. Even though we quarreled over Christopher's attentions to her, I know she wouldn't leave and hide all this long while."

"Things just as strange have happened."

He stared at her in silence. Then he said, "I guess we can't agree on this one."

"So it seems."

"Madge was my wife!" he protested. "Surely I knew her as well as anyone. Why would she do such a thing to me?"

"Christopher's orders. All he need do is threaten to cut off her supply of the drug and she'd agree to anything. I was told by Charles Milano that she was deeply addicted."

"Milano! And so he rescued you?"

"Yes."

The handsome man was grim. "I didn't think he had that much character."

"I have much to thank him for," she said quietly.

"Forgive me," Stephen said. "I know that. I shouldn't have spoken as I did. Where is he now?"

"I don't know."

"He rescued you and then left you?" Stephen said. "If he cared enough to risk his life saving you I can't think that he could walk away from you without some effort."

Enid sighed. "He seemed to find it easy enough to do. It appears he's dedicated to a life of crime."

"At least he was frank," Stephen said.

"Brutally so."

"I'll have to call the police and fill them in on your return and point the finger of guilt at Christopher, Larsen and the Universal Hotel crowd. What do you plan to do?"

She said, "I'll remain a few days to see what happens if you don't mind."

"I want you to remain here for as long as you wish," the handsome man said. "I thought you understood that."

She looked down. "That was before all this happened."

"I have not changed my mind in any way," he said evenly. "And I would expect the house will be a much safer place for you with Christopher out of the way."

So it was arranged that she would continue as a house guest for a short while longer. She was secretly hoping that when the police captured Christopher, the missing Madge might come to light. If she did not show herself, then the chances were that she was dead, either from drowning or an overdose of drug.

Luncheon was a tense affair. As soon as it was over old Edmund Porter went upstairs complaining of a headache. Eleanor followed to make sure he wasn't ill. And Stephen was going in to Hong Kong to have a further discussion with the police.

He asked her, "Will you feel safe here?"

"I think so," she said. "I doubt that Christopher will return."

"Highly unlikely," Stephen agreed. "I'll get back as soon as I can. And in the meanwhile I'd say you should rest."

"I will," she promised.

And she did sleep for about an hour but then she awoke in a restless mood. The house was very quiet and she made her way downstairs without encountering anyone. Her uneasiness was deep-seated and she felt it had its cause in her doubts about what had happened to Madge.

She strolled out across the lawn in the direction of the teahouse with its gilt dome. Very often when she was in a restless mood she found herself heading there. She did not know why but the ornate example of old China seemed to have a morbid attraction for her. She thought it strange that of all the people in the old mansion she was the only one who still believed that Madge might be alive.

She reached the teahouse and mounted its steps to stand in its shade. As she stood there she had the eerie sensation that she was on the verge of discovering some truth, that a mystery was to be revealed to her. She couldn't think why she had this odd sensation when she came within the shadow of the exotic garden house.

She fixed her eyes on the bay, so calm now, and tried to fathom her feelings. She was deep in thought when she heard the wooden floorboards of the teahouse creak behind her. She turned quickly to find herself facing the elderly, stout Wong Lee.

The partner of Edmund Porter was in one of his white linen suits; he doffed his Panama hat to bow to her and say, "Welcome back, Miss Branch."

"Thank you," she said. "You have heard what happened."

"A shocking affair," he said with a shake of his head.

"Do you know Macao at all?"

"I avoid the place," Wong Lee told her with a solemn expression on his broad face. "It is a refuge of criminals from all over the world."

"I'm sure you are right about that," she agreed.

Wong Lee said, "You were fortunate to safely escape."

"A good friend came to my aid," she told him.

"One could do with many such friends," the old man said. "And at last Christopher is revealed in his true colors."

"Old Mr. Porter is taking it badly."

"He ruined the young man by letting him do as he pleased," Wong Lee told her.

"That seems to be the opinion. Why do you think he was so lenient with Christopher?"

The broad face of the stout Wong Lee showed no sign of expression. "Perhaps an obsession with family pride which has gone far beyond the healthy stage. You must remember that Edmund Porter has not been himself since his own wife vanished long ago."

"The Jade Princess."

"Yes," Wong Lee said. "He built this teahouse for her shortly before she vanished. You are standing in her shrine. That is what he has made it."

She gave a tiny shudder. "Just before you came, when I was standing here alone, I was trying to decide why I felt so strangely when I came out here. There is an air of sadness about this tiny building. An atmosphere of tragedy which you can't help but notice."

"You are a sensitive young woman," Wong Lee agreed. "What you say is true. I wonder that you have not seen the ghost of the Jade Princess."

234

"Perhaps I have without knowing it," she said. "I have seen odd shadows and heard strange sounds."

"Porter House is said to have hidden passages," the old man told her. "Built because of Edmund's fear that bandits might attack the house one day. Yet when the Japanese came he did not have time to conceal himself before they took him prisoner, while I was warned by his servants and managed to get away."

She smiled at the stout man. "You two have been the best of friends for so long."

"And yet we were rivals for Regina's hand. And Edmund for a long while was jealous of me. He once accused me of being Regina's lover. He seemed certain of it. Of course it was not true and he discovered this later."

Enid sensed there was something behind the old man's words, something he wanted to say to her but could not quite manage to come out with.

She said, "Forgive my asking, but was Regina unfaithful to him with anyone else? Were you being blamed for another person's evil acts?"

He nodded slowly. "There was another man. Regina had been a flirt from her youth. Marriage could not change her. Having a child did not change her. I do not think she understood the hurt she gave Edmund. At any rate she could not seem to help herself. The affair went on."

"Did Edmund Porter discover who he was?"

"I have never asked him directly," Wong Lee said. "I can not be sure. Regina was captured by the bandits and lost to all of us. Edmund grieved so for her he forgot all about that other business. His grief left no place in his heart for jealousy."

"It is a tragic story," she exclaimed.

"Much of life is tragic," Wong Lee said. "Surely the death of your half-sister was equally sad."

"If she died."

Wong Lee sighed. "I know your thoughts on the matter but I fear I cannot help you. I can only warn you that the history of this house is a dark one. Do not remain here too long and taunt the evil powers which seem to rule it."

"I'll keep that in mind," she promised him.

They walked back to the house together and he told her to

offer his sympathy to Edmund Porter. Then the stout man got in his venerable car and was driven off. She watched the car vanish and decided that Wong Lee was one of the nicer people she'd met since arriving in Hong Kong. Then she went inside and up the stairs to her room.

As she opened the door she had the sensation that there was someone in the room. Hesitantly she entered and looked around. Everything seemed to be in order, just as she had left it. Then as she stood there in the middle of the room she heard a kind of grating noise from the closet. She looked quickly in that direction and saw the closet door was shut. It seemed to her that she had left it open.

Tensely she crossed over to the door and opened it. And she was greeted by a familiar scent from the closet—the scent of jasmine. It lingered lushly in the air filling her nostrils.

She stood there bewildered. The scraping noise and now the strong scent. As if a phantom had passed through the room. She recalled those other times when she'd encountered the odor of jasmine. And now she roughly shoved back her clothing on the hangers to give the walls of the big closet a more thorough inspection.

It took her about three minutes to find it. And when she saw its outline she wondered why she hadn't noticed the secret door before. It was on the right side of the closet but she could not see what controlled it. There was no sign of a doorknob or even a latch. She went close to the mystery door and began pressing it.

She tried several spots on the door but the miracle did not take place until she placed both hands on the left side. Then the door opened inward with the same scraping sound she'd heard before. She found herself staring into blackness. A damp odor now came to replace the scent of jasmine.

Enid came back into the room and debated what she ought to do. She thought of calling Eleanor but knew that the older woman would not want to venture into the secret passage. Old Edmund was surely feeling too unwell to be of any help. And there was no one else at home.

She went to the dresser and saw the emergency candle in its small glass holder. She found matches and, with fingers which trembled slightly, lit the candle. She was eager to discover where the passage led and if anyone might be hiding in there. Perhaps it was Madge who wore the jasmine perfume.

It took some courage on her part to leave the bright bedroom and enter the closet with the lighted candle in hand. She seemed to recall that the jasmine perfume had been associated with the phantom visits of the legendary Jade Princess. But she was now hopeful that the dark passage and the scent might lead her to the missing Madge.

She stepped into the darkness and saw that she was on a narrow landing. The feeble light of the candle showed her the stone walls, damp and mildewed, and there was a winding stone stairway which led downward. She began a descent of the weird stairway. It had been carefully fashioned in a very small circumference so that it would take the least amount of space.

The stone steps were slippery and to help balance herself she touched her free hand to the damp wall. The candle in her other hand gave only a tiny glow of light and its flame fluttered ominously and made her fear she might be left in the grim shadows without any light at all.

So she moved very slowly, descending a step at a time. She felt that she had gone down a very long way. Perhaps to the ground floor of the old mansion, or even the cellar, but so far she had found no other passage, just the downward steps.

When she was ready to give up hope, the steps came to an end and she was faced with another narrow passage. She looked for a secret door which might open into a downstairs room but found none. So she kept on walking straight ahead, timorously staring into the shadows. Uncertain where she was or what might happen in the next instant.

Then from the dark tunnel before her, from a distance, she heard a sound which made her stand frozen with fear. Out of the shadows ahead there came a dry, ghostly cough.

eighteen

The completely unexpected sound from deep in the eerie darkness ahead caused her to stop there in grim fright. The cough had an odd, disembodied sound. It struck her more as being a ghostly echo than a real cough. She had an impulse to turn and try to make her way up that slippery, spiral staircase but she also wanted to know what the cough meant.

Then she wondered, could it be Madge hiding here in the darkness? No doubt her half-sister had lived in the old house long enough to know its secret passages.

At last she called out nervously, "Who is there?"

There was no answering sound. This worried her as much as hearing the cough. It seemed certain there was someone or something lurking ahead in the shadows, someone not willing to reply to her.

She tried again, this time calling out, "Madge?"

No answer. She stood there in the damp blackness of the passage for a few minutes longer as she debated whether to go back or ahead. In the end her curiosity overruled her good judgment and she decided to advance a little further along the passage.

She held the candle up high again and began to walk on with great care. She went about a dozen steps when all at once a dark figure rose out of the shadows beside her, seized her and knocked the candle from her hand. She screamed out her fear as her unseen assailant grasped her and literally hurled her against the side of the passage. She fell screaming,

238

struck her head, and in the next second lapsed into unconsciousness.

When she finally came to she was slumped on the rough stone floor of the passage. She raised herself a little and stared into the blackness of the place for a moment before she realized what had happened. Then terror came flooding back to her. She had been brutally attacked by some phantom figure.

She lurched up to her feet, with her head still spinning. She had no idea where the candle had gone when it fell and didn't feel like looking for it. She pressed a hand against the damp tunnel wall for support. She had no idea where she might be in relation to the old mansion. She had blindly followed the steps and then the tunnel.

Somebody had been expecting her and had waited in the passage for her to come along. She stood there trembling, her elbow sore and feeling as if she might have sprained it in her fall.

Unhappily she had to make some decision. And so she made up her mind to try going on. She did, without meeting any further resistance. The phantom appeared to have fled and she edged forward now without interference, until the passage came to an end at a stone wall.

Must she go all the way back? She stood mulling this when her eyes lifted upward and she saw a faint line of light from directly above her. She reached up and her fingers explored what appeared to be a wooden bulkhead. From the thin line of light it seemed likely it might open in the outdoors.

She made an effort to lift a portion of the bulkhead but she was not tall enough. Even when she strained on her tiptoes it was no good. Then, slumping against the wall of the passage, she worried what to do next. She decided to cry out for assistance.

"Help!" she cried and at the same time pounded a small fist against the bulkhead. She repeated this effort several times before she fell back exhausted.

She had given up the effort as hopeless when she heard a murmuring of voices from above her—voices chattering in Chinese. This gave her new courage to try attracting attention once again.

"Here!" she cried. "Down here!"

The Chinese voices came louder and nearer and then in a moment of startling change which she would never forget, the half-portion of the wooden bulkhead above her was swung open and she had a view of blue, cloudless sky and three or four solemn Chinese faces peering down at her over the edge of the bulkhead.

"Please help me out!" she begged them, raising her hands to them, and doing a wild little dance at the same time.

There was a gabble of Chinese and the faces vanished. From the distance she heard Eleanor's irritable voice as she tried to communicate with the excited Chinese and learn what was going on.

A moment later Eleanor's bleak face peered over the edge of the oblong opening and the older woman showed surprise. "What are you doing down there?" she exclaimed.

"Don't worry about that. Just get me out!" Enid cried back in exasperation.

"One moment," Eleanor said and her head vanished.

Enid waited in the passage hearing other excited consultations between Eleanor and the Chinese. And after a little the Chinese showed themselves again and dropped a ladder down into the passage. As soon as it was balanced against the side Enid gingerly climbed up it to appear on the lawn before Eleanor and the astonished Chinese gardeners.

The bulkhead opened near the house and not too far distant from the teahouse. She saw that she had given them all a shock and stood before the dominant Eleanor apologetically.

Eleanor said sternly, "We have not used that passage to the cellar in years. May I ask how you managed to get yourself down there?"

"I found a doorway from the closet of my room and a secret passage," she said. "There were stairs, a spiral stairway that must have taken me to the cellar regions. Then I found a passage and moved along it until I could go no further."

"Incredible!" Eleanor said. "I never heard of such a passage. I must consult Edmund about it."

"It exists," she said, glancing at the bulkhead. "I had no idea where I was."

Eleanor said, "You should have reported the door and passage to one of us and not gone down there on your own."

And then she spoke sharply in Chinese to the gardeners and they went and retrieved the ladder and closed the bulkhead.

Eleanor told her, "Stephen's grandfather has come down to sit in the left wing patio for a little. Let us go there and tell him about this."

Enid did not argue. She would have preferred to wait and report the incident to Stephen when he returned. But she knew how strong-willed Stephen's mother was and that she would resent any questioning of her authority. So she followed the older woman inside and down the broad, long corridor which led to the screened patio.

Old Edmund Porter was seated there in a wicker easy chair gazing out at the bay. He turned when he saw them join him in the patio. There was a questioning look on his emaciated face as if he suspected there might be some new revelations.

He asked, "What now?"

Eleanor briefly told him as much as she knew of Enid's adventure. She finished with, "I don't know what the gardeners thought! They behaved as if she were a specter rising out of the ground."

The old man sighed. "It seems everything must happen at once. There are some secret passages in the house, placed there for security purposes. They have not been used for years. I'd forgotten there was an entrance to one of them from your room."

She said, "From the clothes closet."

Edmund turned to Eleanor and instructed her, "Have one of the handymen go up there and somehow seal that entrance shut. They can use wood strapping or whatever."

"I'll see what I can do," the older woman replied. "I'm not sure I ought to go ahead with anything until Stephen comes back. He is better able to supervise such an operation than I am."

Enid quickly spoke up, "I don't mind allowing it to go until later. It has been there all the while and I didn't know about it."

Eleanor said, "I'll speak to Ling about it anyway. But I'll let the actual work go until Stephen is here to offer an opinion." And having said this she went back down the corridor leaving Enid and the old man alone together.

He waved a thin hand towards an empty chair and said, "Do sit down for a little."

"You are resting. I don't want to intrude."

"I would enjoy your company."

"Very well," she said. And she sat down near him.

He studied her with a weary look on his thin face. "You have been through a great deal."

"It wasn't pleasant," she agreed.

"And then to stumble on this secret passage must have been frightening," the old man said. "What brought it to your attention?"

"I thought I heard a sound from the closet like a door scraping closed," she said. "And when I entered the closet there was a scent of jasmine perfume filling the air."

"Jasmine!" he said, his rheumy eyes fixed on her. "You are sure?"

"Yes."

"Jasmine was the favorite perfume of my wife, Regina," he said. "I don't think I have smelled it in all the years since she vanished."

She asked him, "Didn't Madge ever use it?"

"Madge?" There was a tremor in his voice.

"Yes."

"Not that I know of," he said, licking his thin lips nervously. "She may have. But not that I recall."

"I wondered."

His clawlike hands were clasped at his waist and now he began to twist them uneasily as he stared at her and said, "You still hope to see your half-sister alive?"

"I do," she said quietly.

He nodded in nervous fashion. "I know how you feel. I have shared the same feeling. Hope dies hard within us. For many months after Regina vanished I was certain that one day she would return. That she had only been taken captive and held against her will."

"And she never did come back," Enid said.

"She never did," the old man said solemnly. "So you can understand that I sympathize with you."

She leaned forward confidentially in her chair and told him, "I didn't give Eleanor a complete account of what happened to me in the cellar."

He frowned slightly and his thin hands grasped the arms of his chair. "No?"

"No," she said. "I thought I had better wait and speak to Stephen. But I don't mind telling you."

"Telling me what?" his voice had a fretful edge.

"When I was in the passage I encountered someone. I heard a cough. I was badly upset. But I went on and I was attacked in the darkness. I lay unconscious for a little while."

"You're telling me you were attacked in the cellar?"

"Yes. Or at least I was thrown roughly against the wall and hit my head so that I fainted," she said.

"Did you see who it was?"

"The candle I had for light was knocked from my hand," she said. "I didn't get even a glimpse of the mystery person."

The old man showed concern. "This means someone is lurking in the hidden passages of the house. Or at least using them when they wish."

"Yes."

He continued to be more upset as he considered this. "It might be a thief from the outside or a murderer. I don't like it at all."

"I knew you had to be told."

"Most certainly," the old man said. "I can understand your not mentioning it to my daughter-in-law. It might have put her in a panic."

"I was afraid of that."

"I will consult with Stephen about this," he said. "We will have a thorough search made of all the hidden passages. I promise you."

"That would make me feel less uneasy," she agreed.

Edmund Porter sighed. "It couldn't be Christopher. He left Hong Kong this morning. You say he is expected back in Macao."

"That is what I understood," she said. And then she asked, "What would you say to its being Madge?"

He frowned at her. "If Madge were alive why should she hide in the cellar?"

"She is supposed to be dead."

"I'm certain that she is," the old man told her.

Enid said, "And I'm not. I think she may be alive and in hiding. Her body is wasted from drugs and her looks are

243

bound to be marred. Perhaps she doesn't want to show herself."

"Hold on to your hopes if you like," the old man said. "I can't blame you. I did the same thing when Regina vanished."

"It is odd," Enid agreed. "That two wives should vanish from the same house under mysterious circumstances."

"The conditions were completely different," Edmund Porter said. "Regina went off to the hills with only an aged servant to protect her. Madge chose to take a boat out on the bay in the face of a storm. Neither of them was seen again."

"What about the servant who went with your Regina?" she asked.

"She vanished also," the old man said. "I expect they were both murdered by the hill bandits."

Enid apologized, "I'm sorry to bring up such a tragic matter again."

"I do not mind," he said. "In fact I was sitting here thinking of Regina and those other days. You have seen her portrait."

"Yes. The Jade Princess."

He nodded. "They have called her that down through the years. I promise you she was an exquisite beauty. Half Chinese, and very fond of the Chinese customs. She never failed to become excited about the New Year."

"I have heard that the Chinese New Year is a most important occasion here in Hong Kong," she said.

"It is important wherever there is a Chinese population. They celebrated it here in Hong Kong even during the period of the Japanese holding the island."

"Isn't it in February?"

"Chinese New Year is the first day of the first moon of the Chinese year," Edmund Porter told her. "It can fall anytime between the last part of January and late February. It is a big event in Chinese life. Religious and family ceremonies go with it. It is very often the only holiday of the year for these people."

"So they're bound to make a lot of it."

"Exactly," he said. "Chinese firms which are run along western lines, or who employ a great number of workers, close down for the day on certain festivals or decreed holidays, yet many of the shops stay open, and factories even work on Sundays. At Chinese New Year, not only does everything close down, but all employees receive a cash bonus. In this house we give one month's extra wages. In some Chinese firms where the pay is small a much bigger bonus is given. This allows the lucky ones an opportunity to celebrate. Wong Lee gives his household servants two months wages, but he is a bachelor and generous."

"He is a fine old man," she agreed.

"A true gentleman of China," Edmund Porter said. "The first day of the Chinese New Year is given up to feasting. Pork and more expensive types of fish are added to the usually austere daily menu, while oranges and candied fruits form the dessert. The second day is spent visiting relations, walking in the parks, and attending cinemas, concerts and plays. The third day is not granted to everyone."

"A sort of extra holiday?" she suggested.

"Exactly," he said. "It is considered a day to rest or for continued festivity such as walking in the parks in brightly colored holiday garb, or going to the tombs to visit one's ancestors. And while at the tomb it is the practice to burn a few joss sticks around the graves without too much soberness being shown. Children, thermos flasks and the Chinese items for a hilarious picnic are thrown in with the symbols of veneration so that a good time is had by both the quick and the dead."

She said, "You have been here so long you have a great knowledge of these people."

"And yet I have never felt I fully understood them," he said. "Not even my Regina, who was only half Chinese." He paused for a moment and then went on, "Of course this first moon of the new year is not a time of rejoicing for everybody. It also happens to be the due date for the payment of any outstanding debts. This results in a good deal of heartache for the individual debtor, while many a shop or even a bank fails to raise its shutters when the holiday is over."

"I had no idea of the holiday's importance," she said. "I wish I had been here for it."

"It's also a bit of a bother for Europeans," the old man said with a wry smile on his emaciated face. "From midnight on New Year's Eve the firecrackers start, and for the next forty-eight hours or so, there is hardly a moment in the day or night when one does not hear them. A blue haze of smoke actually hangs over the large cities and the fire bell is often heard amid the celebrating. The streets are literally covered with the red paper of exploded crackers as they drop from balconies or are thrown down by children. In Hong Kong, British and American sailors join in the fun, and it is a wise motorist who keeps all the windows of his car closed, as he drives through the streets."

She saw that he looked weary and rose, saying, "I must go. I'm tiring you. I'll see you at dinner." And she left him to go to her room.

She found that somebody had examined the closet and removed all the hangers with her clothes on them and placed them in a heap on her bed. But nothing had yet been done with the secret door except that it had been closed. She arranged her clothing on the bed so the dresses would not all be on top of one another and be badly wrinkled.

Then she took a shower and changed into a rose gown which she had not worn before. She had enjoyed her conversation with old Edmund Porter. It had almost made her forget her terrifying experience in the dark cellar. Now she thought about it again and began to believe that she must have encountered a distraught Madge who, in her fear of being revealed in her drug-ridden state, had shoved her against the wall with enough force to stun her.

There was a knock on her door and she went over and opened it. She was surprised to see that it was Stephen, home earlier than she had expected.

He said, "You weren't resting?"

"No," she pointed to the bed. "I don't expect to until those clothes go back in the closet."

Stephen frowned slightly. "Ling must have put them there so he could do the necessary work in the closet. Mother told me about your strange adventure in the secret passage."

"There is more I didn't tell her."

"Oh?"

"Yes. I've spoken to your grandfather about it and I will tell you."

"Later," he said. "Just now I have someone below waiting to talk with you."

"Who?"

"Inspector Sullivan of the Hong Kong police and formerly of Scotland Yard," Stephen said. "He has been assigned to your case and he has some questions to ask you. He was kind enough to come out here rather than have me drag you back to the city when you were still recuperating from your bad experience."

"That was kind of him," she agreed.

Stephen said, "The police had to be brought into this. Christopher can be protected no longer. I'm sorry to put you through this but it is necessary."

"I don't mind," she said.

They quickly made their way downstairs to the living room. When they entered it she saw a man of medium build in a light brown suit standing admiring the portrait of the Jade Princess. He heard them and turned around. He was in his forties with graying hair and a squarish face much bronzed from the sun.

He bowed and said, "Miss Branch."

"Yes," she said, going to him. "Thank you for coming here and sparing me a trip, Inspector."

Inspector Sullivan smiled and his squarish face became quite appealing. "The least we can do for a visitor from London like yourself who has been exposed to the dark side of our life here."

"I'm afraid I was too venturesome for my own good," she said.

"No doubt," the Inspector agreed, studying her with his keen eyes.

Stephen said, "The Inspector wants to get the exact address of the house in which Christopher kidnapped you and he also has a photo to show you."

The Inspector took a notebook from his pocket. "Now about the exact street, alley and house. The details please."

She told him as best she could. "There was no number on the house. But it was the only three-story one in that awful alley."

"I know the house," the Inspector said. "It has been a trouble spot before. You mentioned a captain being there?"

"Yes. He was talking to Christopher when I arrived."

"Describe him."

"Not too old. He had a harsh voice and short brown whiskers," she said, trying to remember. "He dressed very shabbily but wore a captain's peak cap."

The Inspector wrote down all that she had said. And then he gave her a questioning glance, "Was his name mentioned?"

"No. Christopher just called him captain."

"Captain Brand? Does that name mean anything to you?" the Inspector asked.

"No."

"You've never heard it?"

"I haven't," she said.

Stephen asked the Inspector, "Is that who you think it might be?"

"I'd say so from her description," the Inspector replied. "Do you recall the name?"

"Vaguely," Stephen said with caution. "I have an idea that Christopher threw some of our business his way. We use a lot of coastal shipping."

"If so your records should show it," Inspector Sullivan suggested.

"They would," Stephen agreed.

The Inspector turned to her again. "And later this man, Ben Larsen, was involved in your kidnapping."

"Yes."

The Inspector turned to Stephen, "You actually had this Ben Larsen employed here as a boatman?"

"For some time," Stephen agreed, a troubled look on his handsome face.

"I can't think why you hired the fellow," Inspector Sullivan protested. "He has a long criminal record."

Stephen grimaced. "I'm afraid I must give the credit to my cousin, Christopher, again. He was the one who brought him here and recommended him as an expert on boats."

"He is," the Inspector said with a sigh. "It also happens he has the reputation for being expert in a number of other things including robbery with violence, assault with intent to murder and quite a lot more if you'd like to make a list of them."

"Thank you, no," Stephen said, his face crimson.

"You walked into a regular nest of criminals it seems," the Inspector told Enid. "Most unfortunate."

"Ben Larsen was quite shameless about being a criminal," she said. "I tried to talk him into helping me but he wouldn't be bribed."

"Not our Ben," the Inspector said with sarcasm. "You were too big game." He put his hand in an inside coat pocket and drew out a small photo and handed it to her. "Ever seen him before?"

She studied the brown, ancient photo and in spite of the subject looking younger she exclaimed, "That's Mr. Kamasato!"

"I thought so," the Inspector said, taking the photo back from her and himself glancing at it grimly. "He goes under a lot of names."

Enid said, "He was the leader of the gang. I had the feeling that Christopher and the others were afraid of him."

The Inspector put the photo away. "Kamasato is a frightening man and a dangerous one."

"Was, Inspector," Stephen corrected him.

The Inspector nodded and said to Enid, "You are sure that girl killed Kamasato?"

"Charles Milano said so," she told him.

Inspector Sullivan considered this. "I'm not at all sure I can accept the word of Milano."

She found herself becoming indignant. "You can't think of him in the same way as the others."

The inspector studied her with a cynical look. "You mean because he rescued you?"

"Yes, I suppose so," she replied, knowing she was blushing furiously.

"We must regard that as a purely personal gesture," the Inspector warned her.

"He tricked them and set me free. He brought me to Hong Kong to safety," she said.

"Still, purely personal," the Inspector said. "You know he was in with the gang. You saw him there and know that he had been in the drug-running previously."

Lamely, she said, "I only know I saw him there and it was lucky for me that he showed up."

Stephen appealed to her, "The Inspector realizes that Mi-

249

lano probably saved your life. But the point is he did it because he is fond of you and not because he deserted his criminal activity."

"Thank you, sir," the Inspector told Stephen. "Very nicely put if I may say so." He gave his attention to her again. "As far as the police are concerned, young lady, Charles Milano is still a wanted man."

"I see," she said in a small voice.

"And he may well have said that Kamasato was dead to throw us off the track. We've had false reports about Mr. Kamasato's death before. He likes us to read his obituary whenever the situation gets hot, but when it cools off he invariably comes to life again."

She said, "I was in a bad state. But I saw the girl plunge the knife into Kamasato. I don't see how he could have survived such a wound. There was a pool of blood all around him and he lay very still."

The Inspector wrote this down and said grudgingly, "I'm not saying it isn't so. I'm only pointing out that you can't expect your friend Milano to receive any special favors from the Hong Kong police. On our records he is listed as a dangerous public enemy."

"I understand," she said, feeling terribly sorry for the young American.

The Inspector put his notebook in his pocket. "I think that will do for now. I'll depend on Mr. Porter to see you have full protection for the rest of your stay in Hong Kong. How long do you plan to remain here?"

"Not too long," she said. "Before I leave I want to be sure that my sister is dead."

Stephen said embarrassedly, "My late wife, Inspector. She drowned in a storm in the bay. Her boat overturned."

"Yes, I recall that," the Inspector said with a stern look on his squarish face. "An odd case if I may make a comment."

nineteen

"Odd?" Stephen echoed, not sounding pleased. "Why do you say that, Inspector?"

"Sorry, sir," Inspector Sullivan said. "I didn't mean to offend. I meant that it was strange that your wife should take a boat out in the face of a rising storm."

Stephen's face was stern. "Her judgment in such matters was not always good."

"I would assume that to be the case," the Inspector said. And he turned to her again with an interested look on his square face. "So you think Mrs. Porter might somehow have survived the storm? That she wasn't drowned?"

"Yes," she said awkwardly, aware of Stephen's disapproval of her comments. "I may be wrong. But it is hard for me to think of her as dead."

"Have you any particular reason for thinking your half-sister alive? Any special reason?" The Inspector pressed her.

She wanted to tell him of some of the signs which had been left for her, of her strange encounter in the cellar just an hour or so earlier. But she was certain Stephen would make all that she said look like neurotic suspicions on her part and nothing would be gained.

So she made herself say, "I have little real evidence to back up my opinion. Some things have happened which could be ascribed to Madge or alternately to someone who wished to make me think she was still alive. I have found certain items belonging to her in my room. I have thought I've seen

251

her at a distance but I've never been able to catch up with her. She invariably vanishes. So I can't say whether I've seen her or someone who looks like her. It is terribly frustrating."

"I should imagine so," the Inspector said dryly.

Stephen spoke up again, "Miss Branch has been under an unhappy strain since arriving here. It is not surprising that her nerves may have sometimes played tricks on her."

Inspector Sullivan eyed the handsome man doubtfully. "One thing is certain, her nerves did not transport her to Macao and the great danger she was exposed to there."

Stephen crimsoned. "My cousin Christopher must be given full blame for that."

"It would seem so," the Inspector went on. "Rather a novelty to have a Porter wanted by the Hong Kong police. Times change."

"You will handle all this as discreetly as possible," Stephen said in a troubled voice.

The Inspector shrugged. "There are certain procedures. They do not vary. He placed this young woman in great peril. He must expect to pay. The best thing would be if he did not return to Hong Kong at all."

"For my grandfather's sake I hope he doesn't," Stephen said. "He is the one most upset by all this."

"A fine old gentleman," Inspector Sullivan agreed. "I think we have everything we need for the moment." And he turned to Enid again, advising her, "Do be careful while you are here. These drug people are vindictive. If they think of you as in any way being a hazard they will patiently pursue you and attempt to silence you permanently. You understand?"

"Yes," she said quietly.

"The fact that Kamasato may be dead will not really make all that much difference," the former Scotland Yard man went on. "He was the leader of a well-organized gang. There is an associate, Wu Chang, just as dangerous as the Jap ever was. And even though Charles Milano rescued you he may find himself under a death threat to see that you do no talking."

Her eyes widened. "You think Charles might try to harm me?"

"If they corner him and give him the choice of killing you or losing his own life," the Inspector told her.

"But he saved me!" she protested.

"And you may never hear from him again," he said. "But if the organization turns on him he wouldn't be safe anywhere in this part of Asia. In that case he might come after you. If he makes any contact with you let us know at once."

Enid said, "I don't want to be a party to turning him in to the police."

"You can't risk your own life," Stephen told her.

She turned to the handsome man. "But Charles might call me without having any plans to hurt me. I can't turn against him."

Inspector Sullivan sighed. "I think you've missed the point I've been trying to make, young lady. My feeling is that he will only contact you on the instructions of the gang. Normally he would keep away from you and give you a chance to return to England without further complications."

"I see," she said quietly.

"I will go back to the city now," Inspector Sullivan said. "But I will keep in touch. You have my private phone number. I urge that you call me if anything happens to worry you."

"We will, Inspector," Stephen promised as he saw him out.

The Inspector halted at the door to nod at her and say, "I have enjoyed meeting you, Miss Branch. I hope the rest of your stay here will be more pleasant."

She managed a rueful smile. "I hope so."

He went on out with Stephen escorting him. She felt drained by the trying interview and slumped down in a nearby chair and stared bleakly ahead of her. She had not said all the things she should have. With Stephen standing by to hear everything she had felt constrained to go easy on her ghostly experiences. But these moments when she'd been exposed to a phantom Madge had played a large part in her adventures at the old mansion.

There were approaching footsteps in the hallway and then Stephen came back into the room. He saw her in the chair and said, "Sorry you had to go through that."

She shrugged. "I didn't mind all that much."

Stephen frowned and strolled by her to stand with his back to the fireplace. Having taken a stand there with his hands clasped behind him, he said, "I try to protect the ladies of the

253

house. But it is not always possible. He insisted on questioning you."

"I gladly cooperated," she told him. "If there's any hope of solving this mystery I want it done."

Stephen stared at her. "You're still dissatisfied with the explanations as they stand?"

"I'm afraid so."

He looked unhappy. "We've discussed it at length before. I see nothing to gain by further discussion."

"Nor do I," she said. "But I do want to tell you something else."

"What?"

She went on to describe the weird and violent encounter she'd had in the dark cellar passage, ending with, "I know I oughtn't to have gone down there alone but I did."

Stephen studied her with a shadow of despair showing on his bronzed, even-featured face. "So I have come home to another crisis?"

"I don't know what to call it," she said. "But it did happen and it has to mean something. I didn't want to tell the Inspector until I discussed it with you."

"That was considerate of you," the young man said. "Who do you think it may have been in the passage? Perhaps Christopher?"

"No. I'm almost certain he's in Macao."

"Ben Larsen, then? He knows every inch of this old house."

"It could have been Larsen," she admitted. "But I worry that it might have been a near-insane Madge. If she is still alive she must be in a crazed mental state by now."

Madge's husband said, "I have to discount that idea."

"In any case the fact remained I again suffered an attack in this house."

He said, "Perhaps you ought not to remain here for the balance of your stay. I can book you in a hotel."

She said, "A hotel might be safer but I think I will get closer to the truth by remaining here."

"If that is your decision," he said.

"It is," she replied.

"I'll have Ling nail that passage door so no one can get into your room by it or use it as a way of escape," he said.

"If you'll just relax down here for a little I'll have it attended to before dinner."

"Don't you wish to explore the passage? Find out if there is anyone hiding there?"

"Later," he said. "We can do that without using the door and steps which lead down from your bedroom. There are other entrances and exits to the secret passages."

He left her and presumably went to have the handyman, Ling, attend to the carpentry. She was somewhat surprised that he had so accurately described the door and steps down from the closet. He had so glibly given her the description of them she suspected that he was much more familiar with the maze of secret passages in the old mansion than he pretended.

This was how she came to be downstairs when the lovely Sonya Chen returned from her day of teaching in Hong Kong. The black-haired girl came into the living room to join her. And she clasped her in her arms.

"I'm so glad you're safe," Sonya said, her eyes sparkling happily.

"It was a sort of nightmare," she admitted to the other girl.

Sonya stood there with anger shadowing her lovely features. "I never did trust Christopher."

"I know that," Enid agreed.

"Now he has revealed himself as a complete scoundrel," Sonya went on. "He will not dare return here."

"I wonder."

"He had better not," Sonya said sternly. "He was the one who destroyed your half-sister. I have said that from the start. I was surprised that you were willing to go out with him that first night you came here."

"I had no idea the kind of person he was."

"Perhaps it is better that it happened this way," the Chinese girl said. "He was brought out into the open as a scoundrel."

Enid said, "I'm sure in due course he'll fall victim to one of his gangster companions or the police. I'm not worried about avenging myself on him. I'm concerned still that Madge may be alive."

A shadow crossed the other girl's face. "Perhaps you would

255

do better to forget about her. If you did find her alive she would not be the person you once knew."

"Surely she could be saved," Enid insisted.

Sonya shook her head. "I doubt it. And I am one of those who think she is dead."

"What about the ghostly happenings? The phantom female seen here in the night?"

Sonya turned to the portrait of Regina which hung on the wall near where they were standing. She said, "The ghost you have seen was likely the Jade Princess. Many have seen her moving about the house and grounds at night."

"I'm a skeptic where the legend is concerned," Enid told her.

Sonya glanced over her shoulder at the portrait and seemed nervous. She said, "You oughtn't to say that. Especially not within hearing of her likeness."

Enid was fascinated by the Chinese girl's superstition. Sonya was modern in most things but she could not turn her back on the legend with which she'd been brought up since childhood. The two girls went upstairs together and when Enid went to her bedroom she found the passage door had been closed off with boards nailed across it. Her clothes had been returned to the rod in the big closet. All was much as it had been. She need have no more fear of traffic from her room to the secret passage.

Dinner proved a quiet time but at least there was less tension at the table with Christopher missing. There was no mention of him by anyone, probably in deference to old Edmund Porter who was looking most bleak.

When the meal was over Stephen invited her to go out for a stroll with him. They went as far as the wharf and the boathouse and then back to sit in the teahouse as dusk gave way to darkness.

Sitting there beside Stephen, she said, "Thank you for all you have done for me."

"And my apologies for Christopher," he said. "By now he has found Kamasato was killed and you are free."

"Did Madge and you ever discuss him?"

"Many times," Stephen said bitterly. "She saw him as interesting and misunderstood."

"Surely she changed her mind about him later."

"I don't know that she did," he said. And then looking at her earnestly in the growing darkness, he said, "Why don't you change your mind and remain here?"

"Remain here?"

"Yes. As my wife," Stephen said. "You know it is what I've hoped for all along. Many times I remembered our meeting in England."

"You had eyes for no one but Madge then," she protested.

"I saw you very clearly," he said. "And I liked you. True, I was in love with Madge at the time. It did not occur to me that one day I might ask you to be my wife. But with Madge gone everything is different."

She turned from him to gaze at the bay and the lights of a ship out there, twinkling red and white. She said, "Even if Madge is dead it would be no good. Her ghost would always be between us."

"Surely not."

"Yes," she said. "And if you are seeking a wife to understand you, and who will love you, there is no need to look further than right here."

"You're thinking of Sonya Chen?"

"Yes," she said, looking up at him once more. "How can you be blind to her love for you?"

"I don't see that she does love me," Stephen said. "We were brought up together. I have come to think of her as a sister."

"You should look at her with different eyes," Enid told him.

"That's interesting," he said, "I assume it is your way of letting me down easily."

"No, I'm sincere about it! What future is there for Sonya Chen here if you don't marry her?"

"When my grandfather dies I expect she will leave us," he said. "He will see she is well provided for and can do anything she wants. Perhaps she'll marry one of her own race."

"Then the great objection is that you don't want a Chinese wife?"

"I didn't say that."

"Your reaction suggests it," Enid told him. "Yet your grandfather married Regina and it was a great romance.

257

They would probably still be happy together if she hadn't been murdered by the hill bandits."

"I've often wondered about that," Stephen said seriously. "I know grandfather loved her dearly but he was also jealous of her. Wong Lee has told me that. And you must know that Wong Lee was also a suitor of hers."

"Yes. I understand she had many young men who wished to marry her."

"She was a flirt and condemned for it by the prudish European women of the colony at that time. I understand many of them were secretly happy when she came to a dismal end."

"Sonya Chen is dedicated and serious-minded," Enid said. "She would never cause you that sort of problem."

"I'm not at all sure she is interested in marriage," he went on. "There was a young Englishman came out here for Lloyd's of London. He fell deeply in love with her."

"And it didn't turn out?"

"No. She sent him on his way broken-hearted. He asked for and received a transfer to Singapore and at the last hearing I had of him he'd married a Malaysian girl there."

She smiled thinly. "Clearly he'd become enchanted with the East. Perhaps Sonya saw that. He wasn't in love with her so much as with the idea of marrying a girl of the Orient."

"I think he married the other girl in an attempt to forget Sonya," he said.

"I still say she refused him because of you."

"I know she hated Christopher," Stephen said. "From the moment he arrived here from London she distrusted him. Of course she had some grounds. We'd all received advance word that he'd been in trouble in London and was being shipped here to avoid prosecution and a term in prison."

"Yet you all accepted him into the family!"

"My grandfather's idea," Stephen said. "That is why he feels so badly now. At the start I thought even grandfather was disgusted by Christopher's abrasiveness. I was sure he'd send Chris off in a few months. Strangely enough as the months went by Chris began to exert a stronger influence over him."

"I think your grandfather did not want to believe he had made an error in judgment."

"That must have been it," Stephen said. "I only know that my life with Madge would have been happier if he hadn't been here, and not satisfied with causing that trouble he tried to harm you."

She stood up. "We'd best go back. We'll create gossip if we stay out here alone in the moonlight."

"I wish they'd link our names so you'd feel forced to marry me," he said.

"You are almost as devious as Christopher," she teased him.

He said, "Let's not join the others without your giving me a kiss. I need that, at the very least, to remember." And without waiting for her consent he took her in his arms and kissed her with a deep sincerity.

She did not find his embrace unpleasant. He was a handsome man and there was much about him which she liked. But as she remained there in his arms for those few seconds an odd feeling of terror streaked through her. It came quickly and she recalled that she'd had something of the same feeling other times when she'd been in the teahouse. After an initial period of pleasant calm there had come this breathtaking sensation of fear.

Stephen must have noticed the change in her. As he released her, he said, "Is something wrong? Did I make you so unhappy?"

She shook her head. "It wasn't you. It was something else. I've felt it here before. I can't explain it. At the start I'm always very comfortable here and then before I leave I'm overcome by a feeling of terror."

"Your nerves are still frayed from what happened in Macao," he said. "I shouldn't have kept you out here. We'll go inside." With his arm around her he led her out of the teahouse and down its steps. Then they crossed the lawn to the big white house.

When they reached the open French doors leading into the living room she was mildly startled to discover Sonya Chen standing there gazing out into the darkness. The Chinese girl greeted them with her usual courtesy but Enid was left wondering if the girl had seen her and Stephen in each other's arms.

Sonya was casual and friendly. "We have a guest," she told them.

They went on inside and saw the elderly Wong Lee seated with Stephen's mother near the end of the room. Eleanor was telling the old Chinese a long account of Christopher's misdeeds. She halted on seeing them.

"I wondered where you were," she said, studying them with her sharp eyes.

Stephen looked embarrassed. "We walked down to the wharf and by the time we came back as far as the teahouse it was dark. We remained there for a few minutes to watch the ships' lights from the bay."

Sonya Chen had followed them in and, with a knowing glance their way, said, "The view out there is fascinating."

"I have never liked the teahouse, myself," Eleanor said in her emphatic way. "But it was built when I came here and so I had to learn to like it. I often hoped it would burn down. But it never has."

Enid sat down by the older woman and said, "But it is the only touch of authentic China about the estate. How could you not like it?"

"That's precisely why," Eleanor said irritably. "If it weren't for that teahouse I could enjoy the grounds and think I was somewhere in England. That thing always makes me know I'm not at home."

Sonya Chen was standing near Stephen and she said, "It is the same with the club in Hong Kong. Once you step inside it is an exact replica of a London club rather than reflecting some of the background here."

Stephen cleared his throat. "That is so and it is wrong. If these people so resent coming here why don't they go back to England."

The stout Wong Lee chuckled. "Because I suspect that in spite of all their longing for the old country, this has become their home. Few ever return to stay, and I notice that after a few trips back to England they lose their enthusiasm to return."

Eleanor said, "That is because England has changed so for the worse!"

Stephen told his mother, "All the world has changed and

will go on changing. I'm sure the time will come when people here will refer to the good old days in Hong Kong."

"Things have not been the same since the Japs were here in the Second World War," Eleanor said unhappily. "Only old men like your grandfather cling to their pictures of the past and refuse to notice the change."

"How is Mr. Porter feeling tonight?" Enid asked.

"Edmund had a headache and decided to go to bed early," Eleanor said.

"Still concerned about Christopher," Wong Lee said. "He should put the young man out of his thoughts." The old Chinese directed himself to her. "You are feeling better after your bad time in Macao?"

"A good deal," she said. "Much of it is just coming back to me. When I first returned it was a jumble in my mind."

"I'm sure it must have been," Wong Lee said sympathetically.

"That Ben Larsen told me that the gang Christopher was involved with was what they call a triad. What did he mean?"

Wong Lee said, "We have many secret Chinese societies in Hong Kong, most of them in the Kowloon district. Their members range from pimps and shoeshine boys to businessmen and even teachers." He glanced up at Sonya Chen.

The lovely Sonya accepted his words calmly. "I have heard such societies exist."

"They do," the old man said. "Their numbers run into the tens of thousands. Originally the aims of the triads were good. Members were screened, sworn to brotherhood, and dedicated themselves to moral and religious principles. But then the societies began to degenerate. They dabbled in politics and conspiracy and squeeze—our name for extortion. This led to them going into other criminal acts such as blackmail and smuggling. In the same way the Society of Harmonious Fists degenerated into the criminal Boxers over a period of years."

"Triads are not legal here, are they?" Stephen asked.

"No. But they are allowed in Macao. They identify each other by the manner in which they light a cigarette or set teacups before visitors. A true secret society. The largest one I know of is the '14 K,' so called because the ancient address in Canton was Number 14 in Po-wah Road, with the 'K' added later for karat of gold in memory of a battle over protection with a rival triad whose members likened their strength to a softer gold. This '14 K' Triad dates from the seventeenth century and was updated by General Kot Sui Wong as a secret agent for the Kuomintang. He was deported from Hong Kong to Formosa in 1950, but returned incognito to the colony and, before his death in 1953, set up eighteen groups of the triad which now has an estimated membership of eighty thousand in its various branches."

Stephen said, "Doesn't each branch have a particular area in which to function?"

Wong Lee nodded. "The so called 'Sincere' branch is a strongarm group who protect squatter areas in Kowloon. The 'Filials,' who have about fifteen thousand members specialize in the drug and prostitution traffic. And it is with that branch that Christopher has allied himself."

"He surely is in dangerous company," Enid suggested.

"No question," Wong Lee told her. "Few Europeans are allowed to work with the triads. The initiation to the triad can last all night and involves novices in rituals handed down over the centuries. Ten precious articles are featured which include a red lamp, to tell true from false, a red pole, for punishment, a white paper fan, to strike down traitors and a peachwood sword, representing a magical blade which has the power to decapitate enemies, when merely flourished in the air."

"Heathen practices," Eleanor said with a sniff.

"Perhaps," Wong Lee said with a faint smile. "But then you Europeans have your own strange secret societies and rites, haven't you?"

"You are right," Stephen said. "You should not be so critical, mother."

Wong Lee said, "The triads are much like the Mafia. They have the reputation of never talking to the police. They are loyal to each other. That is why they do so well with drug and gold smuggling."

Enid said, "Mr. Kamasato was in with them as well."

"He had power because he was an archcriminal," Wong Lee told her. "The triad would have to accept him and do business with him."

Sonya Chen said, "That sort of corruption would not be tolerated in mainland China today."

Stephen glanced at her in surprise. "You sound like a Peking sympathizer, Sonya."

She gave him a level look. "I approve of much that the Communist Government have done for the Chinese people. Their gunboats constantly scour the islands watching for opium smugglers. And when they catch them it goes hard with them."

Enid turned to the girl and said, "I know that is true because I heard Christopher and the others talking about the sea patrol. They were terrified of being captured by it."

Eleanor said, "It would serve Christopher right if he wound up in a Communist prison."

"It would certainly settle him," Stephen said soberly. "I doubt that we'd ever see him alive again."

The conversation went on for a while longer and Enid found herself impressed by the wide fund of information the elderly Wong Lee was able to offer. He might be eighty, stout and slow moving, but his mind was extremely active. At last the old man rose to leave. Before he went he paused to speak with her.

He said, "I would be pleased if you would be my house guest for a few days while you are recuperating from Macao."

"That is kind of you," she said.

"I trust you will accept my offer," the old man said in his gracious way. Then he bowed and allowed Stephen to escort him out.

Enid and the other two women went upstairs to their rooms. As she prepared for bed she thought of all she had heard during the evening. She realized how thankful she should be that Charles Milano had taken the risk he had to save her. She worried that the Chinese mafia might exact their revenge on him.

Finally, she settled in bed and tried to sleep. But sleep was slow in coming. Her mind went back to the island and the sinister Kamasato. What a villain Christopher had been to leave her to such a fate!

When her eyes closed in a light sleep it was long after midnight. Then her sleep was troubled by weird dreams in which

263

she was constantly being threatened. She awoke with a start to hear a light knocking on her door.

She sat up in bed and asked, "Who is it?"

Something was mumbled from the other side of the door. She thought it was Stephen trying to tell her something but she couldn't be sure.

She rose from the bed and crossed to the door, saying, "I can't hear you."

"Hurry!" the word came clearly and urgently and she was sure this time it was Stephen.

With a sigh she pulled the bolt on the door and opened it only to have an enraged Christopher pounce in on her and seize her by the throat.

twenty

The whole thing happened so swiftly that Enid did not have a chance to scream for help or even think of how to defend herself. The last person she'd expected to see in the old mansion was Christopher. He'd returned much sooner than she'd expected. He was choking her and she was certain that in a moment she would faint.

Then he changed his attack and used one hand to twist her arms painfully behind her back and another to cover her mouth.

"You little demon!" he hissed in her ear. "You thought you'd done for me, didn't you?"

She shook her head and made a painful effort to speak but his hand was clasped over her mouth in such a way as to make this impossible.

She felt his hot breath against her ear as he went on whispering. "You and Milano thought you were clever. You expected them to finish me. Well, you were wrong. Wrong! Wrong!" Each time he echoed "wrong" he twisted her arms so that she moaned with pain.

He went on, "Don't think you're going back to England. Never! You've chosen to battle with me, and I'm not one to back down from a fight."

She was tormented with pain from his cruel handling of her and worse, she imagined that he would not be content with merely threatening her. He undoubtedly planned to kidnap her again and expose her to some terrifying new ordeal.

She fought to keep from losing consciousness, growing weaker every moment.

"Let her go!" The voice which spat out the words was weak but there was determination in the tone he used.

A startled Christopher halted in his attack on her and turned to the doorway. Though still in Christopher's grasp she could see the figure in the doorway. It was old Edmund Porter and he had a gun in his hand which was pointed at Christopher in a businesslike way.

After a moment, Christopher shifted her in front of him to act as a shield and said, "Old fool! If you shoot me you'll have to put a bullet through her as well!"

"I'll kill you both if you make me," the old man told him coldly.

"Maybe that's what you want to do," Christopher sneered.

"I'll give you until I count three to drop her," Edmund Porter warned him. "If you do I'll give you time to get away before I arouse the rest of the house."

"Generous!" the young man sneered. "What about her? The minute I take my hand from her mouth she'll scream her head off."

"She'll be silent," Edmund Porter said. "You hear me, Enid?"

Enid nodded. She knew the old man was taking a desperate chance to get her out of this predicament and she daren't not go along with whatever he said.

Christopher warned her. "If you so much as let out a deep breath I'll have us both shot by that old fool. If you want to stay alive, keep quiet!" And with that he let her slump to the floor. She lay there with her breath coming in painful gasps and her heart pounding crazily, but she attempted no outcry.

"Get going!" old Edmund Porter said, backing a step but still keeping Christopher covered.

The young man moved warily towards the doorway. "You make a great hero," he said derisively.

"Don't tempt me to use this weapon," Edmund Porter warned him. "I will if you make me."

Christopher nodded. "I think you would. In fact, I think you'd like to. You're anxious to be finished with me."

"I'll give you three minutes to get away," the old man told him.

Christopher turned to her with a malevolent smile on his face. "Don't think you've seen the last of me," he told her.

Then he moved warily past old Edmund and ran down the corridor. She heard him racing down the steps. Then the door opened and closed. Almost immediately after that a car door slammed, the motor roared and with screeching of tires the car raced off into the night. Only then did the thin Edmund Porter drop the hand with the weapon in it and lean weakly against the door frame.

She was on her feet. She crossed to him and took his arm to give him support. She guided him to an easy chair and sat him in it.

She said, "I'll find something for you."

"Brandy," he said. His face and lips were purple and he lay back in the chair as if he might collapse.

Enid turned just in time to confront Stephen in pajamas and dressing gown. He'd come racing into the room and now he asked, "What's going on? That car driving off wakened me."

She said, "Get some brandy! Your grandfather's in a bad way!"

Stephen took a look and saw she was right. He rushed out to get the brandy. In the meanwhile she went to the bathroom and hurriedly wet a towel in cold water and brought it out and placed it on the old man's forehead. She was keeping the towel in place when Stephen returned with a brandy bottle and glass. He feverishly poured out some of the amber liquid and touched the glass to his grandfather's lips.

Enid stood back and watched. The old man feebly took a sip of the brandy, then a little more. After a moment he finished it. The effect was next to miraculous. You could almost see the life force returning to him. His face and lips became less blue and he was able to sit up properly in the chair.

Stephen poured a little more brandy in the glass and said, "Better have a drop more."

"I'm all right now," the old man said, but he sipped the brandy.

Stephen glanced across at her. "What happened?"

"Christopher came here," she said.

"What?" he said, incredulously.

"He mimicked your voice and I let him in. He sprang at

267

me and if it hadn't been for your grandfather he would probably have dragged me off again in the car he had waiting. Your grandfather held a gun on him and made him release me."

Stephen listened to her account in a stunned fashion. Then he turned to his grandfather in bewilderment. "How did you know he was here?"

The old man in the chair swallowed the last of the brandy and then in a low voice said, "I wasn't able to sleep. I thought I heard a car in the driveway. Then I heard a noise from down here. I always keep a gun in my room. I came down prepared."

"And found Christopher attacking her?" Stephen said.

"Yes."

"And?" Stephen urged him for more information.

"I threatened to shoot him. He used her as a shield. I told him I'd shoot both of them if I had to. I gave him three minutes to get away quietly. He left."

"You should have shot him as soon as he let Enid go," Stephen told the old man.

Edmund Porter shook his head. "I gave my word. I made a bargain with him and I kept it."

"He did the only thing," she reasoned with Stephen. "If he hadn't suggested that, Christopher wouldn't have let me go and your grandfather would have had to shoot me as well!"

Stephen paced up and down. "But to let him get away!"

His grandfather gave him a look of reprimand. "The main thing was the safety of this girl. Surely you agree with me in that?"

"I guess so," Stephen said, still upset. "The nerve of him coming here so soon."

"I agree," Edmund Porter said with a sigh.

Stephen said, "I guess you were glad to let him go. You have always been lenient with him."

"He is a Porter," the old man said wearily. "Family does count."

Enid crossed to the upset young man. "I wouldn't torment your grandfather any more if I were you. You can see he's not well and this took a great deal from him."

Stephen nodded and went over to the old man. "I'm sorry. I give you credit for what you did."

268

Edmund Porter lifted himself out of the chair. He patted the gun in the pocket of his dressing gown pocket. "It was pure luck that I had this nearby and equally lucky that I heard the noise down here and guessed what it might be."

"You should go back to bed," Enid told him.

"Yes, I will," he said.

"I'll always be grateful to you," she told him.

"You are our guest. While you are under our roof it is our duty to offer you protection," the old man said gravely.

Stephen accompanied his grandfather to the corridor and said, "Will I go upstairs with you?"

"No," the old man said. "I'm fine now. Make no more fuss. We don't want Eleanor and Sonya up, having to explain to them!" And with that he went off to take the stairway back to his room.

Stephen came back to her. "Did Chris hurt you?"

"Only superficially," she said. "I was mostly terrified. Your grandfather was wonderful."

"I know," he said absently. "This will mean talking to the police again. Inspector Sullivan will have to come back."

"Will that do any good?"

"Whether it does or not, this is now a police matter," Stephen said. "We have no choice."

She did not argue since she knew he was right. They returned to their beds and the old mansion was quiet for the balance of the night. But the next morning the story of what had happened spread. Both Eleanor and Sonya were shocked, not able to believe so much had happened while they slept through it all.

Sonya Chen came to her room before leaving for school. She said, "If it were not an examination day at the school I would remain here to see what the police decide."

Enid was dressed and seated on her bed. "I don't think they can do anything but make a report on what happened. With dozens of confederates and planes at his disposal, Christopher can be safely back in Macao by now."

"That is probably just where he is," Sonya said angrily. "We would be better off if Peking took over Macao and all the other islands."

"You really think that?"

The lovely black-haired girl sighed. "Yes. Call me a com-

munist if you like. What we have here now is too corrupted."
And she left to drive to her school in the city.

Eleanor was marching about downstairs in a nervous state when Enid came down. Stephen's mother halted in crossing the foyer to greet her at the foot of the stairs.

Eleanor eyed her stonily. "I hear Christopher was here last night."

"Yes," she said.

"Why didn't you make an outcry so we could have captured him and turned him in?" the older woman asked irritably.

"It didn't work out that way," she replied, trying to be patient with the overbearing Eleanor.

Eleanor said, "To think he was here and got away! It's too much. He'll come back some night and murder us all in our sleep."

She said, "I think his anger was directed chiefly at me. He was ready to kidnap me again."

"And Grandfather saved you."

"Yes. How is he this morning?"

"He is staying in his room," the older woman said. "What can you expect? He hasn't been well for a long time and a situation like that would be bound to tax his feeble strength. I don't know how he held a gun in his palsied hand."

"Strangely enough the tension of the moment seemed to help him," she recalled. "I don't think his hand ever did tremble while he was covering Christopher with that gun."

"That's a small miracle in itself," Eleanor commented. "You must have been born under a lucky star."

"Yes and no," she said grimly.

Stephen emerged from the corridor and told his mother, "I expect the police here any moment. It might be wise for you to go up and keep grandfather company. The police will want to go up and get his version of last night before they leave."

"Surely you and Enid can tell them enough," Eleanor said.

"They'll want a complete account," he said. "And that means talking with grandfather."

"All this will kill him before it's over," his mother said gloomily. "There's been no peace in this house since you married Madge." And with this said she went up the stairs.

Stephen gazed after his mother with some embarrassment

and then said to her in a low voice, "You must forgive her this morning. She's upset about missing the excitement last night."

"So it seems," she said.

"Inspector Sullivan ought to be here at any moment," he said. "I think we'll talk with him in my study. It will be more private."

"That might be better," she agreed.

He gave her a sharp appraisal. "You look very well, considering that you probably had little sleep."

"I surprised myself," she said. "I slept soundly the last half of the night. I suppose I was so exhausted."

They went on talking for a few minutes until the Inspector's car pulled up at the front door. Stephen went out to greet him and accompanied him in to the foyer where she was waiting.

Inspector Sullivan's square face wore a resigned look as he told her, "I gather that this is not going to be one of those easy cases."

"I'm afraid not," she said ruefully.

"I'd hoped that Christopher Porter would move on to some other part of the world and we'd be finished with him," the Inspector said.

Stephen, "I think he's a little crazy. Or maybe those thugs he's associated with won't let him move until he finishes Miss Branch."

"An unpleasant thought," the Inspector said. "Where shall we talk?"

Stephen said, "My study, come along." And he marched ahead with the Inspector and Enid following.

When they were comfortably installed in the study, the Inspector took out his notebook to begin the session. First, he told them, "Kamasato is dead and so is the girl, Yun. That has been confirmed by the police in Macao. So we need have no doubts on that score."

"What about Charles Milano?" she asked, worriedly.

Inspector Sullivan frowned at her. "Strange. But the more we dig, the more we find him to be a mystery man. For one thing it appears that he is travelling on a forged passport. It is probable his name isn't Charles Milano."

271

Stephen said, "He has to be an American. There's no mistaking that accent."

Inspector Sullivan shrugged. "Some people are very clever with accents. When I was with Scotland Yard we had I.R.A. people who could fake American identity and accents as neat as you please."

"I'm sure he is American and that if he is using a fake passport there must be a good reason for it," Enid said, trying to defend the man who had saved her.

"Of course there is," Inspector Sullivan said with irony in his tone. "He's a drug smuggler. What better reason?"

"He's still at large?" Stephen asked.

"You hardly needed to ask that," the Inspector rebuked him. "If we had him I'd be boasting about it. No. Milano is as elusive as ever."

Stephen was seated behind the desk. He said, "I didn't dream that Christopher would be brazen enough to come back here last night."

"Perhaps he counted on Edmund Porter to protect him," the Inspector suggested.

"It was the exact opposite of that. The old man covered him with a gun and saved me," she said.

The Inspector poised his pencil over his notebook. "Let me hear your version of events."

She told him as precisely and yet as quickly as she could. When she finished, she said, "After Christopher left the old man almost collapsed."

Inspector Sullivan looked up from his notebook. "Was it because the old man was so weak that he allowed him to get away?"

"Not really," she said. "The old man made a bargain with him to drop me. He said if he would do that he'd give him three minutes to get away and he did just that."

The Inspector showed surprise. "He could have at least winged him in the leg so he couldn't have gotten away."

Stephen spoke up, "I don't think you completely understand the sort of man my grandfather is. When he gives his word he keeps it."

"Even to a dangerous criminal?" Inspector Sullivan said. "That's like making a pact with a viper."

"My grandfather wouldn't see it that way," Stephen said.

"And then there is the question of family. He probably didn't want to shoot Christopher unless he was forced to."

The Inspector showed disgust. "In other words he had the drop on this would-be murderer, and yet he preferred to take the law into his own hands. Administer his own brand of justice. As a result the criminal is free."

Enid asked him, "Don't you discourage people from taking the law into their hands and killing lawbreakers? Don't you prefer to leave that sort of thing to the police?"

Inspector Sullivan said, "In the normal course of events, yes. But this is a much different situation." He sighed. "In London I didn't even carry a gun as a police officer. But it is different out here. In Hong Kong we have to be armed."

Stephen said, "I think the worrisome thing is that Chris seems to want to avenge himself on Miss Branch."

Inspector Sullivan asked her, "Does this make any difference in your plans to stay on here?"

She hesitated and then awkwardly said, "It does frighten me. But I still don't want to leave until I have some questions settled in my mind."

The Inspector eyed her grimly. "You're not going to bring up that business about whether your half-sister is really dead or not?"

"I'm afraid so. I want to know that before I go back to England."

"If you stay here to find out you're liable to wind up a corpse, too," the Inspector said bluntly. "Haven't you any sense of danger, Miss?"

"Of course I'm frightened," she said.

Stephen got to his feet, his handsome face grave. "May I offer a suggestion?"

"What is it?" the Inspector asked.

"We have a neighbor, who is also a partner in our firm, Mr. Wong Lee."

"I know him," the Inspector said.

"He lives alone on the estate next to ours," Stephen went on. "He has asked Miss Branch to visit with him for a few days. Would this not be a good time for her to do this?"

The Inspector said, "I think she'd be safer most anywhere but in this house. Personally, I'd like to see her safely on a plane for London."

Stephen said, "But if she insists on remaining here?"

"I do," she said.

The Inspector gave her a worried glance. "You're not making things easier, Miss."

"I'm sorry," she said.

"I doubt it," he replied. And he turned to Stephen again. "Is your neighbor's house readily accessible from here?"

"Yes. There's a path through the woods which goes directly to the house. And there's the main road approach."

"So Miss Branch would not be far away yet she would be out of this house. I feel while she is here she presents a kind of target for those thugs. Remember, your cousin is not alone in this drug smuggling."

"I know that," Stephen said. "And I recommend that she accept Wong Lee's invitation and go over there for a day or two at least."

The Inspector asked her, "Are you willing to do that? Be Wong Lee's house guest?"

"Yes," she said.

"Good," the Inspector said, rising. "That will at least get you out of the line of fire. Now I'll go up and get a transcript of what your grandfather has to say, Mr. Porter."

With the end of the questioning she was free to move about downstairs. She went into the living room and found an old copy of the *London Illustrated News*. She sat down and tried to concentrate on an article which told of the various efforts to join England and France with a tunnel under the English Channel and how all the various projects were doomed to failure.

The article was interesting but she had a hard time trying to concentrate on it. She kept wondering what Edmund Porter was telling the Inspector. The old man's story would be plain enough. She was still trying to concentrate on the article when Eleanor came to the doorway of the living room.

"You are wanted on the phone," the older woman said in a tone which was almost accusing.

She put aside the magazine and stood up. "Wanted on the phone?"

"Yes. Some man," Eleanor said studying her with grim suspicion.

"I can't imagine who!"

274

"He's waiting," Eleanor said.

"Thank you," she said. And she hurried out to take the phone in the hallway. Nervously she lifted it up and said, "Enid Branch here."

"Good girl," came from the other end of the line. It was Charles Milano.

"You!" she gasped.

"Didn't you expect to hear from me again?" he asked in his light manner.

"I hoped to," she said. "Are you all right?"

"So far," he said. "You had a visitor last night."

"Yes, Christopher," she said.

"I heard about it. He got drunk after he left your place and talked a lot. Someone passed the word to me. I was worried about you."

"I'm all right," she said. "Stephen's grandfather held him off with a gun and sent him on his way."

"Very heroic."

"It was for a sick old man," she said. "What about you? Are you staying in Hong Kong?"

"Censored," he said. "We don't know who may be listening on the line."

"You ought to get away from here," she told him.

"So should you."

"I mean to. I'm going in hiding for a little."

"Don't tell me where."

"I won't," she said.

"Don't tell anyone where. Christopher isn't finished with you. Remember that."

"I will."

"When I have a chance I'll be in touch with you again," he said.

"The police say you are using a false passport and name," she said, almost in tears.

"Is that important to you?"

"No," she said. "But I don't want them to catch you."

"Don't worry."

"I can't help it. If they don't kill you, Christopher and his crowd will," she lamented.

"At least I have a choice," he told her, and Enid shuddered at his black humor. "I will be in touch again when I can."

"How soon?"

"When I can," he said. "In the meanwhile remember I love you."

"Charles!" she said, but he had hung up.

She put the phone down and glanced towards the stairs and saw that Stephen and the Inspector had been standing there hearing all her end of the conversation with Charles. Her face went crimson and her eyes filled with tears of frustration.

The Inspector came down the stairs and stood facing her. "Well," he said. "That was interesting. You had a call from Milano."

She bit her lip. "You wouldn't believe me if I told you no."

"I would not," the Inspector said, his voice hard. "You must remember that your friend Charles is also one of the gang."

"Not the same!" she protested.

Stephen came and stood by her. "It's nonsense to defend him to the police, Enid."

"It surely is," the Inspector said. "I take it he is in Hong Kong. It wasn't a long distance call?"

"I wouldn't know," she said. "He was on the line when I took the phone."

Stephen's mother appeared in the background. She said, "It was a call from Hong Kong. I took it."

The Inspector said, "Thank you. Now that we have established that, did he ask you to meet him, Miss Branch?"

"No. Nothing like that. He just wanted to know if I was all right."

The Inspector said shrewdly, "So he'd heard about last night?"

"Yes," she said.

"That means that Christopher and he are likely together," Stephen suggested.

"I don't think so," she said. "He told me someone gave him the word. As if they came to him and told him."

The Inspector's square face was bleak. "He'd tell you that anyway. Those rats generally run in a pack. And I heard you warn him that the police knew about his false passport and name. That wasn't nice, Miss Branch."

276

"I thought he should know," she protested. "And realize you're closing in on him."

The Inspector said, "That's the last thing we want him to know. You're not helping us at all."

Stephen said, "Did he give you any idea where he was?"

"No," she said unhappily.

The Inspector asked, "Did he say when he'd try to get in touch with you again?"

"No," she said. "He made no promises."

"But he did show enough interest in you to call you. Did he say anything else?" the Inspector said.

Enid looked down. "He warned me against Christopher."

"You didn't need a warning from him," the Inspector said. He then paused a moment and said to Stephen and his mother, "If you two don't mind I'd like to speak with Miss Branch alone for a moment."

"Of course," Stephen said.

"We can go into the living room," Eleanor said with some annoyance.

"No need," the Inspector said. "Miss Branch and I can go outside. Lots of room out there. I'll be driving back to the city in a few minutes." And turning to her, he said, "Come, along, Miss Branch."

She went with him nervously, not knowing what he was about to say to her. When they were outside he began walking across the lawn with her in the direction of the teahouse. He didn't speak for a moment.

Then he glanced at her and said, "I wanted to talk to you alone because I'm not completely satisfied with everything here. There's something a little strange about this family. Is that why you think your sister may not have died a natural death or that she may be still alive and they're hiding the fact?"

"Yes," she said.

"Tell me all that you've seen and heard to make you feel as you do," he said.

She told him everything she could remember quickly—the mysterious figures, her name being called, the trinkets which had belonged to Madge being left for her as if they were messages. And her seeing a phantom image of her supposedly dead sister on several occasions.

The Inspector heard her out with a troubled look on his face. He said, "I can't say I put much stock in ghosts, Miss. What else did you see that made you suspicious?"

She remembered about the gravestone in the private cemetery. And she told him, "The stone was vandalized. Battered with a rock and the letters broken."

He surprised her, by saying, "Let's take a look at it."

twenty-one

Enid had come to respect the rather stolid Inspector more and more. She felt he was perceptive and took in a good deal on which he offered no comment. This latest suggestion of his took her by surprise.

She said, "We can go look at it if you like."

"I'm sure it might be helpful," he said. "You've told me all these things. I'd like to see one of them for myself."

She glanced back at the white house where Stephen and the others were waiting. She rather embarrassedly said, "Won't they think it strange?"

The square-faced man eyed the house sternly. "Maybe. I don't mind if they do."

"I'll explain it to them when I go back," she said.

"They should understand," Inspector Sullivan replied.

They began walking towards the path which led to the cemetery and she told him, "They are rather touchy about this private cemetery. The first mistress of Porter House has a stone erected for her there although she vanished in the mainland hills. And they erected this stone to my half-sister though she supposedly drowned. Her body is not there either. Stephen claims his grandfather made him do it."

"The old man is a character," the Inspector said. "What did Stephen make of the vandalism of his wife's gravestone?"

They were walking along the narrow, shaded path now. She said, "He thought it might have been somebody who hated her."

279

"And you?"

She gave him an uneasy glance. "I suspected that Madge might have done it herself. Angry at the stone being erected to her."

Inspector Sullivan showed interest. "A rather macabre picture. Someone destroying their own gravestone."

"I felt that she had become a drug addict because of Christopher and at his bidding pretended to have drowned. He may have needed her to aid him in his drug smuggling or perhaps he merely wanted to completely remove her from the house so she would not tell what he'd done."

"The rest of the Porter family stay with the drowning explanation of her vanishing?"

"Yes. But as you say, they are a strange, tense group. Even Stephen eludes understanding at times."

"I couldn't agree more," the Inspector said. "They leave me with the same feeling, that they are banded together in concealing something. Whether it is that your sister is not dead or merely that they are trying to protect the black sheep, Christopher, it is impossible to say."

"I know," she said.

"I think Christopher's returning last night is significant. I can't imagine him coming back to the house if he didn't have at least one supporter there."

"It does make you wonder," she said. "I can thank old Edmund Porter for saving me. Otherwise I'm certain Christopher would have taken me off."

"But you must not count too much on that Charles Milano," the Inspector warned as they came to the clearing with the cemetery. He took in the score or more of tombstones and said, "This is interesting."

"I'll show you Madge's stone," she said, leading him to where it was.

She reached the spot and then stepped back with a gasp. Turning to him in a state of shock, she gasped, "I don't understand!"

Patiently, the Inspector asked, "Are you sure this is the spot?"

"Yes," she said, still stunned. "Next to the stone erected to the memory of Regina."

Inspector Sullivan said, "But there is no grave here."

"I know," she said, staring at the ground where the grave had been. The stone had been neatly removed and so had the mound of the grave. It had all been smoothed out and sections of fresh turf installed so that it looked now as if there had never been a grave there.

Inspector Sullivan said, "Your description of the stone was perfect. You told me how it had been battered by a rock."

She was still staring at the spot. "All that I've said is true. In the meantime they've removed the stone and every trace of the grave."

"Why?"

"I don't know," she lamented, her frustration bringing her to the point of tears. "You do believe me, don't you?"

He studied her with his shrewd eyes. "I do. But if I didn't know you so well I probably wouldn't. I'd think you'd been fantasizing."

"The stone and grave did exist," she protested.

"All right," he said quietly, worrying her that he might be merely humoring her. "So our little trip in here went for nothing."

"I'm sure there has to be an explanation."

He said, "Undoubtedly."

"They must have done it for some reason."

"Even so," he said, "it does spoil this part of your story. Unless I'm able to see that gravestone I have nothing to substantiate what you said."

"Yes, I know," she agreed unhappily.

"Has it ever struck you that your half-sister may have been murdered rather than drowned? And that is what this odd family conspiracy is all about. An attempt to protect the murderer."

"I have wondered about that," she said. "If that were the case the logical suspects would again be Christopher or Stephen."

"Stephen, his wife, and Christopher formed a kind of love triangle?"

"Yes," she said with a sigh. "I'm sure that Christopher caused the trouble. Madge was very much in love with Stephen when they were married."

"People change," the Inspector said.

"I know."

He said, "I think you should get away from Porter House for a while. It might be wise to accept the invitation of that neighbor. What was his name?"

"Wong Lee."

"Yes, Wong Lee," Inspector Sullivan said. "My suggestion is that you go there at once. Perhaps in a few days I'll have found out enough more about the case to know better what is really going on."

She said, "He has invited me. I'm sure the Porters won't mind."

"Then you must go. I imagine you'll be safer there."

They walked back along the path and the Inspector bade her goodbye and got in his car and drove away. As soon as he vanished she went inside to find an irate Stephen waiting for her in the foyer.

"You were gone long enough," he complained.

"I'm sorry," she said.

"What were you doing using the woods path?"

"I told him about the damaged gravestone. He asked to see it. When I took him to the cemetery the stone had disappeared and so had the grave. I'm afraid he must think I'm a little mad."

"You should have mentioned it to me first," Stephen said sternly. "I had the headstone removed."

"You did?" she gasped.

"Yes. You know I was against the idea of it being there from the start. And when I found it vandalized I made up my mind. I had one of the gardeners remove the stone and flatten out the ground by it."

She said, "I took the Inspector out there to show him the gravestone."

Stephen's handsome face showed surprise. "Why would he want to see it?"

"Because of my insistence that she is still alive," Enid told him.

The handsome man took a deep breath. "I wish you hadn't brought the matter up. Now it will mean a lot of explanations."

She said, "I don't think any serious harm was done."

"I don't like it," Stephen said stubbornly.

282

"I was innocent in the affair. I didn't know what you had arranged."

Stephen said, "This continual harping that Madge is alive is becoming tiresome. Surely you've been here long enough to not question this."

She shook her head. "I still have doubts."

"What does the Inspector say to that?"

"He seems to think her vanishing as she did a little strange," she said.

"Mostly because you've brought the matter up so much," he said irritably.

"I have only said what I thought."

"It is unfortunate that you have these doubts," Stephen said.

"The Inspector is worried about my safety here after last night," she said. "He agrees I should go to Wong Lee's for a few days."

"He said that?"

"Yes."

"Perhaps it is a good idea," Stephen said. "Then if Christopher should return you won't be here. And it seems his anger is directed against you."

"Judging by last night," she said. "So if you don't mind I'll make the move before tonight."

"I'll help you," Stephen said. "Pack some of your things and I'll drive you over."

She went upstairs and packed what she thought she would need for a few nights' stay. She was closing her suitcase when someone knocked on her door. She went over and opened it to see Stephen's mother there.

Eleanor said, "I stopped by to tell you that Edmund wishes to see you before you leave."

"Thanks," she said. "When should I go up to him?"

"Are you packed?"

"Yes."

Eleanor said, "I'll have one of the servants take your bags down to the car and you can go up to him now. He's still in bed but he seems much better."

"Is Stephen waiting for me?" she asked.

Eleanor nodded. "Yes. But there's no hurry. He has no

plans to return to the office today. I have rarely seen him so upset."

"That's too bad," she sympathized. "Perhaps after I'm gone the house will settle down to a more normal pattern."

Eleanor looked grim. "Not so long as that Christopher is at large and playing his games."

Enid made her way upstairs. The door to the old man's room was open and so she knocked on the door frame and entered. He glanced up at her from his pillow and she thought his color was much improved from the previous night. He looked more rested.

"You received my message," he said.

"Yes, Eleanor told me," she said, coming to his bedside.

He said, "I'm distressed that you feel it necessary to leave my house."

"Wong Lee invited me to visit him. The Inspector felt I would be safer there."

"I cannot agree," the old man worried. "Never has anyone had to leave here to seek sanctuary elsewhere. It is a sad reflection on us. We have failed you."

"You can't say that," she told him. "You saved my life last night."

"It was a near thing," the old man said. "My hands are so shaky my aim might have gone far astray had I been forced to use the gun."

"You handled the situation very well," she told him. "And I will come back here before I leave Hong Kong."

He gazed up at her earnestly. "You promise that?"

"I do."

He gave a deep sigh. "Christopher has placed us all in a difficult position. I did not think he would so sorely try me. I've done all I can to rehabilitate him. Now he must take his chances with the police."

"That would seem best," she said. "Anything you do for him now might be construed as helping him in a criminal career."

"True," the old man said. "He has placed himself beyond our help."

She managed a weak smile for him. "You mustn't worry. I will be back eventually and in the meanwhile I can always come over for a visit. I'll be nearby."

"You will find Wong Lee a considerate host," the old man said. "And he will enjoy having a beautiful young woman as his house guest. He has always been an admirer of feminine beauty."

Enid thanked him again and he closed his eyes as if to sleep. She quietly left the room and went downstairs where she found Stephen waiting for her. They went out to the limousine and the chauffeur drove them to Wong Lee's neighboring villa.

The portly old Chinese appeared on the front driveway to welcome her. Waiting servants swept up her luggage and she was shown to a bedroom with a view of the bay. It differed from her bedroom at Porter House in that it was smaller and on the ground floor. But it was furnished with just as much taste and with every convenience which she could ask for.

Stephen remained only a few minutes. She unpacked before she went out on the patio to join her host for afternoon tea. She seated herself across from him and he officiated with the teapot. There were some small cakes set out on plates as well.

She sat back with her teacup in hand and said, "It is so peaceful here."

"You do not find this true at Porter House?" the old man said.

"No," she told him. "It is a house full of tensions. I felt that from the moment I arrived. Didn't Madge ever talk to you about that?"

The broad face of the old man darkened. He said, "As I recall it she did mention something of the sort to me."

"Haven't you noticed it yourself?"

"Christopher's arrival did much to make Porter House a place filled with unhappy people. Stephen and Sonya resented him yet the old man insisted that he be allowed to remain. And Eleanor is basically an unhappy person; she has been since her widowhood."

"When Stephen's father was killed in that seaplane crash?"

"Yes."

"Madge must have found it very difficult. Especially after she became infatuated with Christopher. She would be caught between the tensions of the two groups."

"She was, I'm sure," Wong Lee said over his teacup.

285

"I'm still not satisfied about her death."

"No?" the old Chinese said politely and waited for her to go on.

"Something else that is strange," she said. "The teahouse has a weird influence on me. I only remain within it for a short time and I begin to experience a feeling of depression and then fear."

"That is odd," Wong Lee said.

"Have you ever felt that way because of it?" she wondered.

"I have always found it a sad place," Wong Lee told her. "Edmund built it before his wife, Regina, vanished. And after this happened he began to treat it as a kind of shrine to her."

"A shrine to his Jade Princess," she said.

"Don't doubt that he was a man of strong passions then," Wong Lee went on. "He was fierce in his love for his wife. The only other thing in his life that mattered was their little boy. I think I told you that at one time Edmund Porter suspected that his wife and I were having a romance. It almost broke up our partnership. When he came to his senses he was humbly apologetic and he has been my staunch friend since then."

She eyed the stout old Chinese seated across from her in the screened patio. "And you have also been a good friend to him."

"I have tried to be," Wong Lee said. "I am devoted to the Porter family."

"I know you are," she said. "And I'm sure that Edmund Porter has come to value your devotion highly."

They sat in silence a moment, then Enid asked, "He saw his wife off on the day she went to visit her relatives on the mainland, didn't he?"

"We used donkey carts in those days," Wong Lee said. "Fine little beasts they were. There were no motor cars on the island. As I understand it Edmund was worried about her making the trip from the time she mentioned it."

"He knew the danger of the hill bandits?"

"We all were conscious of the bandits in those days," the old man said, his eyes seemingly focused in the distance as he recollected it all. "Regina was stubborn and laughed at his fears."

"She was inclined to like her own way, wasn't she?"

286

"Always," Wong Lee said. "She would only take an old *amah* with her who was nurse to the boy. But Edmund would not allow her to take the child. They left in the donkey cart early so they would not have to travel after dark. I believe that Edmund in a separate cart went part of the way with them. The great tragedy is that he did not make the entire journey. He might have saved Regina. The hill bandits might not have been so ready to swoop down on two carts, especially if a sturdy man was in one of them."

"And neither Regina not the old *amah* was ever seen again," she said, fascinated by the story.

Wong Lee looked at her a long moment in silence. Then he put down his teacup and rose and went over to stare out at the bay. After a short pause he turned to her and said, "I will tell you something that few people know."

"Oh?" she said, a slight chill racing down her spine as she recognized by the gravity of his tone that whatever he was about to tell her was of much importance.

He came back a step towards her and said, "Some years later I was summoned to a sampan in the Hong Kong harbor, where so many of the peasants live and die."

"And?"

"The message was written in Chinese and begged that I come to see someone," he said.

"You went?"

"Yes. I at once sensed the urgency of the message. When I reached the sampan an old man took me to a shrivelled old woman on a bed of straw. She was very thin and dying, but I recognized her. It was the *amah* who had accompanied Regina on that trip. And this was a dozen years later."

Enid was all attention. "What did she want?"

Wong Lee said, "The old man told me she had an important message for me. But by the time I reached her she was unable to talk. All she could do was stare up at me with troubled eyes and moan."

"So you learned nothing?"

"No. I remained by her side until she died. And I provided money for a suitable funeral for her. The family were grateful. I gathered she was an old aunt and had come to them not long after she and Regina had vanished in the hills. From what they said she was mentally unsound and they had to care for her. But as she neared death her mind became clear and it was then she sent for me."

"But too late."

"Unhappily, yes," Wong Lee said, seating himself opposite her again.

"What did you make of it?"

"I think that somehow she escaped," Wong Lee told Enid. "It is possible that the *amah* showed cowardice and deserted Regina when she most needed her. The *amah* was old and the grim experience unhappily unhinged her mind. She managed to remember her own people, so she sought them out and lived with them."

"Did you tell Edmund Porter?"

Wong Lee shook his head. "No. By that time he was reconciled to his loss. At least as reconciled as he will ever be. I felt that to open the matter would be cruel, especially as I had nothing to offer him except the fact that the *amah* had survived."

"Your thought was that this knowledge would torture him needlessly," she said.

"Yes," Wong Lee said. "Had the old woman given me any sort of information I would gladly have passed it on to him. But she didn't."

"And none of the other Porters know about it?"

"No," Wong Lee said. "You are the first person whom I have told. I have done it because I think you deserve to know."

"That is kind of you."

"And I'm sure you can be trusted with the information," Wong Lee said.

"You may depend on it," she told him. "Yet it only makes the mystery surrounding Regina greater. No wonder the legend of the Jade Princess sprang up."

"Many people believe in it," Wong Lee said. "They think the same curse caused your sister to lose her life."

"I know," she said. "And I have incurred the displeasure of most of the Porters by insisting she may be alive, the tormented drug victim of Christopher."

"You are entitled to your opinion. It is evident that Christopher did not want you delving into the matter any deeper. That is why he took you to Macao."

Enid said, "I think that now Inspector Sullivan is growing suspicious about everything. And this is the first time the police have been brought into it. The Porters can't interfere with the police probing the affair. I'm sure it will make a difference."

"Without question," Wong Lee said with a serious look on his broad face. "You have no idea the power the Porters have here in Hong Kong. They exert great political influence. That is why Christopher has been so bold in his criminal acts. He feels no Porter can ever answer to the law."

"I'd say Inspector Sullivan has other ideas," she said. "And I admire him for them."

"Excellent," the old man in the white linen suit said. "I feel it would be dreary for you to have dinner alone with me tonight. So I have planned to take you to the floating restaurant at Aberdeen. Would you be interested?"

"I think it's a fine idea," she said. "If it isn't too much bother for you."

"I shall enjoy dining in public with a lovely young lady," Wong Lee said. "The ideal time to reach the floating restaurants is twilight. They are a fair drive from here and an ideal way to enjoy the evening is to stop about half the distance along the route at Repulse Bay. They serve excellent martinis on the verandah there at sunset. Then one can drive on to Aberdeen."

Enid said, "I look forward to it. I've really seen only a little of the islands."

"We can have dinner out every night during your stay here," he said. "There is the Parisian Grill and the Marco Polo in the Peninsula Court is the most expensive restaurant and is often very good. One of my favorites is Maxim's. They serve bear's paw as one of their special dishes but I do not recommend it."

She could tell that the old man was enjoying the prospect of visiting the various restaurants and so she encouraged him. "I leave it all to you," she said.

"Perhaps we shall also visit a native place one night," he said, rising. "The Cafe de Chine serves Cantonese-style dishes in a restaurant consisting of two large connecting rooms on the top floor of a ten-story building in the heart of Victoria. Their best dish is roast suckling pig, Cantonese style."

She changed and was ready to join him in his ancient, chauffeured car in time for them to make the drive to Aberdeen with a stop along the way. The old man was in an amiable mood and asked her many questions about London.

"I have not been there since just after the Second World War," he confided. "I expect that I would hardly be able to find my way about."

She smiled. "You'd manage. But there are many changes. A lot of skyscrapers and many new hotels."

"Look at Hong Kong," he said. "Who would have dreamed that one day it would also be a city of tall buildings."

They enjoyed the scenery along the way and she thought how different this was from her sojourn at the Porter House. She needed to get away from the brooding old mansion if only to get her thinking in order. She knew that the Porters had not wanted her to leave. Stephen had pretended he didn't care at the last moment. But she was sure that he, along with old Edmund and the others, was a trifle upset.

Suddenly the old man turned to her in the rear seat of the car and said, "Do you mind if I ask you a most intimate question?"

"No," she said. "I'm sure anything you ask will be sensible and in good taste."

"Thank you," the old Chinese said in his courtly way. "One hesitates to intrude."

"Please ask me whatever you like," she said.

"What are your feelings towards Stephen Porter?"

She felt her cheeks warm. She glanced down at her white gloved hands and said, "That is a difficult question."

"Do not try to answer it if you prefer not to," he said at once.

"Let me go on," she said. "It is a complicated question with me. My feelings towards him are ambivalent. There are times when I like him a great deal."

"And?"

"There are times when I have the odd sensation that I don't know him at all."

The old man nodded gravely. "That is strange. He has the same effect on me. I wish to be his friend but there are moments when I sense his drawing away from me."

"Yes," she said. "Because he was married to Madge. And

290

because of my confused suspicions about what happened to her, I find it all that much more difficult to relate to him."

"Can it be that you suspect he may be partly or all to blame for what happened to Madge?"

"I suppose that is lurking in my mind and it is unfair," she admitted.

"Perhaps, but who knows?" the old man said. "I ask you these questions because it is evident to me that Stephen is in love with you."

She smiled bitterly. "You are perceptive. He has asked me to marry him."

"I thought so."

"Of course I told him I couldn't think of it," she went on. "Not with this mystery still surrounding Madge and what has happened to her."

"That is to be expected," the old man agreed.

"Christopher also told me he was in love with me and he was fairly convincing," she said. "Apparently because he had such success with my half-sister, he planned to try his game on me."

"I'm sure you knew how to handle him."

"I managed," she said. "Of course I made him my enemy. But I feel he was that from the start."

"That is a fact," Wong Lee agreed. As the car slowed down, he added, "We are coming to Repulse Bay now. We'll have our cocktails here."

"It's a lovely location," she enthused as the car came to a halt before the ample structure.

"Very popular with the European colony," he assured her.

They left the car and went inside. The headwaiter knew Wong Lee and led them through several rooms to a table out on the verandah overlooking the water. Wong Lee gave him a tip and they seated themselves to enjoy a quiet drink. The place was filled. The old man ordered for them and she glanced about her.

All at once her heart gave a gigantic leap! For several tables beyond them, at the other end of the verandah, she saw Charles Milano seated alone.

twenty-two

Enid's look of surprise on seeing Charles Milano gave her away completely. Wong Lee must have seen that she was excited for he also turned and observed the young man seated alone at the other end of the vernadah.

Wong Lee asked her, "Someone you know?"

"Yes," she said, breathlessly. "And someone I didn't expect to see."

"Would you like to have him join us?" the old man asked.

She thought quickly. "No," she said, "But if you will excuse me for a moment I'd like to speak with him."

"If you would prefer that," Wong Lee said.

She confided in him, "His name is Charles Milano and he is the one who rescued me."

The broad face of the old Chinese showed surprise. "Then he must also be one of them. One of the drug runners."

"I can't help that," she said. "I trust him."

"You're sure it is safe to let him know you're here," Wong Lee worried. "We could leave without his seeing us."

She rose from her chair. "No. I must talk to him."

Wong Lee also stood up. "I shall be waiting here for you. And I shall also be watching in case he should turn out to be an enemy rather than a friend."

"He is my friend," she told the old man confidently. Yet as she walked the long expanse of the verandah, passing the tables of four, she felt some of her assurance draining away.

At last she reached his table and stood there for him to look up and see her.

"Hello," she said, in a voice with a slight tremor in it.

Charles glanced up at her and then jumped to his feet. "Enid! What are you doing here?"

"I could ask you the same question."

"I'm here to meet someone," he said, looking nervously over his shoulder. Then anxiously studying her again, he asked, "Are you alone?"

"No," she said. "I'm with Wong Lee. He is a neighbor of the Porters and a senior partner of their firm."

"I've heard about him," Charles said. He looked down the verandah where the stout man sat impassively watching them. He said, "Is he the one glaring at us? He looks like an overweight Buddha."

"He's a wonderful old man. And he's watching us because he's concerned for me."

"That's good news, after last night," Charles said.

"I'm not at the Porters," she told him.

"You're staying with Wong Lee?"

"Yes," she said. "See, you found out after all."

"You should have left Hong Kong long ago. You must know that."

"So should you," she said. "Did those thugs try to get even with you for rescuing me?"

"Christopher has," he said grimly. "Thus far I've managed to outwit him."

She said, "He's determined that I won't find out what happened to Madge."

Charles frowned. "You know that and yet you remain here."

"I can't leave now."

He glanced at his wristwatch. "Better go back to your own table. There's someone coming here to meet me and I don't want us to be seen together."

"One of the gang?"

"It doesn't concern you," he said almost angrily. "Go back to your fat old man. And get out of here as soon as you can. A lot of Christopher's crowd come here for cocktails. He might even show up."

293

"That would be something," she said grimly. "I had enough of him last night."

"Sorry to be so abrupt," Charles said. "But you must go. For your own good."

"Very well," she said. She touched a hand on his arm. "You can call me at Wong Lee's when you like."

"I make no promises," Charles said. He gave another nervous glance over his shoulder and apparently seeing no one to worry about he leaned close to her and kissed her. "Now, hurry along."

She smiled and turned and made her way back to the table of Wong Lee. He rose to greet her and they sat down together. She said, "He thinks we shouldn't stay here. It is a gathering spot for some of the smuggling crowd."

"I didn't know," Wong Lee said. "We can leave at once." And he signalled to the waiter to bring their check. He paid it quickly and escorted her out.

They did not begin to talk again until they were in the limousine being driven to the floating restaurant in Aberdeen. Wong Lee was hunched at one end of the seat. He looked her way and said, "That young man has a good face. One would hardly suspect him of being a gangster."

"I know," she agreed.

"He seemed very nervous all the time you were with him."

"He was expecting someone. A member of the gang."

"Ah," Wong Lee said. "He was worried about your safety."

"I would say so."

"Perhaps he will reform one day," Wong Lee suggested.

"I wonder," she said with a sigh. "I think he likes the thrill of criminal life. And not too many of those in that kind of game survive many years."

"Unhappily that is true," the old man said.

She glanced out at the water as they drove along the shore road. "He is angry with me for not going back to London."

"But he knows why you're remaining?"

"He doesn't think it important," she said. "It's something we don't agree on."

"You must decide your own values," the old Chinese said.

She sat back thinking about this. It would be terribly easy for her to have Stephen arrange her passage back to London and forget about Hong Kong. Simply put Madge's mysterious death out of her mind and think no more about it. Yet she knew that after she returned to England the whole business would come back to haunt her. She had ventured too deeply into the macabre happenings to back away from them now.

It was just twilight when they arrived at the floating restaurant. It was crowded with well-dressed men and women and the waiters darted about in an effort to keep the many customers satisfied. Enid was impressed at the number of chic Chinese women in Western evening gowns scattered about the place.

Wong Lee was well known and he was familiar with the menu. He ordered for them and soon their table was covered with some of the most succulent dishes she had been exposed to since coming to Hong Kong. The service was excellent and the wine was first class. She relaxed and enjoyed the evening.

It was after ten o'clock when they left the restaurant to begin the drive home. The parking area was crowded with cars and Wong Lee asked the doorman to go to his chauffeur and advise him they were ready to leave.

He turned to her as they waited. "I hope you were not disappointed with the food."

"Everything was perfect," she said.

Wong Lee smiled happily. "It would be difficult to find fault," he agreed.

Their car came and the drive back to Wong Lee's mansion seemed to take less time than that coming to the restaurant. She relaxed and watched the moon on the water, and the elderly Wong Lee dropped his chin on his chest and slept for most of the ride. When they reached the villa he saw her inside and to her room. She thanked him for a pleasant evening and began to prepare for bed.

It was a measure of how much more relaxed she was under Wong's roof that she was able to go to sleep almost at once. Nor did she have troublesome nightmares as she almost invariably had at the Porter mansion. But her uneventful sleep was to be rudely interrupted in a manner completely shocking.

She came partially awake to the distant sound of glass breaking. And before she could become fully alert someone stuffed a sweet-smelling rag over her mouth and nose and held it there. She now knew she was in the midst of a catastrophe and she struggled fiercely to try to escape the nauseous rag which was making it impossible for her to breathe.

She couldn't! And with mounting panic she knew that she was growing weaker, succumbing to the sweet smell which she was involuntarily forced to inhale. Her weakness became so pronounced that she decided it wasn't worth fighting back. And as she reached this decision her mind blacked out.

It was much later. She didn't know how much later but she somehow sensed that hours must have passed. She awoke to the blackness and stench of what seemed a dungeon. She groaned from the aching of her head and the nausea she was experiencing. After the first awful feelings passed she tried to take some measure of where she was.

She sat up and balanced herself with her hands. Her hands were touching a hard, dirt floor. No light came into this place but she began to see something of her surroundings. She was in a square dungeon with bare walls. There was a rough, wooden door directly in the middle of one of the walls.

So she was a prisoner again. In spite of everything they had found her and captured her. What had happened back at Wong Lee's villa? She remembered the sound of splintering glass and not much else. They had used a chloroform rag to subdue her and it had worked wickedly well. She hoped that they hadn't harmed the old man.

She wondered who had captured her? Was it Christopher or some of the thugs who had been loyal associates of the late Mr. Kamasato. How had they found out about her being at Wong Lee's? Few people knew about it. And with a dull sensation of pain she recalled that she had told Charles where she was staying. Could he have betrayed her? Not likely since he had rescued her last time. But what if they had tortured the information out of him?

She braced herself and got to her feet. She stood there weaving a little drunkenly. She was still clad only in the nightgown which she'd been wearing when they captured her. The thought of being exposed to her captors in this sheer gown made her wince.

There was a sound. A key was turning in the door and then it was thrown open and a familiar figure came striding in—the apelike little Ben Larsen.

"Well, my pretty," the boatman said, "you're my guest again. And this is the best room I can offer you." He chuckled.

"You'd best set me free," she told him. "The police will be after you."

"Will they, now?" Ben Larsen mocked her. "Well, we won't worry too much about that since we're in a cellar they're not all that liable to find."

She gripped her arms around her. "I'm cold! It's freezing down here."

"You ain't dressed for it," the little man jeered at her. "If you're very nice to old Ben I can maybe get you some food and some clothing to wear over that nightie."

"I have always been pleasant to you," she told him.

"So you have," the little man said with a grin on his ape face. "But you were cruel to Kamasato. Right cruel. He's gone to join his ancestors thanks to you and that girl with half a face."

"Yun killed him because he'd ruined her beauty," Enid said.

"She did it to rescue you. She and Gentleman Charlie. Well, you've neither of them to help you now," Ben Larsen warned her. "And you don't have a hope of getting out of this place."

"Must you talk so much?" she cried. "I told you I was cold."

"Sorry, my lady," the little man said mockingly. "Come along with your humble servant."

He led her out of the dungeon and down a short corridor with brick walls. They came to another room lighted by an oil lamp on a shelf. Hanging on a rack were some filthy-looking clothes. The little man took down a Chinese-type coat from the rack and threw it at her.

"Wear that over your nightie," he said. "It will keep you warm enough."

She lifted it up with distaste. "It's filthy!"

"Sorry," the little man grinned, showing yellow teeth. "The dry cleaning shop is closed for the day."

She put the coat on, preferring its warmth and covering to standing shivering in her sheer nightgown. She at once felt the benefit of it.

She asked Ben, "Who is behind my kidnapping this time?"

He gave her a wink. "Guess?"

"Christopher?"

"Who else," Ben said gleefully. "He's got an extra debt to settle with you now. His grandfather has warned him never to show himself near the house again."

"That is his own fault," she said.

"Christopher doesn't see it that way," Ben told her. "But you'll hear it from him personal like. He'll be coming by to see you in a little while."

She asked the little man, "How much to let me go?"

"You tried that last time," he said scornfully. "And it didn't work then and it won't work now."

"You said you were going to give me something to eat," she reminded him. "I could do with a strong cup of tea. My head is aching badly."

"Now that's a shame," Ben Larsen taunted her. "I'll call in the cook and her assistants. I'm not alone here, you see. So don't get any ideas of trying to eliminate me and escaping. You never will make it. I've got lots of helpers down here."

"I thought you were my only jailer," she said unhappily.

"It's time you met the others," Ben said. And he went out into the corridor and shouted out something in Chinese. Then he came back to her and stood waiting and grinning.

There was a murmuring in Chinese, a mixture of several voices. Then the sound of shuffling feet coming nearer to the room where she and the little boatman stood facing each other. Suddenly an incredibly ugly face thrust itself into the room. It was the face of a stout Chinese woman literally covered with evil-looking black warts.

Ben Larsen motioned to the stout woman to enter. "That's our cook, the warty wonder. Not too bright, mind you. But good enough for down here."

The stout woman had on a black outfit and she came into the room and stared at Enid with undisguised curiosity. A moment later a thin little man with a black patch over his eye followed the woman in and he also came to gaze at Enid with awe.

"That's our Harry One-Eye," Ben said with delight. "He's been in prison and the looney bin a few times. He likes to choke pretty young women like you and we have him here just to keep his one eye on you."

She turned away to avoid the stares and grimacing of the two Chinese as they gabbled about her in their native tongue. Then a third figure appeared, a short, squat, incredibly hairy creature. You could barely see his features because of his long black hair and straggly black beard. He joined the others in talking, gesticulating, and pointing at her.

Ben said, "We call him the Spider. Looks like one, don't he? Not right in the head but he's able to run errands and the like for us. I think he'd like to get those hairy hands of his on you, Miss." The little man guffawed.

The trio, the Warty Wonder, Harry One-Eye, and the Spider, were now chattering about her in Chinese and laughing. She had the certain feeling that they were not saying anything good.

"We run a neat little place here," Ben Larsen boasted. "Right in the middle of the city but down deep enough so we don't have to worry." He barked out some order in Chinese to the stout woman. The Warty Wonder shuffled off and down the corridor.

She said, "When will Christopher be here?"

"Sooner or later," the boatman said. "Meanwhile you have the benefit of our hospitality. The Dorchester House was never up to us." And he laughed at his own joke.

There was a stool by the wooden table with the lamp on it. She went over and huddled miserably on it. The thin face of One-Eyed Harry showed a greedy leer and the Spider's eyes were visible in his hairy face, following her with a gleam of madness in them. She decided forlornly that she was worse off this time than she had been before.

But she had one thing in her favor. If the little man had spoken honestly she was a captive somewhere in a cellar in the center of Hong Kong. Before she had been on an island a long distance away. Perhaps she was better off in this wretched place here than to be in luxurious surroundings in far-off Macao.

The Warty Wonder came shuffling back with a sullen look on her wart-covered face. She slammed a bowl of brownish soup on the table in front of Enid, without offering her a spoon or anything else to eat it with.

Ben Larsen chuckled and told her, "Drink it, Miss. There's nothing wrong with it. Same fare as we have for ourselves. No class system here."

Desperate for something in her stomach she lifted the bowl and sipped the soup. It tasted much better than it looked and she quickly drank it with Ben and the three weird Chinese observing her. They made gobbling sounds among themselves, shrieked with laughter and enjoyed their mocking of her.

She finished the soup and put the bowl down. Pushing back strands of hair from her face, she asked, "What now?"

"We wait," Ben told her.

"For what?"

"For him."

"Christopher?"

"He'll be along soon," Ben assured her. "And don't you fret, love. He'll have a plan. He always does."

"What fools you are to think you can get away with this!" she said with bitter scorn.

"I don't know, Miss," Ben said. "We're not alone, you know. We've got a regular chain of those helping us. We know what the police are going to do before they do it."

She rested her head on her arms and closed her eyes, ignoring him and the Chinese trio. After a little she heard them leave the room and its door slammed shut. She was alone again but at least she had a lamp and a stool to sit on. She lowered her head again and tried to rest for whatever was ahead. Surprisingly she fell into a light sleep.

She was awakened by the sound of the door opening. She sat up with a start, fear registering on her pretty face. It was Christopher and he was alone. He entered the room and closed the door behind him. He looked as dapper as ever, yet she thought there was the hint of gauntness behind his cool facade. He was wearing a neat brown suit and matching cravat.

He stood staring at her with grim satisfaction. He said, "You don't know how much pleasure it gives me, seeing you here like this."

She remained on the stool and pulled the Chinese coat more tightly around her and brushed back her strands of tangled hair. "I'm sure it seems a great victory," she said with a cold dignity.

"It is a victory," he told her. "I can't think of it otherwise. You managed to get me in trouble in Macao and then with Edmund Porter. I insist on paying you back."

"Whatever happened was your own fault."

"You have neither Madge's looks nor her good sense," Christopher snapped.

"And where is Madge?"

It was his turn to smile nastily. "That's something you'll never know."

"I can guess," she said. "You murdered her."

"Keep on guessing," he jeered.

"How do you think all this will end?" she asked.

"Not with a romantic scene and you in Charlie Milano's arms," Christopher taunted her. "Nothing like that, though I know it's what you want."

"Charles Milano may be a criminal but he could never sink as low as you," she told him.

Christopher looked grim. "It suited him to rescue you. He was playing his own game and you fitted in it. He'll have to settle accounts the same as you."

"You seem to think you're the only one who won't pay for your actions," she told him.

"Stephen didn't do much for you," he taunted.

"I didn't expect much," she said.

"You think old Edmund won't forgive me. But you're wrong."

"I don't care," she said. "I wish you'd go away and leave me alone."

"Don't think your company is any treat," he told her. "I'm holding you here tonight and then we're moving on."

"Where?"

"Macao. I can deal better with you there."

"It didn't work too well last time," she reminded him.

"Because I treated you too kindly," Christopher said. "This time it will be different."

She said, "I don't suppose there's any use in appealing to you."

"Too late for that."

"It always was," she said.

"I wouldn't say that," he told her. "If you'd not kept prying and questioning what had happened to Madge there would have been no trouble. You brought this all on your-self."

"I did what I had to do," she said evenly. "If you hadn't destroyed Madge you wouldn't have had to cover up for your evil."

He said, "We'll have plenty of time to discuss that in Macao." And with that veiled threat he went on out and slammed the door and locked it.

She was left alone in the fetid room. The lamp was smelly and gave off acrid oil smoke. The air had a peculiar dampness in it which made her wonder if she might be somewhere down by the docks. There were many ancient warehouses there, the Porter and Lee properties among them. Perhaps Christopher was using the celler of one of the warehouses as his hideout.

His visit left her in a restless mood. She began to pace up and down. She'd been at this for a while when she heard the key turn in the door lock and the bantam Ben Larsen came in again with a grin on his apeish countenance.

"Mr. Christopher came to see you, Miss."

She halted and said, "You know that."

"Cheered you up proper, I hope," the little man said.

"Why don't you let me alone?" she demanded.

"Boss has give me my orders," Ben told her. "I'm to look in on you regular to be sure you're all right. He wouldn't want you to do yourself in, or anything like that."

"Not when he has his own torture in mind," Enid said bitterly.

"Macao won't be so bad, Miss. Not after you get used to it," Ben assured her. And he took a package of cigarettes from his pocket and lit one with a lighter he'd produced from the same pocket.

It was the lighter which caught her eye. Impulsively she leapt forward and somehow got the lighter from the startled little man. He took a step back and this time produced a nasty looking automatic from his other pocket. He held this on her and said, "No more tricks!"

She stood there in a shocked state. "Sorry," she said. "It was the lighter made me do it."

The little man kept his distance, looking at her with slit eyes. "None of your stories."

302

"I mean it," she said. "This gold lighter. It belonged to my sister, Madge. Her name is engraved on it. How did you come by it?"

Ben Larsen eyed her uneasily. He said, "It's no business of yours. She gave it to me."

"I don't believe you."

"And I don't care!" the little man said nastily.

"I say you stole it from her," Enid said, still holding the lighter.

"What difference does it make?"

"Is she alive or dead?" Enid pleaded. "I must know. Please tell me!"

"Ask *him*," Ben Larsen said, moving his weight from one foot to the other and keeping his eyes and the gun fixed on her.

She stood there with her hands partially raised and the lighter in the right one. It came to her that this was her moment to make the supreme effort. She might wind up shot and killed, but better that than to meekly submit to all that was happening to her. And if she could somehow grapple with the little man there was a chance she might get her hands on the gun. With it she would have at least a fighting chance to save herself.

Ben Larsen must have read her thoughts for he became more uneasy and he began to slowly edge his way out of the room, moving back an inch or two at a time and keeping the gun on her. She watched him retreat, seeing her only hope slowly fading, and made up her mind.

She pounced forward and pounded the lighter into his face. He shouted and as she grappled with him he fired the gun. The bullet went wild and she continued to struggle with him. Her desperation gave her strength she had not known before. But Ben was a wiry opponent and she knew that if the battle between them went on long she would be the one to lose.

As they weaved about she contrived to trip him and they fell to the floor with her on top of him. In the same instant the gun went off again. She fully expected to feel the impact of the bullet and meet her death. But instead the little man under her shuddered weirdly and then all his resistance ebbed. He lay still.

She stared down at his still figure not able to quite take in what had happened. Instinctively she groped for the gun which his hand had released and which was now a foot from him on the floor. As she picked it up she saw that there was a wound in his side and blood was flowing from it in a frightening fashion.

But she knew she had no time for pity or concern. Her only concern had to be for her own life. There was the Chinese trio to contend with and she did not know whether they were armed or not. With the gun in her hand she opened the door and came upon them standing with a frightened air in the corridor. She brandished the gun and they turned and fled.

Apparently they were stupid fools rather than hardened knaves. She remembered this was the manner in which the fallen Ben had treated them. She ran along the corridor after them and came to a rickety ladder. She thought about it for a fleeting second and then began to climb the ladder. It swayed ominously when she was part way up but she forced herself to go on.

At the top she groped up with her hand to find a trap door. She shoved up with all her might and the heavy door gave enough for her to advance up the ladder and finally pull herself through the narrow opening out onto the floor of what seemed to be a room filled with wooden cartons and smelling strongly of tea. She lay there gasping for a moment, a sorry figure in her nightgown with the filthy robe over it and both stained with Ben Larsen's blood.

Then she struggled to her feet and thrust the gun in the pocket of the robe. She made her way to a door and opened it, finding herself in a dark hallway. She slowly walked along the hall not able to think clearly, not able to do anything but keep groping on for freedom. That was her one thought. Somehow to escape!

She came to the end of the hall and there was another door. She tried it and it wouldn't open. All her torment and frustration came to a head. She began to sob aloud and she pounded on the door with both fists.

"Open! Please open!" she cried, as she made her desperate assault on the door panels.

She gave up and leaned against the wall in despair. Then she thought she heard voices on the other side of the door. It gave her a final bit of strength. She pounded on the door once more and cried, "Please, let me out!"

twenty-three

The door suddenly opened to reveal a startled blond man in a khaki coat surrounded by a half-dozen Chinese men in work clothes. Behind them she saw a large room with tea packing equipment. She had been right in her assumption that Christopher had been using one of the warehouse cellars.

The middle-aged man came to her and said, "My dear young lady, how did you get out there?"

She looked at him with gazed eyes. "Call the police! Inspector Sullivan!"

"Yes," he said. "Of course. But first you must come along with me. Let me make you more comfortable."

"Thank you," she said, weakly. And she allowed him to offer her support and take her into the big packing room.

He did not halt there but took her on to a small office and saw her safely seated in a chair. Then he poured her a cup of black tea from a pot sitting on an electric burner. As he offered her the tea he regarded the blood on her weird combination of clothing with shocked eyes.

He said, "Here. This may be of some help. I wish I had a spot of whiskey instead."

"Thank you," she said.

He sat at the desk opposite her and reached for the phone. "Shall I tell the police who you are?" he asked.

"Enid Branch," she said. "Get Inspector Sullivan. He'll know." And she sipped some of the tea and tried to control the trembling which had finally taken hold of her. The impact of what she'd been through was now having its effect on her.

The man was speaking into the phone. "This is Thomas Cullen of Porter and Lee. A young woman has just appeared from an unused portion of our harbor warehouse. She is in a very upset state and asks for Inspector Sullivan. Her name is Enid Branch."

She sat back in her chair and closed her eyes. She vaguely heard the conversation continue with occasional pauses. After what seemed a long while the troubled Thomas Cullen put down the phone.

He told her, "I finally managed to contact Inspector Sullivan. He is on his way here now."

Enid opened her eyes. "You're very kind," she said.

"Not at all," the foreman said. "I couldn't believe there was anyone on the other side of that door. We haven't used that portion of the warehouse for several years now."

She said, "I was kidnapped and held a prisoner in the cellar down there. I managed to escape and found my way up to that door."

"Remarkable!" Thomas Cullen said seriously. "Do you know there is blood on your clothing?"

"Yes. I had a scuffle with my captor. A gun went off and he was either badly wounded or killed." She reached in her pocket and produced the gun. "There's the weapon."

The warehouse foreman eyed it uneasily and made no attempt to touch it. "Dear me!" he gasped. "Well, don't you worry. The Inspector should be here shortly."

"Yes," she said in a dull tone.

"If you will excuse me," Tom Cullen said, rising. "I want to explain the situation to my workers and get them back on the job. I'll return in a few minutes."

She nodded without speaking. Her trembling was easing a bit but she was still in a badly upset state. It was hard to believe that within the last few hours she'd endured another ordeal and only by a lucky chance was not still Christopher's prisoner.

There had been no Charles Milano to help her this last time. She'd had to battle through by herself. Now she began to worry about the elderly Wong Lee and what might have happened at his villa when the thugs came to take her. She

307

was deep in this reverie when she heard voices in the hall outside with Inspector Sullivan's crisp tone prominent enough for her to pick out.

Thomas Cullen returned with Inspector Sullivan and two Chinese police in uniform following him. The Inspector came to her and said, "I thought you were really done for this time."

"So did I," she said.

"Are you all right?" he asked.

"I think so."

"That blood?" he asked, pointing to her clothing.

"Not mine. Ben Larsen's. Christopher had him keeping guard on me in the warehouse cellar. There was a struggle. His gun went off. I don't know whether he's dead or not."

The Inspector turned to the two policeman and told them, "Search the cellar. See about the man down there."

"There may be others still down there," she warned.

"Be ready for trouble," the Inspector warned his two men. And he told Thomas Cullen, "You show them the way to the closed-off section and the cellar."

The foreman nodded and went out with the Chinese policemen on his heels. The Inspector sank down in the chair on the other side of the desk and looked at her glumly.

He said, "Your stay with Wong Lee didn't work out that well."

"Not your fault."

"I was hoping your stay there would solve our problems. I should have known better," the Inspector said. "I ought to have kept men on guard there."

"What about Wong Lee? Was he hurt?"

"They knocked him down and locked him in his room," the Inspector said. "But he wasn't really injured. One of his servants was. Had a knife plunged between his shoulders. But he will recover."

"Thank goodness," she said.

"The old man is very upset," Inspector Sullivan went on. "He blames himself for not having kept a lookout. Not that I think it would have made much difference. How did they get you out of there?"

"Chloroformed me before I could put up a struggle."

He sighed. "Christopher again?"

308

"Yes."

"Feel well enough to give me the details as you remember them?" He took out his notebook.

"There isn't that much to tell," she said. And she offered all that she was able to remember of the grim night.

She'd barely finished her account when a distressed Thomas Cullen returned with the word, "That man down there is dead. And the officers are still searching to see if there is anyone else in hiding."

The Inspector gave her a meaningful look. "Well, that is the end of Ben Larsen."

"The gun went off accidentally," she said.

"I don't think anyone will worry about that," the Inspector said. "Is there anything else you want to tell me?"

"Yes," she said. "Ben Larsen had a gold cigarette lighter which had belonged to my sister. I don't know how he got it."

"It should be down there?"

"Yes," she said.

"We'll have to get you out of here," the Inspector said, rising. "You'll feel better after you've had a shower and a change of clothing. Where do you want to go?"

"Porter House," she said. "I'm as safe there as any place, it seems."

The door of the office opened again and this time it was Stephen Porter who came striding in. He saw her and registered shock. "What have they done to you?" he asked.

"I'm all right," she said rising. "Though not exactly dressed for a fashion show."

Stephen turned to Thomas Cullen and said, "Am I to understand that Christopher has been using the abandoned warehouse and cellar as a gang headquarters?"

The middle-aged man looked frightened. "I don't know, sir. He did hold this young lady captive down there. Whether he has made use of the area before, I can't say."

"I should have suspected he would use that warehouse. It is convenient to the center of the city. There are a lot of questions I'll want answered." His tone was grim.

Inspector Sullivan said, "I think this young woman ought to be taken away from here at once."

Stephen said, "I'll take care of her. I'll drive her home. I have my car outside."

"Your business?" she said.

"I have no business as important as your welfare," he said, his handsome face in shadow.

She rose and prepared to leave with him. She told Thomas Cullen, "Thank you for your help."

"Glad I was here," the foreman said nervously.

To the Inspector she said, "You will look for the cigarette lighter. It's gold with my sister's name on it."

"Yes," Inspector Sullivan promised. "And I'll be out to see you either late this afternoon or early this evening."

With this promise to encourage her she left with Stephen. He helped her into the front passenger seat of the small car he was driving and then got behind the wheel as he explained, "I use this for personal errands. It isn't as comfortable as the big car."

"It will do well enough," she said.

He started the car and they drove along the cobblestone harbor street. He said, "You can imagine my surprise when I found out you were actually a prisoner in one of our own buildings."

"I knew I was somewhere near the harbor and thought about the warehouses."

"Christopher knew the warehouse wasn't in use and he had keys to it," Stephen said bitterly. "I should have thought of it before."

"You didn't because it was so obvious."

"True," he said, as he headed the car along one of the wider streets in the new section of the city which had little of the Oriental about it. "We were wakened in the middle of the night with the news that you'd been kidnapped again."

"It was long after midnight that it happened," she said.

"Of course we all were upset. Particularly my grandfather. He was concerned about Wong Lee as well. We were relieved to learn he wasn't badly hurt."

"I worried about him also," she said.

"We realized it had to be Christopher," the young man at the wheel went on bitterly. "And with the police involved we realized it could only make things worse than ever. Mostly we feared he'd somehow get you off the island and over to Macao again."

"He was planning that," she agreed. "But he couldn't line up transportation until tonight. That alone saved me or I'd likely be on the way there now."

"Lucky break," Stephen said. They were leaving the city now and driving along the broad highway. "You'll feel better after you've had a chance to wash up and put on decent clothes."

"Ben Larsen gave me this Chinese coat. I had no idea then he'd be dead within a few minutes."

"He brought it on himself. He was bound to die violently."

"I know," she said. "But I wish I hadn't been there when it happened."

Stephen said, "The way I see it, if he hadn't put the bullet in himself he might have shot you."

She sat back against the seat with a sigh as the tropical beauty of the islands flashed by their car windows. It seemed odd that such a paradise could hold so much menace and danger.

She said, "I don't think I'd have had the quarrel with him if he hadn't brought out a lighter which had belonged to Madge."

He gave her a brief, sharp glance. "The gold lighter I gave her before we were married?"

"Yes. It didn't turn up among her things. And when I saw him with it I recognized it at once."

"How did he get his hands on it?"

She said, "My guess is he either stole it from her or she gave it to him in exchange for drugs."

"You're saying she's still alive."

"I have kept on saying it," she said. "Seeing the lighter convinced me more than ever."

The man at the wheel said, "I don't agree. However much Christopher gained power over her she would not have left me as she did."

"You were quarreling."

"About his interference," Stephen said angrily. "He set out to take Madge from me the moment she arrived here. He did confuse her but I think she drowned that afternoon in the bay."

311

She said, "Considering the alternative I now almost wish she had."

"What did Christopher say to you?"

"The usual threats. He intended that I should go to Macao. I don't know what his plans were for me after that."

"You can be sure they wouldn't be pleasant."

She said, "He also said something rather strange. He told me not to count on your grandfather withdrawing his support of him, that he still had the old man to depend on."

"Pure bluff!"

"He sounded so sure of himself."

"Part of his game to terrorize you," the young man at the wheel said. "Don't forget it was grandfather who sent him on his way the other night."

"I haven't forgotten," she said.

"Grandfather is sick and old," Stephen went on. "And for that reason he was too easy with Christopher. But that is all changed. He knows he made a mistake and he will make no more."

Enid sighed as they turned into the driveway of Porter House and the car finally came to a halt by the golden dragons guarding the entrance. She said, "I'm sorry to be bothering you again. You must be anxious to see the last of me."

Stephen looked at her with deep sincerity and said, "I wish you would always remain here. You know that." And then he got out from behind the wheel and opened the car door for her.

Eleanor was in the foyer to greet her. The hawk face of the older woman paled as she saw the blood on Enid's nightgown and the Chinese coat. She gasped, "What did they do to you?"

She looked down at the stains grimly and said, "That is Ben Larsen's blood. The gun he had went off in a struggle between us and he killed himself."

"Ben Larsen's blood!" the older woman echoed her and gazed at the stains again in a stunned fashion.

"Don't dwell on it, Mother," Stephen angrily rebuked her.

Eleanor quickly regained her usual cold demeanor as she snapped, "I can only say some good came of the fracas. That Ben Larsen was always a menace."

Enid said, "I think I'll go straight to my room."

Eleanor nodded. "Do you have everything you need? Wong Lee has promised to send your things over here. But they have not arrived as yet."

"I only packed a few items when I went to visit him," she said. "I have most of my things upstairs."

Stephen accompanied her to the stairs. "Do you feel like going up alone? Mother can go with you or send one of the servants."

"I'm fine now," she assured him. "Thank you for deserting your office."

"I'll go back now," he said. "I want to check out that cellar and what's been going on down there."

Enid went upstairs and enjoyed the luxury of a long, warm bath. She deposited the filthy Chinese coat in a hamper used for waste materials, to be burned later, and her nightgown went in the basket for wash. She changed into fresh clothing and for the first time felt more like her old self.

But she was exhausted, so she drew the shades and stretched out on the bed to rest. She slept right through the afternoon. It was a knock on her door which awakened her and when she sat up and invited whoever it was to enter, the door opened and Sonya Chen came in.

Her usual chic self in a blue and silver gown with a high collar, the lovely girl came over and sat on the bed beside her. "We were so worried about you," Sonya said.

She grimaced. "That must be becoming a habit since I'm almost always in trouble."

"To think that Christopher would invade Wong Lee's home," Sonya Chen said angrily.

"Not even I expected that."

"And the poor old man could have been killed," the girl pointed out.

Enid said, "I ought not to have gone there. I placed him in danger by doing so."

"It was at his wish that you were there," Sonya said. "He underestimated the depth of Christopher's villainy. I think we are all guilty of that."

Enid said, "Still, I have the feeling it will all end soon. I thought him haggard when he came to see me this morning."

"The police should try a little harder. He should not be all that difficult to catch," Sonya said.

313

"I think the noose is closing on him. Inspector Sullivan is efficient. He lost no time coming for me today. And he has promised to visit me here this evening."

Sonya stood up. "I don't know where you found the courage to make your escape."

"When things are desperate enough you discover new sources of strength," Enid told her.

The girl left and Enid got up and dressed for cocktails and dinner. And when she went downstairs she was delighted to find Wong Lee on the patio with the others waiting to greet her.

"Two barrels of tears do not heal a bruise," he exclaimed. "How can I tell you my shame and sorrow that you should come to harm while my guest?"

She smiled at him. "It was much more my fault than yours. I brought the danger to you."

"And I failed to protect you," the stout old man lamented.

"It is over and we are both alive," she said. "I think we should put it behind us."

"You are too kind," Wong Lee said. "I have brought your luggage back here. But I hasten to add that you will be my welcome guest at any time you so desire."

"I appreciate that," she said. "Because I know you mean it."

She went over to old Edmund Porter who sat huddled in an easy chair with Sonya on one side of him and Eleanor standing on the other. The patriarch of the Porter family seemed thinner and more pale than she had ever seen him. It was clear that Christopher's vicious behaviour was taking its toll of him.

She paused before the old man and said, "You mustn't worry so, Mr. Porter."

He gazed up at her and lifted a thin, palsied hand in a gesture of despair. "What can I say?"

"You need say nothing," she said. "I understand your feelings. And I'm already indebted to you."

"You are a most considerate young woman," he said. "My family have brought you nothing but pain. Yet you can extend the hand of forgiveness."

"I cannot blame all of you for Christopher's acts," she said.

Stephen came to her with a drink. He said, "Take this. It will do you good."

She thanked him and sipped the drink. It seemed incredible that she should be here in this cool, screened patio surrounded by elegance and people who were good friends. Only a few hours ago she'd been a prisoner in that vile dungeon with Christopher taunting her.

At dinner she sat next to Wong Lee and as usual enjoyed the old man's conversation. During the course of the meal he told her a story about China in the second century.

Wong Lee said, "At Linhuai, a silk merchant was carrying a piece of waterproof silk to the city for sale. There came a rain and he spread it over his head for shelter, and soon another man came to stand under it. When the rain had stopped both of them claimed that the silk was his own. The Chief Minister Hsueh Hsuan said, "This piece of waterproof silk is only worth several hundred cash. Why fight over it?" Thereupon he cut it in two and gave each a half. As he continued to watch them, he saw the owner was protesting that he had been wronged, while the other man seemed self-satisfied. And so he knew to which one the silk rightfully belonged, and the other man was found guilty and punished."

"That is a fascinating little fable," she told him.

"And it has an important point," he told her. "We must not always accept people's words for what they believe and what they are. We must judge them by their actions."

Enid had an idea he was slowly leading up to some comment on her present plight in his own fashion. But she was not able to question him further as Stephen at once began to talk about the warehouse cellar and how Christopher had converted it into a gangster's stronghold.

"The Inspector's men found a hidden cache of stolen goods there," Stephen said indignantly. "It seems that Christopher must be associated with all the criminal triads in Hong Kong."

Eleanor said vindictively, "At least that Ben Larsen has paid for his misdeeds. Maybe Christopher will soon pay for his."

Old Edmund Porter glared at her from the head of the table and said, "You are not his judge!"

Enid was startled by the old man's stern words. And she

315

saw that the others at the table reacted in the same way. She could not help thinking of Christopher so defiantly telling her that the old man would continue to support him. Was it true?

After they left the dinner table they broke up into groups. Wong Lee and Enid strolled out on the lawn, while Edmund Porter went up to his room. Sonya and Stephen sat on the patio talking. Eleanor had vanished in the rear of the house to take up some problem with the servants.

Wong Lee halted as they reached the gilt-domed teahouse. He asked her, "Do you still have strange feelings about this bit of old China?"

She stared at the richly decorated teahouse and sighed. "I find myself depressed, just standing here. I wonder why."

"There must be a reason," the old man said. "I'm sure one of your Western psychiatrists could explain it."

"I'm certain I don't know," she said. "It's supposed to be a happy place, a spot to relax in and enjoy oneself."

"It was that at the start," Wong Lee agreed. "But the tragedies which overtook the family have changed their attitude towards it. I believe Eleanor was seated here when she received the news that her husband was dead. Unhappily she always links the teahouse to her husband's death."

"And in the same way Edmund Porter relates the teahouse to his lost Jade Princess, for whom he built it."

"True," Wong Lee said.

She gave the old Chinese a sharp look. "Did you notice how quickly he reprimanded Eleanor tonight? And came to the defense of Christopher?"

Wong Lee nodded. "But then he does not regard Eleanor as a Porter. He has never been fond of her. He is old and this business of Christopher has confused him a good deal."

"I'm sure it has," she agreed.

A small, black sedan drove up before the entrance. Wong Lee studied it and said, "You have a visitor."

She saw a familiar figure emerge from the car and said, "It's Inspector Sullivan. He promised to come."

"You will wish to see him alone," Wong Lee said at once. "You go on. I will join Stephen and Sonya Chen in the patio."

Enid left the old man and went to meet the Inspector. He came up to her and gave her an admiring look. He said, "No one would guess you were the same bedraggled person I saw in the warehouse office this morning."

"I also feel a lot better," she said.

"I'm sorry to be so late," he said.

"I appreciate your taking the time to drive way out here," she told him.

"My duty to see you," he said. "Where can we talk?"

She hesitated and then said, "What about the teahouse? We will have privacy."

"Good idea," he said and they strolled over to it in the growing twilight. They entered its shadowed interior and sat down together.

He said, "I didn't know old Edmund Porter went in for things Chinese."

"This is the exception," she told the Inspector. "He built the house to remind him of his home in England. And the teahouse was in honor of his Chinese wife."

"The Jade Princess," Inspector Sullivan said in his crisp voice. "She was the first Porter wife to vanish. Your sister was the second."

"With many years in between."

"I suppose so," the Inspector agreed. "You'd call it a long time, and the colony certainly changed much over those years. There are no more hill bandits. The Communists have reformed everyone on the mainland. They tell me crime is almost unknown."

"A poor place for your profession," she said.

"I wouldn't mind retiring in such a society," Inspector Sullivan assured her. "I used to think I wanted to return to England but there is nothing but unrest there now. The last time I went back I was disillusioned."

"It is a different world," she agreed. "But the London of today is the only one I've known. So, to me, it doesn't seem all that bad."

"One of the blessings of youth," Inspector Sullivan said with unexpected gentleness in his tone, "you don't look back."

"That's not completely true," she protested. "I sometimes long for my childhood. Especially since I've been here trying to pick up the threads of what happened to Madge, I've thought a lot about those days."

317

The night was descending upon them and the shadows in the teahouse grew darker. She could barely see the face of the Inspector. And the depression she always knew in the tea house came to bother her once again but she didn't want to burden the Inspector with an account of her neurosis about the place. Bad enough that she'd bored old Wong Lee.

The Inspector said, "I made a through search of the cellar."

"What about the lighter?"

"I'm sorry," he said.

She was upset. "You didn't find it?"

"No."

"But it had to be on the floor. It was what gave me the needed courage to battle with that awful little man. I saw the lighter and recognized it."

"We searched his body and all around the room. No sign of it."

Enid said, "It was gold. One of that unholy three must have seen its glitter and stolen it."

"They had fled before we got there," the Inspector said. "And if they stole the lighter, they took another bit of evidence that Madge might still be alive."

"Yes, I realize that," she said in a tone of dismal frustration.

twenty-four

Inspector Sullivan broke the quiet melancholy of the teahouse by telling her, "That doesn't mean I've lost all belief in your theory."

"Thank you," she said, quietly.

"But my main concern at this time must be with the reality," he went on. "And the reality is that Christopher Porter and the gang he is associated with are a serious threat to the peace of the island."

"Without question."

"So my first efforts must be dedicated to capturing him and upsetting his drug smuggling activities."

"But Madge's fate is tied up in all that," she protested. "It was he who introduced her to drugs."

"We know that," he agreed. "But we don't know that she is still alive or whether he had anything to do with her actual death, if she happens to be dead. Therefore Madge is at the moment of secondary interest to us."

Ruefully she said, "I'm afraid she is still my main interest. And the mystery surrounding her is what Christopher is trying to stop me from penetrating."

"That may be," the detective said. "Our concern now is for your safety. For the balance of your stay here I feel that guards should be posted at the house."

"I'd rather you didn't," she said. "If there is any chance of Madge being alive and presenting herself to me, the guards may spoil it. They'd act as a barrier between her and me."

"They would also act as a barrier to danger for you," the Inspector pointed out.

She gazed off into the darkness. "I would rather take the risk," she told him.

"I'm sorry you feel that way," he said. "I think you are in great danger. I should ignore your wishes and do what I consider best for your safety."

"You won't shatter my last hope of contacting Madge?" she asked plaintively.

Inspector Sullivan was silent for a moment. "I'll give way to your wishes for tonight. But I won't promise to go along with them in future. I have my job to do."

"I'm sure I'll be all right," she told him.

He stood up with a sigh. "I seem to remember having heard talk like that from you before."

She rose also. "This is important to me."

"I'll come back in the morning," he said. "If we haven't captured Christopher by then I'll make some new arrangements. My hope is we may get him tonight. He is said to be seen almost nightly at one of the gambling casinos."

"The chances of his returning here immediately are slim," she said. "He's had two failures in trying to abduct me. I don't think he'll be so anxious to try again."

They walked back to the Inspector's car and he told her, "Feel free to contact me at any hour."

"I will," she said.

"And don't trust anyone," the Inspector went on with a glance towards the house. "I have certain reservations about this family. I won't go into them now but enough to say that power for too long corrupts."

"I think I understand," she said quietly.

The Inspector drove away and she went inside. Eleanor met her in the foyer and asked, "Has that Inspector person left?"

"Yes."

"I don't like him," the older woman said. "He gives you the feeling that he suspects everyone."

"I suppose that is part of his job," Enid said.

"A nasty job! I dislike police generally," Eleanor said in her arrogant fashion. "And his continual showing up here is upsetting to Stephen's grandfather. Why doesn't he concentrate his efforts on trying to arrest Christopher and these crooks he is in league with?"

"I'd say that's exactly what he is doing," Enid said. "But he also has to keep in touch with me."

"Why doesn't he install an officer here to guard you?"

"We discussed that. I don't want a guard."

"Whyever not?" Eleanor wanted to know.

"I have my reasons," she said. "And I assure you they are good ones."

The older woman looked bleak. "I confess I don't understand anything that is going on. Everyone behaving so secretively and making so much of the tiniest happenings." And she turned and started up the stairs with a disgruntled air.

Enid remained standing in the foyer to avoid going upstairs in the older woman's company. Eleanor could be terribly annoying at times. And Enid found her so at this moment. On impulse she stepped outside into the darkness again to enjoy the warm night air and her own thoughts.

She stood gazing up at the stars until a scraping sound from the nearby bushes made her turn in fear. Out of the shadows by the bushes came Charles Milano. The young American held up his hand to beg her silence as he came towards her.

"You!" she gasped.

"Yes," he said in a low voice. "Let's move off into the darkness so we can talk safely."

Her faith in him was such that she did not question this but moved off with him. When they were a distance from the house he halted and said, "I know about last night. I only just found out."

"Your warnings were well founded," she told him, a tremor in her voice.

He took her by the upper arms and gazed at her earnestly as they stood there in the darkness. "I don't know what I'd do if anything happened to you." And then he drew her close to him for a long kiss.

She wanted to be in his arms and yet she knew that he was allied with everything she was opposed to. He was part of the same drug-smuggling ring as Christopher and criminally just as guilty. How could she condemn one and forgive the other,

321

even though it was what she wanted to do. She pulled away from his embrace and gazed up at him with frightened eyes.

"This is all wrong!" she protested.

"I disagree," the young American said. "I saved you from Christopher once and now I'm here to protect you."

"I'd rather you left here and gave up being one of them."

"Don't try to interfere with my life style," he said. "You either care for me or you don't."

"There's more to it than that," she told him unhappily.

"There oughtn't to be."

"How can I make you understand?"

He said, "Don't bother trying. Whether you appreciate it or not I'm going to see you are safe from now on. I'm going to be near to protect you."

"You'll be arrested," she warned him. "The police were just here."

"I saw the Inspector," Charles said. "He doesn't bother me. Since he hasn't chosen to guard you I'll do the job. You know Christopher will be back."

"You are better acquainted with his plans than I am," she said.

"We're not that friendly anymore, but I know him well enough to be sure he means to square accounts with you. That can only be bad news."

"I'm used to it."

"Don't tell anyone you've seen me," Charles went on. "And remember I'll be nearby."

"Leave Hong Kong!" she begged him.

"People have been asking you to do the same thing and you have refused."

"I've a good reason for staying," she said.

"So have I," he told her.

At that moment the front door of the old mansion opened and Stephen appeared in the doorway. Charles did not wait but hurried off into the darkness at once leaving her standing there alone. She turned and walked back towards Stephen.

He stared at her in consternation. "You shouldn't be out here alone!"

She tried to appear casual. "I only went a few steps from the door."

"You oughtn't to be out here alone at all," the handsome

Stephen said irritably. "You seem to like placing yourself in danger."

"Sorry," she said.

They went inside and Stephen shut the door and locked it. He told her, "I was checking for the night before I went upstairs. I hadn't any idea I would find you out there."

"I wanted some fresh air."

"Why didn't you find me?" he said. "I'd have been glad to take a stroll with you."

"Wouldn't it be just as dangerous for us both?" she asked. "If Christopher returns it's not likely he'll come alone."

Stephen frowned. "I don't even like to think about it."

"I'm sleepy now," she said. "I'm going upstairs to bed."

"I'll see you to your door," Stephen said firmly.

She gave him a small smile. "You're not going to risk my changing my mind."

"No," he said. "You're entirely too apt to give in to some other impulse."

He escorted her up the stairs and to the door of her room. They said goodnight and she went inside. She had been afraid for a moment that he had seen her talking to Charles Milano. But she decided she was wrong. He hadn't. For that she was grateful.

The night was unusually hot and humid so she decided to take another shower before going to bed. After her shower she spent an unusually long while placing lotion on her body and face. Following the ordeal of the previous night it was a luxury which she enjoyed. It was after midnight before she put out the lights and slipped between the sheets of the big bed.

Then the heat and her general nervous state served to keep her awake. She lay there staring up into the darkness thinking about any number of things. What had become a new concern was her mixed feelings towards Charles Milano. She was sure the unrepentant Charles was just as closely wedded to his career of crime as Christopher. The only difference was that Charles was in love with her.

Was she in love with him? The question tormented her. She knew she cared more for him than any man she had known before. But did she care enough to forgive him the criminal career which might have played a large part in ruining the lives of Madge and countless others? The idea of being the mate of such a man was repugnant to her.

And yet he was somewhere out there in the darkness being completely loyal to her. She could not ignore that, much as she might want to. It was a story as old as the history of romance—lovers on opposite sides, unable to ignore their passion for each other though faced with a barrier which threatened their happiness.

She knew that very soon she would have to make a decision, and at this moment she knew she wasn't prepared to do this. She could only pray that Charles would give up his evil life and go somewhere distant from Hong Kong for a new beginning. Maybe then she would go to him one day.

Suddenly the stillness of the night was broken by a woman's cry. It came from the area of the lawn. Enid sat up in bed with fright flooding across her lovely face for she thought she had recognized the voice which had uttered this angry cry.

Leaping out of bed she hurried to the window and looked out. She saw a female figure crossing the lawn. And in the teahouse there was a faint light glowing and someone was standing there by the light. As she watched with fascinated eyes she saw the female figure step up into the teahouse and move to whoever it was there.

Enid could stand it no longer. She found her dressing gown and slippers and against all the advice she had been given silently made her way out into the hall and down the stairs. Only a tiny night light served to illuminate the foyer. The old mansion had a silent, ghostly air.

She slowly opened the front door, slipped out, and started across the lawn in the direction of the teahouse. By the time she'd covered half the distance she could hear an exchange of angry voices—those of a woman and an old man. She kept crouched down so as not to be seen. At the same time she strained to see who was having the bitter argument in the teahouse.

Moving a few yards closer she had her first view of the two and it gave her a stunning shock. She had been right. Madge was alive! But a very different Madge from the sister she had known. This was a fragile, emaciated Madge, hollow-eyed and with most of her beauty gone. The man she

324

was having the grim argument with was none other than Edmund Porter. Stephen's grandfather!

The old man was fully dressed and livid with rage as he pointed a threatening, palsied finger at Madge. She made some scornful remark and pushed his hand aside. The old man took a step back and hesitated as if making some dread decision. Enid could see the panic-stricken expression on the pale, old face. Without warning his other hand raised in the air and she saw the glitter of a knife in it.

Madge cried out but it was a useless protest. The old man plunged the knife into her chest. Plunged it all the way to the hilt! Then he stumbled back and watched the unhappy Madge. Madge groped for the knife with her hands as if she were going to make an attempt to extract it, then a glazed look came over her face and she slumped down on the floor of the teahouse.

Enid was on her knees on the grass now watching the grim charade. The incident had happened far too quickly for her to do anything. She knelt there with her knuckles pressed against her mouth to subdue her sobbing. She knew the old man in the teahouse must be mad and if she betrayed her presence to him he would turn on her next.

But she had to do something to try to save Madge. To find her alive after all this ordeal and then lose her to death almost immediately was too much. She watched the old man crouch over Madge's prostrate body and then move the lantern he'd taken out there from the table. Now he was talking aloud to himself, mumbling words which seemed to make no sense. He shoved the table back and bent down and lifted up a trap door.

He stood above the open trap door and lifted up the lantern so he could see down below. Now his gabbling was louder and she could hear the words, "Dear one!," then "Alone." He moaned after this. Then he put the lamp down on the table again and moved over to Madge. She saw what he was about to do—drag Madge's body over and drop it down through the trap door.

If there were any hope of saving Madge she had to act at once, forget her own safety and try to divert the madman in some way.

She raced to the steps of the teahouse and cried, "Stop!"

The old man had already dragged Madge part way to the trap door. He let go of her limp body and wheeled around with a terrified look on his gaunt face.

He saw her and in a madman's voice asked, "What do you want?"

"I want to see my sister," she said.

"Too late," he told her in the rasping monotone which he'd used before.

"No!" she protested. "Please!"

"She's dead!" the old man rasped. "She knew too much and so she had to die. Christopher sent her here to blackmail me. He was wrong."

"She may still be alive," Enid said, edging closer to the madman. "Please let me see if she is still breathing."

"No," he rasped. And he sprang forward with surprising agility and grasped her by the arm. "I mean to put her to rest. And she won't be alone."

Now Enid was faced with the horror of attempting to escape his maniacal grasp. She sobbed, "Please! I mean you no harm!"

The old man lurched over by the trap door opening and dragged her with him. "Look down there."

She glanced down and what she saw gave her another moment of sheer terror. Resting on a funeral bed in regal attire at the bottom of the deep, secret passage was a skeleton figure! A black wig capped the grinning skull and a rich Oriental gown in vibrant colors covered the skeleton. The smell of dusty death wafted up from the grotesque figure.

Enid dragged back. "No!" she screamed in horror.

"My Jade Princess! That is her resting place! Madge knew! So now she joins her," the old madman cackled with insane laughter and the grip on her wrist became more viselike. "And you must go down there, too! You also have learned my secret!"

"Hold it, old Edmund." The voice that came from behind them was familiar. It even caught the old madman's attention, and still keeping his grasp on Enid, he turned to stare at the newcomer. Enid also had a chance to see who it was.

It was a malevolently smiling Christopher who stood on the steps of the teahouse. His gun pointed at them. He sneered at Enid and said, "You haven't done yourself a lot of good this time."

"You!" the old man quavered. "You are a devil! You sent her to blackmail me when you were afraid to come yourself."

"I'm here now, Granduncle Edmund," Christopher went on in his mocking fashion. "And I'm going to do you a favor. I'm going to rid you of another troublesome young woman. And then we'll cover up the bodies and talk money."

"Go away!" The old madman backed away. "No!"

"I'm on your side," Christopher said. "The gun has a silencer. It won't be heard. You'll be safe. The family name will be unstained. You'll give me the money I need and I'll leave Hong Kong."

The old madman hauled her close to him. "I don't trust you!" he rasped at Christopher. "It's another trick!"

"Look!" Christopher said, aiming the gun at Enid as if to fire, but he was destined to get no further.

From the darkness on the other side of the teahouse a gun blazed. The shot rang out loudly and at the same instant Christopher straightened suddenly and the gun he was holding dropped from his hand. His mouth gaped open and he toppled back on the lawn.

Then Charles Milano sprang up from the darkness and climbed over the railing into the teahouse, the gun still in hand. He ordered old Edmund Porter. "Release her or I'll drop you next!"

The old madman hesitated for only a moment. Then with a wild cry he let go of Enid and toppled back into the pit with the skeleton figure of his beloved Jade Princess.

Enid gave a huge sob and fell forward into the arms of Charles. "All right," he consoled her. "It's all right."

"Madge!" she said hoarsely.

Charles gently released her and bent down over the prostrate figure of the stabbed girl. Then he turned to Enid who was kneeling with him. "Sorry," he said. "There's no hope here."

Her eyes blurred with tears and she sobbed violently as he helped her to her feet and guided her across to a place where she could sit. Then he went down to check on Christopher. By that time the entire house was roused. Stephen came across the lawn with a flashlight and a gun in his hand. Close behind him were Sonya Chen and his mother and some of the servants.

Stephen came up to where Charles was bent over Christopher. "What is going on here?" he demanded.

"Bloody murder," Charles said bitterly as he straightened up. "This one is still alive. You'd better call the police. Your grandfather murdered Madge and he fell down into the pit where he hid the body of his murdered wife. I don't know whether he's alive or not."

Stephen stared at him and then at her as she sat there still sobbing uncontrollably. His handsome face showed a blank look. "I don't follow you at all!"

Charles gave him a weary glance. "Call the police," he said. "Inspector Sullivan. Tell him to send an ambulance and a doctor if they want to keep this one alive." He glanced down at Christopher contemptuously.

"I'll call at once," Stephen said and hurried back in the direction of the house.

Charles turned to a pale Sonya Chen and said, "You look after Enid!"

The Chinese girl said, "Of course!" And she at once went to Enid and began to comfort her.

Charles told Eleanor, "The old man is down twenty feet or so in a pit. Get the servants to bring a ladder. I'll find out if he's still alive."

Eleanor was standing staring at him as if she were in a stupor. "Did you say Stephen's grandfather murdered Madge?"

"I did," Charles said abruptly. "If you want proof her body is over there." He nodded to the teahouse behind him.

"But Madge drowned," she gasped.

"We'll talk about that later," he said. "Have one of the servants bring me a ladder."

"Yes," Eleanor said abjectly, all her arrogance gone.

Enid calmed down a little under Sonya's comforting attention. The Chinese girl wisely made no attempt to get her to leave the teahouse but she also restrained her from going over to her sister's dead body.

Charles went to the trap door and waited for the servants to come hurrying back with the ladder. Then he grimly made a descent into the chamber of death beneath the teahouse. He remained down there only a few minutes. By that time Stephen had returned and was standing by the trap door.

He was pale, and trembling. As Charles came up the ladder he asked, "What's the story?"

"Dead," Charles said. "He probably died as soon as he hit the bottom. Heart, I'd say."

Stephen gazed down into the pit. "That skeleton?" he asked tautly.

Charles Milano brushed back some strands of dishevelled hair and gave him a sardonic look. "I thought you knew. That's your grandmother."

They were interrupted by the arrival of the police car and the ambulance. Stretcher bearers and the doctor hurried across the lawn to find Christopher. He was placed on the stretcher and taken back to the ambulance.

Charles asked the Chinese doctor, "He's alive, isn't he?"

The doctor nodded. "Serious wound. But his chances should be good."

"Give us a report from the hospital," Charles said.

The doctor nodded again and rushed back to the ambulance which at once drove off. At the same time Inspector Sullivan and several uniformed officers came up to the teahouse.

The square-faced Inspector examined Madge's body and then stared down at the body of Edmund Porter in the pit, and the elaborately-clothed skeleton beside him. He said grimly, "Something like the last act of Hamlet."

"Just a little," Charles acknowledged.

Inspector Sullivan went over to Enid and touched her gently on the shoulder. He said, "Well, you were right. You found your sister."

"I didn't even have a chance to speak to her," she said brokenly.

"Maybe it's better this way," the Inspector said. "She'd become completely his puppet. Her mind and body were ruined by drugs."

Enid said, "She and the old man were quarreling. Then he stabbed her."

Charles came forward. He said, "She knew about the body in the pit. Christopher had found out about it long ago and

329

that was his hold over the old man. He put her up to coming here and blackmailing him."

Enid stared at him. "How do you know so much about it?"

"I enjoy putting together puzzles," Charles told her.

Inspector Sullivan interrupted to say, "I owe you an apology, Miss Branch. I have kept some pretty important information from you. Charles Milano is an American agent for Interpol. He was sent here to fight the drug traffic."

Charles looked embarrassed. "Sorry. I had to keep you in the dark."

Enid tried to think of something to say but couldn't. She knew she was thankful but too much had happened for her to accept this welcome shock in a normal fashion.

Sonya said, "I think it is time you came back to the house."

Inspector Sullivan said, "Yes. We have work to do out here."

And so the nightmare came to an end. The newspapers had a field day heralding the murder of Madge, the strange secret which Edmund Porter had kept for so many years, and the break-up of the drug ring. Quiet private funerals were held for Madge and Edmund Porter. And there was some irony in that Stephen insisted they both be buried in the small private cemetery in the clearing.

He also arranged for the transfer of Regina Porter to the grave marked by the headstone her murderer husband had erected nearly a half-century earlier. It was a strange homecoming for the long-dead beauty.

Christopher Porter recovered from the gun wound and was scheduled to stand trial at the next session of the court. Stephen humbly begged Enid's pardon for being so deaf to her pleas that Madge was still alive and asked her once again to marry him.

He told her, "The way is clear now."

She shook her head. "I like you, Stephen. I won't marry you."

"Charles?" he said.

"Yes," she replied. "Not that he's asked me since I found out who he really is. But I'm sure he will. Or at least I hope so."

Stephen smiled sadly. "I hope so too. It isn't pleasant to be alone."

She said, "You needn't be alone. You have someone here who loves you and would ask for nothing more than to be your wife."

"Sonya Chen?" he said.

"Yes."

"I doubt it," he said worriedly. "I don't think she cares for me in that way."

Enid smiled. "We've become very good friends. Sonya has spoken frankly to me. I know you need only ask her."

Stephen's handsome face lit up. "Count on it that I shall."

Enid's own proposal of marriage came in an unexpected way and in an unexpected place. She and Charles were having dinner with Wong Lee before leaving for London. Charles took her out to the garden for a stroll and asked her to go on to New York with him and be his wife. She accepted the offer at once and they were in each other's arms when the stout old Wong Lee joined them.

A smile showed on his broad face. "So there is to be a romance?" he said.

Enid went to him happily. "Charles has asked me to marry him."

"That is excellent," Wong Lee said approvingly. "And I am happy that he asked you here in my garden."

"The ideal place," Charles said.

Enid gazed up at the old man wistfully. "I've always seen you as a romantic."

"I am a fat old man," Wong Lee said.

"You are much more than that," she insisted. "You were in love with Regina, weren't you?"

"Yes, I loved her deeply," Wong Lee said, his broad face shadowed. "But she chose to marry my friend and partner. My code of honor would not allow me to think of her in that way again."

Her arm linked in his, Enid went on, "But Regina was not as honorable as you. She had to test her beauty with many men. She tortured Edmund Porter with her flirtations and he came to think that you two were having an affair."

"Yes," Wong Lee said heavily. "But soon after he accused me he learned the identity of her lover."

331

Enid said, "Later he came to you and apologized. After Regina vanished."

"Yes. I accepted his apology," Wong Lee said.

"And ten years later when the old *amah* who was supposed to have gone with Regina sent for you, you learned from her dying lips that Regina had never left Porter House. And then you guessed that Edmund Porter had murdered his wife in a fit of jealousy."

"It is so," Wong Lee said. "I guessed that he had hidden her body beneath the teahouse."

"But you told no one. Why?"

"I was sorry for him. He was my partner and my friend. I could not bring our Jade Princess to life. I did not realize he would become dangerously mad. I was wrong."

"I knew it," she said. "You came near to telling me the truth that day you spoke about the *amah*."

"I wish I had," Wong Lee said sadly. "I might have saved lives."

Enid said, "It's hard to say. I think fate meant it to happen as it did."

The old man nodded. "Man concocts a million schemes. God knows but one!"

Enid reached out and took Charles's hand as the three of them stood there in the silence of the lovely garden.